MW01178263

About the Author

Raised in Ottawa, Ontario, Brianna Shea moved to England to pursue a degree in law and human rights. While studying for exams, she did what anyone would do while procrastinating studying for said exams… she wrote a book. Ever since she was a child, Brianna had the dream of seeing her name printed on one of those covers in the bookstore. To reach and inspire even just one person to read, just like you.

The Beauty of Power

Brianna Shea

The Beauty of Power

Olympia Publishers
London

www.olympiapublishers.com
OLYMPIA PAPERBACK EDITION

Copyright © Brianna Shea 2023

The right of Brianna Shea to be identified as author of
this work has been asserted in accordance with sections 77 and 78 of
the Copyright, Designs and Patents Act 1988.

All Rights Reserved

No reproduction, copy or transmission of this publication
may be made without written permission.
No paragraph of this publication may be reproduced,
copied or transmitted save with the written permission of the publisher,
or in accordance with the provisions
of the Copyright Act 1956 (as amended).

Any person who commits any unauthorised act in relation to
this publication may be liable to criminal
prosecution and civil claims for damage.

A CIP catalogue record for this title is
available from the British Library.

ISBN: 978-1-80074-876-7

This is a work of fiction.
Names, characters, places and incidents originate from the writer's
imagination. Any resemblance to actual persons, living or dead, is
purely coincidental.

First Published in 2023

Olympia Publishers
Tallis House
2 Tallis Street
London
EC4Y 0AB

Printed in Great Britain

Dedication

To you, thank you for helping my dream come true.

Chapter 1

"Start from the beginning." The woman leaned back, her green eyes piercing into me. I cleared my throat and opened my mouth. I then proceeded to shut it, suddenly feeling a strong sense of stage fright.

"In as much detail as possible," the brown-haired woman chimed in, smiling widely. I looked between the two and began picking at my thumb.

"How much detail is that?" I choked over the words and intently stared at the water in front of me.

"We understand this is hard, as much detail as you can manage," the green-eyed woman prodded.

"I don't know, I was just going to class, I stopped to get a muffin like I did every day."

***

I stood there in shock. My hands trembling from the deprivation of food as I stared intently at the empty muffin basket. My morning ambition suddenly shattered at the idea I could not have my favorite muffin, the only thing that motivated me to get out of bed in the morning. The only thing that has allowed me to hang on to the tiny amount of sanity left in me during midterm week. "Do you have any chocolate muffins?" I called to the cashier.

"We ran out about an hour ago," she shouted back tiredly.

"Are you going to make any more?" I asked, desperate to

cling on to a ray of hope.

"Not until tomorrow," she responded, obviously getting annoyed at my line of questions. I opened my mouth to dispute this fact, turning around prepared to beg for any possibility of a fragment of the muffin.

"Try this," a woman popped out of nowhere holding a wrapped donut. Her blue eyes eager to help with the tragic scene unfolding in front of her. I paused and shut my mouth. I opened my mouth again to decline this disgusting substitute for the muffin. Then shut it realizing that would be a very abrasive response to a kind gesture. I took the wrapped donut in my hand and turned it a few times. The sugar glaze almost made the donut hard beneath the wrapping. "I know it's not as good, but I like them." She smiled and turned around, her dark brown hair flowing over her shoulders. She walked to the cashier and began to purchase her black coffee. I was filled with panic realizing she wasn't going to wait for me to respond to her. I needed to thank her, to open the possibility of a conversation. She was remarkably beautiful, obviously had terrible taste in baked goods, but that's neither here nor there.

"Wait," I called to her. She turned around as the cashier processed the cash she paid, another odd thing, who carries cash? She smiled at me expecting me to continue to speak as humans typically do after calling "wait." I held up the disgusting donut determined to say thank you. "Donut!" my mouth decided to say. My eyes grew wide in embarrassment.

"My name's Stephanie," she giggled and grabbed her coffee. Walking away to continue on with her day.

"Are you going to pay for that donut?" The cashier spat impatiently. I nodded, walked forward and placed it in front of her. I tapped my card instinctively as I heard the total, my mind still engaged with the embarrassing interaction that had just occurred. I walked away checking my phone to see the time.

"Shit," I began to sprint as I realized how late I was. I had an English exam, now. Or I should say ten minutes ago. How could I have been so callous with my time?

I barged into the class completely out of breath, my legs trembling, not used to the exercise. My English professor stood up from his desk, prepared to usher me out of the class.

"Why are you late, Mr. Davis?" His gruff voice echoed in my head as I attempted to find a valid excuse for being late.

"They were out of chocolate muffins," I said pitifully. I was never very creative in my excuses. But I guess the truth worked. Either out of pure understanding of the muffin tragedy or complete indifference, Mr. Williams gestured for me to take a seat. I sat down, putting my bag at my feet, my eyes glancing around the class. My friend met my eye contact and mouthed the words 'where were you' to which I shrugged and turned back to my English exam.

"Where were you?" My friend caught up to me as we left the class.

"Getting a muffin, but they were out, so this girl handed me a donut." I ruffled through my bag to find it, determined to eat as my stomach growled ferociously.

"A girl? Was she hot?" His eyes lit up with excitement, obviously thinking there was more story to come.

"Very hot, managed to tell her 'donut' before she left." I sighed at the disappointing memory. My friend stared at me in utter confusion, not sure how to even follow up that statement. Luckily for him, our other friend joined up with us.

"How did your English exam go?" My friend chimed.

"Well, Levi met a hot girl while getting his muffin this morning."

"Shut up, Aidan. Not even worth talking about." I unpeeled the donut, throwing out the wrapper in the garbage.

"That's not a muffin?" my friend questioned.

"No duh, Lucas, they were out," Aidan corrected as if he hadn't just learned that same information. I took a bite of the donut and quickly regretted it.

"Anyone hungry?" I asked with a look of disgust on my face from the pure sugar which was the donut. Both Lucas and Aidan were quick to nod as we trekked across campus to the cafeteria.

We split up instantly going to our favorite food areas. My university may not be known for any school programs but they certainly had an excellent selection of food.

"Ah, the muffin man!" Stephanie exclaimed, nudging in beside me and grabbing an apple. I looked up from the fruit selection as she was leaning against the counter. She gently moved her hair to her back revealing the straps of her black crop top, and two long matching scars on the underside of each of her forearms. Huh. I brought my eyes back to hers, not wanting to stare. She was gorgeous. Breathtakingly gorgeous.

"Ah, terrible donut girl!" I teased, rather proud of myself for being able to communicate this interaction.

"Look at you being able to say more than 'donut.'" She winked and looked around the cafeteria. "Where are you sitting?"

"Oh, with my friends over there," I pointed at the table by the right at the windows. Aidan and Lucas sat there chatting among themselves.

"I'm joining you." She took a bite out of the apple and began walking to my friends. She adjusted her shorts while looking back at me curious as to why I wasn't following her. I grabbed an apple and began walking quickly, intent on catching up to her. I met her just as she sat down at the table. "Hi, I'm Stephanie." She smiled at my friends. Lucas and Aidan looked at me, confused as to what was happening.

"We met this morning," I sat beside Stephanie and looked across at Lucas and Aidan as the dots connected.

"You're donut girl!" Aidan exclaimed. "Welcome to our table."

"Thank you, I do go by terrible donut girl though." Stephanie threw a smile at me. I laughed. "How's everyone's day going?"

"Meh, pretty boring," Lucas crunched loudly on his fries. "You should come to our gaming hangout tonight."

"I'm sure she has better things to do," I cut in quickly.

"I literally have no friends," Stephanie smiled, unperturbed by my efforts of cutting her out of our hangout.

"Well, I'm Aidan, this is Lucas and Levi," Aidan quickly introduced then nudged toward me to clarify that she should in fact come.

"I can bring some beer?" Stephanie bit her fingernail.

"Well, I am sold, took you long enough to prove your worth, Stephanie," I teased. Stephanie pushed my arm slightly and giggled. Was she flirting with me? "Do you have a car?"

"A Rolls-Royce." She grabbed a fry off my plate. Lucas put his hands on the table in utter amazement, his mouth hung open as he made eye contact with Aidan and me, seemingly not too impressed that our reactions were not equal. "I'm joking, I drive a beat-up Toyota." She laughed at Lucas as his expression fell almost instantly into pure disappointment.

"There was no reason to break my heart like that," Lucas grumbled.

"Then you can drive Levi, he is the worst backseat driver."

Aidan gestured to me with the half-eaten sandwich in his hand.

"I am a perfectly fine passenger, you are just a terrible driver, Aidan!" I protested remembering his intolerably slow driving.

"You have been warned," Aidan nodded at Stephanie.

"If you don't drive, you don't have an opinion." Stephanie stared at me challengingly.

"Thank you!" Aidan enthusiastically hit the table and pointed at Stephanie excited for some back up on his point. "These two boys are so terrible, but they still expect to be able to cram into my truck whenever they damn well please."

"You're creating a monster," I whispered to Stephanie. She leaned in slightly.

"I think you may be right," she smiled. "I have a class, when and where should I pick you up?"

"Six, and in front of the sign. Here, give me your phone number," I passed her my phone. She typed in her number and saved it under Stephanie. She got up and quickly disappeared into the crowd. "She's odd." I turned back to Lucas and Aidan and quickly got a firm smack on the arm. "What? She is!" I protested.

"Boy wouldn't know fun if it strangled him to death," Aidan muttered.

"It's freezing, where are you?" I jumped around slightly.

"Literally a few seconds away, you drama queen." Stephanie's voice echoed through the phone. I saw a faded red Toyota pull up to the curb. The dents on the front and rear of the vehicle were distinct. If I didn't like Aidan's driving, I doubt this would be up my alley. I paused, not sure if I should get into this possible death trap. The passenger window rolled down, Stephanie was leaning forward pointing at a large case of beer. I opened the door.

"You promise me you won't kill me?" I pointed at the front dent. Stephanie rolled her eyes.

"I don't make promises I can't keep." Stephanie winked. Not really the answer I was hoping for but I swallowed my instincts and got into the vehicle, placing the beer on my lap. I closed the door and was quick to inspect my surroundings. The inside was in far better condition, everything was perfectly clean, not a speck of dust anywhere. "This is Delila." Stephanie checked her blindside as she pulled out onto the street.

"You named the car?" I spoke, unsure on whether it was endearing or just weird.

"Yes, it's more fun that way." Stephanie leaned back in her seat. It was weird. "You know how to get me to where we're going?"

"Yes," I tapped on my temple.

"You have it memorized? Weird." Stephanie shook her head in disbelief.

"I've only been going there almost my entire life."

"Oh, you grew up here?" Stephanie glanced over at me.

"We all did, thought we would stick around here together," I looked down at the beer cans jiggling in the box on my lap.

"That's awesome, good for you guys," she smiled.

"Take a right here," I pointed to the stop sign approaching. "We're going to Aidan's place tonight, his parents have this sweet set up in the basement, surround sound and everything. They keep to themselves too. We normally take turns going to each other's houses, so the parents don't get too annoyed with all of us always hanging around." The car veered right; the beer started to slip off my lap before I grabbed it. "Left here," I motioned to the street in front of us. The car gently turned.

"That's really cool you guys are so close," Stephanie said. I couldn't help but hear some envy in her voice.

"What do you study?"

"History," Stephanie looked over and smiled at me. Ew.

"It's the house with the horse mailbox." I repositioned my legs, the weight of the beer making them fall asleep.

"Excuse me?" Stephanie questioned, laughing. "A horse?" She looked at me in disbelief.

"Ya, his family used to own a horse farm or something like that." I had never thought of it as odd until this moment. I pointed forward at the large white horse mailbox that set Aidan's house apart from every other one. Stephanie giggled in surprise as she pulled into the driveway. We pulled behind Aidan's blue truck. I opened the door to get out but struggled under the awkward positioning of the beer.

"Ah you found it!" Aidan called, quickly walking to the car to take the beer off my lap. He held it up victoriously showing it to Lucas like they had never drank beer before. Lucas cheered. I shook my head at them as I got out and shut the door. Stephanie walked up the driveway repositioning her hair.

Aidan was quick to pass the beer to Lucas and turned back to Stephanie. "The kitchen is over there if you need anything." Aidan gestured unimpressively to his left. "But where we're playing is down here." Aidan led the party down the stairs where Lucas had already set the beer down and cracked one open. The basement had been carefully designed around Aidan's wishes. A large flat-screen was mounted on the left wall and a massive sectional couch to the right. A cabinet full of snacks and a bar fridge full of drinks were placed to the right and were always full of whatever Aidan wished except, of course, alcohol, which under strict instructions from Lucas's parents was forbidden. Aidan grabbed a beer and plopped down on the couch, putting his feet up.

"What are we playing?" Stephanie sat down on the other side of the couch. I grabbed a beer and sat beside her, awkwardly jutting it out. She took it from my hand, quickly opened it.

"Deciding that is our first order of business," Lucas pointed to the game selection underneath the television. "Have you ever played any of those?"

Stephanie placed her beer on the floor and crawled over to the games. My eyes glided over her perfect ass. Holy fuck. I looked over to Aidan who was hitting Lucas on the arm, gesturing to Stephanie. Lucas looked over confused, then his face changed to disappointment as he whacked Aidan. "*Call of Duty*, *GTA*, is this a dance game?" Stephanie looked at Aidan judgingly. Aidan smiled and rubbed his injured arm.

"I like what I like, it's good exercise!" Aidan shrugged. Stephanie nodded while smirking as she placed the game back on the shelf. My eyes returned to her, completely in awe. She was here. Playing games with us. Holy fuck.

"Let's do a *Mario Cart* tournament," Lucas suggested, pointing at the old Wii to the left side of the games.

"Oh man, we haven't done that in a while!" Aidan nodded encouragingly, quickly getting the game organized. "Okay, me and Lucas, then you and Stephanie, then the finals." Aidan passed the controller to Lucas and took one for himself. Stephanie made her way back to the couch, grabbing her beer along the way.

"It's been a while for me," Stephanie took a sip of her beer. I looked at her confused as to what she was referring to. She stretched out, pushing her chest up. My eyes were on her, transfixed. "Since I've played Mario Cart." She gestured to the aggressive game ensuing beside us. "The guys I live with are more into the aggressive 'man' games." She mockingly posed like a bodybuilder. I opened my mouth to question what she meant by 'the guys she lived with', but then shut it not wanting to pry into her personal life just yet. I would hate to come across as controlling or possessive over the term 'guys.' I stayed quiet hoping that she would volunteer that information, but she was already distracted by the game between Aidan and Lucas which erupted in swearing as Lucas fell further and further behind.

"Then I look forward to beating you," I commented, bringing her attention back to the conversation.

"Ha, I'll still smoke your ass." Stephanie shrugged.

"Fuck ya! Suck my dick!" Lucas screamed, standing up on the couch. "The underdog becomes the VICTOR."

"Shut up, man, it's just a game," Aidan muttered tossing the remote to Stephanie who caught it without hesitation.

"You're saying that because you are a loser," Lucas mocked passing the remote to me.

"Let's see what you got," I nudged Stephanie. Her eyes were already zeroed into the game. Stephanie had seriously over-estimated her abilities. Within a couple of minutes, I had nearly lapped her. She stood no chance as the sweeping victory became mine.

Stephanie sighed. "Fine, you win, let's see who's victorious, you or Lucas." She passed her controller over to Lucas who switched places with Stephanie. I was eager to prove that I was superior but quickly realized that Lucas's skills were unmatched. Lap after lap, the gap between Lucas and I increased.

"I. Am. The. KING," Lucas announced. We all bowed.

"Where's your crown?" Stephanie laughed. Lucas grabbed his empty beer bottle and attempted to balance it on his head. Stephanie giggled. "I should go," she said, looking at the time on her phone.

"No, the night's just started!" Lucas complained.

"Maybe I'll be able to stay longer next time," Stephanie smiled, organizing herself. "See you on Monday!"

"See you on Monday," Aidan called, taking another sip of beer. "I'll say this, Stephanie has excellent taste in beer."

The weekend passed with its usual mix of procrastinating studying and stressing about the procrastination which leads to further procrastination, my parents asking if I was doing okay in school, leading to further stress and, you guessed it, further procrastination.

My Monday morning alarm went off with a ferocity only matched by my hatred of the sound. "No," I muttered to myself, snoozing it. I rolled over and fell back to sleep quickly.

Another few seconds passed, and the screeching of the alarm rang out again. "Uh," I growled. "No." I stopped the alarm. A fatal mistake. I rolled over and fell asleep only to wake up on my own about an hour later. Now late to my first class. "Better than being late to an exam," I murmured to myself. I rolled out of bed angrily, threw on some clothing and ran down the stairs.

"Do you want some breakfast?" Mom called.

"I'm late," I called back, quickly running out the door and began the trek to class. There was no need to run, I was already late, why be late and sweaty?

I stood outside the class, about twenty minutes late. I contemplated if it was worth the embarrassment to go in. I shrugged and walked away from the door texting Lucas to meet up.

"Dude, where were you?" Aidan tossed his bag at his feet as he sat down at our table in the cafeteria. By the time Lucas woke up we decided it was best to just go to lunch.

"I didn't wake up on time." I shrugged.

"I wonder if Stephanie is going to join us today." Lucas smirked at me.

"Ya, can I ask your opinion on something?" I asked, taking a bite out of my burger.

"She's out of your league man, never gonna happen." Lucas patted my arm sympathetically.

"Thanks, not what I was going to ask." I rolled my eyes. "She mentioned that she lives with 'guys.' What do you think that means, like brothers?" It had been slightly annoying me all weekend.

"Why does that matter?" Aidan and Lucas exchanged a confused look.

"I mean, I'm just curious," I backtracked knowing immediately I should have just let it go.

"Again, she's out of your league, it is never going to happen!" Lucas stated.

"Not why I was asking!" I protested.

"Then why?" Aidan quizzed. I looked down and prodded my fries trying to think of a valid reason for asking such a bizarre question. "Wait, Levi may have a point."

"I do?" I looked up confused.

"Ya, I bet that—" Aidan began to explain his reasoning but was quickly cut off by Lucas.

"Hey, Stephanie, how are you?" Lucas inquired loudly to shut Aidan up. Stephanie looked around the table somewhat disorientated by this interaction but decided to ignore it and sat down next to Aidan.

"I'm good." She settled in and put her purse at her feet.

"So, Stephanie, Levi, Lucas and I all live with our parents," Aidan began. Shit. I wish he would just leave it. I was so stupid for telling him, he has no boundaries. "What is your living arrangement?" Aidan and Lucas looked at her inquisitively. Stephanie met my eyes and gave me a confused look.

"I live with my foster brother and a few friends," Stephanie explained.

"I thought you said you had no friends." I prodded.

"Well, I mean I do, but they're basically family." Stephanie shrugged.

"So, no parents," Aidan smiled at the group, excited about this revelation.

"No parents," Stephanie repeated, taking a bite of her pizza. She seemed completely ignorant to why we were all staring at her expectantly.

"No parents at all?" Aidan prompted.

"No parents," Stephanie looked up from her pizza, confused. "Oh, do you guys wanna come over?" she guessed.

"Hell ya," Aidan hit the table victoriously.

"We own a cottage a little out of town if you guys want to have a sleepover with complete privacy." Stephanie met my eyes and smiled.

"Yes, this girl is the answer to our prayers!" Aidan shook Stephanie's shoulder. Stephanie giggled.

"No guys, my mom already bought our snacks," Lucas whined, suddenly meek.

"What about next Saturday then, we can meet here in the morning?" Stephanie suggested, peeling a piece of pepperoni off her pizza. The table erupted in excitement at the plan.

The week flew by in its typical frenzy. Stephanie's red Toyota, or should I say Delila, pulled up at the sign. She was instructed to not bring alcohol this time. "Lucas's house is the other way," I advised, getting in.

"No warning?" Stephanie complained looking around before completing a U-turn.

"Lucas's parents are very hands-on. That's your warning for the night." I pointed to turn left.

"Is that why they're so excited to be away from adult supervision?"

"Yes, it's our life's ambition to hang out with the same people, doing the same things, without adult supervision." I laughed. "No, they're just excited to get drunk."

"Ah, the truth comes out." Stephanie smiled. I pointed to the right, prompting another turn.

"Just stay on here for a while," I directed. "So what does your brother do?"

"What kind of conversation starter is that?" Stephanie laughed.

"You have a better one?" I challenged.

"I do! What do you want to be when you grow up?"

"Oh damn, you're right, I've never heard that conversation starter before," I joked. "I don't know. I'm studying English, mostly because that's what Aidan wanted to study and I wasn't sure what I wanted to do. What do you want to be?"

"Rich," Stephanie stated then laughed. "I want to own a museum, I can pick out the artifacts and structure the exhibits. Completely create something that impacts people's lives."

"You're such a nerd!" I teased. "What is it with history students liking what they're studying?"

"I was going to say I'd hire you but now, I don't know."

"I'll bring beer." I smiled at her.

"You're definitely not going to be hired then," Stephanie giggled, shaking her head.

"How do you take your coffee?" I questioned.

"Black."

"Answer me honestly…"

"What?"

"Are you a psychopath? My God, one cream, one sugar is the only way to have it." I threw my hands up in exasperation. Stephanie laughed and shook her head vigorously.

"That's not coffee!" Stephanie protested.

"For a job at your fancy museum, I will swallow my humanity and bring you a black coffee every morning," I pitched. Stephanie wobbled her head back and forth.

"Fine," Stephanie relented.

"Oh shit, that was Lucas's house." I looked at the brick home in the side mirror.

"Your one job!" Stephanie exclaimed, throwing the car in reverse and backing up to the driveway.

"For your information, I now have two jobs, you just hired me," I corrected. Stephanie pulled the car into the driveway and parked behind Aidan's vehicle. "Are you ready?" I undid my seatbelt and sat forward. Stephanie nodded. We got out of the vehicle and walked up to the large brick house. Stephanie knocked on the painted red door. We heard rustling from inside and the door clicked unlocked.

The door creaked open showing Lucas's mom standing there. Her blond hair was in big waves and makeup splattered on. "Come in, sweety," his mother exclaimed.

"Hello Mrs. Butler, this is Stephanie," I introduced her. Lucas's father came around the corner hearing that a new person was arriving. Stephanie shook both Mrs. and Mr. Butler's hands.

"Hello," she said shyly. A tone I had never heard her use before.

"Well, welcome, make yourself at home." Mrs. Butler extended her arm pointing past the entrance. Stephanie nodded and I began to walk past the entrance feeling their eyes on our back.

"Are they together?" I heard, Mr. Butler ask.

"No way," Mrs. Butler scoffed. Guess it's an accepted fact that Stephanie was out of my league. I gestured to the left, knowing that Aidan and Lucas were waiting at the kitchen table. I noticed that Stephanie was trying her best to not break down laughing.

"What?" I asked not sure if she had heard what they had said.

"You were just insulted by Mrs. Butler," she whispered to me snickering.

"Glad you found that funny."

"I did." Stephanie giggled, waving to Aidan and Lucas. Lucas was setting up a board game while Aidan waved back at Stephanie vigorously. We sat down facing Lucas and Aidan. "This looks fun, I love board games," Stephanie commented.

"They don't allow Lucas to play video games," Aidan whispered.

"Shhhh," Lucas was quick to cut in. "They have hearing like Satan."

"I didn't know Satan had good hearing."

"Mommy coming in with snacks!" Mrs. Butler announced loudly. She carried a tray full of chips, vegetables and grapes. "I'll be right out with your juice!" She set the tray down and hurried back to the kitchen. Stephanie quickly grabbed a handful of grapes. Mrs. Butler carried in another tray full of orange juice and set it down on the table.

"Thank you, Mrs. Butler!" Stephanie exclaimed. Lucas rolled his eyes. Mrs. Butler turned around, surprised to hear someone thank her. Stephanie glared at us.

"Thank you, Mrs. Butler!" We all called. Mrs. Butler was taken aback and smiled.

"I like this girl!" She exclaimed quickly leaving the room to tell Mr. Butler.

"Look at you, daughter of the year," I nudged Stephanie in the arm.

"I mean you guys make it easy to win!" Stephanie jousted.

"Okay, Stephanie, focus, this is a complicated board game." Lucas leaned forward. It was not a complicated board game, but he proceeded to explain the rules in the most complicated way possible. "Stephanie, you start so we know if you understand."

"Okay." She rolled the die and picked up the card.

"Do you have anything to fight it?" Lucas asked.

"Can I borrow Levi's axe?" Stephanie asked, pointing to the card laid in front of me.

"No, you cannot borrow Levi's axe," Aidan sighed.

"She can borrow my axe." I picked up the card and began to pass it to her.

"She cannot borrow your axe," Lucas corrected, "Levi, put your axe down." Lucas pointed to my side of the table. I slowly lowered it. He leaned forward to grab the card from Stephanie's hand. "You just lose two health, that's fine."

"I'm going to get a glass of water, anyone want anything?" Stephanie stood up.

"Stephanie, we just started!" Lucas whined.

"I'll take a glass of water," Aidan said. Stephanie nodded and looked around the table.

"We have juice!" Lucas exclaimed and pointed at the liquids that would not cause the game to pause.

"Let her get a water!" I defended. Lucas sighed then

motioned that she could go. "You literally explained the game for so long everyone got dehydrated."

"The game is complicated!" Lucas protested.

"Dude, what the fuck are you doing?" Aidan demanded, staring at me. My smile disappeared and was replaced by a confused expression. "'You can use my ax?' You know those aren't the rules."

"It's her first time playing!"

"We don't want you to get hurt, she's not interested in you," Lucas stated.

"We don't want to lose her as a friend because *you* think you stand a chance." Aidan crunched on some chips.

"What is with this spontaneous intervention?" I hissed.

"We don't want you falling for someone who obviously sees you as a friend." Lucas looked seriously into my eyes.

"I'm not falling for her, and even if I was, why is it so unbelievable that she could like me?" My voice raised slightly, as my annoyance turned into anger.

"We don't mean it as an insult, man," Aidan said, attempting to defuse the situation.

"Just, girls like that don't end up with guys like you," Lucas chimed in. They looked at each other then back at me, attempting to figure out if what they were saying was sinking in. "We really don't mean it as an insult, we just don't want you to get hurt."

"It's okay guys, literally Stephanie and I are just friends." I protested. "I'm going to see if she needs help in the kitchen." I needed to breathe. I stood up and walked to the kitchen, taking a deep breath in. I saw a movement from my peripheral vision and turned to my left. Stephanie was leaning against the wall by the entrance to the living room.

The entrance to the place we were just talking about her in. Shit.

She was staring at me but not saying anything. Her floral

crop top moved as she took a deep breath in and walked over to the counter, placing the two glasses of water down. She stood there for a second, not moving, debating what she was supposed to do in this situation. She turned toward me and picked at her fingernails.

"I'm sorry if my intentions weren't clear," she smiled nervously. I opened my mouth to reassure her that I indeed did not want anything more than friendship. But she stepped closer to me. "I don't want to be friends," she murmured, taking my hand and putting it on her hip, as she nervously cupped my face. I leaned into her hand, processing what had just happened. She leaned forward and kissed me.

Her lips hesitated for a second before my instincts kicked in; and I pulled her close to me, embracing her tightly as I deepened our tender kiss. I grabbed at her, trying to get her as close as possible. She backed up until she was against the counter. She quickly pushed the glasses to the side and jumped up wrapping her legs around me. One hand gripping my hair, one hand holding my chest against hers. Our lips locked together, moving with my pounding heartbeat. To my left, I heard a noise and became hyper-aware of my surroundings.

All of a sudden, the shock of the situation rushed back to me. I pulled away abruptly. Stephanie looked at me, confused. I heard her say something but the words were jumbled as I tried to make sense of everything.

"No," I said, the only word I could muster. I rubbed my face before realizing that Stephanie had grabbed the glasses of water and quickly walked out of the room. I looked after her. What? What did I say no to? I walked back into the room. Stephanie was slouching in her chair, arms crossed, refusing to make eye contact with me.

"Are you okay, man?" Aidan said, looking at me in concern.

"Ya, I'm okay, just needed some air," I replied. I needed to talk to Stephanie, but I didn't want to say anything in front of Aidan or Lucas. I wasn't sure if she wanted them to know.

The game continued but my mind was on what had just happened. I managed to have a relationship and lose it within seconds. Call the world record people. Before I knew it Stephanie was leaving for the night. I tried to follow her out but she had no intention of slowing down or talking to me.

What the *fuck* did I say no to?

"Are you sure you're okay?" Lucas asked.

"Stephanie kissed me," I muttered in disbelief.

"Mom, Levi and Aidan are staying over tonight," Lucas called. We trekked upstairs to his bedroom. I told them everything.

"Are you sure she kissed you?" Aidan asked, throwing a bouncy ball in the air. "Maybe you hallucinated it."

"She definitely kissed me." At this point, I wished she hadn't.

"And you randomly said 'no' without knowing what she asked. Are you an idiot?" Aidan abruptly threw the bouncy ball at me.

"I was surprised."

"Who says 'no' when they're surprised!" Lucas said, frustrated. He had a point there.

"And now she's mad, but you don't know what you did." Aidan continued his summary.

"Pretty much," I sighed.

"You're such an idiot," Lucas muttered.

"Yup," I agreed, exasperated with myself.

Chapter 2

"So, your friends were close to Stephanie?" The green-eyed lady paused her writing and looked up at me.

"They loved her," I responded.

"We will need to speak with them too," the green-eyed lady said to the brown-haired lady. The brown-haired lady nodded.

***

The week slipped by without Stephanie talking to us. Lucas, Aidan and I made the decision to meet Saturday morning at the cafeteria just in case she still wanted to take us to her cottage. We all knew it was a long shot, but as our texts and calls went unanswered, I was grasping at straws and Lucas and Aidan were trying to support me. They were going through a loss of their own desperately hoping that freedom from their parents was not shattered because of my stupidity.

I walked into the cafeteria, the sudden explosion of noise rang in my ears as I looked around for my friends. There was Aidan and Lucas sitting at our usual table next to Stephanie. My palms were sweaty as I approached, not sure if she was there to tell me to stop bugging her. She sat back as she saw me approaching, her smile unwavering. She was wearing a pastel blue corset top, her hair in waves. My jaw dropped slightly as my eyes glided over her. She was magnificent, perfect. How could she have possibly kissed me?

"You're late," Aidan scolded me. I nodded.

"Lucas, you're with me, Aidan, I'll drive over to your car, you can follow me and get Levi to call me if you lose me," Stephanie instructed cheerfully. Lucas and Aidan looked at me, knowing that I would be disappointed by the seating arrangement. I tried to hide my visible disappointment and nodded. We all stood up and joined our designated groups heading to the vehicles. I hopped into Aidan's passenger seat.

"How are you doing?" Aidan looked at me solemnly, doing up his seat belt.

"I'm fine, it's not like I didn't know she was out of my league," I said pointedly.

"Look man, I'm sorry, we should have stayed out of it. We shouldn't have assumed her intentions," Aidan apologized, turning the vehicle on.

"Doesn't matter now." I rested my head against the seat. My heart straining to beat under my anxiety and disappointment.

"Talk to her this weekend."

"I've tried to talk to her this entire week."

"If you guys can't talk this out, you had no chance of forming a relationship anyway," Aidan muttered. We heard a honk and turned to see Stephanie's red car waiting. Aidan began to follow it.

"You're such a pessimist," I looked both ways as Aidan stopped at a two-way stop sign. "There's a car coming to your left."

"Shut up, Levi. I will kick you out if this is going to be the entire drive," Aidan threatened. I rolled my eyes. "What do you think this cottage is like?"

"Probably nothing much, I can't imagine her brother being that much older than her."

"I will bet you a full five dollars that her brother is rich as fuck." Aidan grabbed his wallet out of his pocket. The tradition was to put the money on the dash until we knew the rightful winners. He handed it to me, focusing on the road. I put it on the dash. I reached into my own and grabbed a five-dollar bill and tossed it on top.

"You're gonna lose those five dollars," I said smugly. Aidan gave me the finger.

"I bet they're stocked up on alcohol too."

"Now that I agree with," I laughed.

The suburbs gradually became thicker and thicker forest, the roads became more uneven and brittle. The ride becoming louder and louder from the bumps to the dirt and the stones hitting against the vehicle as the rest of humanity trailed further and further behind us.

"They could kill someone out here," Aidan murmured, looking around at the forest that surrounded us. The blinker went on Stephanie's vehicle as she turned.

"Don't try to foreshadow our deaths, you stupid English major," I muttered, having to admit to myself that I was also uncomfortable. The car turned as we entered the driveway. The gate opened in front of Stephanie's vehicle.

"A gate, looking good for me." Aidan smiled. The car inched forward until we were clear of the gateway. We followed Stephanie's car as it winded up the long driveway. "Holy shit," Aidan whispered to himself as we caught a glimpse of the cottage for the first time. It was a mansion made of black tinted windows and stone. Aidan parked beside Stephanie's vehicle and quickly grabbed the money off the dash. "What the fuck does her brother do?" Aidan tucked the money back into his wallet as we got out of the car.

"I thought she was going to murder us!" Lucas exclaimed, his hands in the air victoriously as he gestured to the large cottage behind us. Stephanie giggled, grabbing her purse. We all grabbed our bags and followed Stephanie into the house. The hardwood flooring was shiny and followed into the open concept rooms. A winding staircase to the left, a large empty living room to the right.

"I'll show you guys around," Stephanie started to the left in the hallway that passed the staircase. It opened into a large room with floor-to-ceiling windows. "Lucas, you should sleep here," Stephanie pointed at the door to her left.

"Sweet," Lucas looked in and set his bag by the door. I popped my head into the room. The hardwood carried into it; a black carpet laid beneath the king-sized bed with white bedding. Above the bed was an art nouveau painting. On the far wall, the floor-to-ceiling windows continued revealing the forest outside. To the right was a wall full of wood closet doors.

"This is my room," Stephanie continued pointing to the room next to it. Stephanie continued walking, I peeked into her room. The full-size windows continued, the king-size bed with white bedding was against the window and to the right were the closet doors. I heard the steps continue away and I rushed to rejoin. The large room that held the entrances to the two bedrooms opened up to a large kitchen with white marble countertops and white cabinets. The kitchen was against a backdrop of the dark brown and green that echoed through the forest shown in the windows that had carried through.

"This is the kitchen," Stephanie gestured and continued her tour. The kitchen opened back up to the living room. The ceilings went to the roof and held a massive art nouveau chandelier at the top. The living room was just a massive empty space. It held no furniture; the wood flooring was unnervingly bare.

"Is your brother single?" Aidan joked in awe of the building.

"He is, I can put in a good word for you," Stephanie winked at Aidan. She circled us back to the steps and we continued on to the next story. The upstairs held three massive bedrooms to the left. Aidan and I placed our bags in the chosen ones. They all had the same layout. Bed to the left, closet to the right, windows straight on.

Stephanie showed us back to the main floor. "So, this is where the 'hangout' room is," Stephanie walked across the living room and through the open door frame to the next room. This room was equal to the size of the living room and held a large card table and to the right, a massive black sectional couch pointed toward a flat-screen television that was mounted onto the wall. To the left was a doorway that went outside. But in the far corner was another door that was not surrounded by any windows. It was painted black, my eyes narrowed on it, it was odd. The entire house being open concept except that singular small area.

"What does that door lead to?" Lucas asked curiously, pointing at the off door.

"Just the basement, it's not very safe," Stephanie quickly dismissed it. Lucas seemed satisfied and jumped onto the couch. Aidan was quick to follow.

"This is literally in the middle of nowhere," Aidan paused, taking in the freedom. "Ah!" Aidan screamed at the top of his lungs. He laughed to himself. We all looked at each other and screamed at the top of our lungs knowing no one was going to be disturbed by us. It was completely freeing.

"Is your brother going to be joining us?" I turned to Stephanie.

"No, I told him to not come up this weekend." Stephanie smiled. She turned and jumped on the couch with the others. Aidan was quick to blast some music and soon everyone was up on their feet dancing.

"Do you have any alcohol?" Aidan called.

"In the fridge, my foster brother stocked us up," Stephanie continued to dance. Her hair was flying all over the place. I followed Aidan into the kitchen. He stood at the fridge looking at all the goodies.

"She wasn't kidding." Aidan started to take out beer and cocktails. I looked around feeling hungry. There was a sticky note on one of the cabinets: "For Stephanie's friends."

"Huh, look," I said ripping off the sticky. I opened the cabinet. It was chalked full of junk food: cookies, chips, a delivery menu for pizza.

"Sick, pizza." Aidan grabbed the menu. "Wonder how long they take to deliver." Aidan looked at both sides of the menu. "We're ordering pizza!" Aidan called, running into the room. The music was quickly paused for the debate on what pizza. I brought in a few bags of chips. One was quickly stolen by Stephanie.

All pizzas that weren't just pepperoni were quickly shot down by Stephanie. The end order was two large pepperoni pizzas. We were all hungry from the lack of lunch. "Should we watch a movie?" Stephanie suggested.

"Yes, debate time!" Aidan shouted.

"Debate time?" Stephanie whispered to me.

"We each choose a movie and pitch it, whoever gets the most votes win, you can't vote for your own," I whispered back. Stephanie nodded. You could see her competitive wheels start turning.

"I'll start," Lucas stood up and cleared his throat. "*Die Hard*, an iconic movie, has some good violence in there, some lovely romances, some comedic characters, it is perfectly paired with beer and pizza." Lucas bowed slightly.

"Boo! It's not Christmas!" Stephanie shouted, throwing a chip.

"Tough crowd today." Lucas sat down. Aidan was next, he stood up and straightened his clothing.

"*Mamma Mia*, a fun movie, delightful mother-daughter relationships, heartwarming, perfectly paired with the cocktails, pizza and this lovely audience right here." Aidan motioned to us.

"You're such a suck-up!" Lucas shouted. Stephanie stood up next.

"*The Autopsy of Jane Doe*, a horror movie, full of adrenaline rushes, best paired with alcohol and a cottage in the middle of nowhere where people can't hear your scream." Stephanie curtseyed and sat down. We all nodded in agreement.

"Hard to follow that one," I stood up. "*Scream*, a horror movie that we can make fun of as it's old. Full of screams and laughs, best paired with a lot of alcohol." I bowed and sat down.

"Okay all those for Lucas's *Die Hard*?" Aidan called. The room was silent. "For my *Mamma Mia*?"

"Aye!" Lucas shouted. Aidan nodded pleased with his one vote.

"For Stephanie's *Autopsy*?" Aidan called.

"Aye!" I called out.

"Looks like Levi has won with *Scream*," Aidan announced.

"Thank you, I would like to thank my mother and father for raising me with such good taste," I joked. Stephanie promptly threw a chip at me. We quickly rented the movie.

The movie was worse than I remembered. The doorbell rang

loudly in the middle. Stephanie grabbed my arm out of fear before snapping out of it and walking over to the door. A few moments of hushed whispers between the pizza man and Stephanie were concluded as she excitedly brought over the large boxes of pizza. The room erupted in happiness.

Once the movie was done, and we had more than our fair share of pizza we all split up to go our designated ways. I stayed back picking up empty cans and bottles. Stephanie came out in her robe to do the same. Without her makeup on, a scar along the right side of her jaw could clearly be seen. I paused, my curiosity wanting me to demand where she got her scars. They were odd, not the typical 'I fell' kind of scars. They all seemed distinct and linear.

"Oh, I have that," she smiled, grabbing the leftover pizza to put in the fridge.

"Look, can we talk?" I followed her to the fridge.

"Ya, what's up?" she asked, seemingly ignorant to what had been going on.

"I don't know what I said 'no' to, it obviously made you angry." I put the cans on the counter. Stephanie began walking to her room.

"I'm not mad, you're not interested, I was embarrassed, but we're okay, you're allowed to not like me." Stephanie retreated to her room and began to close the door. I stopped it with my hand. She looked up in surprise, her blue eyes on me.

"That's just it, I am interested," I murmured, my nerves preventing my tone from being louder than a barely audible whisper. "I was surprised that you kissed me, everyone said that you were too far out of my league. And you are. So you kissed me and I panicked. You're so far out of my league Stephanie, you're beautiful, funny—" I blurted out, the flustered speech barely making sense with the overlapping syllables. Stephanie moved closer, pressing her lips against mine, shutting me up from my speech.

She pulled me into her room; and I pushed the door shut. My hands quickly on her as she gripped my hair and pulled herself close. My lips collapsed over hers as my fingers glided along her body. Desperate to feel every inch of my skin against hers. She pulled away in a moment that felt like forever. I let out a whimper, somehow everything felt so cold without her lips on mine.

Stephanie got down on her knees and undid my belt, her eyes on me as she pulled down my pants, slightly exposing my neon pink boxers. I opened my mouth to explain that if I knew this was going to happen I would've worn something sexier but shut it realizing that this was not the time. My internal monologue was quickly suppressed as I felt my erection enter her mouth. I let out a loud gasp, that egged her on as she continued more ferociously. My hands went through her hair, I felt her head bob, her tongue flick and her lips move along me, the slight suction. I moaned loudly, completely captivated, still in disbelief that the sexiest woman I'd ever set eyes on was on her knees, pleasuring me. I didn't last very long before making a grunting noise as I finished.

"Thank you," I panted.

"Thank you?" she laughed, standing up. My face turned red in embarrassment. She pulled me close to her and leaned into my ear. "You're welcome," she whispered, nibbling at my ear.

"Fuck, you're so sexy," I whispered. She grabbed my hand and led me to the bed. "I, uh, I don't think I can go again just yet."

"I was meaning to cuddle," Stephanie undid her robe revealing a nightgown. I stripped down to my boxers and crawled into bed next to her. She cuddled up next to me. I put my arms around her, falling asleep almost instantly next to her.

I woke up to an empty bed, and stretched out slowly recalling what happened last night. I smiled to myself, getting out of bed and throwing on my jeans and T-shirt, walking out of the bedroom. Aidan, Lucas and Stephanie were all huddled around the kitchen counter, eating toast and fruit. I walked up to Stephanie and gave her a kiss on the cheek.

"Good morning, sleepyhead," she giggled. "I'm going to get dressed." She turned and kissed me on the lips before walking back to her bedroom. I looked, beaming at Aidan and Lucas. Their expressions were of complete fear.

"We did stuff last night," I smiled and winked. Aidan and Lucas looked at each other. Lucas looked down and began to prod at the fruit bowl. "You're not still going on about how she's going to break my heart are you?" I sighed.

"No, man, shut up for a second." Aidan took a deep breath.

"Because we did stuff last night," I said, attempting to lighten the mood.

"We know!" Lucas stated, frustrated.

"We need to show you something." Aidan looked at Lucas, Lucas slowly got up and began walking to the room he slept in last night.

"Guys, this isn't funny." My heart began to pound. What were they on about? What could possibly require such a somber occasion? I stepped into the room Lucas slept in to find him standing by the closet. The closet doors were pulled open, the male clothing pushed away from the center.

"I promise I didn't watch or anything," Lucas tried to explain, pointing at a light part of the closet. I approached it. "I just heard you guys talking, so I wanted to try to make out what you were saying and I found this." Lucas choked out. My heart sank, the tenseness collapsing around it as I stared blankly at what he was pointing to.

This couldn't be happening.

This couldn't be real. I heard Lucas sniffle as my breath quickened. My palms became sweaty, my body became numb.

The spot of light was a grate.

I stepped closer, still stunned, still in complete disbelief. There was a thin mesh darkening the vision, but you could very clearly see Stephanie getting dressed in front of her floor-length mirror.

"What the fuck is this?" I whispered. My heart pounded loudly in my chest. I looked around the room to Lucas and Aidan, both looking solemnly at me, knowing what it was. "Did you tell Stephanie about this?" My mind was racing.

"No, we wanted to show you first," Aidan explained.

"No one tell her," I ordered, closing the clothes over the grate. Aidan and Lucas looked at me, a bewildered expression sliding over their miserable expressions.

"Her brother is watching her, she has a right to know," Lucas protested.

"We don't know that this is his room, we don't know that he put that in."

"Then let her explain that to us," Aidan argued. His face hardened with anger. Aidan and Lucas continued to speak, but their words fell into a blur as my mind spun out of control, my heart feeling weak as the pace became uncontrollable. I felt like the world was collapsing around me.

"You shouldn't have been snooping." I gained composure for a second and walked out of the room and to the kitchen running my hands through my hair. Trying to calm down my breathing.

"Are you okay?" Stephanie came over resting her hand on my arm as I tried to breathe.

"Uh, Lucas and I are going to head out, Stephanie," Aidan called.

"Okay," Stephanie replied. The door slammed behind them. "Did something happen?"

"We just had a fight," I wiped the tears from my eyes, my breath nothing but a wheeze. My mind spiraling in a thousand directions as I tried to make sense of it. Was she okay? Was she safe? Was I doing the right thing? My whole perfect moment with her now seemed dirty, my joy of last night came pummeling down. Our moment fracturing into shards that sliced at my chest. I had never encountered something like this. How do you possibly tell someone there was a grate that looked into their room? How do you possibly break someone's safety like that? I tried to hide my face from Stephanie, unable to qualify this reaction to her. I wanted to seem strong. "They're worried about losing you," I lied. "I'm just going to straighten up."

I walked out and back into her room clinging on to the hope I would see just a bad cover-up job. But when I looked to the left, I saw an art nouveau painting. I walked closer to it peering through and when I stood close enough I could see that not everything was painted. In those parts, it was a thin black mesh. I lifted the painting up to look behind it and saw the grate. I hung it back up and stepped back staring at it. Could all of this just be a mistake? Surely it must be. I desperately pulled this veil of ignorance over myself, not wanting to admit something might be wrong. I barely knew her. I wasn't the one to question this.

"What are you looking at?" Stephanie whispered, hugging

me from the side.

"The painting, it's interesting."

"That's Raphael's, my foster brother. He loves art nouveau, me not so much. But when we bought this cottage, he wanted his favorite piece in my room. He thought it would make me appreciate it more or something."

"We should probably get going too, there's a long drive ahead of us."

Chapter 3

"Why didn't you tell her about the grate?" The brown-haired lady cut in.

"Knowing what I know now, I would have told her. But I was terrified of having her feel her privacy was invaded," I responded.

"Why would her brother invading her privacy affect you?" the green-eyed lady questioned.

"I was worried she would feel that I invaded her privacy," I corrected. "I tried to reason that her brother didn't know, but I was scared of losing her. I was the new person in her life, who was she more likely to turn on, me or her foster brother?"

***

I sat at the kitchen table of my home, early Monday morning in the darkness. My brain still not able to catch up to what happened. I felt like a helpless child. This moment, this *thing*, eating away at me. The lack of sleep made it difficult to process it anymore. My brain only coming together for one singular thought.

This was fucked up.

But how fucked up? Every morsel of my being wanted to tell Stephanie, to shake her and say she needed to get away from her supposedly trusted companions. But what if she chose them? What if they made up a lie and she fell for it and I was thrown out of her life like garbage. I couldn't do anything then. I couldn't help her then. At this point I wasn't sure if I was being selfish or protective. Perhaps I just didn't want her to think negatively of our first time together. No. That couldn't be it, right? I was a better man then that.

Right?

I heard footsteps approaching. The distinct pad of my mother's slippers echoing down the wooden stairs and to the kitchen doorway. I heard her stop, inevitably confused by what her son was doing. My nails continued to pick at the kitchen table, unwilling to look up and have to acknowledge the fact that I had to make a decision about this. About what I should do with this disgusting and massive piece of information that had been dumped on me. I felt like I needed to claw my way out, or maybe I could just lay down and let it pile over me. Maybe I could suffocate, then I wouldn't have to figure out what kind of man I was. Maybe then I wouldn't have to be confronted with this test of morality. I could just – suffocate.

"Sweetheart, what are you doing sitting in the dark?" Mom asked, flipping on the light switch.

"Am I a bad person, Mom?"

"Is this about the girl you've been seeing?" she asked, starting the coffee. I heard more footsteps approaching.

"No way is this my son sitting here early on a Monday morning!" Dad mocked ruffling my hair.

"He's having girl trouble." Mom smirked excitedly at dad.

"Nothing we can't help you fix," dad sat down beside me, patting my shoulder endearingly.

"What if you had a really bad secret, but you decided not to tell the person it impacted? But now if you tell them, they'd know you didn't tell them immediately," I explained vaguely. Mom and dad looked at each other.

"If it's serious, you have to tell them the truth," mom reasoned hesitantly.

"Can you fix this bad thing?" Dad smiled. "If it's fixed, there's nothing to tell." Dad stood up to help prepare breakfast. I quite preferred his rendition of things.

"Mom, can we go shopping?"

The week went by slowly. Aidan and Lucas were avoiding me. Stephanie and I hung out every day. She was going up to the cottage this weekend with the intention of writing a paper. Apparently, she had procrastinated significantly and needed peace and quiet in order to sit down and get it finished. I understood the feeling. All my assignments were done with a few energy drinks the night before it was due. I was rather impressed she was so stressed when the paper was due on Tuesday.

I sat beside my mom in the car, a large bag at my feet. The drive seemed longer than before. Maybe I was nervous about surprising Stephanie. When the stones began to pummel our car and the loudness of the drive became somewhat unbearable so did my anxiety over the situation. "Are you sure you want to do this, sweety? It seems like kind of a grand gesture," mom reasoned. She had a point, there was a massive chance Stephanie would yell 'creep' and slam the door in my face but it was something I had to do. "We can turn back at any time."

"I want to do this mom; she's going to really like it." I insisted, more to convince myself than her. My mom pulled up to the gate. "This is good," I got out of the passenger seat.

"Good luck, sweety," mom called as I trekked through the trees beside the gate. I walked up the driveway where there were a few cars, a mattified black Cadillac, a black Range Rover, a black Rolls-Royce and Stephanie's red Toyota. Her vehicle stuck out like a sore thumb next to these pristine, expensive vehicles.

I immediately panicked and realized that I hadn't thought this plan all the way through. I turned and looked back to my mom, only to find that she had already taken off.

Shit.

There was only one way and that was forward. I walked up the stones to the large door. It seemed far more looming this time. I took a wavering breath in and knocked. I heard shouting come from inside and the door creaked open.

"Levi?" Stephanie looked at me confused.

"Surprise!" I smiled.

"I have a paper to write," she said somewhat annoyed. "Who dropped you off?" Her confused attention turned to glancing behind me.

"I know, I will be very quiet, I promise," I reassured. "I come bearing gifts." I gestured to the large bag in my hand.

"Ya, I guess. Come on in." Stephanie opened the door wider and continued to walk to the hangout area. I set the bag down and followed her. "Hey, guys, uh, Levi's here, he'll be staying for the rest of the weekend."

"You're kidding right?" came a man's voice. I rounded the corner and saw a group of four men with cards in their hands. None of them much older than Stephanie or me. "No fucking way." The man leaned back in his chair staring at me and at Stephanie almost looking confused. His tussled hair was a dirty blond. His dark eyes looked vehemently annoyed with my presence. His short sleeves showed a few tattoos on each arm, his muscles were large and somewhat flexed as he kissed his teeth while glaring at me.

"I know she's out of my league," I joked, hoping to make

this encounter less uncomfortable.

"You got that right," another man snickered. The blond-haired man put his finger up, which quieted the snickering man. He slowly leaned forward, tossing his cards on the table and standing up. He puffed out his chest and walked toward me.

"Be nice," Stephanie whispered to him protectively. The man nodded at her then placed his daunting, vicious gaze back at me. I swallowed hard, trying not to show my fear. I looked around seeing that the other men were leaning forward waiting to see what the leader's reaction was going to be.

"Welcome to our home," the man smirked, extending a hand to me.

"You must be Stephanie's brother," I shook his hand.

"Foster," the man clarified, squeezing my hand tighter. "Foster brother," he let go of my hand. The other men snickered.

"His name is Raphael and he's a bit of a drama queen," Stephanie stated, frustrated, guiding me out of the room.

"I have another surprise for you,." I whispered to her. She smiled.

"Can we do it tomorrow? It's late and it's been a long Friday, I just kind of want us to go into the bedroom." She bit her lip.

"It won't take long, stay here." I placed her at the entrance and grabbed the bag, rushing into her room.

After everything was prepared, I guided her in with my hands over her eyes. Once positioned I removed my hands revealing a new painting in place of the old art nouveau one that previously covered the grate. I had spent the week lining the back of the painting with as much insulation that could fit to give her some audio privacy too. "I thought this was more to your taste," I wrapped my arms around her from behind and placed my chin on her shoulder.

"I love it," she whispered. The painting was of the inside of a museum, it wasn't a real painting, but it was a beautiful print.

"See, I like to imagine I'm working right over here," I pointed to the right-hand side of the painting.

"It's perfect," she beamed, turning around to face me. Her head turned as footsteps approached in the hallway. She walked over and shut the door, then turned back to me. Stephanie slowly undid her oversized see-through white blouse to reveal the black lace bra that showed through more plainly. I swallowed hard, amazed that I was looking at such perfection in person. She took off her short shorts revealing a black thong. My eyes glided over her; she had a long scar over her left hip. Another scar. I ignored it, desperate to turn my brain off and enjoy her.

I threw off my shirt and removed my pants quickly, sitting down on the edge of the bed. She straddled me and moved her hair over her right shoulder. My eyes slowly glided up her body, taking in every divot, freckle, line and scar.

"You're perfect," I whispered as my hands began gliding up her body. She gently pushed me down on the bed. She stood back up and took off her underwear revealing herself to be completely shaved. I crawled back a bit repositioning myself at the top of the bed and removed my boxers. She unclasped her bra and tossed it to the side. Stephanie went to her closet and opened a drawer. She came back with a condom in her hand and crawled on top of me opening the package. She placed the condom on my tip and rolled it down. We were really doing this.

"Do you want me to fuck you?" She bit my ear. I put both my hands on her thighs, my fingers nervously massaging them.

"Yes," my voice came out as a weak beg. She gently grabbed my erection and positioned it, slowly pressing down. I gasped with pleasure. Her movements started out slow so I could feel every inch go inside her. She gradually sped up, holding the headboard for leverage. Her perfect body lifting and lowering as I drew closer and closer to climax. I moaned loudly with every beat. My eyes on her, unable to close them or look away. I was captivated by her movements, the way she glid along me, the way her head tilted back slightly whenever I was fully inside her. The way her breasts looked whenever she took a breath in. My mind was unable to stray from what was happening. I tried to pull it away. I tried to think of anything else to prolong this. But I could not resist her. Her lips were slightly parted as she rolled her hips, a soft moan parting the air between us. That was it. The indulgent fucking became too much. I gripped her thighs tightly as the pleasure overtook me. I jerked forward slightly. Stephanie lifted and lowered herself one more time as I groaned loudly. I lay there out of breath as she removed herself. I sat forward and took off the condom, going into the washroom to throw it out. I stumbled out of the washroom and dove into the bed. Stephanie turned off the light and cuddled up to me.

I woke up to Stephanie putting on her sweatshirt and shorts. I've never seen her so casual. I beamed to myself, amazed that I had fucked *her*.

"Good morning, beautiful," I said groggily.

"Look at you, up early," she joked. I rolled out of bed and threw my clothes on. We walked out to the kitchen. Raphael's friends all turned and stared at us. The silence was shattered as they cheered loudly pounding on the countertops. "You guys are perverts," she scolded.

"How did you know?" I asked, my voice managing to come out in weak terror instead of the strong demand I intended.

"We assumed," the guy closer to me stood up. He reached

his hand out to me. He was wearing a black T-shirt, showing arms bigger than my face, his black tattoos ran all the way to his neck. I reached out my hand to shake his. "And you just confirmed it to us." He laughed loudly. The gang of men cackled. "I'm Jace, that is Eli." He pointed at a man eating a Pop-Tart. He had a dark shade on his head. He looked strong, his arms and chest muscles defined but smaller than the others. Compact. He had no visible tattoos and light brown eyes. "That's James." Jace pointed to a man eating an apple. His left arm was covered in burn scars, his blond hair was combed back, his eyes a clouded blue.

"Okay, coffee time," Stephanie announced, dolling up the various coffee orders.

"So Levi, what are your intentions with Stephanie?" Eli smirked. James and Jace sat back, curiously awaiting my response.

"Oh, shut up Eli," Stephanie rolled her eyes. "Don't answer that," she instructed.

"You'll quickly learn that Stephanie runs this house," James cut in. "We are all at her mercy," he laughed.

"Don't let Raphael hear you say that," Eli joked.

"Where is Raphael anyway?" Stephanie looked around the room.

"Maybe he decided to sleep in?" James suggested. The kitchen roared with boisterous laughter.

"Let's go ask him if he has some clothes you can borrow," Stephanie suggested.

"You came all the way out here without bringing a change of clothes?" Jace gave me a confused glance. "Damn, Stephanie. You know how to wrap them around your finger."

"Do any of you have any extra clothing?" She looked at all the men sitting at the table. They all shrugged. She rolled her eyes

49

and walked back through the hallway. I followed. She turned into her room which confused me until I stepped in.

"This is new," Raphael was staring at the painting I had brought yesterday. A bucket of ice felt like it had been dumped down my back as I looked at him. His body was tense as he rocked on his heels. I glanced around the room, plotting a quick escape.

"Ya, Levi bought that for me," Stephanie sat down on her bed, ignorant to the panic that was slowly gripping me. Raphael slowly turned around and smiled at me.

"Well, I much prefer the old one, but as it's already been changed, I guess there's no going back now," Raphael said, not breaking eye contact with me. I looked over to Stephanie who opened her mouth to say something but was cut off by Raphael. "Since you have to work on your essay today, I thought I would take Levi out for a hike." Raphael stepped toward me, a seemingly unperturbed grin on his face.

"If he wants to," Stephanie looked at me, trying to give me an out.

"Okay," I croaked, not convinced there was another option. If I said no, he'd probably kill me some other time anyway.

"He'll need different clothing," Stephanie pointed out.

"Yes, I can see that, I'll bring it over." Raphael gave me a brisk nod before leaving the room, dropping off a stack of clothing before disappearing into the hallway.

"That's really good!" Stephanie announced. "It typically takes him a while to warm up to people." She passed me the shirt from the pile.

"Has your brother ever killed someone?" I asked, trying to sound joking but a bit of panic slipped into my speech.

"What kind of question is that?" Stephanie laughed.

"That's not a no," I said, my voice breaking slightly.

"I mean, maybe." Stephanie sat down on her bed. Not a reassuring answer. "You'll find this out soon enough, my foster brother isn't like a 'good guy.' He's done a lot of shitty things. I get he's scary, but he's loyal, he won't touch you, none of them will."

"Like robbing a store kind of shitty? Or murdering multiple people shitty." I did up my belt.

"Like robbing banks type shitty," Stephanie said pensively. Does that mean he's robbed banks, or that it's something equal to it? "You look really good," Stephanie charmed. I stepped in front of the floor-length mirror. I looked very good.

"Let's go," Raphael pounded on the door. Stephanie nodded to me and I left the bedroom. Raphael tossed a jacket at me and I followed him out through the hangout room. We walked into the forest. I was hyper-aware of what was happening. The sticks breaking beneath our feet, the birds flying overhead. The bushes moved as creatures ran away from us. My palms were sweaty, my breath shaky. Raphael's coat went past his knees and was a dark gray. His black boots crunched the terrain under him. He had dressed me up similar to him. I had black pants, a black shirt and a past knee-length black jacket. Raphael moved his coat back, taking a handgun from his back pocket. He took out the clip and stopped, reaching into his pocket and loaded it up with bullets. I froze. Maybe it was for protection? Maybe they had dangerous animals around here? My mind whirled trying to come up with a reasonable explanation. Raphael looked up and snapped the clip back in. He continued walking. So did I.

"You know the reason I bought this place?" Raphael paused and looked at me, smiling. I shook my head. "Completely in the middle of nowhere, no one around to hear a gunshot." Raphael's grin disappeared. He looked at me with complete seriousness. His eyes were vicious. There was a long period of silence.

"Very useful for a man in your field," I tried to joke, my voice breaking every few syllables.

"I don't like people that cause me problems." Raphael stated, his eyes focused on the terrain in front of him. I stayed quiet. "Will you be one of those people?" Raphael stopped and looked at me.

"No," I choked out.

"Good." Raphael continued to walk. My body and brain were completely numb in terror. There was no running from this, my feet weren't functioning well enough. The only thing I could do is aimlessly follow this man. "You know, if you were nervous about your..." Raphael paused for a second, choosing his words carefully "...bedroom performance, you could have asked any of us for advice, you didn't have to do something so rash."

"What the fuck? I wasn't worried about my bedroom performance," I retorted, my brain shocked out of its coma. Raphael stopped walking.

"You should be," he smirked. "First time I've ever heard her silent." Raphael's eyes danced at the prospect of humiliating me. He was trying to distract me from what he had done. Make me feel belittled. The years of being raised by a therapist kicking in just long enough for me to fight.

"I was worried about the fact you were fucking watching her."

Raphael's uninhibited smile widened. "Well, that couldn't have been the case." His voice became smooth. "If that were the case, you would have told her." He laughed quietly to himself. "You are just as bad as I am."

"Maybe I was planning to tell her today," I argued. "Maybe

I'll tell her now." I began to walk back, desperate to not be compared to him. I heard a click behind me. I turned around to see that he had his gun pointed at my head.

"I'm so sorry, Stephanie, it was just an accident. He got in my way," Raphael made a pitiful face at me.

"Okay," I said, my hands partially up.

"You saw that grate and you thought to yourself 'Stephanie won't want to be with me if I show her this.' How the fuck do you think she would feel now after you didn't tell her? You can't say you didn't know, there's insulation in the back of the painting. You fucked yourself over and pissed me off in the process. You can either run back and lose Stephanie, and maybe I'll kill you. Or you can man up to what *you've* done and maybe gain a tiny bit of respect from me."

"You're right," My voice broke, realizing that every word he said was true. Raphael lowered his gun and continued walking. I followed. "What did you use the grate for?" I asked, trying to find a new way to justify it to myself.

"Why does that matter? Tell yourself what you need to hear."

"What?"

"Tell yourself what you need to go to sleep at night. I use it to protect her, I use it to watch her, I use it to watch her fuck others. Tell yourself whatever you need to hear like I did when I put in that fucking grate." Raphael put his gun in his back pocket.

"Okay," I agreed. Probably best that way.

"Let's head back, this wasn't a good idea." Raphael turned around and began walking back to the cottage.

"You're important to Stephanie," I stated.

"Glad you have a brain to compensate for your weakness." Raphael rolled his eyes.

"I don't want you to hate me," I continued.

"Why are you here?" Raphael snapped. "Was it just to swoop in like a savior? She doesn't need *your* protection."

"Look I'm sorry I angered you; I'm just trying to protect her," I replied. Raphael laughed.

We walked the rest of the way to the cottage in silence. I entered the cottage as Raphael stayed back. I came in to find Stephanie at the hangout table with her laptop open. Eli was sitting next to her with two history books propped open.

"Ah, you have a team." I smiled, my pulse beating rapidly. Stephanie looked up and giggled.

"Ya, Eli's really good at this stuff." She gestured to Eli who was completely encapsulated in one of the books.

"Found another nerd like you," I joked. Stephanie smiled. There was loud gunfire outside. Raphael stormed in.

"I don't like him," Raphael muttered to Stephanie. Stephanie looked at me confused, then walked after Raphael.

"You have barely met him." Stephanie grabbed his arm. "You need to calm down." Stephanie looked at him intently. Raphael yanked his arm away from her and continued walking. Stephanie followed. I heard a door shut.

"What did you do?" Eli laughed. I shrugged. "It's okay, Stephanie will get him sorted out."

"What did the boy do?" Jace chuckled while walking into the room with James. They both patted my shoulder and sat down at the table.

"He doesn't know," Eli mused. "Stephanie brought me into this family. My introduction to Raphael went even worse than yours."

"Hard to imagine," I replied. Eli pulled the top of his shirt down to reveal a gunshot scar on his left shoulder. "Holy shit." I muttered.

"I was crashing at Stephanie's place; he swears he thought I was breaking into her apartment. He'll get over this, he's just territorial." Eli nodded at me.

"Like a wolf with too much testosterone," Jace joked.

"I'm going for a drive," Raphael shouted. The front door slammed behind him.

"Urg," Stephanie shouted walking to the hangout room.

"Guessing that didn't go too well?" I asked.

"No, it's fine, you did nothing wrong." Stephanie sat beside me.

"We've already established that, you're late to the party," Eli laughed.

"The drive will calm him down, it always does," Jace reassured me.

"What do you guys want to do?" Stephanie leaned back in her chair.

"I'm going order us all burgers, then get high as fuck," Jace smiled.

"I'm craving pizza," James said.

"You're always craving pizza, we're getting burgers." Jace left the room.

"Knock on the door when the burgers arrive," Stephanie instructed. She grabbed my arm gently and gestured for me to come with her. I obeyed. We went back to her room. "I'm sorry about all this, Raphael can be such a dick."

"It's not your fault, he doesn't like me. I shouldn't have sprung myself on you guys this weekend," I replied.

"No, it was sweet, he'll come around." Stephanie wrapped her arms around my neck. She leaned forward and kissed me gently.

"Did Raphael say why he didn't like me?" I asked.

"No, he's just being protective. Nothing to do with you, it's something Raphael has to work out." Stephanie kissed my cheek. "Let's take your mind off this, what do you want to do?"

"I want to learn more about you." I smiled and sat down on her bed.

"I want to learn more about *you*."

"We can play 'never have I ever'?"

"A drinking game this early? Mr. Davis, I think you'll be a bad influence on me." Stephanie laughed. "I'll grab the vodka." Stephanie winked and skipped out of the room, returning with a bottle of vodka.

"Is that Crystal Head Vodka? A little too proper for a drinking game don't you think?" I smiled.

"Why get normal drunk, when you can get proper drunk?"

"Fair enough, okay you go first," I encouraged. Stephanie sat down on the bed, putting her legs over mine.

"Never have I ever climbed a tree."

"Excuse me? You've never climbed a tree? That is just sad." I shook my head. I took a shot of vodka straight from the bottle. "Never have I ever driven a car."

"I'll make you drive one day," Stephanie stated. She took a shot of vodka. "Never have I ever owned any pets," Stephanie smiled. I took a shot.

"A small hamster, it managed to drown in a jug of water after escaping," I replied. Stephanie started to laugh. "It was traumatic!"

"No, I know, it's just a ridiculous death."

"It was. Never have I ever done any recreational drugs." I was curious about her response to this question. Stephanie took a shot. "What have you done?"

"I've done a lot, I don't do any currently, I've done weed, cocaine, ecstasy and meth."

"Any particular reason you don't take them?"

"Just don't like the feelings they give me." Stephanie smiled. "Never have I ever had a threesome."

"I have never done that, no, never have I ever committed a crime," I said. Stephanie took a shot. "What crime?"

"I'm not out here trying to get arrested," Stephanie giggled. "Never have I ever had sex with someone hotter than you."

"That's true," I joked. I took a shot.

Stephanie took the bottle and put it on the floor, her eyes on me hungrily as she pulled off her top revealing a light blue lace bra. My body immediately filled with need as I stared at her. She stood up, slowly undoing her shorts and allowing them to drop to the floor showing a matching lace thong.

"Holy fuck," I breathed.

Stephanie straddled me, gently pushing me back as she bit my ear. I let out a soft groan, pressing my erection up, desperate to find some release. She kissed me, her tongue immediately flicking the inside of my teeth. I could taste the vodka on her, my senses on full alert as I touched her bare skin. Her fingers stroked along my chest and moved lower, beginning to undo my belt.

"Touch me," I pleaded, my erection painful with anticipation. She flicked my pants open, her fingers darting in and gliding along me. "Yes." I gasped.

"Food is here," Jace announced. Stephanie and I turned sharply. Jace was leaning against the open doorway, a smirk firmly on his face.

"Jesus fuck, Jace. How long have you been there?" Stephanie bit out, stomping over to him.

"Long enough." Jace winked at her. Stephanie slammed the

door in his face. "You look great!" Jace yelled through the door. Stephanie rubbed her face. I did my pants back up, a mixture of embarrassment and frustration making it impossible to regain the moment.

"I'm so sorry," Stephanie said. Grabbing her shorts and putting them on. I sat up motioning for her to come closer. She obeyed, a small smile on her lips.

"You do look great," I said. She promptly hit me with a pillow. I laughed. Stephanie pulled on a shirt and walked out of her room and into the hangout room. James passed me a tinfoil-wrapped burger.

"Oh damn, we forgot to order one for you," James smiled mischievously. Stephanie put her hand out. James shrugged.

"I'm hungry," Stephanie whined. I held out my burger for her. Stephanie grabbed it. James reached into his bag and passed me one.

"Damn, wasn't expecting the boy to give up his own dinner." James laughed. "If I found a man like that, maybe I would settle down."

"You're not allowed to settle down, I would be so lonely," Jace voiced.

"You know if you switched teams, we could settle down together," James winked.

"The minute I do you'll be my first call," Jace blew him a kiss.

"Ew, stop, I don't want to picture that," Eli groaned. "Movie tonight?"

"Ya, sure. I want something violent," Jace said.

"*Saw*?" Stephanie suggested.

"Gross Steph, I said violent, not disturbed," Jace replied.

"*Saw* sounds good," James nodded. Eli nodded.

"You guys disgust me." Jace shook his head. "What about you, Levi?"

"*Saw* sounds good," I lied. I had never been able to sit through it.

"Are you sure? It's kind of a mood killer." Jace raised an eyebrow at me.

"Not to Stephanie," James replied. Stephanie hit him on the arm. "What?" he laughed. "I'm sharing my wisdom."

"That's a lie." Stephanie giggled looking at me.

"I mean, whatever works for you." I joked. James roared with laughter. Stephanie gave me the finger playfully. I kissed her on the cheek.

"So *Saw* it is," Eli announced. I nodded, taking a bite out of the burger. It was amazing the beef was juicy and gushed when you took a bite. The lettuce was crunchy, the cheese gooey. I ate it quickly, unable to stop from downing it in seconds.

Jace had rolled up the tinfoil and was throwing it at Eli's head, it would bounce back slightly and he would swoop in and grab it and continue.

"Are we in elementary school?" Eli raised his head annoyed. The tinfoil hit him on his forehead.

"Yes, this is all a dream, you're going to wake up in class in three, two, one."

"Wish I could go back so I wouldn't have met you dorks." Eli laughed mockingly. He picked up the tinfoil and chucked it at Jace's head.

"This is what I have to put up with," Stephanie whispered to me.

"It's terrible, everyone's worst nightmare," I replied.

"Okay, movie time, who's on popcorn?" Stephanie asked.

"Me." Eli stood up and went to the kitchen. We all went and

sat on the couch, talking amongst ourselves until Eli brought the popcorn.

"May I suggest we don't put ourselves through such terror and watch something else. We have a few DVDs here. We have *Saving Private Ryan*, aggressive but it has a storyline, *Fast and Furious*, a classic, and from Raphael's collection we have *The Notebook*. All better options." Jace proposed.

"We can smoke weed and watch *The Notebook*," Eli suggested.

"That actually sounds pretty fun." James replied. Jace smiled. James grabbed the weed. "Do you want some?" he asked me.

"Maybe next time," I replied. James nodded, rolling three joints. He passed them out. Jace put on the movie. The smell of weed filled the room within seconds. "This a normal Saturday night?" I whispered to Stephanie.

"Pretty much," Stephanie whispered back. She cuddled up to me. I put my arms around her. We were all mesmerized by the movie. Not a word was said until the anger at the ending.

"Why did they have to make it such an awful ending?" Jace shouted.

"It's beautiful," Stephanie defended. "They spent their lives happily together."

"Then show that to us, not this." Jace growled.

"It's okay to be sad, Jace." Stephanie laughed.

"The movie is crap." Jace stood up and left, followed by James. Stephanie sighed, shaking her head. I looked over. Eli was sound asleep on the couch.

"To bed." Stephanie winked at me. We went to her room. "Where were we?" Stephanie took off her shirt and shorts. I leaped on the bed, removing my pants quickly. Stephanie crawled on top of me removing my shirt. She pulled off my boxers and licked my erection gently. I grabbed onto the bedsheets, moaning loudly. Stephanie placed her mouth around my rock-hard cock, suckling the tip, her fingers gliding along me softly. Her mouth moved further down, her lips tightly moving along me. She stood up abruptly and went to her dresser. Stephanie returned with a condom. She striped down, her mouth returning to my erection, this time it was deep, her mouth moving quickly as she massaged my balls with cold fingers. The distinct temperature drawing more pleasure from me. I let out a groan, shifting in ecstasy. She pulled her mouth off me, the cold air shooting through my nerves. Her fingers quickly put the condom on, kissing up my body and nipping at each of my nipples.

"Oh," I breathed at the unexpected, all-consuming pleasure. I felt her position my throbbing erection and press down. "Fuck," I moaned. Stephanie bit at my neck, keeping a steady rhythm. I was putty in her hands as she slowly fucked me. My right hand glided to her breast as my left went to the small of her back. I could feel her muscles working. I pinched her nipple gently.

"Baby," Stephanie moaned. Her voice drooling with desperation. My breath hitched, the sounds of her enjoyment driving me wild.

"Fuck," I whispered. She began to speed up, her muscles working more quickly as her breath became uneasy. Her hips rolling, her muscles tensing as she chased her pleasure. I wanted to give her what she wanted. The climax she was chasing. I pushed my hips up, feeling her slide down my hardened length. She let out a small gasp, her hand going to the center of my chest for stability. I could tell she was almost there, my fingers pinched at her nipples as she continued to move along me.

Without warning, my body betrayed me. Unable to hold

itself back from the image of her in heat. My body filled with pleasure as I grunted loudly, finishing.

"I'm sorry," I stammered, completely embarrassed by the abrupt ending to our intimacy.

"That was phenomenal." Stephanie breathed, locking our lips in an indulgent kiss.

Chapter 4

"Why did you not tell Stephanie that Raphael had threatened you?" the brown-haired lady asked. I sighed.

"I would then have had to explain why he had threatened me," I replied.

"So keeping that secret was more important than a gun pointed at your head?" the brown-haired lady demanded.

"That gun would have shot me if I told Stephanie. Another reason why I didn't say anything." I rolled my eyes.

"We're trying to help you," the green-eyed lady critiqued.

"You're right, I'm sorry," I muttered.

"Did you get the impression that Stephanie was scared of Raphael?" the brown-haired lady tapped her pen on a pad of paper.

"I don't think so, the others were cautious around him, but not her. I think she thought she was untouchable." I leaned back in my chair.

"So you don't think she had any idea Raphael could do this?" the green-eyed lady quizzed.

"I don't think any of us had any idea that Raphael could do this."

***

I was pulled from sleep by a tap on the door, followed by the very unwelcomed feeling of Stephanie leaving my embrace. My brain tiredly lurched in distress, trying to get my body to follow her and see what was going on. Unwillingly, I was betrayed by my fatigue and slipped back into sleep.

I woke again, already completely aware that Stephanie hadn't returned to my side. My eyes flung open; my body responding to my brains determination that something was wrong. My feet stepped out before I became aware I was still just wearing my boxers. But that was fine, Stephanie could be in trouble. When I reached the kitchen, I glanced over at the clock. Three a.m. The sound of faint voices punctured the morning air. It was coming from the hangout room. What if she was in danger?

No.

My mind lazily became aware of the fact the voices seemed friendly with each other. No yelling or angry tones. I allowed my feet to take me to the doorway of the hangout room.

"Oh, shut up," Stephanie giggled.

"I remember quite clearly," Raphael laughed. Stephanie was sitting in her robe, Raphael fully dressed next to her. A bottle of whiskey sat in front of them, they both had near empty glasses.

"Your memory is shit then," Stephanie mused. There was a long pause.

"I wish it didn't have to be this way," Raphael muttered silently.

"It's for the best," Stephanie replied. Raphael nodded. Stephanie leaned in and whispered something in his ear. Raphael laughed and looked up at Stephanie then turned to me in surprise. She turned around. "Come tell Raph that I wouldn't do this." Stephanie smiled at me, beckoning for me to join their conversation.

"What is it?" I asked, walking over and sitting beside Stephanie.

"I was reminding her that when she introduced me to Eli—" Raphael began.

"This being after you shot him?" I asked.

"Yes, immediately after, Eli was laying there bleeding, probably dying, but instead of going to help him she turned to me and said, 'Raph, your shot's gotten worse.'" Raphael chuckled. Stephanie shook her head.

"I wouldn't have done that," Stephanie shook her head. "Tell him." She nudged me.

"She wouldn't have done that," I smiled.

"See!" Stephanie beamed, pointing at me in success. Raphael sighed.

"Ask Eli in the morning, I guarantee this is what happened." Raphael stated, taking a sip of the whiskey. "I think I acted a bit too rashly in judging you." Raphael looked at me. "Maybe a clean slate is a good idea."

"I would like that," I replied, pulling Stephanie closer and giving her a kiss on the neck. Raphael cleared his throat.

"Well I think I got your girlfriend drunk enough." Raphael downed the rest and placed his empty glass on the coffee table, abruptly leaving the room.

"How much did you drink?" I teased, trailing my fingers along her spine.

"Not a lot," Stephanie replied, her big eyes looking at me innocently.

"Let's get you back to bed," I whispered. We crawled back into bed. I held her tightly as we drifted back to sleep.

"Fuck," Stephanie whispered as she woke up. She slid herself out of bed and pulled on underwear, a long shirt and her shorts. I got out of the bed and got dressed quickly.

"A little hungover are we?" I joked, wrapping my arms around her.

"Shh," Stephanie pleaded. I laughed loudly as we walked into the kitchen. Stephanie hunched over the counter.

"When did you get drunk?" Jace demanded.

"Raphael and her had an early morning whiskey tasting," I taunted.

"And you didn't invite me? Shameful," Jace muttered.

"Everyone was sleeping," Stephanie replied. Jace hit the counter next to Stephanie. "Don't be a dick." She aggressively pointed at Jace.

"Oof, someone had a rough night, what did you do to her?" Eli chuckled.

"I didn't do anything. Raphael got to her," I shrugged.

"Okay, that makes more sense." Eli gently rubbed Stephanie's back. Raphael walked in pulling his shirt over his abs. He cackled when he saw Stephanie slumped over.

"How many times do I have to tell you, you can't keep up with me?" Raphael leaned next to her.

"Lecture me quieter, please," Stephanie mumbled.

"Ah, well, have no fear. Raphael is here." Raphael took two shot glasses and a normal glass out of the cupboard.

"I don't think she needs more alcohol," I stepped in.

"It's not more alcohol. It's Raphael's hangover cure," Jace explained. James walked in and paused when he saw Stephanie.

"What'd I miss?" James asked the room.

"Stephanie drank with Raphael," Jace replied. James nodded understandingly.

"Okay, you know the drill, hot sauce, egg, ginger," Raphael ordered. He motioned to a shot glass full of hot sauce, a normal cup with a raw egg and the other shot glass filled to the brim with chopped ginger.

"I would rather not," Stephanie replied. She held her head to the side and gave Raphael a puppy dog face.

"Doesn't work on me when I know I'm right," Raphael flicked the tip of her nose. "Hot sauce, egg, ginger."

"Chug it, Stephanie, don't think," Jace instructed. Stephanie nodded. She shook her hands like she was getting ready for a marathon. Stephanie lifted up the hot sauce and took a deep breath. She chugged it down then moved on to the next two without flinching. Raphael passed her a glass of water after the ginger.

"Like a fucking champ," James smiled.

"I'll make my famous scrambled eggs," Raphael murmured to Stephanie. She clung onto him, Raphael wrapped his arms around her protectively. "Okay, go sit down."

"Do you think weed would taste good in eggs?" James asked Jace.

"To you, probably," Jace muttered. We all left Raphael in the kitchen and walked to the hangout room table. Eli grabbed the whiskey off the coffee table and put it away. He returned and sat down next to me.

"So is Raphael going to give you a second chance?" Eli grinned. I nodded. "See, told you."

"Looks like Stephanie sacrificed her brain to get you that second chance." Jace prodded.

"I'm fine, Levi is happy so I'm happy," Stephanie smiled.

"Are you?" Jace yelled. Stephanie crippled over and leaned in to me.

"Don't be a dick," I replied, wrapping my arms around her . Stephanie gave him the finger.

"Just having fun," Jace shrugged.

"We can go shooting if you want, Stephanie," James suggested. Stephanie mumbled. "I'll take that as a yes, we can go now."

"She'll kill you guys when she's back to normal," Eli stated.

"That's a later problem," Jace laughed. "The problem now is how to make this worse for her."

"Do we have an airhorn?" James asked.

"I don't ever remember Stephanie doing anything like that to you guys every single hangover you've had," Raphael placed a glass of water in front of Stephanie.

"This is a rare opportunity, Raph," Jace replied.

"Whatever mean things you do to her now, I will do to you every hangover you have for the rest of your life," Raphael warned. Jace and James nodded. "Eli," Raphael turned to him. "Stephanie and I were having a disagreement this morning. Did she immediately rush to your side after I shot you or did she stop to make a comment on my shot?"

"Sorry to disappoint you, Raphael, but I was literally dying and can't remember." Eli sighed.

"Guess you'll never know how wrong you are," Raphael joked, squeezing Stephanie's shoulder before making his way to the kitchen again.

"Did it hurt?" I asked Eli, gesturing to his shoulder.

"Not really, I went into shock pretty quick and passed out soon after that. The pain afterward was remarkable. We got our hands on some morphine so that helped," Eli replied.

"You didn't go to the hospital?" I asked.

"We would've taken him in if it got worse, Eli's on a few lists, you can't show up with a gunshot wound and not expect people to ask questions," Stephanie mumbled. "I mean, we're not all criminals and of course we took him to the hospital."

"Nice catch, Stephanie," Jace laughed. Stephanie gave him a thumbs up.

"I'm sure Stephanie knew exactly what she was doing." I kissed her on the cheek. Stephanie smiled at me.

"No further questions?" James asked, surprised.

"I mean, I'm curious," I replied.

"Nope, not doing this until Stephanie is in full working order," Raphael announced. He placed a plate of scrambled eggs in front of Stephanie.

"Thank you," Stephanie looked up at him graciously.

"Eggs are in the pan for the rest of you," Raphael said. Everyone stood up and went to the kitchen.

"I think Stephanie's his favorite," James joked. Jace laughed, before shrugging.

"I think Levi is." Eli gestured to me. I breathed a laugh. We grabbed our eggs and returned to the table. Raphael was sitting in my seat speaking with Stephanie in hushed tones.

"Okay, I am off, safe driving you two." Raphael nodded at me and left. The front door shut behind him.

"Where is he going?" I asked, sitting down beside Stephanie.

"He's going to church," Stephanie replied. Jace and James broke out in hysterics. "I'm not joking," Stephanie whined.

"I'm sorry Stephanie, no way." James shook his head. "Raphael could see God face to face and would shrug and not go to church."

"He has a meeting in a church. Guess the guy is super religious," Stephanie explained.

"Guess it's immediate forgiveness," Eli shrugged.

"A man of efficiency then," Stephanie smiled.

"Does anyone else think Raphael's eggs taste like shit?" James asked.

"These eggs make me believe in God," Stephanie said passionately.

"Guess your habit of getting on your knees will come in use then," Jace joked.

"I would say it came into use before," I replied. Jace and James roared with laughter.

"Ew, don't encourage them," Stephanie groaned.

"Come on Stephanie, that was pretty fucking quick," Jace laughed.

"Guess it matches you then," Stephanie quipped. James and I laughed.

"And she comes out swinging." Jace winked at Stephanie. "I'll drive you two back."

"I'm fine to drive," Stephanie insisted. Jace clapped loudly beside Stephanie's ear. Stephanie whimpered.

"I'm driving," Jace stood up and grabbed his keys. He left, shutting the door behind him. Stephanie and I got up and followed him out. We approached the vehicle, Jace honked. "Raphael isn't here to protect you anymore," Jace shouted victoriously. I got in the back.

"I hate you," Stephanie sat in the passenger seat.

"Nope, I am your favorite human," Jace replied.

"My favorite human is sitting in the back." Stephanie pointed at me.

"I am honored to even be nominated," I joked. Stephanie put her sunglasses on and leaned her head against the seat. We drove the long way home. Jace pulled into my driveway. My mom stood outside and waved.

"Your mom is kinda hot," Jace said, waving back.

"Ew, stop." Stephanie looked at him in disgust. "His mom is off-limits."

"She's also happily married to my dad," I said.

"Explains you," Jace muttered.

"Yes, how dare he actually have good parental figures," Stephanie snipped before getting out of the car to say goodbye to me. My mom started to walk over. "Oh fuck, I look like a trainwreck," Stephanie whispered, trying to organize her hair.

"Ya, you do," Jace laughed. Stephanie shot him a dirty look.

"Are you Stephanie?" Mom greeted her, my dad trailed behind.

"Yes," Stephanie smiled uncomfortably.

"This is my mom and dad," I introduced them.

"It's very nice to meet you," Stephanie extended and shook their hands.

"I would love to have you over for dinner sometime," mom beamed. "Maybe your parents too?"

"I would love to come to dinner, my parents aren't in the picture, it's just me and my foster brother," Stephanie explained.

"Oh, that's right, I'm sorry, sweety." Mom looked at her pitifully. "Is this your brother?" Mom gestured to Jace.

"Nope, just another misfit," Jace grinned.

"Well, we would love to have your brother over for dinner." Mom nodded at Stephanie.

"Oh, he's not really the 'dinner' type," Stephanie insisted.

"I'm the dinner type though," Jace stated, winking at my mom. Stephanie shot him another dirty look.

"We'll talk about that later; it was lovely to meet you." Mom smiled and walked back to the house.

"She'll wear you down in no time," dad whispered to Stephanie. He left us to say our goodbyes.

"I'll see you tomorrow," Stephanie said, stepping closer to me. I kissed her deeply, pulling her into me, my hand slowly going lower until it was on her ass. I grinded my growing erection against her. Stephanie placed her hand on my chest, pushing away gently. "I don't want them to hate me, so I'm going to go." She gestured to my parents watching us from the porch.

"What don't you want to fuck him in the driveway?" Jace shouted. Stephanie glared at him as she got in the vehicle. I waved as her car pulled out of the driveway, walking to my house.

"That was quite the kiss," mom grumbled. "And the misfit seems... lovely." We entered the house and sat down at the kitchen table. "What happened to her parents?" Mom prodded, curiously. I shrugged. "Well, I'm assuming it went well?" Mom asked.

"She loved the surprise," I replied.

"Oh, that's fantastic, tell us all about it," Mom beamed.

"She was at first confused about why I was there, but we had an amazing weekend together, I met her foster brother and friends. Her friends seem to like me, Raphael seems to... hate me," I explained.

"Oh, no one can hate you," Mom cooed.

"What did he do to make you think that?" dad queried.

"He said 'I don't like him' to Stephanie. I mean, this morning he said we can start with a clean slate, but I don't know if that's true," I replied.

"What is there to wipe clean? You just met him?" Dad inquired.

"He didn't like that I just stopped by. All of their friends said he'll get over it and that he's just protective of Stephanie," I explained.

"Well, I would believe their friends, he just needs to get used to you being around," dad said smiling.

"Ya, probably," I shrugged.

"Your grandpa hated me until I gave him a grandchild." Dad chuckled.

"I gave him the grandchild, you barely did anything," Mom rolled her eyes.

"Doesn't matter, I got a cigar and a pat on the back." Dad shrugged enthusiastically and kissed my mom on the cheek.

"So, your advice is to just stick around?" I clarified.

"Worked for me." Dad shrugged.

"No it didn't, my father didn't like your dad because your dad was a detective. He was concerned with the long hours and safety concerns that he wouldn't be a great husband. He quit that job not long after you were born, that's why he started to warm up to him," mom explained. "If he's protective, there's a reason he's protective, find that out and you'll win him over."

"Were you listening to my client's sessions again?" dad joked. My mom giggled. "I went through years of schooling to learn what your mom instinctively knows."

"How do I find out why he's protective?" I asked. Mom shrugged.

"My money's on asking Stephanie," dad smiled. I nodded and left for my room. I quickly sent a message to the group chat with Aidan and Lucas that everything was fixed. They agreed to meet me tomorrow morning.

I groaned and slowly rolled out of bed at the sound of my third alarm. Why did I agree to meet them in the morning? I made my way to the university and to the cafeteria. Aidan and Lucas were already sitting at our usual table. I sat down, placing my bag at my feet.

"Please explain how you fixed it," Aidan asked, his hands firmly on the cafeteria coffee.

"I bought her a different painting and insulated it," I stated. "I replaced the other one already."

"Did her brother say anything?" Lucas demanded.

"No, didn't say a word," I lied. It was easier that way. The minute they heard the word 'gun' I was certain they would call the police. I wasn't about to let that happen. I had no idea how mixed-up Stephanie was with all of this.

"Guess that means we may have overreacted," Lucas said. "We missed you."

"Aw, I missed you too," I took a sip of my coffee.

"How are things going with Stephanie?" Aidan asked.

"We had sex," I whispered to them. Their faces lit up with excitement.

"Where? Her cottage?" Aidan leaned forward inquisitively. I nodded.

"It was amazing." I bragged.

"Look at that, the gang's back together," Stephanie said gleefully.

"Ya, Levi was just telling us about your sex this past weekend," Lucas announced. My face turned bright red.

"Better be saying good things about our sex this past weekend," Stephanie bit down on a carrot, smirking at me.

"Why would I say good things; I want you all to myself," I winked.

"Ah, that's your tactic, make me un-dateable so I'm stuck with you."

"Caught me," I pulled her in closer, pressing our lips together. She shyly wrapped her arms around my neck as my tongue pushed her lips open.

"Ew," Lucas said. Stephanie pulled away.

"No, ignore them," I whined, collapsing my lips over hers as I glided my fingers up her leg.

"Stop," Stephanie giggled, pushing away from me. "Come with me to the cottage again this weekend, we can do whatever you want," Stephanie whispered to me. I audibly gasped, completely starstruck.

"We're right here." Aidan waved at us. "Are we invisible?"

"Yes," I replied. "I would love to go to your cottage this weekend, would Raphael be okay with that?" I turned to Stephanie.

"He'll have to be." Stephanie ran her fingers along the inseam of my jeans.

"If I said that about my parents, they would kill me," Lucas complained.

"The joys of having no parents are not lost on me," Stephanie snipped.

"I thought Raphael was a parental figure to you?" Lucas defended himself.

"He's not that much older than me."

"No fucking way does he own that cottage then," Aidan stated.

"He does, yes," Stephanie said. "I helped, I used to be a very expensive stripper, Raphael used to be a very expensive drug dealer. We worked until we felt safe," Stephanie shrugged.

"Why are you here? Just continue what you were doing!" Aidan replied.

"I want something more," Stephanie smiled at me.

"I think I could be a stripper," Lucas pondered.

"You'd be the only stripper to pay the audience for being there," Aidan laughed.

"Hey, women would love this," Stephanie gestured to Lucas.

"See? Women would love this," Lucas stuck up his middle fingers while doing a little dance. Stephanie giggled. I kissed her on her cheek and reached for her hand, clutching it tightly.

Chapter 5

"Why did you not get concerned when Stephanie said Eli was on lists?" the green-eyed lady asked.

"If I wanted therapy, I would be paying for a fucking therapist," I snipped. "Probably because this shit was normal for them, this didn't seem odd and neither did Raphael shooting Eli. They spoke about it so casually that it felt casual."

"But it wasn't casual for you," the brown-haired lady stated.

"No and maybe if I was just talking to myself the entire time, alarm bells would have gone off." I leaned forward aggressively. "But I wasn't by myself, I was with these people that exude strength, and I was fucking intrigued."

***

Friday rolled around quickly. The days felt shorter, the mornings felt easier knowing I would see her. Stephanie's smile lit up my entire life. I stood out by the sign eagerly awaiting her vehicle to drive up. A black Rolls-Royce pulled up next to me. The passenger window unrolled.

"Get in," Raphael ordered. Stephanie sat in the passenger seat smiling at me. I got in the back, setting my bag at my feet.

"Sorry to ambush you with Raph, my car broke down," Stephanie turned to look at me.

"Because it's a literal piece of shit," Raphael muttered.

"I love that car," Stephanie whined. Raphael shook his head, annoyed.

"I mean compared to this, your car is a literal piece of shit," I said. Raphael laughed looking at Stephanie.

"Stop, don't encourage him," Stephanie giggled, sitting crossed-legged in her seat.

"Get your bare feet off the seat," Raphael instructed. Stephanie promptly wiped her bare feet on the seat and dashboard. "A heathen, who raised you?" Raphael chuckled.

"Wolves."

"I believe it," Raphael smirked.

"I was thinking I would teach Levi how to shoot."

"What like a BB gun?" I asked.

"You have a brilliant shot, you're a terrible teacher," Raphael replied. "I'll teach him."

"You'll teach him?" Stephanie repeated.

"I mean I taught you, no one can be more annoying," Raphael joked.

"Like a gun?" I asked from the back. They continued to ignore me.

"Shut up, I'm not *that* annoying." Stephanie hit him gently on the arm. Raphael nodded vigorously, a wide grin curling his lips.

"Like a gun," Raphael replied to my question. I stared blankly at the back of the seat.

"A legal gun?" I queried. Raphael breathed a laugh and rubbed his face.

"Like a handgun," Stephanie replied.

"Do I get a choice in this?" I asked, my voice more spineless than I intended.

"Nope, this is our family, if you can't help protect it, you're dead weight, we don't carry dead weight," Raphael stated.

"A little harsh, Raphael," Stephanie critiqued, glaring at him.

"What do you guys do?" I demanded.

"You don't have to learn to shoot if you don't want to," Stephanie looked back at me.

"Yes, he does, we both agreed." Raphael turned toward Stephanie frustrated.

"It's too soon," Stephanie replied.

"What do you guys do?" I raised my voice slightly.

"Raphael don't—" Stephanie began.

"We steal," Raphael sighed.

"Steal what?" I picked at my thumb, nerves overcoming me. Like robbing a bank? That's what she said. Stealing. Better than killing. Better than a lot of criminal activity, I guess.

"Whatever's in season, we've done weapon plans, bank security plans, we help our clients acquire whatever they need to complete their intended purposes," Raphael replied vaguely.

"Have you ever killed anyone?"

"Many," Raphael smiled and looked back at me. "All deserved it."

"Would you shut up Raphael?" Stephanie hissed. "Killing people is not what we do." Her voice was a weak plea as she stared at me, desperate for some understanding. Desperate for me to commit to her. I could see for the first-time fragility in her eyes. She wanted me. She needed me to understand, to tell her she didn't disgust me.

"Just an unfortunate side effect of the job," Raphael continued. "All people who think they can harm our family."

"That's why it's important I know how to shoot?" I murmured, my eyes leaving Stephanie's for a second.

"To be able to protect yourself and Stephanie," Raphael

nodded. I went quiet. My mind mulled over what I had just learned. I looked at Stephanie, remembering the scars that were on her body. And for some reason that was all I could think of in the backseat of a Rolls-Royce owned and driven by a professional criminal. Her scars, there were four of them, all almost perfectly straight.

"You're such a fucking idiot," Stephanie said viciously to Raphael.

She had been hurt, she didn't fall, or get into a crash. She had been hurt by *someone*. Four scars. Four fucking scars. Was this what she meant by working until she was safe? Is this why she does this?

I stared into her eyes as I saw her look at me pleadingly. What had she gone through? Maybe I couldn't imagine. I probably couldn't imagine. The arguing ensued between Raphael and Stephanie.

I wanted to say I wouldn't do it. That this was a life of crime, and I didn't want to partake. But the scars, the grate, *her*. She *needed* me. She needed me to protect her.

"I want to learn," I announced. Stephanie blinked in surprise. "I want to learn how to shoot," I confirmed.

"See, not too early," Raphael shrugged.

"Are you sure?" Stephanie demanded.

"Ya, I am," I nodded. Just as surprised as she was to hear the words topple out of my mouth. But I was okay with it. The small portion of my mind echoing for me to run was trampled by the excitement and love I felt.

"Okay," Stephanie replied, nodding at me.

"I'll take you out tonight," Raphael announced. I nodded. The rest of the drive was quiet as I thought about the decision I had made. Was I sure? Yes. At the same time, I knew it was a terrible decision.

We pulled into the driveway. Stephanie took my bag and went inside as Raphael took me back to the trail. I could see that the forest was beautiful now. The crunching twigs and leaves no longer making me jump. The rustling of the bushes making me look to see any cute animals that might be running. Everything seemed to feel different. I knew what was happening. I was in on the joke.

"Thank you for doing this," I said, breaking the silence. Raphael looked over in surprise like he had forgotten I was there.

"Just don't make this a waste of my time," Raphael muttered. We continued to walk until we reached a large clearing. "Our shooting range." Raphael took the gun out of his pocket and cocked it before passing the gun to me. "Let's see what you got." He pointed to one of the targets, then led me closer.

"I've never shot a gun." I stared blankly.

"I mean, it's not nuclear science. It's loaded and cocked. Just point and shoot." Raphael pointed at the target. I raised my arm with the gun in it. "Both hands, it's not like the movies. One hand on the gun, use the other to support your wrist. Helps you keep steady, better for the kickback." Raphael grabbed my hands and positioned them. He went behind me kicking my feet to a wider stance. "You want to be as sturdy as possible." He looked over my shoulder. "Okay, shoot." Raphael stepped back slightly. I pulled the trigger. I felt my pulse quicken as a feeling of pure power waved over me. I had never felt such strength before.

I was a fucking king.

No, I was a fucking god.

The spiraling feeling of pure intensity was quickly followed by a ringing in my ears. I moved my mouth, trying to hear something over the deafening sound. It was replaced by a sudden, sharp pain as my nerves came down from the ecstasy.

"Mother fucker!" I screamed as my ears stung with the noise. I looked up to see Raphael unfazed by the noise. He was looking over at the target to see if it hit.

"Go again," Raphael called, backing away from the target then walking back to me. I repositioned myself and shot again. My ears buzzed from the abrupt noise. Then a different pain hit, my shoulder. I put my hand on my shoulder. "Kickback's a bitch." Raphael said. "Hand on to your wrist. Again." Raphael showed from the sidelines what he meant. I repositioned myself again, careful to have the correct stance. I shot again. The pain in my ears echoed in my head. "Shoot on your exhale, calm your breath," Raphael ordered. I repositioned myself and shook my head trying to get my ears to stop ringing. I let out a series of shots hoping one would hit the target. Raphael yelled something back and I couldn't make it out, my ears were ringing so bad. I felt a hand on my shoulder and lowered my gun, turning around to see Raphael pointing at his ear. I nodded figuring he was asking if my ears were hurting. Raphael nodded and sat down. I sat down next to him and we waited for it to pass.

"Do you ever get used to the noise?" I asked when the ringing died down.

"You do, your ears don't," Raphael smiled. "When your ears do, you don't have any hearing left."

"Here," I passed Raphael the gun. He didn't take it.

"If you learn anything from me, learn to always wipe your fingerprints off the gun. Especially if it's not yours. I could shoot someone, but the only complete fingerprint may be yours." Raphael took the gun from me and pulled his shirt up using it to show me how to clean it. His lifted shirt revealed his eight pack. Raphael passed me the gun back, gesturing to show what he did back. I self-consciously pulled up my shirt, tensing what little abdominal muscles I had and cleaned the gun.

"I bet I'm the worst person you've taught." I passed the gun to Raphael using my shirt.

"Nope," Raphael stood up putting the gun in his back pocket. I stood up and we began walking back.

"Who was the best person you trained?" I asked.

"Stephanie, hands down. Within seconds, she had it down. I make fun of her because the entire time I was teaching her she kept getting distracted. Still somehow absorbed the information. Jace took months to master it, I didn't teach Eli and James still has a terrible shot, explosives and knives are more his thing," Raphael listed.

"They don't tell you how powerful it feels to hold a gun."

"Pretty addictive," Raphael replied. "Phenomenal feeling to play God."

"I can understand that," I nodded. We walked back to the cottage and in the door.

"How'd he do?" Jace asked.

"Better than your first go," Raphael laughed. Stephanie stood at the kitchen speaking with James. She smiled at me as I walked over.

"How did you like it?" Stephanie asked.

"Holy fuck, it felt amazing, why didn't you tell me the feeling you get when you fire it?" I asked, moving close to her.

"I remember the first taste of power I got," Jace walked over laughing. "Pretty damn awesome."

"Can't have you getting too addicted," Stephanie giggled.

"I'm already addicted," I whispered, pulling her into me. I cupped her face, catching her lips in mine. My mouth moved to her neck, pressing my erection into her as I bit and sucked.

"Jace, let's go," James urged. I didn't pay attention to them. My hand crept up her body to her breast. Stephanie's fingers intertwined in my hair.

"Let's go to the room," Stephanie breathed in my ear, gently biting it. I nodded and pulled away. She took my hand and led me to her room.

I undid my belt and pants as she shut the door, dropping them to the floor and taking my shirt off. Stephanie undid her shorts pulling them down, revealing a red thong, then pulling off her shirt showing a red bra. My jaw dropped, still not believing that *this* was the woman I was fucking. She took my breath away. I was completely infatuated with her. I sat on the bed, my eyes not leaving her. Stephanie straddled me, I could feel her warmth. "So you like the power?" she whispered in my ear. I turned her and pushed her onto the bed, crawling between her legs.

"Fuck yes," I growled into her ear. Stephanie kissed me deeply, pressing her chest into mine. I could feel her heart pound as she looked at me.

My fingers glided down her body, until it rested between her legs. I stroked along her thong, feeling the dampness. She wanted me. I felt my cock pulsate at this; she was soaking for me. Her hands went into my boxers as she started to gently stroke me.

"Yes," I moaned. My body wanted desperately to stay in this intimate embrace, but I forced myself away, grabbing a condom. Our eyes were locked as I took off my boxers, my erection bouncing out. Stephanie took a breath in, pulling off her bra and thong. I climbed back on top of her putting the condom on, my eyes gliding over her. I was captivated, entranced. My eyes delighted, my brain still having difficulty understanding that I was about to fuck her. She was so out of my league, untouchable.

"Fuck me, Levi," Stephanie pleaded as she positioned me

correctly and I entered her. She bit her lip as I began to pound her. Her legs wrapped around me. My right arm supported my weight beside her head, my left hand glided up her leg. She squirmed at my touch, her chest raising and falling as she slowly succumbed to me. Slowly becoming *mine*. I continued to fuck her, rolling my hips as I entered her. Stephanie gripped onto my back, her head tilted back as she moaned. Her moan drove me wild, every nerve of my body perking up and spiking with pleasure. I pounded her deeper, purposefully, wanting her. Needing her. Craving her.

"Say my name," I breathed.

"Levi," Stephanie begged, her voice filled with lust. I gripped onto her hip, pulling her to meet my thrusts. She tilted her head back, her nails digging into my ass as she desperately pulled me into her. "Levi," she repeated. Her voice a wanting plea. The slapping noise echoed through the room, adding to the pleasure driving me forward. Stephanie's mouth opened slightly, her eyes closing.

"Look at me when you come." I asserted, driving my rock-hard erection into her. Her eyes fluttered open, lazily, glazed over with indulgence. I felt her nails dig further into me, her hips grinding to force me deeper into her.

"Yes, yes, Levi, baby," Stephanie moaned, a gasp filling the air as I drilled her. Success flooding me as her body shuddered, her voice falling to whimpers.

"Yes," I groaned as my body filled with pleasure as I finished. My entire body giving in to her. She moved her hips along me until my body convulsed. "Oh, yes, baby." I cried out at the feeling of her hungrily wanting every second possible.

We lay in bed, coming down from the pleasure-filled high. I

stroked her arm, my eyes still on her in disbelief. My heart still pummeling in my chest. Pure love filled me. I froze. *Love.* But it was there, it was undeniably there.

"How are you so perfect?" I kissed her neck gently.

"I'm actually a robot," Stephanie replied. I tickled her. Stephanie arched her back and tried to push me away giggling.

"I want to be a part of your life," I murmured.

"You are a part of my life." Stephanie looked at me, a confused expression on her face.

"I want to be a part of all of your life." I kissed her on the cheek.

Stephanie nodded slowly. "It's dangerous."

"I know," I replied, nuzzling our noses before dragging my lips along hers. "I want this," I purred.

"You can have all of it." Stephanie smiled at me, lovingly caressing the side of my face.

"Pizza?" Jace shouted through the door.

"Okay!" Stephanie yelled back.

"You managed to train him to not intrude?"

"No, no one can possibly teach him that. Just a fluke," Stephanie giggled, her hand pulling my face to hers. Our lips meeting before her tongue diving into my mouth. I sucked on it gently, groaning as I felt her hunger start.

"We should probably go out there," I whispered to her.

"Or we can stay here," Stephanie suggested her hand trailing between my legs.

"Fuck, you don't know how hard for me this is to say right now." I took a sharp breath in. "We should probably go out there."

"Okay, just let me know when you want to come back in." Stephanie winked at me, lifting her hands over her head and stretching, curving her back upward, her body on full display. I watched in awe.

"Fuck them," I stated. Stephanie giggled, gleeful that she won the battle. Our lips returned to their embrace, my tongue stroking along hers. Her hand returned to between my legs, her fingers stroked along me. Stephanie straddled me kissing my neck, still stroking me.

"You drive me insane," I groaned. Stephanie smiled at me and began biting down my body. She took my growing erection into her mouth. My hand trailed to her hair feeling her head move up and down. The sloppy suction making me weak. I could feel the back of her throat as she took me all in. She continued to move until my body swelled with pleasure. "Holy fuck," I bit out as I finished. Stephanie licked me clean and lay back beside me. "What did I do to deserve you?" I placed my hand gently on her chest.

"Must have sold your soul." Stephanie sighed, slipping out of bed and getting dressed. I followed suit, pulling on my jeans and T-shirt. We walked out to join the rest of them. They were all sitting down at the table.

"There they are," Jace smiled. "Post first shooting sex. I know I had the same reaction."

"I did too, but mine was delayed," Raphael laughed.

"Delayed?" I asked, sitting down next to Stephanie.

"I had no one to fuck until a later," Raphael lit a joint.

"Raphael's somewhat of a romantic," Jace chuckled.

"Why fuck around when you know what you want?" Raphael shrugged. "Eli, what was your reaction?" Raphael asked, taking a puff. Eli grinned to himself.

"I just kept shooting," Eli replied. "Why fuck around when you know what you want?"

"Eli's soulmate, the gun," James replied jokingly.

"Well, it won't break my heart at least," Eli sighed. I reached out and held Stephanie's hand.

"Don't break my heart," Stephanie whispered to me. I shook my head. The doorbell rang.

"I'll get it," Raphael muttered, getting up.

"No, I can get it," James offered, running toward the door. He returned with a few boxes of pizza.

"Not the right pizza delivery man?" Jace prodded. James shook his head solemnly and placed the boxes on the table.

"What's your vice?" Raphael turned to me taking a long puff on his joint.

"My vice, uh, I don't know?" I replied, stunned by the question.

"I think mine would be coffee," Stephanie put in.

"You literally steal for a living and your vice is coffee?" I laughed looking at Stephanie.

"I agree with her, she needs coffee, you don't want to be near her if she doesn't have her morning cup," Eli jabbed. Stephanie giggled.

"You're one to talk. I'm not *that* bad," Stephanie persisted.

"You're terrible," Jace said. Stephanie shook her head smiling. "Mine would be… oh God, I'm realizing I have a lot. I think drugs."

"Guns," Eli shrugged. Predictable.

"Maybe money," James said. "What's yours, Raphael?"

"I don't have one, I'm perfect," Raphael leaned back in his chair.

"Really? I can see one in your mouth right now," Stephanie gestured to his joint. Raphael smirked.

"This is coping," Raphael grinned, leaning on the table and

staring at Stephanie.

"Some people would call that addiction." Stephanie rolled her eyes.

"Maybe I do have a vice, but it isn't this." Raphael gestured to his joint. "And it's one you have too," Raphael simpered, his eyes not leaving from her. He paused for a second, licking his teeth. "Driving."

"Driving isn't a bad habit," I replied.

"How we do it, it is." Raphael leaned back in his chair.

"He's not talking about normal road driving," Stephanie explained.

"What, is there a different type?" I looked around the table, a confused expression plastered on my face.

"We race," Raphael clarified.

"How is that a bad habit?" I asked.

"What car did you take out last weekend Raphael?" Jace asked.

"A Ferrari," Raphael chuckled.

"Paid outright?" Jace asked. Raphael nodded. "So why isn't it here?"

"Rolled it," Raphael sighed.

"Raphael drives like an insane person on the track, paired with Stephanie they have a death wish," Eli muttered.

"It's just for fun," Stephanie laughed. "No one has a death wish."

"Have you ever left the track with a working vehicle?" Jace asked.

Stephanie leaned back in her chair. "No," Stephanie lamented.

"Death wish," Eli repeated. "I think you have to change your top vice to that, Stephanie, it's a terrible habit."

"I'll take you out to do it sometime," Stephanie smiled at me.

"Don't agree to it," Eli pointed at me warningly. "The last time I sat in a car with her during one of their races I threw up."

"We're not that bad," Raphael shook his head. "You're being dramatic."

"No, he threw up, made me lose," Stephanie muttered.

"And the excuses come out," Raphael joked.

"It sounds like fun," I shrugged.

"See!" Stephanie stared victoriously at Eli.

"We'll see if he thinks the same after," Eli replied.

"What's your vice, Levi?" Raphael repeated the question to me.

"Uh, video games?" I replied unconvincingly. Everyone broke into laughter.

"Better put Stephanie down then," Raphael chuckled. "She's gonna corrupt the fuck out of you."

"I will not, he will stay as innocent as he was when I met him," Stephanie giggled.

"I taught him how to shoot today," Raphael said dryly.

"He hasn't shot anyone," Jace remarked. "So, still just as innocent, just with a new hobby."

"Well, I for one volunteer to be corrupted," I laughed pulling Stephanie closer. Stephanie giggled, putting her head gently on my shoulder.

"Well, in that case, I'm going to blow your fucking mind," Stephanie winked at me.

"Boy won't be innocent for that much longer," Jace announced, boisterously hitting the table. I kissed Stephanie gently on the forehead.

"Keep the noise to a minimum," Raphael grumbled, rolling his eyes.

"Get ear plugs," I retorted. Jace and James laughed in shock.

"I'm getting a beer." Raphael stood up and left for the kitchen.

"Your desire to impress him didn't last long," James commented.

"I like this Levi better," Jace smiled at me and nodded.

"We're doing a workout tomorrow." Raphael returned into the room, joint in his mouth, beer in hand.

"We do a workout most days," Eli shrugged.

"Levi's joining us." Raphael sat down. "We're going to start working out every day again."

"No, why?" Eli whined, placing his head angrily against the table.

"Because we've been slacking for too long," Raphael replied.

"I didn't bring any workout clothing." I protested.

"I doubt you own any," Raphael scoffed.

"Raphael will give you some," Stephanie stated, giving Raphael an unimpressed look. Raphael sighed loudly before nodding.

"Well, what should we do tonight?" Eli asked.

"The beach," Stephanie beamed at the idea.

"Isn't it kind of late in the year for a spontaneous beach trip?" Eli voiced.

"Come on, bonfire, alcohol, swimming," Stephanie encouraged.

"Hypothermia," I added.

"It's warm today, you'll be fine." Stephanie rolled her eyes.

"Well, I'm in." Jace stood up and left for his room. James and Eli followed.

"I'll get the beer," Raphael smiled and left for the kitchen.

Stephanie and I headed to her room.

"Don't suppose the guys have an extra bathing suit laying around?" I questioned.

"Doubt it, just wear your boxers, it'll just be us," Stephanie replied. I looked to make sure they weren't a light color. I was okay, they were black. Stephanie stripped down and changed into a yellow string bikini. "Raph, I need a shirt," Stephanie yelled. Raphael's footprints echoed through the hallway. He opened the door.

"You have shirts," Raphael stated.

"I don't want mine to get dirty from the sand," Stephanie whined.

"Why don't you use your boyfriend's shirt?" Raphael gestured to me.

"He only brought two," Stephanie rocked back and forth on her heels. Raphael nodded and left. Stephanie and I went out to wait by the door.

"Damn!" James shouted at Stephanie. Stephanie giggled. I immediately felt possessive. Raphael walked out of his room tossing a shirt to Stephanie. She pulled it over herself, it fit like a short dress on her.

"Let's get drunk!" Jace shouted running down the stairs.

"I'll be the designated driver," Eli volunteered walking down the stairs.

"Thank God." James followed Eli down the stairs.

"Okay, let's go." Raphael grabbed the cooler and pulled the keys from his black swimsuit pockets.

"I'm driving, you're high." Stephanie grabbed the keys from his hand and her purse off the floor. We walked out to the Rolls-Royce. Raphael opened the trunk, putting the cooler in the back. I got in the back as Stephanie got in the driver's seat. Raphael got in on the passenger side.

"A man who knows his place," Raphael laughed, gesturing to me sitting by myself in the back.

"Thought you would be a pain in the ass if I sat in the passenger seat," I retorted.

"You thought right." Raphael shut his door. Stephanie turned on the car. Eli reversed the van quickly and sped off. "Don't scratch my baby."

Stephanie giggled and reversed the car. She slammed on the gas; the car hummed as we sped off. Raphael laughed, pounding on the hood of the car enthusiastically.

We sped along the country roads. The trees whipping by. I tried not to pay attention to the speed. The whole idea made me want to throw up when I thought about it. Raphael shouted words of encouragement as Stephanie powered on. My nerves on edge with the irresponsible driving. Sirens suddenly blared behind the car.

"Fuck," Stephanie cursed, pulling over.

"Oh, you're fine, it's a male," Raphael laughed. The cop approached her window. Stephanie rolled it down, turning the car off.

"License and registration please," the cop asked. Stephanie nodded, undoing her seat belt and leaned over Raphael to grab her purse stationed in between his legs. The cop's eyes went to her visible ass in the thong bikini. His eyes rested there. Stephanie slowly popped open the glove compartment and grabbed the registration. She sat back in her seat, popping her chest up slightly. Stephanie passed him the documents, touching his hand gently as she pulled away.

"This car is registered to a Raphael Carter?" the cop questioned.

"Oh, that's my brother, he drank a bit too much so I'm driving." Stephanie gently moved her hair to her right shoulder. Raphael waved but the cop was transfixed with Stephanie.

"Do you know why I pulled you over, Stephanie Gibson?" the cop asked.

"I was speeding. I'm so sorry officer, they wanted me to show them how fast the car goes," Stephanie flirted, nibbling her nail while leaning onto the windowsill.

"Then I don't think you were going fast enough," the cop laughed. "I'll let you off with a warning for now, but I expect you to drive faster." The cop winked at Stephanie. He passed her the paperwork back.

"Oh, thank you officer, how could I ever repay you." I saw Stephanie bit her lip gently. The cop took a sharp breath in.

"Just make that car sing, maybe I'll catch you on your way back." The cop winked at Stephanie and walked back to his car. Stephanie turned the car back on and rolled the window back up. We sped off.

"Like fucking putty in your hands," Raphael scoffed, shaking his head. "How predictable."

"He encouraged you to speed," I said, amazed. Stephanie shrugged.

"One day, you'll be pregnant and have consequences for your actions," Raphael stated.

"Oh, that cop would still want to fuck me if I was pregnant," Stephanie replied. Raphael shook his head. We sped onto the beach and parked, getting out of the vehicle. Raphael grabbed the cooler from the back. Eli, James and Jace had the bonfire already started. We walked over.

"I got a fucking ticket," Eli whined in disbelief.

"Oh, we got pulled over, Stephanie handled it," Raphael

announced.

"Well, that explains why he seemed uninterested when I flirted with him," James chuckled, grabbing a beer from the cooler.

"He told her she wasn't going fast enough," I muttered.

"What, did you fuck him?" James asked Stephanie.

"No, just let his imagination do some work," Stephanie giggled.

"Jesus, Stephanie, you have it so much easier sometimes." Jace grumbled. Everyone took off their extra clothing getting ready to swim. The shedding of layers exposing toned bodies and tightened or bulky muscles. I looked down, realizing just how out of place I was. They all had intriguing scars, demonstrations of strength, I had nothing. My muscles nonexistent, my skin unflawed. I tightened the grip on my arms, covering as much of my clothed body as possible. Stephanie glanced over to me; her eyes glinted with excitement. I'm certain she could see through the fake smile I flashed, but she didn't let on. Or maybe she didn't care.

I was weak.

I couldn't protect her. Why would she even give me a second glance? I held no use to her, no security, no attractive muscles. There was no way she could choose me over these men. It was a fluke. *I* was a fluke. She certainly noticed it now.

No. Stop.

She was probably ignorant to what I was feeling. I mean, she was perfect. I doubt she ever felt anything less than the stunning angel she was. How was such a radiant piece of art meant to understand why her hideous boyfriend felt uncomfortable?

"You coming?" Raphael kicked my leg. I looked up, giving a meek shake of my head before looking emptily back at the fire.

"No, go ahead, maybe I'll go swimming later," I croaked, grabbing a beer and sitting down.

"Okay, you guys go on," Stephanie stated, plunking her alluring body next to me.

"No, you go ahead," I told her. Stephanie shook her head, those blue eyes on me.

"You're coming," Raphael picked Stephanie up effortlessly and swung her over his shoulder. James and Eli raced to the water. Jace sat down next to me, his fingers gliding through the sand as he took a breath in.

"If it's any consolation, you're exactly James's type," Jace joked.

"Too bad I'm not with James," I muttered.

"If Stephanie didn't like the way you looked, she wouldn't be fucking you," Jace reasoned.

"Yes, but when she sees me naked, she's not looking at me next to you guys," I retorted. "She's never been with someone that looks like me, I can tell by Raphael's comments."

"Ignore Raphael, he's an asshole. I've also never seen her this happy, so who fucking cares." Jace shrugged. "Don't let yourself get in the way of your relationship with her." Jace looked at me sincerely. I nodded. He ruffled my hair before getting up and walking to the water.

"How did you know that I was feeling self-conscious?" I called.

"You have it easy, I have to pick up girls standing next to him," Jace shot me a pained smile before walking to the water. I watched, taking a few breaths, Stephanie and Raphael were in an aggressive water battle. Their faces made it obvious that this wasn't fun, this was life and death. I took off my shirt and pants stepping across the cold sand.

"Finally." Eli grinned. I stepped in the water. It was fucking freezing. Nope. No fucking way. I quickly retreated to the safety of the sand. Raphael started to walk up to the beach.

"Nope," Raphael chuckled, grabbing me harshly and tossing me into the water. I went fully under. The cold water shocked my system.

"You decided to join us," Stephanie smiled.

"Couldn't let you have too much fun without me." I grabbed her and gently pulled her closer. Stephanie wrapped her legs around me. My hands glided along her back as she kissed me. I felt my erection jump to action, my body reacting to the warmth of her touch. Suddenly, I felt a pressure on my side, both of us toppled into the frigid water. I came to the top to see Jace laughing.

"What the fuck man?" I laughed, splashing him aggressively. This meant war to Stephanie. She pounced on him, taking him down into the icy cold water. Jace rose from the water, his angry glare resting on Stephanie as she desperately tried to swim away, she was no match for him. Jace grabbed her foot, pulling her back, picking her up and tossing her.

"Glad you decided to join us," James squeezed my shoulder. "What do you study?"

"English, third year."

James nodded. "I wanted to study mechanical engineering for a bit," James commented. "Always kind of wonder what would've happened if I hadn't met Jace."

"Why didn't you pursue it?"

"Well, Jace and I started our work and it became too dangerous to stay long enough to start. Also, why would I? I have money."

"Do you regret starting work?"

"No, not for a second. I'm meant for the fast life; I would have been bored working the same job every day." James shrugged. "I'm meant to do this."

"I get that, going to classes seems so dull now."

"We can use another hand."

"Can I ask?" I gestured to James's burnt up arm.

"Oh ya, we were trying to get information from someone, a real piece of shit, traded children, Jace and I were being paid to find one of them. The guy hated fire. I held him in our little bonfire too long. Now I have a souvenir," James flexed triumphantly. I looked at him in shock. He killed someone. That's what that meant. No. He tortured someone to death.

"This career isn't all pretty girls and fast cars." Jace sighed, raising an eyebrow at me as he stepped over.

"I mean, he deserved it," I shrugged, regaining my composure.

"Yep, my favorite one of our kills." Jace gave James a high five.

"Did you find the child?".

"Ya, little girl, around five. Occasionally we'll get updates and money from the dad," James said quietly. A grin slightly parting his lips as he looked at the water. A moment of pride. A moment of victory. "Probably one of the best jobs we got to do."

"Why didn't they go to the cops?"

"We're more efficient." James sighed.

"Hard to find someone through cops when no one wants to talk to cops," Jace explained. I rocked on my feet, my mind catching up in a melancholy fashion. The reality I thought I knew seemed to shatter around them. With every story, the sheltered blanket that kept my life warm and comfortable was yanked off.

"Are we talking about previous war stories?" Raphael

demanded, stepping out of the water and gesturing to the bonfire.

"He asked about my scar," James replied. We all got out, eager for the story time. Like kids at camp getting excited to tell horror stories around a campfire.

"I have quite the story," Raphael laughed, grabbed a beer and sat down next to the bonfire. "Our first job with Stephanie, this was before Eli."

"Oh no," Stephanie shook her head. Raphael nodded, smiling.

"He'll enjoy it. We were being paid to get a message to a witness in a massive trial. The man felt that killing her would have been too obvious, so we were just to kindly remind her that he can, at any point, get to her. We thought it would be an easy job, a good start for Stephanie, so we took it. We plotted everything to a tee. She was being watched by a police officer and had a guard in her apartment complex. Stephanie's one job was to distract the police officer while we did this, we were going to turn off the power so it was harder to see us, so we needed the police to be distracted long enough not to notice," Raphael began.

"Which was a long time." Stephanie put in.

"It was a long time," Raphael agreed. "We figured Stephanie could flirt with him and he wouldn't notice what was going on. Anyway, we missed a detail. The police officer was gay. So we come out of the building, turn the power back on and I walk over to her to tell her we can go. And she smiles at me and says, 'This is Mark, he's the one I've been talking about.'" Raphael shook his head, smiling at Stephanie. Everyone laughed. "She had spent the entire twenty minutes talking me up to this police officer."

"I'm resourceful." Stephanie shrugged.

"Resourceful would be telling me to get James, you wanted revenge." Raphael rolled his eyes. "So, this police officer says he's off duty in five and he wants to take me out. We had just finished the job and I didn't want to seem suspicious, so I agreed. Terrible experience, he was so pushy."

"Because I spent twenty minutes saying how loud the men you were with are," Stephanie giggled.

"So generous talking up my sex skills with him," Raphael frowned.

"Did anything happen?" I laughed.

"No, left the poor guy with blue balls." Raphael took a sip of his beer.

"Shameful Raphael, you should've helped him out," James winked.

"I'm not one to put out on the first date!" Raphael joked. "Eli, any cool stories?"

"If we're talking about Stephanie's first job, I can tell you the first job Stephanie and I worked together," Eli offered. "It was a stereotypical diamond heist."

"How unoriginal," Jace mocked.

"Yep," Eli shrugged. "We were supposed to steal them from the fencer's house. That went without a hitch, but we made it to the drop, and they had their jeweler there to evaluate it. Turns out they weren't real, so they say, 'you're not going to be paid.' So we get back in our car. They get in their car and they start leaving and Stephanie starts driving after them. Butting their car, ramming it from the side, using the driving that Raphael taught her. She's telling me to shoot, so I do, I shoot one of their tires, and they go spinning. They come out, hands up, terrified. We take our money and leave. That's when I knew I wanted to continue to work with her,"

"Pretty fucking cool," I grinned, my eyes on Stephanie.

"See, driving does come into use," Raphael stated.

"How did you get your scars?" I asked Stephanie. I heard everyone shift in uncomfortable silence. My eyes didn't leave from Stephanie.

"Oh, that's not a nice story," Stephanie shook her head, her body immediately shrinking as she retreated into herself. The smile slipping from her lips as her muscles tensed, her eyes turning to the fire. Her nails absently picking at the scar that marked her jaw. Like her subconscious believed that it could claw it off and erase the memory. I watched her, wanting to shake her and demand what had happened. In the stories she was a reckless joy, completely without fear. Why did this one topic make her surrender to her thoughts? What was so powerful about those scars?

"An accident on one of the jobs," Jace murmured, interrupting the secluded moment with an intense demand for me to stop the line of questions. "She pushed through though, managed to still complete it."

"I had no idea you were such a badass," I murmured, my eyes on her intently. Stephanie's gaze didn't stray from the fire, her hands began to shake. I looked around at the men, all of them not acknowledging her shattering. "So how did you all meet, is there like a Tinder for criminals?" I joked, trying to distract from her reaction.

"As you know, Stephanie and I met in foster care. I aged out soon after and I completed jobs by myself for a while. Then I kept hearing about these two guys who were running me out of business. So finally, I demanded to be brought to them and that's how I met James and Jace. Then Stephanie aged out, so she joined. How did you meet Eli?" Raphael grabbed Stephanie's shaking hand forcefully. She winced before yanking herself out of her trance. Taking a wavering breath as she pulled her hand from his grip and clutched onto herself tightly. I could see her nails puncturing her skin as she moved her gaze from the fire, her fun, lighthearted personality plastered itself back on her face with a vivacious smile. The glint in her eyes displaying an ignorance to her moment of imprisonment.

Where did you go?

She breathed a laugh, rubbing her face before turning to me. I searched her face, desperate to understand her, to be part of the dark moments. But nothing was there anymore. The fleeting moment of pain, replaced by her normal bright demeanor.

"Oh, kind of an odd story. I was working a job and I was speaking to the man who was meant to give me some information. All of a sudden, I heard a bang and there was blood all over me. I was pissed. This was meant to be my informant. Turns out Eli had been paid from the other side to stop the information from getting to me." Stephanie shook her head at Eli.

"I had heard of Stephanie; their group is kind of legendary in the business. So, I brought a towel and a change of clothing for her." Eli grinned. "So, I run up to her and hand her the stuff and she's pissed. I explain that I was paid to take him out. And she demands half of what I was supposed to make. I agreed because I didn't want to be hunted. I found out after that she was temporarily on her own and I slid in and convinced her to work with me."

"And now you're part of the legendary group." Jace took a sip of his beer.

"I am honored every day," Eli bowed dramatically.

"We call him the puppy," James stated. "Basically, only talks to Stephanie, we don't hear many of his stories."

"The first person I talked to other than Stephanie shot me!" Eli defended.

"How did Raphael think you were an intruder if he talked to you?" My brows furrowed, a confused expression running over my face.

"He didn't answer my questions quick enough," Raphael sighed.

"It's a long-debated topic," Stephanie explained.

"You didn't introduce yourself, why would I tell you information?" Eli replied.

"Levi, are you sleeping with Stephanie?" Raphael demanded.

"Yes," I answered.

"See? Look how easy it was for him to respond to that!" Raphael laughed.

"Have you slept with Eli?" I tried to cover my nerves with a smile.

"Are you jealous?" Stephanie winked, seeing through my façade instantly.

"No, just curious," I replied, scratching my head to distract by from my miserable expression. Eli stood up and brushed himself off, walking over and sitting behind Stephanie. He pushed me gently to the side and embraced Stephanie.

"Are you jealous?" Eli egged me on, slowly running his fingers up her leg. Every nerve in my body stood on edge. An itch to stop this disgusting behavior. She wasn't *his*.

"Now I'm getting jealous," I grabbed his hand.

"Then you should know, Stephanie disgusts me," Eli laughed, getting up and walking to the other side of the bonfire.

"Rude," Stephanie rolled her eyes.

"You're just not my type," Eli shrugged.

"For your information, I would blow your fucking mind," Stephanie smirked.

"Tell us more about that process, Stephanie," Jace winked.

"It's a process you'll never experience," I growled, my voice coming out more vicious than I intended.

"Ya, Jace," Stephanie laughed, staring at Jace.

"Oh yes, of course, it's a process I will never experience," Jace remarked sarcastically. I opened my mouth to challenge his sarcasm.

"What are you kids doing?" A male voice rang out from the beach. We all turned in shock. A flashlight blinding us.

"Nothing to see here, Officer," James called. The officer stepped closer, the light making it impossible to tell his expression.

"This is a public beach, you cannot have a bonfire," the officer stated. Raphael stood up slowly and walked over to the officer.

"Hey, didn't you pull us over earlier?" James inquired.

"Yes, I believe so," the officer muttered. His eyes zeroed in on Stephanie. "Stephanie right?" The officer shone the flashlight in Stephanie's face. She squinted and nodded. "Oh, sorry." The officer turned off the flashlight. "You seem to be quite the troublemaker," the officer joked.

"Trouble is my middle name," Stephanie laughed uncomfortably. Raphael stepped in front of Stephanie who quickly put Raphael's shirt back on.

"Did you orchestrate this?" the officer asked.

"Yes, I did, officer," Raphael replied. "Levi, go with the others, we'll take care of this," Raphael ordered, looking over his shoulder at me. James, Jace, Eli and I quickly packed up and headed to the vehicle.

"Always fun until the cops break it up," Eli let out an exasperated sigh while getting into the driver's seat.

"Will they be okay?" I demanded.

"At most, they'll be given a fine," James shrugged.

"Why send us away?" I questioned.

"Less people they can recognize now and later," James explained. "You saw that he knew Stephanie's name? We don't like that. The fewer people around, the fewer that will be recognized," James stated. I nodded.

"I want to watch *Jaws*," Jace announced.

"Why? Because you were just swimming in a body of water? Kind of a weird reaction to that don't you think?" I laughed.

"Don't psychoanalyze me," Jace replied.

"It probably has something to do with your father," James joked. We walked into the cottage. I quickly departed to shower the sand off me. The warm water felt so nice after being in the cold for so long. I dried off and put on clean clothing. Jace and James were on the couch getting *Jaws* set up.

"Eli has gone to sleep," Jace stated. James pressed play. We watched the movie quietly. I barely paid attention, my mind on Stephanie. What would happen if she was arrested? Would we break her out of prison? How does that work? Do I smuggle a little pickaxe in for her to dig away at the wall?

Finally, the front door opened to Stephanie laughing loudly. I let out the breath I was subconsciously holding. Thank God. I wasn't sure what type of pickaxe I would buy. My knowledge in that area was non-existent at best.

"We've returned!" Raphael shouted victoriously.

"I'm going to go shower," Stephanie declared. I walked over to Raphael, wanting to know what took so long.

"I'll tell the story after, I really want to shower too." Raphael walked to his room. I headed into Stephanie's room.

"Who is it?" Stephanie called from the shower.

"Me." I stepped into her bathroom, the steam hitting my face.

"You wanna come in?" Stephanie popped her head out.

"I just had one," I replied. The water stopped and Stephanie stepped out. She grabbed the towel and dried herself off, I caught her face in my hands, planting my lips on hers with a sensual vigor. My fingers glided up her body until my hand was on her breast. She moaned against my lips, the steamed filled tension sliced as she pulled away from me. I smiled as I watched her slip on some underwear, sweatpants and a crop top. "You're so sexy," I praised, my brain lunging at her casual appearance. I loved when she was like this. I felt like I was being honored by witnessing a side few people got to experience. She was always so done up, but here in the safety of her cottage, with me, she felt comfortable to shed that. Stephanie stuck out her tongue mockingly. "I'm not joking." I kissed her neck gently. My lips savoring the taste of her warm, damp skin.

I grabbed her hand and we walked out to the hangout room. James and Jace had paused the movie, turning towards Raphael who was on the sofa beaming.

"There you are," Jace sighed. "Raphael refused to tell the story until you got here," Jace whined. I sat down, putting my arm around Stephanie as she curled into me.

"It's not much of a story, I just don't want to repeat myself," Raphael stated. "He was going to write us up so I bought him off," Raphael shrugged. "Figured it's better to have him on our side."

"That's it? Why did you take so long?" I demanded.

"The cop was mesmerized by Stephanie, wouldn't let her leave," Raphael grumbled.

"He kept offering to give me a ride home," Stephanie

murmured. "Eventually, Raphael used the 'her boyfriend is wondering where she is.'"

"What did you do, Raph? You're too happy for this to be the story," Jace commented. Raphael shrugged.

"Raphael called the cop a pervert and he's pretty proud of it," Stephanie giggled.

"Good, I'm glad someone said it," I said.

"He was so shocked that I dared to say something to him," Raphael chuckled. "Doesn't know who he's dealing with." Raphael puffed his chest out.

"It's the only minute that he wasn't staring at my tits," Stephanie muttered. "Can we go to bed?" Stephanie asked, smiling faintly at me. I nodded. We left for the bedroom and crawled into bed. I pulled her close to me, clutching on to her.

"Are you okay?" I asked her gently.

"Ya, why?" Stephanie turned to me, a confused look on her face.

"I mean, that police officer was creepy," I stated.

Stephanie shrugged. "It's fine." Stephanie kissed me on the cheek.

I woke up, the sun pouring through the windows, my hand instinctively searching for the warm body. My eyes frustratedly opened with the acknowledgement of the empty bed. I groaned, dragging myself to my feet. I pulled on clothing and stumbled out to the kitchen. Jace and Eli were leaning on the counter whispering to Stephanie. She giggled and nodded.

"What are you guys gossiping about?" I asked.

"We're talking about Christmas," Stephanie replied.

"You made me go swimming yesterday and you're talking about Christmas today," I laughed.

"Did you get hypothermia? I don't think so. Stop being a little bitch." Jace shook his head at me disapprovingly.

"I could have," I stated, pouring myself a cup of coffee. "So what are the Christmas plans?"

"Well, we were hoping you could join us." Stephanie smiled at me.

"I'll ask my parents if they're okay with that," I responded.

"That's right, I keep forgetting you have normal familial relationships," Raphael chuckled, walking into the kitchen. "Well, we can celebrate the day after if that would work better for you."

"No, we can't, I have a gift that can't wait an extra day," Stephanie replied.

"Okay, you weirdo, what did you get them, bread?" Raphael poured himself a cup of coffee.

"I'm not telling you," Stephanie said, a smug smile slithering across her lips.

"So, it's my gift. Well, Stephanie, I'm now intrigued, tell me. What did you get me?" Raphael grinned slickly, leaning on the counter.

"I'm not going to tell you," Stephanie repeated. "Anyway, Levi, please come, it'll be fun," Stephanie pleaded, grabbing my arm like a child about to have a temper tantrum.

"Are we talking about Christmas?" James asked while walking into the kitchen.

"He said he'll ask. Anyway, it's Stephanie's turn to go grocery shopping, you can either go with her or stay back and hang out with us." Raphael looked at me.

"We will be very insulted if you choose grocery shopping over us," Eli advised.

"Then I guess I'll stay back," I replied. Stephanie nodded,

chugging the rest of her coffee.

"Any last-minute requests?" Stephanie queried.

"Chips," Eli said. Stephanie gave a quick thumbs up before snatching the key to the Rolls and departing. I turned to the guys. We drank our coffee in an uncomfortable silence. They didn't know me too well and I could see their brains trying to work out any topics that would make me uncomfortable.

I was probably like a child to them. This innocent, whiny, stupid kid intruding on their space. I tapped my mug, looking between them. My body itching to prove myself. Maybe I should get a tattoo. Would Stephanie find that hot? I could get a rose for Stephanie, my beautiful flower. Or maybe a wolf, Raphael had animals tattooed on him. So did Jace. Maybe a bunny, Stephanie and I were going at it like bunnies. I bit the inside of my mouth to keep from laughing at my own internal joke.

"Good thing the policeman came when he did, would hate to have him deal with drunk Raphael," Jace's voice broke through the uneasy silence.

"What's drunk Raphael like?"

"The biggest asshole you'll ever meet," James stated.

"Oh, come on, I'm not that terrible," Raphael rolled his eyes.

"Last time you were drunk you robbed a convenience store for fun," Jace kissed his teeth, giving Raphael a confused look.

"I was craving chips," Raphael shrugged.

"You had enough cash on you to buy the convenience store," Jace retorted.

"Okay fine, I'm an asshole," Raphael groaned.

"I can't wait to know how Levi is drunk, I bet he's going to be weird," James smiled at me.

"I think he'd be an asshole," Eli analyzed me.

"So, what are you like?" Raphael demanded.

"I don't think I've ever gotten completely drunk," I murmured, rocking back on my heels. "I live with my parents."

"I know what we're doing this morning." Jace laughed and went to the cabinets pilling an assortment of alcohol into his arms. He walked to the table. James grabbed the glasses and we all went to the table in the hangout room. "We need a drinking game."

"Never have I ever?" I suggested. Everyone nodded. "What kind of drunk is Stephanie?" I asked.

"You've seen her drunk." Raphael looked at me confused.

"For like a few minutes, I put her to bed," I replied.

"When she's tipsy, she's horny," James chuckled. "When she's drunk, she's like an aggressive version of her tipsy state."

"She becomes a narcissist." Jace leaned back smiling. "She can't fathom that someone wouldn't want to fuck her."

"Stephanie is not like that when she's drunk, what the hell are you guys talking about?" Raphael grabbed some whiskey and poured it into his cup.

"Stephanie is most certainly like that when she's drunk," Eli stated. "Why, what is she like when she gets drunk with you?"

"Just like a more relaxed version of herself," Raphael muttered.

"Damn, sucks for you. Narcissist Stephanie is hilarious," James snickered. "After Levi rejected her, she got drunk and made it seem like Levi was an alien for not wanting her."

"To be fair, I was an alien for saying I didn't want her," I commented.

"How often do you guys get drunk without me? I feel kind of left out," Raphael frowned.

"Our ambition is to get drunk every night you're not here." Jace smiled at Raphael. I reached forward and poured Sambuca in my cup. "Everyone ready?" Jace asked. Everyone nodded. "Okay, never have I ever had sex with a man." Jace stared at James who promptly gave him the finger while taking a shot.

"Never have I ever had sex with a woman," James grinned, leaning back in his seat. Everyone, other than James, took a shot.

"Never have I ever had cocaine," Eli said. Raphael, James and Jace all took a shot.

"Never have I ever killed someone," I said. Everyone at the table except for me took a shot. I tried to cover my stunned expression. I knew they weren't great. I knew they had killed but having every person at the table drink to that punched me in the face with the sobering realization that I was next to killers. The guilt filling me that the only thing I felt was envy. They were strong, they could protect her.

"Hmm." Raphael paused, his fingers toying with his glass. "Never have I ever gone to university," Raphael said, looking at me. I took a shot.

"I'm home," Stephanie announced.

"Need any help?" Raphael called.

"No, just two bags." Stephanie quickly put the stuff away and walked over to the table. "It's morning, why are you drinking?"

"We're trying to get Levi drunk," Jace announced.

"I leave you for less than an hour, and you're trying to get my boyfriend drunk?" Stephanie rolled her eyes, sitting beside me.

"How are you even back so quickly?" James demanded.

"Just went to the gas station, we didn't need much."

"Okay, never have I ever sent a naughty photo to someone," Eli said. Stephanie, Jace, James and Raphael all took a shot.

"Excuse me, Ms. Gibson, I have yet to receive a naughty

photo from you," I laughed.

"You've never asked!" Stephanie giggled. "I do not send unsolicited nudes."

"I will remember that." I kissed her on the cheek.

"Okay, if our intention is to get Levi drunk, I don't think this game is the way to go," Stephanie teased.

"I will chug an entire glass of any alcohol they choose, if you do the same," I winked at Stephanie.

"Agree," Jace nagged.

"Mr. Davis, you have a deal," Stephanie smiled. Jace immediately grabbed the vodka and poured us glasses to the brim with it. We clinked the glasses and chugged the contents. Everyone hit the table encouragingly. I muddled through and set my glass down, entering into a coughing fit. Stephanie laughed.

"Will I finally get to see Narcissist Stephanie?" Raphael prodded.

"What are you talking about?"

"We were telling him how you become a narcissist whenever you drink with us."

"Firstly, I am always a narcissist, and secondly, you are absolutely correct, it does get worse when I drink with you." Stephanie laughed.

"How come I have never seen this drunk alter ego?" Raphael demanded.

"Because Jace and James stroke my ego until I reach my true self," Stephanie sighed.

"Damn Stephanie, you are looking so fucking sexy tonight," Jace commented, his eyes hungrily running over her.

"See?" Stephanie gestured to Jace. "They get worse the more they drink, I get worse the more they drink."

"She's our little puppet," Jace joked.

"I'm going to get us some water." Stephanie kissed me on the cheek. There was some bustling around the kitchen. Stephanie returned with two tall glasses of water. James whistled at her when she returned. I put my arm around her when she sat down, my frustrated eyes on the guys. "Did any gossip get spilled when I was gone?"

"Nope," Raphael shrugged, taking a sip of his whiskey. "Except for the fact that I turn into an asshole when I'm drunk."

"When you take any substance you turn into an asshole. I literally tell you this all the time," Stephanie scowled.

"At least I'm not a narcissist." Raphael stared at her challengingly.

"Because you have no right to be a narcissist, Stephanie is an image of perfection," James cooed.

"I would give everything I have to sleep with her," Jace licked his teeth.

"Fuck off, Jace," I muttered. "She's not interested."

"How do you know that?" Jace challenged. I knew he was trying to get under my skin. Despite my best efforts, it was working. I turned to Stephanie, leaned in and kissed her. My fingers gliding through her hair as I clutched her close to me.

"That's how I fucking know," I replied, pulling away from her abruptly. Jace's face flashed annoyance before quickly covering it with a smirk.

"Look at that, Levi has grown some balls," Raphael let out an annoyed breath.

"Let's see if that's the case." Jace placed his drink on the table and moved his chair back. "Stephanie, come here."

"Ew, no," Stephanie retorted. I brought my lips victoriously to hers, my fingers gliding up her leg. "Do you want to go to the room?" Stephanie whispered to me.

"No, I'm good here," I replied, pouring myself a glass of whiskey.

"You want a show?" Stephanie purred. She gently bit my ear her lips gliding down to my neck. I felt her fingers run along my inseam.

"Yup, let's go to the room." I stood up abruptly and walked to Stephanie's bedroom. She entered a few minutes later. I stepped over to her, aggressively throwing her against the wall as I collapsed my lips on hers. Her hands scrambled to undo my belt and pants. I pulled away from her, tearing off my clothing and grabbing a condom. My breath was unsteady as I walked back to her. My eyes gliding over her now naked body. Her eyes were fixed on me like I was the only man in the world. Those blue eyes made it impossible to breath. I felt my heartbeat in my throat. She grabbed me, pulling me on top of her.

"Fuck me," Stephanie murmured, our eyes locked. I felt my erection pulsate at her voice. The throb she immediately brought on as she looked at me, desperate for me to fuck her. My fingers raced to put on the condom, a millisecond after succeeding I shoved myself into her.

"Oh," my hands stumbled to her hips as I gripped on to her. I let out a deep growl as I began to pound into her. My vision became foggier with each thrust. Stephanie pulled me into her, her nails puncturing my ass as she hungrily yanked me into her I could hear the wet smack each time I plunged my rock-hard cock fully into her tight hole. Her body stretching to meet my demands.

"Don't stop," Stephanie pleaded, her voice no more than a soft whimper. With that I was gone. My body swelled with pleasure as I finished.

Stephanie threw on a thong, shorts and Raphael's shirt. My

heartbeat harshened, my chest restricting as my blood rose. She was wearing *his* shirt? After I fucked her, she was going to throw on another man's shirt?

"Do you have to wear that?"

"You bring me one of your shirts, I'll stop wearing it," Stephanie looked at me innocently, her eyebrow raised in ignorance. Music seeped through the bedroom walls. Stephanie's eyes lit up with excitement.

"Let's go." I slapped her ass. We walked out to the kitchen. Eli, James and Jace were dancing to "Dancing Queen." Raphael stood against the wall watching while drinking a beer. I walked over to him as Stephanie began dancing with the others.

"Looks like you're a possessive asshole when you're drunk," Raphael stated.

"You're a possessive asshole all the time."

"Fair enough," Raphael shrugged. He cleared his throat. "I hate when new men come into her life. An endless barrage of questions are always in my head. Are they here for her or sex? Will they physically hurt her? Will they break her heart? James, Jace and I have been abandoned so many times it's hard to hold optimism. But Stephanie," Raphael smiled to himself, his eyes dazedly watching her, "she sees the world as bright and colorful, even after everything she's been through. And everything in me just wants to preserve that. She's all I have."

"I'm not going anywhere," I declared.

"Good, because Stephanie's in love with you," Raphael passed me his beer. "Stephanie, *Dirty Dancing?*"

"It's been a while, you sure you can still do it, old man?" Stephanie prodded.

"Hell fucking ya." Raphael laughed. Stephanie ran forward and leaped into his hands. Raphael effortlessly lifted her over his head. I stood there in shock. Stephanie was in love with me? How? I slowly took a sip of beer. Raphael gently put her down and whispered something to her. Stephanie's attention turned to me. My mind raced, what did he say? Raphael chuckled and went to speak with Jace. Stephanie walked over to me.

"You look disorientated," Stephanie observed, taking the beer from my hands. "I think that's enough alcohol."

"Ya, I was thinking about how amazing you are."

"If I knew you were going to shower me with compliments, I would have come over sooner," Stephanie giggled, resting her head against my shoulder. I wrapped my arm around her. She was in love with me. Is this reality? Will I wake up in a few seconds? Will I wake up alone in my bed, her feeling like a distant and unattainable dream?

"What did Raphael say?" I queried, kissing her gently on the head.

"That he's starting to like you."

Holy fuck. I puffed my chest out with pride. Raphael nodded to me, I nodded back.

Chapter 6

"So this is when your friendship with Raphael started?" the green-eyed lady asked.

"I wouldn't call it a friendship," I scoffed.

"You've previously stated," the brown-eyed lady shuffled around her papers, "'I can't believe he would do this, I thought he was my friend, I thought he was family,'" the brown-eyed lady read then looked back up at me quizzically.

"Ya, sorry, it's hard to think of a time that I didn't hate him," I replied, looking down at my water.

"It's important we understand where your mind was during all of this. It's hard, but push away what you currently know and focus back to where you were at the time," the green-eyed lady leaned in.

I nodded.

"This is when my friendship with Raphael started."

***

I felt something soft against my left arm. I glanced over to see Raphael was passing me workout gear. My head was pounding, angry with me for drinking that much. I opened my mouth to protest but closed it not wanting to give up on him starting to like me. I took it and nodded toward him.

"Let's get ready." Stephanie and I headed back to her room. She slipped on a two-piece pink workout set and put her brown hair in a ponytail. I slipped on the joggers and loose shirt that Raphael had passed to me. We walked back out to the hangout room. Jace made a fighting gesture toward Stephanie which she jokingly returned.

"Look at those muscles!" Jace commented holding up her arm. "They're bigger than Levi's." Jace gestured toward me. The rest laughed in a boisterous and unhinged way that shattered what little confidence I held next to them. Raphael came in, keys in his hand. He turned toward me.

"That shirt's tight on me," Raphael prodded. The guys roared with laughter. I felt like shrinking, disappearing into thin air. Stephanie came over and put her head on my shoulder. Raphael unlocked the strange door in the far corner and held it open as everyone filed in.

"Welcome to our playpen," Raphael said to me as I went past. He followed us in. The stairs were unfinished wood and looked rugged. When we got to the bottom, everyone went to the right which had opened into a massive workout place. The floor was all black padding. Raphael placed his hand on my shoulder and gestured to come to the left. Stephanie walked further into the big room and went to the boxing bag. Raphael unlocked a door set slightly to the left. "The rest know about this," he explained. The door opened and he flicked on the light allowing me to enter first.

The room was equal to the size of the hangout room upstairs. It was set up like a massive walk-in closet, with lights above each section and drawers underneath. But instead of clothing, it held guns and ammunition. They had everything: guns, grenades, knives. "If at any point you need protection, we have you covered." Raphael grinned. I couldn't imagine why they would need to know how to use all of this. I felt like a kid in a candy store. My fingers glided over a gun, the power it exuded was intoxicating. The power emanating from this room was enchanting. This was a different world, a different existence. If you weren't respected, you stole that respect. You demanded that respect. I looked back at Raphael; his tattooed arms crossed as he watched me with an amused expression on his face. His presence was one that was felt, even if you weren't looking at him. I stared at him for a couple of seconds, pure envy seeping into my bloodstream.

I wanted that presence.

I wanted to commandeer power by a glance, by a subtle flick of a finger. I needed that aura of dominance. The knowledge that the second you walked into a room; eyes would turn in pensive silence waiting for your instruction. What must it feel like to not step around in uncertainty with your head down? For no one to snicker when your arms were around a stunning woman. One click of a gun could give you that, everyone bowing in terror.

I nodded to Raphael respectively before stepping out of their hidden chamber. Raphael locked the door behind us, gesturing for me to go into the workout room. Stephanie stood there, patiently waiting as she bit her nail.

"We can do sit-ups together and pass a weight," she offered.

"I'll be the one training him," Raphael instructed. Stephanie nodded and walked to Eli. "We'll have that shirt fitting right in no time." Raphael and I strolled into the room. I realized very quickly that this must be a punishment. I was dripping with sweat and gasping for breath. "I'll give you a twenty-minute break." Raphael walked away and began sprinting on the treadmill. Stephanie walked over, finally seeing an opening to talk.

"How are you doing?" She sat next to me.

"Well, frankly I think dying would be better." I pushed my

soaking wet hair out of my face. "How long do we do this for?"

"Two hours, every day."

"How long has it been?" I asked desperately searching for an end.

"Thirty minutes," Stephanie said, her voice full of pity.

"No," I whispered lying down. "I'm good."

"Okay, let's get back to work." Raphael stood over me.

"That was not twenty minutes," I moaned, my face still pressed firmly against the mat.

"You're right, but you're distracting Stephanie, so back we go." Raphael clapped encouragingly. Stephanie disappeared to the treadmill. "Maybe you need to put your strength in perspective as motivation," Raphael said as I continued to lay on the ground.

"Push up competition!" Raphael shouted. I dragged myself off the floor. Everyone gathered into a circle. I took my spot in between Raphael and Jace. Everyone got down on the ground. "Go," Raphael shouted. They all went in unison. I got five in, the sixth was impossible and I flattened on the floor. I watched all the group continue. Raphael was watching while effortlessly performing his. It took what seemed like an eternity before there was any sign of weakness. "Stephanie, butt down," Raphael shouted. Stephanie was starting to struggle and fell out of the competition next.

"Damn," Stephanie shouted, removing herself from the circle. James was close after, a few minutes later Eli slipped and dropped out. He stood up and walked out of the circle, sitting beside Stephanie and whispered something to her. Stephanie giggled. Jace and Raphael looked at each other. Raphael pushed himself up and clapped. Jace groaned but followed suit. A few seconds later, Raphael messed up the landing and face planted on the floor. Jace stood up victoriously.

"Fuck ya," Jace roared, his fists raised in the air. Raphael stood up smiling and shook his hand.

"Damn man, well done," Raphael praised before walking over to me. "Soon enough you'll be the one to win," he patted my shoulder.

It was the motivation I needed to continue on. The muscles in my body were burning and my lungs were aching, but I persevered. I wasn't close to keeping up with Raphael, but I tried. With every gasp for air, I felt my heart quicken. The strenuous exercise made my stomach throb.

"Good workout today," Raphael praised me. "Go stretch with Stephanie." Raphael gestured to Stephanie who was on the other side of the mat. I let out a grunt of pleasure. It was done. The torture was done. I stumbled over and plopped myself down beside her.

"You survived," she pointed out.

"Barely," I mustered up a smile. I looked around, everyone was stretching now.

"You should be working out every day from now on," Raphael helped me up. I nodded. "We want you prepared for the worst-case scenario." Raphael patted me on the back. Everyone filed back upstairs.

"You can shower first." Stephanie grabbed my hand.

"I am honored," I replied, kissing her hand.

"You should be, my favorite part of a workout is the shower." Stephanie smiled at me. We went to her bedroom and I immediately went to the shower, desperate to wash off the pools of sweat. I hopped in the shower, the hot water felt so nice against my sore muscles. My head tilted back as I savored this moment, this feeling of pain and pleasure. The shower curtain rustled.

Stephanie stepped in. "I can help clean you, I know my arms are always a little too stiff." She grabbed the loofah and gestured for me to turn around so my back faced her. With a mixture of the soaped-up loofah and her hands, she gave me a back massage. Her hands worked meticulously. I let out a moan, captivated by the unbelievable sensation. "You were so hot when you were working out today." She continued up to my shoulders. There was a knock at the bedroom door.

"They'll go away," she whispered to me, kissing my shoulder and moving one of her hands down and to my front. Her loofah hand continued to work my left shoulder as her right hand began to stroke me. My hand reached out, attempting to steady myself, her indulgent strokes engulfed my tired and shaky body in ecstasy.

"I let myself in," Jace's voice called. Stephanie rested her head frustratedly on my back.

"Uh, we're in here," I replied hoping Jace would get the idea to leave us alone. I heard his footprints going toward the bathroom. Stephanie stopped her movements.

"Jace, some privacy please," Stephanie scolded.

"Don't stop on my account, I'm sure Stephanie's giving you a hell of a reward after the workout," Jace said from the other side of the curtain. "And you deserve it, you did well." Jace complimented.

"Thank you," I murmured, hesitantly. Very uncomfortable with the current situation.

"Jace, why are you here?" Stephanie demanded.

"Oh, just here to take orders for dinner," Jace stated.

"Jace, can this not wait?" Stephanie put the loofah down.

"I'm very hungry," Jace responded.

"What are the options, Jace?" I asked, feeling my stomach

jump at the idea of food.

"Hamburgers or pizza."

"Uh, pizza," I responded.

"Jace, can you pass me a towel? I'm getting cold." Stephanie whined. There was some movement and Stephanie reached past the curtain to take the towel Jace was passing her. She wrapped herself up and left the bathroom.

"Raphael and Stephanie don't allow anything but pepperoni pizza in this household, so I guess that means pepperoni pizza." Jace chuckled.

"Uh Jace, can you pass me a towel?" I asked, turning off the water. Jace pulled back the curtain, passing me the towel. I quickly grabbed it and covered myself. "Jesus, Jace."

"How was it?" Jace smirked and gestured to the shower. It took me a few seconds to connect what he was talking about.

"It was fantastic until you interrupted." I wrapped the towel around me and stepped out of the shower.

"Oh, I'm sorry man, I really thought she would have continued." Jace patted me on the arm, excitedly leaving to put the order in. I quickly put on my pants and top, walking out to the kitchen. Stephanie was standing next to Raphael in a red long-sleeved crop top and her jean shorts. Raphael looked up at me.

"Are you also mad at Jace?" Raphael sighed.

"I mean, it was an invasion of our privacy." I put my arm around Stephanie.

"I'll talk to him about boundaries, I can't say it will help," Raphael whispered. Stephanie nodded and walked to the hangout room.

"Do you want me to put the workout gear straight into the wash?" I asked.

"No, that's yours, you need something to work out in."

Raphael stood up and began to pour a glass of water. "I also have a chin-up bar for you to take."

"Thank you," I blinked in shock.

"You're family now." Raphael passed me the glass of water. He walked away to join the rest of the group in the hangout room. I followed, placing the glass of water on the table and slumped on the couch next to Stephanie.

"Are you leaving tomorrow?" James asked Stephanie. Stephanie nodded.

"I have classes starting Monday, and I need to drive this guy back too." She ruffled my hair.

That was all I remembered. I woke up to the light shining in through the window and noise coming from the kitchen. The pure vindictive ache of my muscles making it impossible for me to move. The dull pain lulling me back to sleep.

"I'll wake him up in a bit," Stephanie's voice rang out.

"I'll take the stuff out to the car," Raphael stated. I heard the door shut, maintaining the façade of sleep. All of me longing for Stephanie to come over, snuggle into me, and allow herself to sleep in.

"Is sleeping beauty awake yet?" I heard Jace call as his heavy steps came down the stairs.

"Not yet," Stephanie replied. "Don't…" Stephanie started as I heard footsteps sprinting toward me. I moved slightly to show that I was indeed awake and slowly got up, every muscle in my body screamed out for me to not move. Jace pouted as I hobbled over to the kitchen slowly. "Good morning, you fell asleep so we thought we would leave you." Stephanie passed me a travel mug full of coffee. "We should get going."

"All loaded up!" Raphael announced. Stephanie and I

walked out of the house. Raphael walked to the Rolls-Royce.

"Did I miss anything?" I asked.

"Absolutely nothing, we ate pizza then went to bed, we didn't want to disturb you."

"Oh, I'm sorry."

"We've all been there," Stephanie giggled. "How are your muscles feeling?"

"Stiff, I am very stiff." We got into the vehicle, Raphael turned it on and we began driving back. I slept through most of the car ride. We pulled into my driveway. Stephanie opened the trunk and handed me a bag, which held the workout clothes Raphael gave me. She also handed me the coat I wore earlier and the chin-up bar. Raphael sat in the car waiting. I waved and went into my house.

"What is this?" Dad asked, motioning to the chin-up bar.

"It's a chin-up bar. Raphael, Stephanie's foster brother, gave it to me." My parents nodded. "Uh, can I talk to you about Christmas?"

"It's a little soon to be spending Christmas with Stephanie don't you think?" dad pondered.

"How did you know I was going to ask that?" I sat down at the kitchen table.

"I used to be a detective," dad laughed, sitting across from me.

"I don't think it's too early," I stated.

"You love her," dad said, analyzing me.

"Would you stop that?" I spat. I looked down at my hands. "Raphael said that Stephanie is in love with me," I murmured. Mom joined us at the table intrigued by this development.

"And how do you feel about this?" dad quizzed, leaning back in his chair and watching me closely.

"Like I'm the luckiest man on this planet." I smiled to myself. "She makes me feel important, you know? Like, I could take on the world."

"That sounds like you love her." Mom grinned, moving the hair out of my face.

"I'm scared that she'll wake up one day and realize she could do better. Because she can. She's constantly surrounded by these guys who exude power and strength. I just don't understand how she could fall for me," I whimpered. My parents paused, glancing to one another, I knew they were having an entire conversation in silence. A language only they understood made from the subtilties of facial expressions. Dad's focus returned to me, shifting as he chose his words.

"I think the same about your mother, I mean, not the part where she's surrounded by other men, but every morning I count my blessings that she chooses me over everyone else. Besides, she's obviously not interested in those guys." He smiled tenderly at me.

"What if she's slept with one of them, Jace made a—" I began to blurt.

"If she's slept with one of them, but she's with you, doesn't that speak for itself?" dad shrugged.

"Her brother said she loves you; he would know better than anyone." My mom rubbed my back gently. "Don't let her past inhibit your future."

"Okay," I replied. My mom and dad looked at each other, continuing their unspoken conversation.

"What if you spend Christmas with them and we'll move our Christmas dinner to Boxing Day?" mom suggested.

"That would be fantastic," I beamed, kissing my mom on the cheek. I went upstairs and set the coat on my bed, looking at the tag: Armani. I chuckled and shook my head. I eagerly set up my chin-up bar.

My Monday morning alarm went off. The most painful alarm. I snoozed it. I stared at my roof contemplating if Stephanie and her misfit family ever needed to set alarms. I smiled to myself thinking that was a reason by itself to become a criminal. I slowly rolled out of bed, my muscles still sore and begging me to just stay among the cozy blankets. I got dressed and grabbed my bag, walking to the cafeteria. Aidan and Lucas were seated at the typical table.

"How was the cottage?" Aidan asked as I joined them.

"It was fun. We went to the beach, got drunk early on Saturday and had amazing sex," I bragged.

"You got drunk early Saturday morning and her brother was...?" Aidan inquired hesitantly.

"Drinking with us, so were the other guys," I shrugged.

"Good morning," Stephanie sat down beside me.

"Can we have a party at your place?" Aidan demanded.

"Uh ya, I can ask my foster brother if he would be okay with that," Stephanie shifted.

"We can do it as soon as we get back from Christmas break," Aidan suggested.

"Did you ask your parents?" Stephanie looked over at me. I nodded.

"I get to spend Christmas with you, I just need to be back by dinner on Boxing Day," I grinned. Stephanie's eyes lit up with excitement.

"Everyone's going to be so excited!" Stephanie hugged me tightly. "I love Christmas."

Chapter 7

"So, you joined out of love?" the green-eyed lady queried.

"I think it was the excitement, and the need to prove myself."
I pondered. "When Raphael spoke, people listened, people
obeyed. It was a power that was intoxicating. I was so easily
overlooked, Stephanie showed me what it feels like to be looked
at, Raphael taught me how to get that from every person. It was
so unlike my life before."

***

Stephanie's beat-up red car pulled up at the sign. I got in the door
and placed my bag at my feet. I leaned in and gave Stephanie a
quick peck on the cheek, the intimate greeting making her giggle.

"Are you ready?" Stephanie smiled at me. The Saturday
morning sun was directed straight into my eyes. I squinted and
nodded to Stephanie.

"Where do you even live? We always go to your cottage?" I
asked. Stephanie did a U-turn.

"I'll show you, it's not far. We'll just drive by." Stephanie
continued straight until we were in the suburbs. She pointed at a
small townhouse.

"No way do you guys own a normal house," I looked at the
light stoned house, its right wall sharing with the house that
looked identical beside it.

"We need to look normal," Stephanie made another U-turn.

"Raphael drives a Rolls-Royce? You also showed us your cottage before you knew us very well." I stated pointedly.

"Raphael is less concerned with the outward image, and no offense, but you're not really the people we're trying to fool." Stephanie laughed. I stuck my tongue out at her.

"Any news on the party?"

"No, I asked Raphael, and he said he'd think about it," Stephanie replied. "I'm expecting it to be a 'no,' hard to make sure a whole bunch of people aren't going to try and investigate the cottage or ask too many questions."

"That makes sense," I nodded with agreement. Aidan would be heartbroken. The cottage, in his words, was the ambiance needed to have a party people talk about for years to come. His house seemed boring in comparison to this mansion in the middle of nowhere.

We pulled into the driveway and entered the cottage. I dropped my bag off in Stephanie's room before walking to the kitchen.

"Welcome back," Jace enthused, walking across the empty living room.

"Anything fun happen?"

"We have a lead for a new job, Raphael is looking into it," Jace leaned on the kitchen counter.

"What's the job in?" I inquired. Jace acted out injecting a needle into your shoulder. I rocked on my heels, racking my brain to figure out what he meant. "Heroine?" I asked. Stephanie and Jace looked at me dumbfounded and laughed.

"You don't inject heroin in your shoulder," Jace said, grabbing my arm. "You inject it here." Jace pressed on my veins mid-way up my arm.

"Or he doesn't inject it at all," Stephanie pushed Jace's

hands off me. "Something pharma." Stephanie clarified. "He was pretending to inject a vaccine."

"Oh, okay." I felt my face turn bright red in pure embarrassment.

"More vanilla than I thought." Jace hit me gently on the shoulder. Stephanie opened the fridge.

"Do we have anything good?" Stephanie's eyes trailed over the fridge, disappointed.

"James went shopping this week, so unless you want a snack of sardines and peanut butter on bread, you are out of luck." Jace walked back to the hangout room.

"He's so weird," Stephanie complained and shut the door.

"Stephanie!" Eli yelled excitedly turning the corner from the direction of the entrance. "How was the drive up?" Eli asked, wrapping his arms around her.

"It was good," Stephanie replied.

"We should work out now," Jace called, holding up a bag.

"Ah, yes, James bought a fuck ton of weed." Raphael pointed to the bag. "Let's do the workout so we have time to smoke it before the pizza place closes," Raphael suggested excitedly, hitting the counter then walking to his room. Stephanie and I quickly changed before walking to the hangout room.

Raphael was standing there propping open the door waiting for us. Everyone had already gone to the workout room. The smell of sweat hit me the minute I walked in. Now that the excitement had dwindled and all that I felt was fear of the impending pain, my nostrils were working normally. I made a face, surprised I hadn't noticed it last time, and upset I was smelling it this time. It was enough that you could taste it.

Raphael worked me to the bone. My muscles shook, my breathing uneasy. I sat there drenched in sweat as he went to go pick on Stephanie. He stood behind her as she was doing weighted squats and shouted for her to go lower. Stephanie eventually put the weights down and, out of breath, motioned that she was done. We called it quits soon after. I walked over, embracing Stephanie tightly.

"Ew, you're sweaty," Stephanie complained.

"And you're stinky, but I still love you." I continued to embrace her chuckling as I nuzzled her neck with my nose. I froze realizing I had never said those words to her before.

"I love you too," she whispered to me.

"Stretch out!" Raphael shouted at us. Stephanie pulled back and smiled. We proceeded to stretch.

"How are you feeling?" Jace asked, taking a glass out of the cupboard. I pushed my wet hair from my face. My damp body, red from the steaming shower, prickled at the chilled air. It felt nice after nearly dying from heat exhaustion from Stephanie's requested shower temperature.

"Not as bad as last time." I leaned against the counter.

"I'm going to give you something that will help with the muscles," Jace said opening the fridge. He took out a large carton of eggs and cracked four in the glass, handing it to me. I took a sharp breath in, looking at the gooey mess. "Do this every day and you'll look like me." Jace posed showing off his massive arm muscles. I looked down at the glass one more time and chugged it down. I gagged. "Keep it down, you get used to the texture."

"I'm okay," I choked, swallowing hard.

"Well done," Jace enthused, taking out another glass from the cupboard and making his own glass of raw eggs. He took it like a shot without even flinching.

"Let's order that pizza!" Eli called as he came down the

stairs. James was already sitting at the kitchen table and we joined him.

"Have you ever smoked?" James asked, gesturing to the large bag of weed. I shook my head. "Have you ever done any drugs?"

"Only ones prescribed by my doctor," I joked, uncomfortable. James smiled. I wasn't quite sure if he was amused at my joke or humored by my naiveté.

"Make sure you take it slow; this is good stuff," James said, beginning to grind it up and rolling the first blunt. Raphael walked in, snatching it from him before sitting beside me.

"Are you guys starting already?" Stephanie inquired from the open doorway.

"We're starting in a bit," James continued to grind the weed for the next blunt.

"Okay, I'll swing by to grab some pizza later then," Stephanie gave a quick thumbs up before disappearing.

"She doesn't smoke," Raphael clarified, taking the joint in his mouth.

"She doesn't like babysitting us when we smoke either," Jace continued.

"Should I not be smoking then?" I turned to Raphael.

He looked at me, confused.

"She doesn't care, stay and hang with us," Raphael said, lighting it.

"It's his first time," James mentioned.

Raphael nodded and took a breath in.

"Try this one first," Raphael passed me his joint slowly expelling the air. I took it from him.

"Breathe in slowly," James instructed. I breathed in slowly, filling up my lungs and then proceeding into a coughing fit. I meekly passed the joint back to Raphael.

"Good job, always difficult the first puff," Jace encouraged. James handed out the rest of the joints and everyone lit them up.

"It's your friends that want to have the party here?" Raphael looked at me.

"Ya, they're used to a lot of parental supervision so having a party is kind of a big deal," I stated, fully aware at how ridiculous and childish that must seem to him. Raphael nodded slowly.

"They can have it, on one condition," Raphael tapped the table, his eyes on me in an intense and protective glare. "We have to all be here, I don't want anyone snooping around."

"Thank you, they will be thrilled," I beamed.

"Figured it was important to Stephanie; she hates parties," Raphael murmured.

"She hates parties?" I clarified.

Raphael looked away from me.

"This is good shit," Raphael said to James holding up the joint. James nodded, leaning back. Raphael passed the joint back to me. I took a drag and coughed minimally. I passed the joint back to Raphael. The doorbell rang. James got up, placing his joint on a plate in the middle of the table. He ran to the door.

"Good, I'm so hungry," Eli groaned.

"I wouldn't worry about it too much, Eli. You'll be asleep in a few minutes," Jace chuckled.

"Jace, can you get the pizza boxes off the floor?" Raphael pointed at the pizza that was resting at the bottom of the stairs. "James picked up the pizza man again." Raphael laughed. James's door abruptly closed. Jace ran over and carried the pizza back.

"How the fuck does he do that that quickly?" Jace

complained.

"I think I could," Raphael puffed up his chest.

"You'd be stumped as soon as you got him into the bedroom." Jace grabbed a slice of pizza and passed the box around.

"Seems pretty straightforward to me." Raphael shrugged.

"Jesus Raph, it's been a while for you has it?" Jace laughed.

Raphael gave him the finger.

"I'm just saying, men are easy, women it's a technical process," Raphael leaned forward like he was unraveling a conspiracy. We all looked upstairs as moans began to echo through the house.

"I mean it doesn't have to be," Jace commented.

"It does, hearing her scream, nothing better," Raphael rolled the joint in his fingers, his eyes dazedly staring at it, his mind obviously captivated by a thought.

"What the fuck did I walk into?" Stephanie laughed, grabbing the pizza box. Raphael looked up at Stephanie and smirked. "Pizza man?" Stephanie asked, pointing upstairs to the noise. Jace nodded.

"What was your best sexual encounter, Stephanie?" Raphael looked connivingly at her.

"You're high, I'm not doing this," Stephanie rolled her eyes before quickly stepping out of the room. I went to stand up to go after her. Raphael grabbed my shoulder and pulled me back down.

"Don't worry, she's just no fun," Raphael gestured to where Stephanie had just stood. I looked at him confused, what the fuck was that? "Sucks she didn't say you though." Raphael kissed his teeth, before a grin slithered across his lips. Jace laughed uncomfortably.

"You're one to talk, how many girls have you slept with?" Eli challenged. Raphael shrugged and leaned back.

"Two the last time I counted," Jace put in.

"When I do it, I do it well," Raphael arrogantly smiled.

"The last girl left crying." Jace raised an eyebrow. A confused expression plastered itself on my face. Jace gestured to Raphael to tell me the story.

"I wasn't over the first girl," Raphael raised his hands in a smug defense.

"He told her he couldn't finish looking at such an ugly face." Jace pointed at Raphael with his joint.

"Ah, I don't remember that," Raphael protested.

"Easy for you to forget, she cried on my shoulder for two hours," Jace frowned.

"Like I said, I wasn't over the first girl," Raphael chuckled. Jace shook his head disapprovingly.

"And that was a while ago," Jace continued.

"Why sleep with other people when I'll be disappointed? No one can top the first girl," Raphael smiled to himself. "Love of my fucking life." Raphael leaned back in his chair letting his face point upward exhaling smoke to the air.

"Okay, get a room," Jace shook his head. Raphael gave him the finger. "What's your count?" Jace turned to me.

"Three," I smiled.

"My boy!" Jace yelled, giving me a fist bump. "More than Raph."

"Still doesn't know how to do it," Raphael mocked.

"So, Stephanie says you're studying English?" Eli turned to me.

"What? Are you going to write a book?" Raphael taunted.

"Maybe, I don't know yet," I responded.

"I can be your main character," Raphael derided.

"I think I can find a more interesting main character," I retorted. My blood froze as I realized my mistake. The foolish loss of temper. I opened my mouth to beg his forgiveness. Raphael and Jace roared with laughter.

"Fair enough," Raphael snickered. We sat there in silence for a few seconds.

"What happened to Stephanie's parents?" I asked.

"Why haven't you asked Stephanie?" Raphael sighed.

"I don't want to upset her," I picked at my thumb. Maybe this was a stupid thing to ask him. Obviously, it could be sensitive for him too.

"We don't know, she was a kid when she entered foster care, never wanted to try to find them," Raphael shrugged dismissively.

"No one adopted Stephanie? I can't imagine that," I stated.

"Ah, innocence. She was too old. People out there only care if you just came into this world or are just about to go out," Raphael murmured, his demeanor shifting to a pensive sadness. A moment I wasn't sure if we were meant to see.

"Or if you kill a few people, they really start caring then," Eli smirked.

"Don't think care is the right word there, Eli," Raphael shook his head, snapping back to his previous light hearted grin.

"I think that's the right word. You know how many fucking essays I've read about how, with a little love, I was perfectly 'fixable'?" Eli teased.

"Oh I love those people, you know how many girls have tried to fix me?" Jace simpered. "I kindly escort them to my bed and they show me the love that can fix me. Never seems to work." Jace shrugged, a cunning smile on his face.

"Did you also enter foster care at that time?" I inquired, reverting the conversation back. Raphael laughed then looked down at his joint.

"No, I knew my parents, they died, rightfully so, and I entered into the system." Raphael took another drag. "Jace, your turn." Raphael pointed at him trying to get my attention off him.

"My parents were pretty cool, strictly religious, I wasn't too into it, so I left," Jace shrugged.

"I'm going to head to bed," Eli stood up, putting his joint out.

"I think this is the longest you've ever stayed awake after smoking," Raphael prodded. Eli gave him the finger while leaving.

"Well, I'm going to head to bed." Jace nodded at us and left up the stairs hitting James's door on the way by. The moaning quieted down.

"Stephanie seems really happy with you." Raphael looked at me.

"I'm really happy with her, too," I replied. Raphael nodded slowly. Then put out his joint. He waved his hand and left for his room. I walked to Stephanie's bedroom.

"Are you feeling okay?" Stephanie asked, sitting up in bed. I nodded and walked over taking off my clothing and getting into bed. "Was Raphael mean? He can get that way when he's high, he gets so sorry for himself."

"No, he said you seemed happy with me." I cuddled up to her shoulder.

"I'm glad he has eyes," she said, stroking my hair. I was asleep within seconds.

I woke up to the light from the windows shining on me; the bed was already empty. I crawled out and threw on my clothing walking out of the room.

"—are you doing?" Eli's voice echoed through the hallway. I paused, curious to hear their conversation. Not out of suspicion or jealousy, Eli was curious to me. Even though his manner seemed weak and reserved, it was evident something dark was lurking underneath. I couldn't quite place my finger on it, but his brown eyes always seemed somewhat sad, somewhat preoccupied with something. Like he was reliving a horror he couldn't unsee.

I snatched myself from the thought. I had obviously spent far too much time with dad. It was simply my imagination running wild. Probably my jealousy of her friendships finding a way to convince her to push them away.

I didn't want to share her.

That's what it was. Eli was innocent, it was just my mind trying to convince me otherwise. I willed myself to move, to make myself known and be the better person. Not one that listened in to his girlfriend without her knowledge. But I couldn't budge. My muscles were morally deficient and ambitious to hear how the 'puppy' spoke to *my* girlfriend when I wasn't there.

"Do you want an honest answer?" Stephanie replied.

"Well, yes, I don't want you to lie to me," Eli chuckled. "Like I'm tiptoeing around a herd of angry emus."

"You've spent too much time with my friends."

"How are you?"

"Oh, I'm brilliant," Eli answered. "As a self-professed angry emu hunter, I just want to say I am at your service," Eli joked. "And if you don't laugh at my brilliant joke, I will have no choice but to start singing."

"No," Stephanie giggled.

"Oh yes, too late," Eli said amusedly. "You can dance, you can jive, having the time of your life," Eli began to belt. "See that girl, watch that scene, diggin' the dancing queen," Eli sang. I walked in. Stephanie was laughing hysterically as Eli spun her around, holding a ketchup bottle to his mouth. Eli's eyes gleamed as he watched her laugh. I leaned against the wall. "Not going to cut in?" Eli chuckled.

Stephanie giggled and grabbed my hands, pulling herself into me as Eli got a Billy Joel song up on the phone and hopped onto the counter. Eli sang terribly over the music. I spun Stephanie around the kitchen, we laughed and sang along to it.

"What the fuck is going on here?" Raphael walked in rubbing his head.

"Not up for some fun?" Eli prodded.

"No, turn it off," Raphael ordered. Eli's smile faded quickly, and he turned off the music, hopping down from the counter.

"Hungover?" Stephanie's eyes watched Raphael closely. Like she was inspecting the movement of a dangerous lion. The air immediately thickening with intensity as she retreated into herself.

"No, just don't appreciate coming in and having a zoo surround me," Raphael snarled, his cold glare resting on Eli.

"Sorry, Raph." Eli patted Raphael on the shoulder.

"Did Levi tell you my one condition to have the party?" Raphael asked Stephanie, a gentle smile crossing his lips.

"No." Stephanie turned to me.

"I've decided it's fine, as long as we're here." Raphael grabbed the ketchup bottle, putting it back in the cupboard.

"Won't that be weird?" Stephanie queried.

"They're literally university age." I gave her a confused look.

"See Stephanie? I'm young!" Raphael laughed.

"Thank you!" Stephanie embraced Raphael. "Have you texted the boys that we're having a party?" Stephanie asked excitedly. I shook my head but immediately did so. Aidan and Lucas immediately went to work planning it.

Chapter 8

"He said he's read multiple essays about himself?" The green-eyed lady looked at me surprised. I gave her a confused look. "Eli," the green-eyed lady specified.

"Ya," I shrugged. The green-eyed lady looked at the brown-haired lady. "What?" I asked.

"Nothing, just something to note," the green-eyed lady stated.

"So, Raphael thought that a party for young adults in an armed house was a good idea?" the brown-haired lady commented skeptically.

"You can't see into the future when you make these decisions," I bristled. "Ya, it was a stupid idea."

"Why did he allow this?" the green-eyed lady asked.

"The same reason he did everything. Stephanie," I retorted.

"You don't think you were part of that decision?" The brown-haired lady questioned. "It seems like you guys were getting quite close."

"If he was close to me, he wouldn't have taken her away." My voice broke.

***

Stephanie entered the cafeteria and sat with Aidan, Lucas and me. I wrapped my arms around her, nuzzling my nose against her cheek. Stephanie cupped my chin, biting the tip of my nose playfully before resting her head on my shoulder.

"I am so fucking excited for Christmas break," I announced to the table.

"Speaking of which, I won't be here for the rest of the week. Raphael's gift is more difficult than I had predicted. So, I brought your Christmas gifts today," Stephanie stated excitedly.

"What did you get Raphael?" I demanded.

"Shut up, Levi. What did you get us?" Aidan asked eagerly. I truthfully had not thought of getting a present for Stephanie yet. She pulled two small boxes from her purse and put them in front of both Aidan and Lucas.

"I got you both the same thing, I always found it more fun to do it with someone else," Stephanie explained. Aidan and Lucas looked at each other, confused. They slowly opened each of their boxes. It was a piece of paper with a number scribbled on it. "So, this is the number for where Raphael goes and drives. They have any car you can imagine. Call and set up a time and you can take your dream cars for a spin. I rented it out for two hours, you can try as many vehicles as you want. Lucas, I know you don't drive so I called Ahmad and he'll set you up with either a teacher or a driver, whatever you want."

"Holy shit, that is so cool Stephanie." Aidan stood up and gestured for her to give him a hug. Stephanie stood up and embraced him. Lucas joined in.

"This is literally the best gift I've ever gotten," Lucas murmured in complete disbelief.

"Okay, well I have to be off, but drive safely you two." Stephanie smiled at them. She walked over and kissed my forehead. "I'll pick you up on Christmas Eve, eleven a.m. at the sign."

"Okay, I'll be there," I smiled at her. Stephanie left,

disappearing into the crowd.

"I think I'm in love with her," Lucas smiled to himself. I gave him the finger.

"I don't know what to get her," I complained, rubbing my face with my hands.

"You haven't gotten a gift for her yet?" Lucas shook his head disapprovingly. "See, I wouldn't treat her like that."

"Shut up Lucas, help me think. I've never been in a relationship over Christmas, I forgot I needed to get her something," I mumbled.

"Dude, you're fucked, look what she got us. She probably bought you a country," Aidan laughed.

I groaned. "I'll figure it out, can't imagine the guys being great present givers," I muttered. "Maybe I'll look good in comparison." I grabbed my bag from my feet. "I'm going to figure this out." I stood up and began to leave.

"You have classes," Aidan called.

"I'll see you guys later," I replied, ignoring Aidan's comment. I left the cafeteria and walked home.

"I need to go shopping," I yelled as I entered the house. Dad put down the paper and looked at me from the kitchen table.

"You have classes," Dad stated, annoyed.

"I haven't gotten Stephanie a Christmas present." The panic seeped into my voice.

"Christmas is next week." Dad shook his head disapprovingly.

"Exactly," I replied. Dad nodded and grabbed his coat. We hurried out to his car.

"What do you want to get her?" Dad asked as we drove down the street.

"I literally have no idea, she got Aidan and Lucas this

amazing gift." I shook my head, frustrated at myself for not thinking of this earlier.

"What did she get them?"

"A two-hour session at this racetrack where they can try whatever vehicle they want, as many as they want," I replied looking out the window intently looking for ideas.

"Lucas doesn't drive."

"I know, she set him up with a driver or teacher, whichever he wants."

"You're fucked." Dad shook his head.

"Thanks, Dad. I appreciate your optimism," I rubbed my face. "Fuck, will I need to get the guys something?"

"Don't use that kind of language. Yes, you will need to get the guys something," dad stated. My heart sank, what could I possibly get them?

"Maybe I'll just say I'm sick." I sank into my seat.

"No, what does Stephanie like?"

"Uh, history, board games, beer."

"What about like a historical book? You're an English major, she's a history major," dad suggested.

"I like that idea," I nodded. "And for the guys?"

"I don't know, poker set?"

"That works." I shrugged.

"Okay, let's find a bookstore for you," dad stared at the stores around us. We finally happened across a rugged bookstore. Dad pulled into the parking lot. We walked in; a bell rang notifying the owner of our presence. It was one of those old ones where the musky smell hit you when you stepped in. I loved that smell. A lady walked out to greet us. "What is the oldest book you have?" dad asked pleasantly.

"The Bible," the lady replied. Dad looked over at me.

"I'm not getting Stephanie a Bible," I gave him a bewildered glance.

"Seems like a perfect Christmas gift," my dad grumbled.

"I am not going to try to convert Stephanie to Christianity," I pinched the bridge of my nose.

"Okay, fine. What is the oldest edition of a book that you have?" dad asked. The lady nodded and returned with a book in her hand.

"First edition of *Great Expectations* by Charles Dickens." The lady smiled at me.

"Holy shit," I took the book gently from her.

"Language," dad critiqued. "How much is it?"

"Two thousand," the lady replied.

"For a book?" dad scoffed.

"This is a first edition, Charles Dickens," I defended. "I'll take it."

"Uh, no you won't," dad said.

"I will," I walked to the counter.

"You haven't known her for that long, Levi. You can't just fork out two thousand dollars on a girl you barely know," dad reasoned.

"I am about to," I retorted. I paid for the book using my savings account. We left the bookstore, my dad visibly annoyed at me.

"That was stupid," dad muttered.

"Maybe, but I feel great about it," I snipped.

"You don't even have a job."

"I made a lot of money this past summer," I shrugged. "I can always get a job."

"Don't do something that stupid again please," dad pleaded.

"I won't," I promised. Dad pulled into another store.

"Don't spend over a hundred on this poker set." Dad got out of the vehicle. I followed. We walked into the store and went to their game's selection. I picked up their only poker set and purchased it. "Okay, panic averted," dad sighed as we left the store. "Are you going to spend a lot of time with Stephanie before Christmas?" dad asked, getting in the car.

"No, she's gone until Christmas Eve, said that Raphael's present was more difficult than she thought." I did up my seatbelt as dad started the car.

"That's an intriguing statement, do you know what she got him?" dad wondered as we pulled out of the parking lot.

"No, only that it's time-sensitive," I shrugged.

"You need to tell me what she got him as soon as you know, I'm very curious," dad stated. I nodded. "Well, I am happy we get you all to ourselves for a bit, it's weird not having you around."

"Maybe we can break out our own poker set." I smiled.

"I would love that," he replied. We pulled into the driveway. I unloaded the gifts and went to wrap them.

The week went by slowly. There were no classes to break up the day. Lucas and Aidan were busy with their families. My parents and I played poker, card games and board games. But a few days in, it seemed monotonous with nothing else going on. I woke up Christmas Eve morning and walked down the stairs, the gifts in my hand determined to not forget them.

"I am going to miss you at Christmas," mom hugged me tightly.

"I'm going to miss you guys too." I hugged her back, the poker set weighing down my arm.

"Make it clear to her brother that next Christmas we have

both of you." Mom pulled back from the hug. I nodded.

"Have a good time son." Dad hugged me. I nodded and waved goodbye as I left. I walked to the sign and waited. Finally, the red Toyota pulled up beside me. I got in.

"Which one's mine?" Stephanie asked cheerfully. I held up the wrapped-up book. She reached for it.

"It's not Christmas!" I protested keeping the present out of her reach. Stephanie sighed and began driving. She wore a tight red sweater and shorts, a pair of fabric antlers sat on her head. "What did you get Raphael?" I demanded.

"It's not Christmas," Stephanie mocked me. "I don't trust you to keep it a secret, he hates not knowing. What did you get the guys?"

"A poker set," I shrugged.

"Oh, they'll love that." Stephanie grinned. I sighed in relief. "I am so excited," Stephanie squealed. She blasted the Christmas carols as we drove to the cottage, belting the lyrics. We pulled into the driveway. Eli ran out of the house and to Stephanie, lifting her up and hugging her tightly.

"I hate when you leave us," Eli muttered. We all walked into the cottage. In the typically empty living room sat a massive pine tree. Decorations were set beside it, and the kitchen chairs sat looking at it.

"We're home!" Stephanie yelled. Raphael rounded the corner with a slick grin on his face as he embraced Stephanie.

"Are you going to tell me what you got me?" Raphael smirked.

"Nope," Stephanie replied. Raphael turned his gaze to me, he embraced me tightly. I patted his back, disorientated by this gesture.

"Do you know what she got me?" Raphael asked, pulling

away. I shook my head. "Damn!"

"Stephanie's home!" James yelled, he ran forward picking her up and spinning her. James nodded at me. I nodded back.

"Okay, so tonight we decorate the Christmas tree," Raphael announced. I nodded.

"And tomorrow we get the treat of my favorite tradition," Jace smirked, walking into the living room. He embraced Stephanie and me.

"I was thinking we should drop that tradition," Stephanie sighed.

"What tradition?" I questioned.

"Jace, the first year he met Stephanie, bought her Mrs. Claus lingerie. The tradition is that Stephanie puts it on and hands out the gifts," James explained.

"I am nothing but a piece of meat," Stephanie rolled her eyes.

"Pretty much," Jace chuckled.

"Can I see it?" I asked. Stephanie nodded and disappeared into her bedroom. She came back with a hanger in her hand. It held a short red velvet dress with fluffy white trim. "Oh, that's not too bad," I shrugged.

"The boy has spoken, the tradition lives on," Jace announced gleefully. Stephanie groaned.

"Presents under the tree," Raphael gestured to the looming green fixture. I walked over, knelt down and placed them under. I looked around to see what was under there. They were all varying sizes. A small box sat under the tree. "To Raph, from Stephanie." My interest peaked. So, it was something small. I looked around and saw another small box "To Levi, from Stephanie."

"They always say good things come in small boxes,"

Raphael commented. I hit my head on the branches in shock. "Don't worry, I do the same thing, can't figure this one out though."

"Because I am brilliant," Stephanie laughed. "Did you make eggnog?"

"Have I ever not made you eggnog? It's in the fridge," Raphael smiled. I stood up managing to avoid the tree this time. Stephanie ran off to the fridge.

"Raphael, I have seen no present to Stephanie from you," Jace walked over, beer in hand. "Did you forget to get her something?"

"No, just don't trust it around you criminals," Raphael joked. "I will bring it out Christmas morning."

"What did you get her?" Jace demanded.

"I know Stephanie is paying you to ask these questions, Jace. It's not going to work." Raphael shook his head disapprovingly.

"You're terrible, Jace!" Stephanie yelled.

"Still owe me." Jace shrugged.

"It's, uh, a weird tradition Stephanie and I have, if one of us guesses the present before Christmas, the loser is forced to do whatever the winner wants for all of Christmas," Raphael smirked and looked at Stephanie. "Stephanie has never won."

"Fuck off, you're a cheater, that's why," Stephanie muttered. "Last year he guessed mine and the entire day he made me polish his boots," Stephanie pouted. Raphael chuckled. "This year, there is no fucking way you're going to figure it out." Stephanie walked over with two glasses of eggnog in her hand. She passed me one.

"So, Raphael, what did you get Stephanie?" I queried.

"Vultures," Raphael muttered and walked to the fridge.

"Let's figure out what he got you," I grinned, pulling on her sweater until she was in my arms.

"Okay, so he went to a few 'appointments' and I think that has something to do with it," Stephanie stated.

"That's literally no information Stephanie, is that all you have?" I asked.

"He's a professional criminal, it's hard to get information." Stephanie defended.

"You're also a professional criminal whose job it is to get information. You live with him!" I laughed.

"There's a lot of judgment coming from you," Stephanie giggled and pushed me gently. "Maybe we can find it in his room. He's protective of his closet."

"No, I don't think he's that stupid," I blurted, frantically attempting to keep the panic from my voice.

"You're right, damn." Stephanie took a sip of her eggnog. Jace blasted the Christmas carols. Stephanie smiled and immediately and started dancing. Raphael joined in, spinning her around. Everyone was quickly on their feet dancing to the music. In seconds, the large room was filled with laughter and loud singing to the classic songs. The opposite to the typical stiff family dinners that had decorated my prior Christmases. Stephanie grabbed my hand and started dancing with me. Her face was pure joy as she giggled.

The doorbell rang. Stephanie sprinted to the door. Raphael immediately saw it as a possible hint and followed her. Stephanie popped her head out and quickly shut the door. Raphael picked her up and placed her on the other side of him as he opened the door looking out. Stephanie laughed hysterically as she grabbed her purse. Raphael shook his head at her, giving her the finger. Stephanie paid the delivery man and brought in the bags of food.

"Tacos!" Stephanie announced. Everyone cheered and

scrambled over for the food.

"You're such a bitch," Raphael flicked her forehead.

"You're too easy," Stephanie teased, shaking her head. Raphael grabbed her antlers and put them on his head. Stephanie reached up to grab them and was promptly tickled by Raphael.

"Aren't you orphans meant to be sad during Christmas?" Jace called.

"Fuck off, Jace," Raphael gave him the finger. Stephanie promptly stole the antlers back and ran behind me. "You think Levi can protect you?" Raphael laughed, shaking his head. He walked over. "Move, Levi."

"No, go get a taco," I instructed. Raphael shook his head and walked to the side. I stepped around Stephanie so I was facing him.

"Fight, fight, fight," Jace chanted from the kitchen.

"No one is fighting," Stephanie stated.

"Raph, where did you put the Christmas cookies?" Eli asked.

"In the fridge," Raphael didn't remove me from his gaze.

"Come on guys, let's eat," I urged. Raphael sighed and walked to the kitchen.

"My savior." Stephanie kissed me on the cheek.

"I will give you a grand to tell me what Stephanie got me," Raphael leaned on the counter staring at Eli.

"I learned from last time, I don't tell anyone anymore." Stephanie grabbed herself a taco. Raphael stared at Eli inquisitively.

"Give me five grand and I'll give you my best guess." Eli negotiated.

"Five grand for a guess? Fuck no." Raphael scoffed. I grabbed my taco and ate it, eyeing up the massive Christmas tree we were expected to decorate.

"Can we decorate the tree please?" Stephanie pleaded. Everyone nodded and walked over to the tree, taking out the varying generic store-bought decorations and placing them on the tree, the Christmas carols still blaring in the background.

"I made them before I left." Stephanie handed me a shortbread cookie. I took a bite. It melted in my mouth, the smooth butter flavor covering my tongue.

"These are amazing," I commented. Stephanie beamed.

"I'm so happy I get to spend Christmas with you." Stephanie wrapped her arms around me. I kissed the top of her head as Raphael turned the Christmas tree lights on. The tree looked beautiful. It was vividly dressed in only gold and silver, with white lights shining through.

"Damn we're good at this," Raphael grinned at the tree.

"*Christmas Carol?*" Stephanie suggested.

"I'll get the tequila," Raphael smiled at Stephanie.

"Uh, can I get an explanation?" I murmured as Stephanie dragged me to the couch.

"You take a shot whenever anyone says 'Bah Humbug' or 'Merry Christmas,'" Stephanie explained. "And you chug the rest of your drink at the end."

"Okay," Raphael said, walking in with a large bottle of tequila and glasses. He poured each of us a cup to the brim with tequila. "Stephanie, normal-sized sips this time."

"I will chug this entire glass right now if I damn well please," Stephanie retorted.

"I mean, if you want to make it easier to find out what my gift is. Actually please do, you having a hangover when I have control would be brilliant," Raphael shrugged.

"Fine," Stephanie muttered in defeat. James played the movie. Everyone cheered whenever one of the phrases was said.

At the end, we all chugged what we had left in our glasses.

"After I die, I'll force this scenario to happen to Stephanie every year," Raphael laughed.

"That would be very fun," Eli commented, smiling at Stephanie. "We should all haunt her."

"Christmas at Stephanie's every year postmortem!" Jace announced.

"Why do you think you're all going to die before me?" Stephanie demanded.

"The man sitting beside you, Steph," Jace laughed.

"No, Levi and I are going to die with all of you," Stephanie hissed.

"Uh, do I get a say in how we're going to die?" I asked.

"Levi is going to die with us, you're going to be the only one living," Jace stated.

"Why won't I be there?" Stephanie scowled, insulted that they weren't looping her into our death plan.

"You're going to get pregnant," Jace snickered. Stephanie threw a pillow at him.

"You are all planning to leave me when I'm pregnant?" Stephanie growled. "You guys are assholes."

"Fine, Eli can stay back," Raphael relinquished.

"Okay." Stephanie smiled and leaned back into my arms.

"What, you're not going to fight for me to be able to stay back?" I muttered.

"Not happening Levi, you're with us." Raphael stood up. "Eggnog?" he offered. Stephanie nodded, and everyone proceeded to get up. They walked over and sat on the kitchen chairs at the Christmas tree. Raphael went to pour the eggnog.

"I wish you all the luck with raising the child with Eli." I kissed her on the cheek.

"I'll teach the child everything I know," Eli sighed, sitting back in the wooden chair.

"To fucking hell you will," Stephanie retorted. Eli acted out shooting a gun before winking playfully at her. Raphael handed out the eggnog.

"What are our Christmas wishes this year?" Raphael enquired, finally sitting down with us.

"Our next job to go successfully and without anyone getting hurt." Jace raised his glass.

"Hell ya," James shouted. Everyone raised their glass to Jace's wish. I followed suit. "To make more money this year than the last," James raised his glass. Jace cheered loudly as everyone raised their glasses.

"For our enemies to die and our friends to succeed," Eli smiled, raising his glass. Everyone cheered as we raised our glasses. Stephanie nodded to me.

"To shoot the target in the center," I raised my glass. Everyone chuckled as they raised their glass.

"For our family to have all the happiness and love possible." Stephanie raised her glass.

"Soppy," Jace coughed. Stephanie giggled and gave him the finger. We all raised our glasses. I kissed Stephanie on the cheek.

"For our family to pursue any job that makes us fucking happy," Raphael laughed, raising his glass. Everyone cheered and met his glass.

"I'm going to order us some pizza," James announced standing up.

"On Christmas Eve? James, some would call that almost a commitment," Stephanie mused.

"I'm horny," James dismissed. "He's a good fuck, that's all." James walked to the other room. I looked at Stephanie confused.

"The pizza man," Stephanie explained.

"It's just sex," James yelled from the kitchen.

"Whatever you say," Stephanie shouted back. "They're in love," Stephanie whispered to me.

"I've literally only ever heard them say two words to each other," Jace commented.

"I'm with Jace on this one Stephanie, they don't speak, it's just sex," Raphael stated.

"They're up there for hours, they aren't just fucking," Stephanie took a sip of her eggnog.

"I think Levi has ruined sex for you Stephanie, I seem to remember you having sex for hours too," Raphael prodded.

"And that man and I were together, it wasn't just sex," Stephanie replied.

"Don't you get sore?" I turned the glass uncomfortably in my fingers.

"You feel it the next day. So worth it though." Raphael grinned. "Complete satisfaction."

"I don't feel it the next day, ready for another go," Jace remarked.

"Ready for another go does not mean you're not sore," Raphael chuckled. "The second I get *that* look, I could be on the brink of death and still fuck her until she's satisfied."

"James, are you sore the next day after pizza man?" Jace called. "Raphael's saying he is."

"Of course, Raphael would be, are you forgetting the hickeys and bruises? He's aggressive as fuck." James walked back in the living room and sat down on the chair.

"Ah right, the daddy issues," Jace sighed.

"Fuck off," Raphael rolled his eyes.

"Parent issues," Stephanie corrected Jace smugly.

"You can't talk, Stephanie, you're terrible," James shook his head disapprovingly.

"I don't know what you're talking about, I'm an angel," Stephanie replied, taking a sip of eggnog.

"I guess the devil was technically an angel, so yes," I laughed. Stephanie opened her mouth in shock.

"It's almost Christmas, Stephanie. Any guesses on your present?" Raphael leaned back, a knowing grin on his face.

"Can I get a hint?" Stephanie asked.

"Why the hell would I give you a hint?" Raphael laughed.

"Because I'm your favorite." Stephanie widened her blue eyes, a firm pout on her lips.

Raphael sighed, shaking his head at her. "Eli knows what it is," Raphael kissed his teeth. Stephanie's eyes shifted to Eli.

"No, I'm not getting involved in this," Eli stated quickly.

"Come on Eli, Raphael shot you," I exclaimed.

"Playing dirty!" Raphael looked at Stephanie in surprise.

"I'm not saying anything," Eli grumbled.

"What will you give me to get the information out of him?" James asked Stephanie as he cracked his knuckles.

"This is not an aggressive game," Stephanie shook her head. "No one is forcing any information out of anyone."

"Fine," James muttered, leaning back in the chair.

Stephanie went under the tree looking for her gift from Raphael. We all watched as the wheels in her brain tried to work out what he got her. Stephanie suddenly sprinted, her bare feet sounding on the wooden floor. Raphael sprinted after her, stopping her from entering his room, throwing her effortlessly over his shoulder and bringing her back to the living room.

The doorbell rang suddenly. Everyone turned and looked at the door. James cracked his neck and stood up. He opened the door and leaned against the frame.

"How is your day?" James asked.

"It's going," the pizza man replied.

"Want me to make it better?" James smirked. The pizza man said nothing but entered the house. James dropped the pizza on the floor and shut the door.

"Let me pay you before," Stephanie said, running to grab her purse. She walked back and handed him some money. "You're welcome to join us," Stephanie offered, trying desperately to prove there was something more between them. The pizza man looked back at James. James looked at him intently then gently bit his lip.

"Maybe after," the pizza man replied, beginning to run up the stairs. James slapped him on the ass and followed him slowly, taking off his shirt and undoing his belt.

"What a fucking legend," Jace muttered. Loud moaning began to echo through the living room.

"Ah, the Christmas ghosts," Stephanie laughed. We sat there uncomfortably making small talk as the noises persisted.

"Okay, twenty minutes to midnight," Raphael announced. Stephanie stood up and walked upstairs. She gently knocked and went in. The moaning stopped.

"So, what did you get Stephanie?" I asked and turned to Raphael.

"I'm not stupid," Raphael laughed and shook his head.

"Worth a try," I smiled and leaned back in the wooden chair. "What happens at midnight?"

"We cheer in Christmas," Jace explained. I nodded. Raphael grabbed the eggnog and topped up everyone's glass. Stephanie finally emerged, she closed the door behind her and took a few seconds standing there, taking a few deep breaths. Raphael stood up. Stephanie smiled and ran down the stairs.

"I have gossip," Stephanie announced. Raphael sat back down, eyeing her carefully.

"What took you so long, did you join in?" Jace joked.

"No, shut up, I have gossip," Stephanie whispered. Everyone leaned in. The moaning upstairs restarted. "They were fucking slowly."

"They're in love," Raphael exclaimed. Stephanie nodded and took a little bow.

"So Jace, are you going to accept defeat now?" Stephanie stared at Jace challengingly.

"You can have slow sex without being emotionally involved with someone, so no, I am sticking to my guns," Jace stated. Stephanie sighed. The noises increased in volume then stopped. James emerged from the bedroom, shirtless and doing up his pants. He bowed. Jace cheered. James pulled his shirt on as he sat down in his chair. He reorganized his hair and winked at Stephanie. The pizza man emerged and walked down the stairs looking at our gathering.

"Come sit on my lap," James instructed. The pizza man walked over, obediently sitting on James's knee. James wrapped an arm around him. "This is Jace, my best friend, Raphael, our fearless leader, the exquisite beauty you just met is Stephanie," James gestured to each of them. Stephanie shifted uncomfortably. Raphael was now looking at Stephanie more intently, trying to read what was going on. "That's Levi," James gestured to me.

"Stephanie's boyfriend," I put in. The pizza man smirked. Raphael whispered something in Stephanie's ear.

"Oh ya, just a little too much eggnog," Stephanie replied. Raphael looked toward me, gesturing discreetly toward

Stephanie. I nodded.

"Come here, you're too far," I smiled at Stephanie. Stephanie moved her chair closer to mine. I wrapped my arm around her and kissed the top of her head. James smirked.

"See, exactly how I told you," James kissed the pizza man.

"James?" Jace murmured.

"Everyone relax, Stephanie and I are having fun, aren't we Stephanie?" James turned his head toward her.

"Yes," Stephanie replied smiling. "Five minutes to midnight, Raph, what's your guess?"

"You're pleased with it," Raphael leaned back analyzing Stephanie. "Something sentimental." Raphael paused reading Stephanie's expression. He nodded to himself knowing he was on the right track. "Ireland."

"Nope," Stephanie giggled. "Lost your touch, Raph."

"Your turn, what's your guess?" Raphael smiled at her, knowing there was no way she was going to guess it.

"Your smugness tells me it's expensive and not sentimental." Stephanie laughed. Raphael shrugged. "Hmm." Stephanie leaned back, evaluating Raphael's smile. "Uh, I really don't know, fuck. Um, a vacation?" Stephanie guessed.

"Nope, not even close," Raphael grinned.

"Fuck," Stephanie groaned.

"Merry Christmas!" Eli yelled, raising his glass. Everyone cheered and raised their glasses to Christmas Day. We all chugged down our drinks and went to bed. The door shut behind the pizza man as he left. Stephanie and I went to her room.

"Did James say something to you?" I asked, finally able to clarify the situation without an audience.

"No, literally nothing, just tired," Stephanie shrugged. "Fair warning, I'm going to leave really early to get

Raphael's present. I should be back before you wake up. Don't tell anyone I left, it may give it away," Stephanie instructed.

"What the fuck did you get him?" I demanded.

"You'll have to find out when everyone else does," Stephanie leaned into me, kissing me tenderly on the lips. We both got into bed and fell asleep.

Chapter 9

"You were comfortable with Stephanie wearing lingerie in front of everyone?" the green-eyed lady asked.

"I didn't think I could say no." I shrugged. "I knew Jace, and James would make comments, but they were harmless, not like Stephanie was James's type."

"You didn't feel uncomfortable with her wearing it in front of Jace, Raphael or Eli? From what you told us, they're all straight males." The brown-haired lady leaned in, fiddling with her pen.

"No, at the time they all seemed harmless," I replied.

***

I woke up to Stephanie in full makeup, heels and her Mrs. Claus costume. She was putting on Christmas earrings looking in her full-length mirror.

"Well, this is my favorite Christmas morning ever." I sat up. Stephanie giggled and walked over to me. "Did you already get Raphael's present?" I asked. Stephanie nodded. I rolled out of bed and pulled on my clothing.

"Wait." Stephanie went to the drawer and got a shirt and brought it back to me. It was a red shirt with a Santa uniform printed on it. I laughed and kissed her on the cheek. I changed my shirt and we left the room. Stephanie passed me her phone for safekeeping. The minute Stephanie entered the kitchen, the room erupted in cheers and the guys banging on the counter. Stephanie rolled her eyes. Raphael passed us both coffees.

"Merry Christmas," Raphael beamed. Stephanie smiled and walked to the tree. Everyone hurried to the wooden chairs in anticipation of presents. Stephanie entered the circle and knelt down beside the tree, grabbing her present for Raphael. She handed him the small box, a wide grin firmly on her face. Raphael took it from her hands with a smile and unwrapped it. Raphael's smile turned to a look of confusion as he pulled out a blindfold.

"Kinky," Jace grinned.

Stephanie took the blindfold from his hands motioning for him to stand up. Raphael obeyed. Stephanie repositioned her brother's chair to face the door. Raphael sat down. Stephanie went behind him and gently did his blindfold up. She ran to me and mouthed the word "phone." I passed her it, she sent a message and went back to Raphael.

"Are you going to kill me?" Raphael chuckled. Stephanie leaned on his shoulders gently.

"That would be a Christmas present for everyone else, not you," Stephanie giggled. Jace's eyes were fully on Stephanie's ass; the short dress barely covered her. He leaned back, smirking. Eli hit him hard on the arm, his eyes viciously tearing into him. Jace frowned at Eli, opening his mouth to complain. The squabble was interrupted as both their attentions shifted to the door being opened. I turned around. A large man walked in. Stephanie smiled widely and undid Raphael's blindfold.

"No fucking way," Raphael's eyes widened as he quickly stood up and hugged the man. "Holy shit man, how long has it been?"

"Too long," the man replied. I looked around the room to

figure out what was going on.

"This is Barry," Raphael called to the group, his eyes not shifting from the man. Barry motioned for Stephanie to come closer to him. He took her hand and spun her around, Stephanie tittered.

"My childhood crush standing in front of me in lingerie," Barry licked his teeth, his eyes transfixed with Stephanie. I stood up and walked over. "Ah, a man walking protectively over, you must be the boyfriend. Levi?" Barry extended his hand. I shook it. "You are one lucky man," Barry murmured.

"I know," I replied.

"Shall I introduce you to the group?" Stephanie offered. Raphael walked ahead to get Barry a chair. Barry nodded and walked over with Stephanie. "So that's Eli, Jace and James," Stephanie pointed at each of them.

"You know, if I brought any one of you in I would get an award," Barry teased, sitting down in his chair. The guys all stiffened.

"You're so funny," Stephanie said sarcastically.

"I like to think so," Barry smiled up at Stephanie. Stephanie and Raphael sat on either side of the man. My brain muddled the statement over.

"You're a cop?" I wondered, sitting down on the other side of Stephanie.

"Not a very good one with the company I keep," Barry chuckled, gesturing to Stephanie and Raphael.

"How in the fuck did you pull this off without me knowing?" Raphael demanded, staring at Stephanie completely impressed.

"We've been planning this for months, she picked me up and drove me out because I crashed my car unexpectedly. Stephanie was determined to make this work." Barry put his hand gently on

Stephanie's shoulder.

"Presents," Jace said to Stephanie. Stephanie rolled her eyes and returned under the tree. She grabbed my present to the guys and placed it in front of them.

"For all of you from Levi," Stephanie smiled. Jace bent forward and unwrapped it.

"Aw sick, thanks Levi," Jace beamed. The guys all nodded in agreement. Eli stood up and took Stephanie's seat.

"Any fun stories about Stephanie's childhood?" Eli asked Barry.

"I met her when she was sixteen, not really her childhood." Barry shrugged.

"This is from Jace and James," Stephanie passed Raphael a box. Raphael opened it and quickly shut it, shaking his head at them.

"What was it?" Barry asked.

"A male pleasure device," Jace cackled. "You need it." Jace winked at Raphael. Every gift Jace and James gave was sex-related, every gift Eli gave was weapon-related, except Stephanie who received a stuffed sheep, seemingly no one understood the gift.

"This one is from Levi," Stephanie smiled and opened the book. Her eyes lit up with excitement. "No fucking way."

"First edition," I grinned. Stephanie sat on my lap and kissed me. She placed the book beside my chair and went under the tree again.

"This is for Eli, from me," Stephanie passed him a massive box. Eli opened it eagerly.

"Holy fuck, no fucking way," Eli muttered, lifting the barrel of a rifle out of the box. Stephanie did a little curtsey. Barry stiffened uncomfortably.

"Stephanie, you need a break," Raphael stood up and gestured for her to take his seat.

"Boo! You're not the one wearing lingerie!" Jace heckled. Raphael took off his shirt and tossed it at Jace. Jace and James cheered. Raphael reached under the tree and brought back a small box that he gave to Stephanie. He positioned himself behind her and leaned over her shoulders as she opened it.

"Raph, this is beautiful," Stephanie breathed.

"One of a kind, just like you," Raphael moved her hair gently over her right shoulder.

"It's a little mouse," Stephanie giggled, shaking her head. Barry broke into boisterous laughter.

"A mouse?" I asked.

"He made everyone in foster care call her Mighty Mouse," Barry explained.

"Raph was my childhood bully," Stephanie prodded.

"It was the perfect nickname. Stephanie was the only one who stood up to me and called me out. Out of all these guys, she's the only one who dared. She's a Mighty Mouse." Raphael gently put the necklace on her. He knelt beside her, looking into her eyes. "If anything happens to me, sell this, it should fetch enough to start out again."

"If something happens to you, I swear to God I will resurrect you and kill you myself," Stephanie retorted.

"Mighty Mouse," Raphael mocked. He stood back up and went to the tree, grabbing a small box and bringing it over to me. "From the guys and me." Raphael handed me the box. I opened it. A document and key lay in the box. "I imagine if something happens, you'll go with Stephanie, but in case she's dead or arrested—"

"It's Christmas, stop talking about death," Stephanie

interrupted.

"Fine, if something happens, we all own our own apartments as 'safe houses.' You're family now, this is yours," Raphael explained.

"You bought me an apartment?" I clarified, suddenly feeling self-conscious about the poker set I gave them.

"Yes, I hope you don't mind. Eli signed the legal forms for you," Raphael replied.

"Jesus fuck, this is so generous," I choked out, complete surprise clutching my throat.

"You're family," Raphael repeated, patting me on the shoulder. I managed a brisk nod.

"Fuck, you should have given him mine first!" Stephanie complained. She stood up and knelt under the tree grabbing the last box there. She carried it over to me and sat on my lap handing me the box. I opened it. "It's not an apartment, but it's a very quiet, and intimate treehouse. Thought it would be nice for us to get away just the two of us. I didn't book any dates. I know you'll have to get your parents' approval for the date."

"Just us two? Alone? For a couple of days?" I probed. Stephanie giggled and nodded. "Fuck Stephanie, this is amazing." I kissed her, my hand on her bare leg, trailing my fingers along her soft skin.

"Let's go for a drink, Raphael," Barry said. I heard movement and the door shut as they left.

"Thank you," I whispered to her.

"Thank you, I love Charles Dickens," Stephanie replied. "My first display item." Stephanie winked at me. My heart swelled. I pressed my lips against hers gently.

"Do you think they would mind if I crashed their talk for a bit? I want to learn more gossip about you," I joked.

"Don't judge me too much." Stephanie smirked and stood up. I laughed and went out the front door after them. I slowly made my way around the building.

"Fuck, why wouldn't she have told me?" Raphael's voice rang from behind the corner. I stopped walking and listened.

"Probably because she's terrified," Barry replied.

"Fuck man, I'm so fucking done with this shit," Raphael muttered.

"So is she, I don't understand what the issue is, leave," Barry stated.

"This is everything we've built up—" Raphael started.

"That won't fucking matter when your dead or arrested," Barry retorted. "You guys are ghosts now, that won't last forever. If you're worried you'll get bored, I can get you a job on my team?" Barry suggested. I smiled to myself thinking of Raphael as a police officer.

"I'm not worried I'll get bored, this is my family, man.," Raphael said gently. "If we stop working, they'll move on."

"That's not family then," Barry replied quickly. "They're your coworkers." Barry's voice came off as angry. "What you, Stephanie and I have, that's family. These men you have hanging around? They wouldn't hesitate to turn you in or kill you."

"No—" Raphael began.

"You don't think they're just waiting for a chance? You don't think they imagine what they'd do to Stephanie if you weren't protecting her? You're being a fucking idiot," Barry hissed.

"Don't go there," Raphael growled. There was a long breath of silence.

"You two are torturing yourselves for people who wouldn't do the same for you," Barry murmured. "Get out while you're ghosts, you have a chance at being happy, don't ruin it for an idealized version of reality."

"I know you're right," Raphael sighed. "Is this why Stephanie brought you here?" Raphael laughed.

"No man, I'm just tired of hearing Stephanie cry and you being miserable over things that can be changed. You're my family. My only family. I don't want to lose you to something you don't even enjoy." Barry stated. I heard movement and pats on the back. "How are you—"

"I figured you guys would be here," Stephanie's voice rang out. "Is Levi not with you?"

"No," Raphael replied.

"Oh, he said he was going to get some gossip on me." Stephanie stated. I heard clinking.

"Probably decided he didn't want to hear about your ghosts," Barry teased.

"What are you guys talking about?" Stephanie queried.

"Retirement," Raphael answered.

"My favorite subject," Stephanie giggled.

"I'm going to find the boyfriend, I want to know his ghosts," Barry announced.

"Be gentle, he's normal," Stephanie advised. I heard footprints walking toward me. Fuck. Shit. What do I do? I froze. Barry rounded the corner. He stopped when he saw me and took a long sip from the beer in his hand.

"Let's go inside," Barry smiled at me.

I turned and followed him into the cottage. We sat in the kitchen together. "I'm going to pretend I didn't see you there and you're going to pretend you didn't hear anything," Barry instructed. I nodded.

"How did you become a police officer and Raphael and

Stephanie become criminals?" I picked at my thumb.

Barry laughed. "I'm too boring for this type of life." Barry shrugged. "They wanted the thrill, the power, the money. What about you?"

"Well, this life they have is anything but boring," I chuckled. "I don't know yet, I guess whatever Stephanie chooses."

"Smart man, she's not one to be trifled with." Barry asserted. "Do you want a family?"

"What, like kids?" I replied, surprised by that question. Barry nodded. "I mean ya, I've always seen myself as a dad."

"Then there's your answer." Barry leaned back in his chair. "Stephanie would never want to risk her child going into foster care. If you decide on kids, you choose the boring life," Barry declared.

"Fair enough," I shifted. "Must be weird to hang out here, with all these criminals." I gestured to the house.

"Ya man, there are some pretty fucked-up people here," Barry muttered, taking a sip of his beer.

"Can I ask you a question?" I looked down at my hands, fidgeting as I knew I was about to ask about the topic he didn't want to acknowledge.

"Ya, can't promise I'll answer."

"If Stephanie wants to leave this, why wait for Raphael?" I pondered. Barry laughed.

"You have parents don't you?" Barry commented, smiling at me. I nodded. "Try for a second to imagine having no one consistent in your life, then someone promises you that they will always be in your life and, better than that, they prove it to you. Every fight, every mistake, they were there. Raphael and Stephanie can be terrible to each other, but they will always be there when the other person calls. Stephanie won't leave this profession without Raphael, as Raphael wouldn't leave the profession without Stephanie."

"Okay," I murmured.

"Would only mean good things for you, man, do a few jobs, get paid, then you and Stephanie can have a normal life," Barry stated.

"Would she get bored?" I faltered, my nerves about my future with her blatantly on my sleeve.

"A normal life is all she wants," Barry asserted. "This life is exhausting when your heart is in it, I can't imagine doing it while wanting to get out."

"What made them even consider this life?" I muttered. Barry took a deep breath and sat back on the chair.

"Raphael was meant to come with me to become a police officer, we had it all plotted out. He did something that was completely justified, but very illegal, and he felt he couldn't become a police officer after that. So, he went a different route while I pursued the one we were already on. Stephanie was always closer to Raphael so it wasn't a surprise that she went with him." Barry shrugged.

"What did he do?" I leaned in.

"You're very curious."

"Well, I'm new to all this."

"Want some advice?" Barry rubbed his face. "Really think if you want the answer before you ask a question. Everyone that lives here has done some terrible things, some more than others. But they'll tell you what they've done, some proudly, some ashamed. Until you get used to all this, just be careful."

"I've heard some of their stories."

"Can almost guarantee they're the toned-down ones," Barry shook his head. "How did an innocent fucker like you get involved in all this?"

"Stephanie," I replied.

"You love her?" Barry kissed his teeth.

"I love her."

"No better reason," Barry smiled and patted me gently on the shoulder. "Have the guys backed off at all?"

"No, I doubt they will."

"You know Stephanie's first year with James and Jace were actually worse than it currently is. Raphael was constantly fighting with them, Stephanie was constantly fighting with them. Some boundaries were put up. Eventually, Stephanie just got tired of fighting and so Raphael stopped. So the comments just never went away. Obviously, they're still perverts because she's wearing lingerie while they gawk." Barry rolled his eyes.

"There you are, Levi," Stephanie sat on my lap wrapping her arms around me. "I was looking for you."

"Levi got lost looking for me," Barry winked at me.

"Sounds about right," Stephanie joked. James and Jace walked into the room. "I think I'm going to get changed." Stephanie smiled and kissed me on the cheek. I nodded. James zeroed in on Stephanie and quickly walked over. Stephanie stood up and went to leave for her room.

"Stephanie, can we please fucking talk?" James huffed.

"It's Christmas." Stephanie continued to walk. James grabbed her arm aggressively. Stephanie didn't flinch. She looked at him holding his gaze for a second then slowly looked down at her arm. James let go like she had burned him. Stephanie continued to walk off. James looked back at Jace sheepishly.

"I'll talk to her." Jace shrugged and began walking to Stephanie's room.

"Uh no." I stood up, stepping in his way. "She's changing."

"Fuck off, Levi." Jace puffed out his chest and moved closer to me. I stood my ground. I wasn't going to budge. I wasn't going to allow him to intimidate her.

"I would fucking listen to him," Raphael laughed. "Did I miss something?"

"No, we were just joking around," Jace grinned, patting my arm.

"Ah right, seems to be a lot of having fun around here," Raphael smiled at James. "I think you and I should have a little talk tonight."

"It was a fucking joke," James retorted.

"Let me put it this way, we have a little talk tonight or I'll tell Eli the joke. I bet he would find it very funny." Raphael's smile was unwavering. James stiffened. "I'm not hearing a yes. Eli!" Raphael called. Eli's footprints trotted down the stairs. James nodded.

"Yes?" Eli asked. "Is something wrong?" Eli blinked in confusion at the tension driven standoff.

"No, nothing's wrong, Stephanie wants to talk to you, she's in her room." Raphael stated.

"Okay," Eli replied slowly.

"Stephanie's changing," I commented.

"Not really his thing." Jace quipped. Eli walked to Stephanie's room. Raphael's vicious gaze went back to James. James left through the hangout room slamming the door behind him. Raphael nodded toward Barry and left for the kitchen. A few moments passed, Stephanie walked out in a red dress and sat on my lap, Eli beside her. I wrapped my arms around her and kissed her neck gently.

"Barry, you should stay here," Stephanie urged.

"God, I would hate that so much," Barry mused. "You and

Raph, I love you guys. I like Levi but, no offense to the others, you guys are fucking terrifying."

"I take that as a compliment," Jace boasted.

"I don't," Eli muttered.

"You are literally the devil," Jace scoffed.

"Fuck off," Eli's head rolled back in exaggerated exhaustion.

"You are not the devil, Eli," Stephanie turned, the gentle smile that felt like home protectively on Eli. Eli grinned and squeezed her shoulder gently. Stephanie took the whiskey from my hands and took a sip.

"That's mine, you thief," I joked. Stephanie chugged the rest of the whiskey. "Now that is just cruel." I laughed and tickled Stephanie. Stephanie shrieked as she tried to push me away. A conversation between everyone else began. My attention was on Stephanie. I collapsed my lips around hers, my tongue darted into her mouth, the taste of smooth whiskey sparked on my taste buds. I savored the taste, my senses invigorated by her as my fingers glided up her leg.

"Want me to make it up to you?" Stephanie whispered into my ear.

"You're gonna have to work for it, it was good whiskey," I quipped.

"I know how to work." Stephanie's hand gently glided down my body, gently squeezing between my legs. I gasped, my body immediately firing in complete and unignorable lust. Stephanie stood up and ran toward her room. I ran after her, catching up to her in the hallway, forcing her against the wall, my lips going to her neck. Stephanie's hands rushed to my belt and undid it. She unbuttoned and unzipped my pants, and got on her knees. My hand pressed against the wall for stability as she took me into her mouth. I moaned as her tongue ran along me, her lips stroking me. My left hand went lower and I gently interlocked my fingers with her hair.

"I need to fuck you," I growled in a deep and frantic order. Stephanie removed me from her mouth and licked the tip gently. Pleasure shot down my spine. "Fuck," I moaned. Stephanie stood up and pulled me into her.

"You need to fuck me?" Stephanie bit my ear.

"Yes," I replied. I was throbbing, desperate to get into her.

"Wait here," Stephanie breathed. I obeyed and stood there completely exposed as she ran into her room. She returned with a condom. "Then fuck me." Stephanie smiled devilishly as she removed her thong. I looked both ways in the hallway. We were feet from her bedroom, but that felt like a distance I couldn't muster. I put the condom on, lifted her up gently and allowed gravity to push her down onto my erection.

Stephanie gasped as I entered her. I began to pummel her, my animalistic desperation overtaking me as I ruthlessly shoved myself into her. One arm holding her up, the other hand intertwined with hers. Stephanie moaned into my ear. It drove me insane, my body needing her to take every inch. Her nails dug into my back and my hand.

"Fuck," Stephanie's head tilted back as I pounded her. With each pound I lost more resolve, my body slowly giving in to her. I wanted to give her pleasure. I needed her to feel ecstasy. I bit her neck as her breath quickened. I felt pleasure surge through me. I continued steady, her eyes opened and she looked at me, her eyes glazed over. I couldn't control myself any longer. I tried desperately to hold back, but I was hers. I grunted as I climaxed.

"Uh, where's Stephanie?" I asked, walking into the living room as I reorganized myself. I had already checked her room. My eyes glided over the living room, the guys all looked at me.

"I'm here," Stephanie called from the kitchen. "I was replenishing the whiskey I stole," Stephanie smiled, bringing me a glass of whiskey.

"Look at that, wife material!" Jace cheered.

"Ya, where's my ring?" Stephanie joked.

"Do you know how expensive engagement rings are?" I laughed, kissing her on the cheek.

"A few jobs with us, he'll be able to buy as many diamond rings as you want, Stephanie," Jace mused.

"And the biggest wedding this world has ever seen," I grabbed her hand, twirling her before capturing her in my arms.

"We should start cooking," Raphael stood up.

"Oh, I'm helping, we can do it like the good old days," Barry stated. Stephanie, Barry and Raphael went to the kitchen. I followed. Raphael grabbed a bottle of wine from the fridge. He poured four glasses. Stephanie opened the fridge and grabbed a large turkey, placing it on the counter.

"Raph, this turkey is the size of a toddler," Stephanie whined. "It's going to take forever to cook."

"It'll be fine," Raphael replied. "We'll get it in, then start on dessert, then side dishes," Raphael instructed.

"Aye, Captain." Barry took a sip of his wine and passed me a glass. Stephanie unwrapped the turkey while Raphael tossed a lemon to Barry.

"Are you not going to wear an apron?" Raphael asked Stephanie.

"I'm too far gone," Stephanie giggled.

"Am I supposed to just hold this lemon?" Barry voiced confused. Raphael turned his attention back to him and passed him a few more lemons, a cutting board and a knife. Barry got to work cutting the lemons.

"You want to melt the butter?" Raphael asked me. I nodded and grabbed a pot and a stick of butter. I cut it in half and popped it into the pot. Stephanie reached her hand inside the turkey as Raphael grabbed a garbage bag. Raphael gagged as she pulled out the innards and chucked them out.

"You have no right being grossed out by this," Stephanie prodded. Barry offered the cut lemons to Stephanie who popped them into the cavity of the turkey. Raphael passed her some rosemary, which she placed inside as well. Stephanie went and washed her hands and arms, she reached into a drawer and pulled out an apron, putting it on over her dress.

"What are we making for dessert?" Barry rocked on his heels like an excited schoolboy.

"What else would we have for dessert?" Stephanie smirked.

"Why would you keep that tradition?" Barry sighed.

"Stephanie loves it," Raphael replied. "It's not that bad."

"I think the entire world but you loves sticky toffee pudding." Stephanie rolled her eyes.

"Do you like it, Levi?" Barry asked.

"I've never had it," I replied.

"One of our old foster parents was British, it was always sticky toffee pudding at Christmas." Barry gagged jokingly.

"Barry used to try to rally the kids into a revolt." Raphael shook his head disapprovingly.

"You were such an asshole. They were so sweet," Stephanie frowned.

"What did they say to you when Raphael picked you up?" Barry raised an eyebrow.

"That I was going to hell," Stephanie sighed. "Raphael was

terrible, I don't blame them for saying it."

"Hey, stop projecting, I was an ideal foster child." Raphael took the butter from the stove and started brushing the turkey.

"Both of you destroyed their house consistently." Stephanie commented.

"Okay, now my memory is coming back, I was not the ideal foster child." Raphael shrugged and set the temperature on the oven. "But Barry was worse. I only got them to leave, Barry was the one to host the parties."

"No way was I worse," Barry laughed. "Look what he's become."

"We're not talking about now, you were so much worse! You know how many times they sat me down and told me they knew I was a good girl and that you were a bad influence on me?" Stephanie giggled, gesturing to Barry.

"They literally had the same conversations with me," Raphael leered.

"Okay no, Levi, listen to this story. There was another kid with us too, Freddy. Raphael would literally terrorize him. Freddy had this massive paper due, it was worth almost all of his mark. Raphael, the night before it was due, snuck in his room and deleted it off his computer." Barry argued, twirling the wine in his glass.

"After all these years, I'm finally learning the truth!" Stephanie hit the counter enthusiastically, her eyes locked on Raphael. "Freddy was sweet!"

"Freddy was a fucking nerd," Raphael scoffed.

"Did he get an extension?" I demanded.

"No one believed him." Barry chuckled. The oven sang and Raphael put the turkey inside.

"That's pretty bad, Raphael," I commented.

"Why would you do that to Freddy?" Stephanie questioned.

"He overheard him bragging to his friends that he slept with you," Barry gave an exasperated sigh. .

"I never slept with him," Stephanie gave both of them confused glances.

"I know, that's why I deleted his paper." Raphael shrugged.

"You had him fail a class because he lied about sleeping with me?" Stephanie hissed, biting her tongue before shaking her head disapprovingly.

"I was young and, to defend myself slightly, he went into a bizarre amount of detail," Raphael justified.

"Did you listen to his entire conversation?" Stephanie thumbed her glass.

"Yes, I was trying to figure out if he was telling the truth or not," Raphael replied.

"What gave it away that he was lying?" Stephanie took a sip of wine, looking at him quizzically.

"He, uh…" Raphael shifted uncomfortably. "He said you have a birthmark on your right hip."

"Seems like a weird detail to make up," Stephanie pondered pensively. "Wait, how did you know that was wrong?"

"I was hoping you wouldn't catch that part," Raphael's voice faltered. "Uh…" Raphael looked at Barry.

"It's been years, just tell her." Barry shrugged.

"Remember that guy you used to like way back when. Shit, what was his name?" Raphael tapped on his glass.

"Oh, uh, Steven," Barry stated.

"Oh, I remember Steven," Stephanie nodded.

"He, uh, he was selling your naughty pictures at school," Raphael explained.

"Ew, did you guys buy one?" Stephanie looked at them in

complete disgust.

"No, ew, of course not. No, we ruffed him up a bit, then I deleted the photos, but I saw them when I was deleting them," Raphael stretched slightly, not making eye contact with Stephanie.

"You know I always wondered why he wouldn't have sex with me," Stephanie giggled.

"Raphael made him cry," Barry grinned.

"Why the hell did you guys not tell me?" Stephanie demanded.

"We knew you liked him," Raphael remarked.

"Not the reason, nope, no reason to lie, Raphael," Barry shook his head.

"That was the reason!" Raphael whined.

"Nope," Barry pointed at him aggressively. "I remember this so clearly, man. You looked at me after and said, 'she can't know,' and when I asked you why, you said, and I quote, 'she'll kill us for not allowing her to handle it by herself.'"

"Well, you're right about that," Stephanie muttered. "I was going to lose my virginity to Steven."

"Well, I am certainly glad you didn't," Raphael smiled gently at Stephanie.

"What else are you two keeping from me?" Stephanie taunted. Jace and Eli walked overhearing the possible gossip.

"Barry never had a girlfriend during high school," Raphael declared. "He thought it would make you jealous and want to sleep with him."

"No, no, no, no, no." Barry stammered. "Well actually, kind of," Barry admitted.

"You thought me thinking you were sleeping with someone else would make me want you?" Stephanie scoffed. "Who gave you that advice?"

"I mean that's a pretty common tactic," I put in.

"Thank you, Levi," Barry praised.

"What, do you men have meetings on how to get girls to sleep with you?" Stephanie giggled.

"Ya, you men are disgusting," Raphael critiqued.

"Okay Levi, what tactics did you use on me?" Stephanie mused.

"I think you're forgetting you picked me up, you kissed me and told me you didn't want to be friends," I boasted.

"I don't think 'tactics' are used outside of stupid high school boys," Raphael stated.

"Okay man who's basically a virgin, picking up a woman is an art," Jace leaned on the counter. "We use as many tactics as we need to."

"You may need to," I chuckled. "Stephanie, do you want to go fuck?" I asked as I walked over to her wrapping my arms around her. Stephanie nodded.

"That doesn't count," Jace announced.

"Anything else you guys would like to admit to me?" Stephanie inquired. Barry and Raphael thought for a few seconds.

"I don't think there's anything—" Raphael began.

"Oh yes there is," Barry laughed.

"She can go her entire life without knowing this," Raphael said quickly. Stephanie grinned, completely intrigued.

"Remember when your laptop broke, and Raphael convinced you that I did it?" Barry pointed at Raphael.

"I yelled at Barry for days. You bought me a new one and I thought you were the greatest person ever." Stephanie shook her head disapprovingly.

"It was an accident, and it wasn't long after I first met you," Raphael groaned.

"This is how my best friend treats me," Barry snickered. "Immediately threw me under the bus."

"I was young!" Raphael said defensively.

"How did you even break it?" Stephanie asked.

"You left it on the counter, and I was trying to break into the alcohol cabinet. So, I was concentrating on picking the lock and the girl I was with, walked in and it scared me, so I stepped over and onto your laptop." Raphael looked at Stephanie sheepishly.

"My laptop broke because you wanted to get some action." Stephanie rolled her eyes.

"Pretty much, ya." Raphael shrugged. "I felt really bad."

"So bad you blamed it on Barry. Your true colors are showing, Raph," Stephanie giggled.

"Was she at least worth it?" Jace joked.

"No, told her to leave after. I was too busy trying to figure a way to get out of Stephanie being mad at me.," Raphael replied.

"I feel like I don't even know you anymore," Stephanie mused. Raphael lunged forward, ruffling up her hair.

"I bet you have a few things you've never told us," Raphael stared at Stephanie, challenging.

"Nope, I told you guys everything," Stephanie smugly took a sip of her wine.

"Oh really? Okay, funny, I don't remember ever having chlamydia," Raphael smirked.

"How did you know?" Stephanie's eyes widened.

"I asked around until someone finally told me that you were telling all the girls that I had chlamydia." Raphael rolled his eyes playfully.

"Why didn't you get mad at me?" Stephanie's face flushed

in embarrassment as she turned the wine glass nervously in her fingers.

"I figured you had your reasons," Raphael grinned.

"You were the one who spread the rumor that Raphael had chlamydia?" Barry fell into hysterics.

"He constantly had girls over, the noise was unbearable," Stephanie whined.

"You've said you only slept with two girls," I said, confused.

"I wasn't fucking them, I was known for something else, and they would return the favor," Raphael extended his tongue, licking dramatically.

"Ew, stop," Stephanie fake gagged.

"My whole setup was ruined because of Stephanie." Raphael shook his head at her.

"That was such a bitch thing to do, Stephanie," Jace chimed.

"Nah, it was good prep for the next bit," Raphael laughed.

"How is your right arm not bigger than the left?" Jace joked.

Raphael looked down at both of his arms. "I think it may be."

"Okay, we are changing this conversation topic," Stephanie voiced, uncomfortably.

"So, Levi, how long do we have you?" Jace asked.

"I am dropping him off tomorrow morning," Stephanie leaned into me. I kissed her on the head.

"And Barry?" Jace looked over.

"He's sleeping on the couch tonight, I'll take him home tomorrow," Raphael stated.

"No Raphael for a couple of days?" Jace grinned.

"Would you stop? Enlighten me on something I don't allow you to do," Raphael rolled his eyes.

"It still feels like a parent is leaving you with unlimited

freedom. Just accept the fact you are our daddy," Jace joked.

"Ew, what the actual fuck."

"Being a dad makes you that disgusted?" Eli prodded.

"I think being a dad to you guys is every person's worst nightmare."

"Not *dad*, daddy," Jace clarified. "He's a daddy to us," Jace winked at Raphael.

"Okay, please stop, this is disgusting." Raphael started taking out the ingredients for the pudding. Stephanie grabbed a mixing bowl, and they began to work on the pudding. We all continued to talk about nothing.

Finally, dinner rolled around. Everyone had been starving themselves all day for this meal. We all helped set the table, Stephanie brought out the turkey and Raphael cut it. It felt like a normal family.

"Everything is delicious guys, thank you," Jace complimented. Everyone scoffed down the food. The massive turkey was almost completely eaten within minutes. The plates and dishes were cleared and the sticky toffee pudding was brought out. Barry groaned.

"We won't force you to eat it," Stephanie laughed.

"Oh yes, we will, a small piece for old times' sake," Raphael joked. The sticky toffee pudding was distributed. I took a bite. It was delicious.

"What the fuck are you on about, Barry? This is amazing!" I grinned. Stephanie smiled and stuck out her tongue at Barry.

"The worst dessert to possibly exist," Barry muttered, shaking his head at me.

"You don't like this?" James asked. Barry shook his head. "You're wrong."

"See, Barry, only you," Stephanie giggled. We finished

eating and everyone worked together to clean up.

"Movie?" Jace offered. Everyone nodded in agreement.

"*Die Hard?*" Stephanie suggested.

"Well, duh," Raphael replied. We all went into the hangout room. James started the movie as Stephanie curled up to me.

Toward the end of the movie, she was gently stroking my thigh. I could feel myself getting harder. I stopped her hand and held it still. Stephanie looked up at me, confused. I let my eyeline drop, subtly gesturing to my penis. Stephanie smiled and stifled a giggle.

"Jace, I'm cold," Stephanie complained. Jace reached behind him and tossed her a blanket. She put it over herself and my lap. Stephanie's hand continued to gently stroke my thigh. My heart began to pound as her stroking became closer and closer to between my erection. I swallowed hard trying to focus on the screen.

"Let's go." I finally broke, unable to ignore her anymore. I got up and left for her bedroom, stripping down to my boxers. I grabbed a condom and sat on the bed. My heart pounding in my chest as I waited for her to enter. After what felt like an eternity, Stephanie walked in, closing the door behind her. She turned around, I stood up to undo her dress. She moved her hair over her right shoulder. I unzipped the dress slowly, kissing her neck tenderly. My arms went into the dress as I flicked it off her shoulders. The dress fell to the ground. Stephanie was braless, she pulled off her thong and stepped out of her dress. "Merry Christmas to me." I purred.

I ran my hands down her body, Stephanie leaned against me. I roughly turned her around and kissed her deeply. My right hand squeezed her ass and pulled her into me. Stephanie's hands glided through my hair as her tongue flicked into my mouth. She hopped up and wrapped her legs around me. I walked her over to the bed, placing her on the edge. I dropped to my knees in front of her, kissing her thighs hungrily. My teeth glided up until I was inches from her. Stephanie took a sharp breath in, the anticipation cutting into the air between us. I had never done this before.

My tongue reached out and licked her, Stephanie let out a whimper. I shoved my mouth against her, now frantic to taste her, to feel her wetness coat my tongue. Her fingers rushed to my hair, clutching so tightly it hurt. I suckled her clit, my tongue probing as her hips rhythmically rocked into me. My erection pulsated at the tone of her whimpers. Every muscle in my body wanted to ram into her. I felt my pre-cum drip onto my thighs, my desperation soaking through my boxers. Her chest pushed up as I harshened my vigor. I felt her body give into me as her moans crescendo.

"Fuck, fuck, fuck." Stephanie groaned, her body convulsing as I lapped up her juices.

Stephanie stood up and pushed me to sit down, pulling off my boxers and biting along the trail. My jaw dropped, the temptation of her driving my being. She straddled me, raising herself above my throbbing erection. My eyes trailed over her perfect body. My hands moved along her, taking her all in.

"You are so fucking sexy," I whispered. Stephanie giggled and lowered herself onto me. I gasped in pleasure. She moved herself up and down, one hand in my hair pulling gently, the other on my back. Stephanie quickened her pace and gently pushed me down. I fell back, my hands glided to her back. I could feel her muscles working as she fucked me. My moans increased in volume. My right hand ran over her body until it reached her breast. I began to toy with her nipples. Stephanie kissed my neck down to my chest, then bit down, hard. I gasped in shock; my hand tightened around her breast. I groaned in delight. Stephanie kissed me deeply, her hands yanking at my hair as she fucked me faster and harder.

"Fuck," I moaned. Stephanie bit down on my lip, the taste of blood filled my mouth. I grabbed her ass hard, gripping it as she moved up and down. She kissed my neck and let out a slight moan. My hands tightened their grip on her ass as my pulse quickened, my body craving every touch she gave me. She continued to kiss down until she reached my chest again. I took a sharp breath in anticipation. Stephanie bit down. Pleasure rushed through my body with the sudden pain.

"I'm gonna come," I grunted. Stephanie quickened her pace again. "Fuck!" I yelled as my body filled with pleasure as I finished. Stephanie flopped down beside me.

I lay beside her, staring at her in amazement. My heart pounding in my chest, my breath a pant after the excitement. There was no doubt, as I stared at her, I was completely in love.

"What?" Stephanie giggled. "Too much?"

"That was amazing." I placed my hand on her chest.

"It was," Stephanie smiled in agreement. "How would you feel if I went with Raphael to drop Barry off? It's a couple-day trip." Stephanie asked.

"Ya, I mean, my parents will want a couple of days with me anyway. They'll be more open to the vacation possibility if I spend time with them," I laughed.

"Okay, what are your typical New Year's plans?" Stephanie queried.

"My parents are hosting a little party; do you want to come? Lucas and Aidan would be there so it's not like a dinner or anything," I explained.

"I would love to, I want to be your kiss," Stephanie stroked along my nose.

"Damn, Aidan will be disappointed," I joked. Stephanie giggled. "Can I request something from you?"

"I will only kill someone if you give me a good reason."

"Well damn," I chuckled. "No, uh, as Raphael and Barry will have you for the next few days, can I request that I get some naughty photos each night you're away? To keep me on your mind."

"Took you long enough to ask," Stephanie sighed. "Of course, but for the record, you will always be on my mind." Stephanie bit her lip. "Especially when I'm alone." Her hand trailed down between my legs.

"Do you masturbate to me?" I smiled at this development.

"Yes." Stephanie began to stroke me. I grinned widely, unable to contain my pride. "What, does that surprise you?"

"Kind of." I shrugged.

"I fantasize about you all the time, you fucking me, me fucking you, what your tongue just did will definitely be something I think about during the next few days." Stephanie propped herself on her elbow, looking at me while she continued to glide her fingers along my length. My penis jumped back to action. "Do you masturbate to me?"

"Yes," I stated, my voice louder then I intended. "All the fucking time, our sex, your blowjobs, just you. Do you realize how amazing it is that you would even look at me?" I asked. Stephanie looked at me with a confused expression on her face. I opened my mouth to clarify. Stephanie dove down and took my growing erection in her mouth. Fuck.

My hand trailed to her head as she moved up and down. Her perfect strokes, her twirling tongue and the suction was something I don't think I'll ever get used to. She used her hand to hold me in the right position as she mouth-fucked me. It wasn't long until I finished inside her mouth. "Holy fuck, Stephanie," I breathed in complete bliss. Stephanie giggled and got into bed, I turned off the light and cuddled up to her, holding her naked body tight to me.

"I love fucking you," Stephanie playfully bit my nose.

"I love fucking you too," I murmured. Stephanie curled up beside me and we fell asleep.

I woke up to Stephanie getting out of bed. She grabbed some clothing from her closet and walked to her mirror to get dressed. She giggled, tilting her body slightly.

"What's so funny?" I sat up. Stephanie turned and pointed to a grip mark on her ass. "Did I do that?" I asked, suddenly feeling panicked. Stephanie nodded. "Fuck, I'm sorry."

"Why are you apologizing, this is hot." Stephanie grinned. "I got you too." Stephanie gestured to my chest. I stood up and walked over to the mirror, two bruises had formed.

"Damn, why does this turn me on?" I laughed, running my fingers over the bruises. Stephanie winked and pulled me into her lips.

Stephanie put on a white lace bra and thong. She pulled on a short white dress over it. I pulled on my underwear, shirt and pants. Stephanie disappeared to the bathroom and quickly did her makeup. We walked out of the room, she grabbed my hand and kissed me on the cheek.

James and Jace were standing in the kitchen, coffee in hands. Half of James's face was almost black with bruises. I blinked in complete horror. Stephanie let go of my hand suddenly and took off to Raphael's room.

"Want coffee?" Jace started pouring me a cup. I nodded, my eyes still on James's face.

What did he say?

Jace passed me a cup. The air was quiet between us. He could see me staring, but to them I wasn't owed an explanation. I swallowed, more angry then concerned for him at this point. Eli's footprints echoed down the stairs.

"What the fuck happened to you?" Eli demanded, staring at

James.

"Slipped and fell down the stairs." James shrugged. Eli looked at him for a while then slowly scanned the kitchen.

"Where's Stephanie?" Eli glanced over at me.

"She needed to talk to Raphael about something," I replied. Eli nodded and looked at James again, his eyes narrowing before he turned sharply on his heels and walked to Raphael's room. I heard the door open.

"What did he fucking do?" Eli snarled, slamming the door behind him. James put his face on the counter.

"I'm going to die today," James muttered. "Please kill me before Eli gets to me."

"James, you know I always will. But, it's fine. You saw Stephanie's reaction, Eli won't touch you without her permission," Jace cooed.

"How could I have said that? Like Jesus fucking Christ, what was I even thinking?" James groaned.

"Can't help you justify it," Jace murmured. Raphael's door opened.

"Eli, no, I'm safe," Stephanie's voice echoed through the hallway.

"You'll be fucking safer if I deal with this," Eli hissed.

"I can handle it," Stephanie replied. "Actually, Raphael handled it already."

"You think a couple of bruises will stop this?" Eli growled. "You are strong, he is stronger."

"Eli, look at me please," Stephanie pleaded. There was a long period of silence.

"If he ever—" Eli started saying.

"Yes," Stephanie said quietly.

Barry walked into the kitchen from the hangout room, naive to what was going on. Eli walked out from the hallway, gun in hand. Stephanie followed. Eli placed the barrel of the gun on

James's head. James didn't flinch and took a sip of coffee.

"You know exactly who I am," Eli began, his voice a low rasp. James nodded. "Then you know I like to take things slow, I like to... take it all in," Eli continued. James nodded, clenching his jaw. "If you ever lay a finger on her, you will be begging me to die."

"I know," James croaked. Eli shot beside James's head, the bullet implanted into the bulletproof glass. Eli glared viciously at him before storming out of the cottage, the door slammed behind him. James's breathing suddenly quickened as he buried his face in his hands.

"I think you've learned your lesson," Raphael asserted, stepping into the kitchen. His domineering presence filling the room. The unquestionable leader, the king, the God. His eyes didn't lift from James until a slight assent was given. An admittance of the power Raphael held. An acceptance of the untouchability of the angel that stood beside him. Those were the rules of the game.

He made the rules.

He was the judge and executioner of anyone who dared question or break them. I wish I could have been happy that it had been taken care of. The only feeling pummeling through my veins was envy. She had trusted him to take care of this. Not me, *him*. I wasn't even granted the privilege of knowing what was wrong. Jace passed Raphael and Stephanie a coffee.

"Can I please know?" I asked. Everyone turned to me.

"No," Stephanie replied. "It's taken care of." Stephanie leaned against me and kissed my shoulder.

Right.

It wasn't *my* game.

"How was the couch?" Raphael asked Barry.

"Oh, it was great, I think that thing has better support than my mattress back home," Barry laughed.

"Stephanie, are you coming with us?" Raphael flicked her forehead.

"Yes, I certainly am," Stephanie swatted at his hand.

"A road trip like the good old days!" Barry cheered.

"Cheap motels!" Stephanie did a little dance.

"Can we please update that part?" Raphael mumbled.

"Oh, come on princess, don't be a stick-in-the-mud," Stephanie mocked.

"Okay fine," Raphael rolled his eyes. "We'll drop you off on the way," Raphael looked over at me. I nodded. "Okay, let's get going," Raphael announced. I went and grabbed my backpack. Stephanie grabbed a bag and stuffed a few items in it. We went out, Barry and Raphael were waiting at the doorway.

"We're taking your car, Stephanie," Raphael stated.

"Yes!" Stephanie cheered. We walked outside. "Eli, I'm leaving," Stephanie called. Eli ran around the corner and lifted Stephanie into his arms. Stephanie giggled as he spun her around.

"Be safe," Eli murmured, setting her down.

"Don't kill anyone," Stephanie joked.

"I don't make promises I can't keep." Eli winked at Stephanie. We all got into her red car. Raphael, of course, rode in the passenger seat and I was banished to the back.

Chapter 10

"They did try to track down Barry, the police couldn't find the man you were talking about," the green-eyed lady stated.

"I figured." I shrugged.

"That was quite the threat Eli made." The brown-haired lady leaned in slightly.

"It was the only time I ever saw him like that," I murmured.

"You said Eli was smaller and less muscular than James, why would James be so afraid of Eli?" the brown-haired lady asked.

"I did ask later, Stephanie said it was dark, that I wasn't ready to know. All I know is that he was a contract killer before he joined them," I replied. The brown-haired lady nodded, noting it down.

"If he is such a dark killer, why are you assuming Raphael did this? Is it not possible that it was Eli?" the green-eyed lady suggested.

"No, Eli would never do this," I croaked.

***

We made it back to my house. Stephanie got out, I pulled her into me and kissed her deeply. My hands on her back, pulling her closer.

"Come on Stephanie, road trip!" Raphael yelled out the window. Raphael and Barry started to chant "road trip!" very loudly. My parents came out, confused. They walked over to us.

"Stephanie, how was your Christmas?" mom asked sweetly.

"Oh, it was lovely. How was yours?" Stephanie smiled.

"It was lonely without Levi, but we'll make up for that today. What a lovely necklace." Mom gestured to the necklace draped around her neck.

"Oh thanks, Raphael, got it for me," Stephanie replied.

"Is that a mouse?" mom asked, taking the charm in her hand.

"Ya, Raph used to call me Mighty Mouse," Stephanie rocked on her heels.

"Is that your brother in the car?" Mom's focus shifted.

"Yes." Raphael stepped out of the car. Barry did the same.

"That is Raphael and Barry, another friend from foster care." Stephanie gestured to each of them.

"Sorry to interrupt, but we have to be on our way. We have a cheap motel to get to," Raphael laughed.

"Oh, of course, have fun," mom grinned.

"Merry Christmas!" Stephanie waved goodbye.

"Road trip!" Barry shouted as Stephanie got in the car. Stephanie giggled and shook her head, starting the vehicle. They took off.

"Why are they staying in a cheap motel?" mom queried.

"They're driving Barry home, he lives a bit away," I explained.

"How did she like your gift?", Dad demanded.

"She loved it," I boasted. We entered the house and sat at the kitchen table.

"How did the guys like their gift?" Dad questioned.

"They really liked it too," I smiled.

"Okay and what gifts did you get?" mom asked. Shit. I can't say I got an apartment. The hairs on my arm jolted up as I began picking at my thumb.

"They all went in together, including Stephanie and got Stephanie and I a little vacation at a treehouse resort," I stated, managing to successfully cover my failing voice.

"Uh, will Raphael be there?" mom asked.

"Oh, ya, of course," I lied.

"The question I have been dying to know the answer to, what did Stephanie get Raphael?" dad demanded.

"Barry. She brought Barry out. It's been years since they've seen each other," I grinned.

"Well, that is awfully sweet," mom commented. "How was it in total, did you have fun?"

"Oh it was so much fun, there was a little scuffle with one of the guys, but that seems to have resolved itself," I smiled. Dad leaned forward, the expression I knew so well plastered on his face. He was about to interrogate me. I looked at him confused before my brain caught up to what I had just admitted.

Shit.

"What kind of scuffle?" Dad quizzed.

"He, uh, made a 'joke' to Stephanie that didn't sit well with her," I shifted.

"What did he say?" Dad's eyes watched my face.

"I don't know, they refused to tell me." I shrugged.

"You must have an idea," dad urged.

"It seemed like a sexual... threat," I replied slowly. I caught my tongue in my teeth as I saw dad's back stiffened.

"And how was it resolved?" dad's eyes dug into me. I couldn't lie to him, he could tell. I certainly couldn't tell him about the threat Eli made, or the extent to which Raphael had injured James.

"Uh..." I took a deep breath. Dad leaned even closer,

193

watching my every move closely. "Raphael punched him, and uh, Eli told him he'd do worse if he ever laid a finger on Stephanie." I swallowed hard, knowing full well my parents wouldn't be too pleased by this response.

"Wait, this is one of the guys that lives with her?" Dad clarified. I nodded. "And their solution wasn't to kick him out? It was to threaten him and punch him?" dad scoffed. I nodded. "Jesus fucking Christ, Levi, I don't like this."

"I don't either, nothing I can really do," I mumbled. My dad nodded slowly.

"Her brother doesn't seem like a good person to have around," dad stated.

"You don't know that, you met him for two seconds and we don't know the dynamic of their house. Raphael and Stephanie might not own it, they may have to put up with it to have somewhere to sleep," mom frowned. "Can you blame him for reacting with violence? Someone he cares about was just threatened."

"The punching is not what concerns me, it's why this man is able to sleep in the same house as Stephanie after he threatened her," dad specified.

"Because of Stephanie, he would have been gone if Stephanie hadn't insisted it was 'just a comment,' and that she was safe," I justified.

"That poor girl, to think a threat is just a comment." Dad rubbed his face. "I want a dinner with both Stephanie and Raphael soon, I don't want it getting too serious before we figure out what type of guy he is."

"What does that matter? I'm dating Stephanie, not Raphael," I retorted.

"Two things, son, first, if you get involved you are stuck in that family, second, if Stephanie's in danger, she needs to get out before something happens." Dad leaned back in his chair, tapping the table.

"I'll ask her to come to dinner first," I said. Dad nodded in agreement. "Can Stephanie come to the New Year's Eve party this year?"

"Oh, of course." Mom smiled. "Go get cleaned up, I laid out your nice clothing for dinner tonight," mom instructed. I nodded and left.

The hours passed slowly. Mom was in the kitchen preparing the meal. I was promptly told to "get out of the way" if I tried to help. I sat there and scrolled aimlessly through social media waiting for people to arrive. Eventually the family started rolling in. First grandparents, then my cousins who were around my age. I sighed, happy to have some company.

"Hey man." Jack gave me a fist bump.

"Let's go to your room." Ben took a small bag of weed out of his pocket. I rolled my eyes and we went to my room. Ben lit up a joint and hung out the window. "Did you have fun on that summer trip?" Ben asked.

"Oh, ya man, I have photos." I unlocked my phone and got up the photos of the trip my parents and I went on during the summer. "Swipe right. I instructed. I sat there as Ben nodded at the photos. He passed the phone to Jack. There were a couple of dings from my phone. I ignored it, probably Aidan and Lucas.

"Holy shit man, who is she?" Jack's eyes widened. I looked up confused. My brain suddenly sprinted to knowledge I didn't want to have. Fuck.

"Give that back." I reached for my phone. Jack kept it out of my reach and tossed it to Ben.

"Holy fucking shit, I'm gonna send these to myself," Ben laughed.

"Don't you fucking dare," I blustered.

"Damn, I think I need to be excused for a second," Ben joked. "Ah, a message. 'I know it's a little early, but I can't stop thinking about you.' Dude, how much are you paying her? I want in." Ben beamed, shaking his head in disbelief while staring at my phone. I managed to grab my phone back. I looked down to see what I thought I would see. There were a few sexy pictures of Stephanie, two in her white bustier and thong, one completely nude. "Don't worry I have them saved in my mind." Ben gleefully tapped his temple.

"Man, stop, that's my girlfriend," I rasped.

"No way are you fucking her," Ben shook his head. I pulled my shirt down revealing the hickeys. "When did you become interesting?" Ben snickered.

"What's it like? I bet she's a wild one." Jack leaned forward.

"The sex?" I clarified.

"No man, the conversation," Jack retorted sarcastically.

"The sex is mind-blowing," I bragged. "She's fucking amazing on her knees too."

"Holy shit." Ben took a drag on his joint. "How did *you* possibly land *her*?"

"No idea, she pursued me." I shrugged. "She's coming to the New Year's Eve party if you want to meet her."

"We'll certainly be coming to that now," Jack laughed. "Is she, like, eager?"

"Had sex twice yesterday and she gave me a blowjob," I boasted.

"Holy fucking shit." Ben murmured.

"She got me a trip. Just the two of us in this secluded

treehouse cabin," I grinned. Jack and Ben gawked. "I'm getting photos every night until she gets back from a family road trip." I paused, making sure they were taking in everything I was saying. "Oh and her gift to me was delivered to me while she was wearing Christmas lingerie." I leaned back feeling like a king. Jack and Ben looked at me in complete envy.

"That woman we just saw is doing, and has done, all that for you?" Jack clarified. I nodded. "Jesus fuck man, you are a god." Jack praised. My phone dinged again. Jack grabbed it out of my hand. "'Any requests?'" Jack read from my phone. "Any requests, Ben?"

"Stop guys," I grabbed my phone back out of his hand.

"What's the point of you having a shiny new toy if you're not willing to share." Ben sighed.

"She's not a toy." I blinked.

"She's—" Jack started.

"Dinner!" My mom shouted. We all got up and went downstairs. I quickly texted Stephanie that she was remarkably sexy and I had no further requests. We all sat down at the table.

"So, Levi, I hear you were spending Christmas with your girlfriend?" My uncle smiled at me.

"Yes, she is such a sweet girl," Mom put in.

"She's smoking hot," Jack stated. My uncle gave him a dirty look. "What? We were just looking at pictures of her! She's completely out of his league."

"Not appropriate," my uncle glared at Jack. "So tell me a bit about this girl."

"Uh, she's studying history, she wants to open a museum when she's done her studies," I grinned.

"The poor girl is an orphan, lives with her brother—" mom started.

"Foster brother," I corrected.

"Sorry, yes, she lives with her foster brother and a few other guys."

"A few other guys? I bet that brother is on edge," my aunt laughed. "That must be a difficult situation to break into."

"At first, Raphael didn't like me, but he's come around. The other guys never had an issue with me," I replied.

"What do they all do?" my uncle asked.

"They all work together, they pick up different jobs." I shrugged. "They consider themselves family."

"Are they all orphans?" my aunt inquired.

"None of them have parental figures in the picture, not all of them are dead," I commented.

"So they created their own family, that seems natural, what does the psychologist think?" my aunt turned toward dad.

"I mean we are pack animals, it's our instinct to cling to familiar relations," dad analyzed. "Would be very natural to make your own family if you don't inherently have one."

"Can we please not psychologically evaluate my girlfriend?" I requested.

"She is a very sweet girl," dad dismissed. "We are fighting with this one to have her and her brother over for dinner."

"That sounds like a great idea, why are you resistant to that idea?" my grandma asked. "I would love to meet her too."

"I'm not resistant to the idea, Stephanie wants to come. Her foster brother just really isn't a dinner person." I shrugged.

"Well you will get to meet Stephanie, Mom. She's coming to our New Year's Eve party," mom announced.

"Great, we'll see if she's suitable to carry our great-grandkids," my grandpa laughed.

"I think it's a bit early for that kind of evaluation," my uncle put in.

"I knew within the first week I wanted to marry your mother," my grandpa smiled and leaned over, kissing my grandma on the cheek. "You both knew before you let on, too, the boy knows." My grandpa nodded toward me.

"Well, let's not scare her off by talking about giving you great-grandkids." Mom smiled at my grandpa.

"The girl doesn't have a family, I bet she's already thinking about that," my grandpa chuckled.

"Why ruin a body like that with pregnancy?" Ben muttered. My uncle promptly hit the back of his head.

"Where have your manners gone?" my uncle hissed.

"You haven't seen her!" Ben retorted.

"You are so close to being grounded, young man," my uncle stated. Ben fell silent. "Sorry about him, I think I need to review proper communication skills with him." My uncle frowned. We ate dinner and dessert to the typical stiff family small talk. Eventually, everyone left. I helped clean up from the dinner, then went upstairs and fell asleep.

Days passed without much communication from Stephanie. I received nightly photos of her, but no calls or messages regarding the trip other than the vague "it's going well" here and there. Finally, New Year's Eve rolled around. I was excited to see her, it felt like forever, the days went by so slowly with nothing else but parental communication. Aidan and Lucas were off with their families and I was left alone.

Aidan and his parents walked into the house. Aidan waved to me. We went downstairs to my basement which had a single couch and a couple of lounge chairs facing each other.

"How have you been? It's been forever!" I smiled at Aidan.

We sat down on the couch.

"It's been such a cool Christmas break, we did the car thing Stephanie gave us. It was so cool. We drove a Ferrari, Aston Martin and Porsche. Man, she is so cool," Aidan smiled at me. "What did she get you?"

"A vacation to a secluded cabin thing, just the two of us." I grinned.

"Damn, are your parents okay with that?" Aidan asked.

"I told them Raphael was coming too," I laughed. Aidan nodded.

"What did you end up—" Aidan started.

"Let's party!" Ben shouted, walking into the room. Jack was at his heels. "Where's the girl?"

"She hasn't arrived yet," I called. Ben and Jack stood in the corner talking to each other. Snickering in hushed tones, their eyes on me intently.

"I hate your cousins," Aidan muttered.

"Ya, they're dicks," I nodded. "I got Stephanie a first edition version of *Great Expectations*," I replied to what I assumed would be his question.

"That's neat, did she like it?" Aidan queried.

"Loved it." I smiled to myself. Lucas walked into the room.

"Stephanie's being interrogated by your grandparents upstairs," Lucas laughed looking at me.

"Oh no," I muttered. I stood up to go rescue her but she walked in the room. She wore a flowy short black dress with gold sparkles and black stilettos. Her makeup was done slightly more dramatic than usual, I couldn't help but stare, completely in awe of her. She was *mine*. Stephanie beamed at me and put her purse down running and pouncing on me. I held her up and kissed her.

"Welcome back," I giggled, setting her down on the ground.

Stephanie went back and grabbed a bottle of whiskey out of her purse.

"What would we do without you?" Lucas grabbed the whiskey from Stephanie. Ben and Jack came over, their chests puffed out.

"Is that whiskey?" Ben demanded, grabbing the bottle from Lucas's hand. Stephanie grabbed it back from Ben and handed it to Lucas. "You are quite the naughty girl." Ben smirked, stepping closer to Stephanie. I stepped forward, Stephanie pushed me back.

"Don't call me that," Stephanie ordered, an unwavering smile on her face.

"Why not? From what we've heard and seen you fit the description." Jack winked at her.

"I don't fit the description for you. No, to you I am a girl that you can fantasize about, you can masturbate to me if you want. But men like you don't land girls like me. You can try to intimidate me, you can try to intimidate my friends, but at the end of the day you'll be using your hand while I fuck Levi," Stephanie stated, that smile not parting from her lips. I wrapped my arms around her from behind.

I always looked up to my cousins. They were always bragging about the women they had been with or the fights they wanted to get in. My fingers trailed along the scar on Stephanie's left arm, her words shattered through my idealized version of their masculinity. As I stood there, feeling the scars from her fights, knowing what her misfit family had done, my cousin's just seemed pathetic. These two boys trying desperately to be seen as tough.

They looked at each other, breathing a laugh and shaking their heads. Not sure how to react to someone questioning their façade. But this tiny woman in my arms could take them down without blinking an eye.

"You're not that hot," Ben scoffed.

"This personality you two have is not unique," Stephanie smirked and undid my arms, she grabbed my hand and pulled me to the couch.

"Holy shit, that was badass," Lucas sat down with us. Aidan followed suit, both of their eyes were locked on Stephanie in complete amazement.

"I'm far too used to guys like that." Stephanie shrugged. "I live with two of them."

"Ah yes, Eli and Raphael, terrible personalities," I joked. Stephanie laughed.

"James and Jace," Stephanie clarified to Aidan and Lucas.

"How did it go with the family?" I asked, wrapping my arms around her.

"Your dad interviewed me about my living situation. So that was a bit odd," Stephanie giggled, leaning against me.

"You get used to the interviews," Aidan laughed. Lucas popped open the whiskey bottle and took a swig.

"This is nice," Lucas commented, passing the bottle to Aidan. Aidan chugged a bit and nodded in agreement before passing me the bottle. Jack and Ben sat in the lounge chairs still pouting from Stephanie calling them out. Stephanie took the bottle from me and chugged a bit.

"Hey now, don't forget what happened the last time you stole my whiskey," I joked and kissed her cheek.

"I don't think we can do that here," Stephanie winked and passed me the bottle. I took a swig and passed it to Jack.

"How are the guys doing after the Christmas incident?" I questioned.

"What happened at Christmas?" Aidan asked.

"James was an asshole to me so Raph and Eli got all uptight." Stephanie shrugged.

"I heard your brother punched him out and someone else threatened to do worse," Jack chuckled. Stephanie's jaw hardened.

"My dad can tell when I lie, I accidentally said there was a little scuffle," I explained quickly.

"Jack, can you go into detail about what you know?" Stephanie smiled at him, biting her nail.

"Just that one guy threatened you, your brother punched him out and the other guy threatened to do worse," Jack responded.

"Someone threatened you?" Aidan demanded, a look of horror crossing his face.

"I'm leaving," Stephanie stood up.

"Stephanie, please stay," I pleaded.

"We handle these matters within our family, Levi," Stephanie hissed, grabbing her purse and walking up the stairs.

"I didn't mean to. Please stop and talk to me," I begged.

"Sorry I have to leave, truly wonderful party," Stephanie called, she opened the door and slammed it behind her. The room was silent. I ran after her, chasing her into the driveway.

"Stephanie, stop and talk to me," I whimpered.

"They're my family Levi, what happens when the rest slips? You think your family will ignore it?" Stephanie whispered angrily.

"Stephanie, it scared me, he's a big guy. Why are you protecting him?" I pressed. Stephanie looked over. I turned around to see that the party had moved outside to watch us.

"We deal with these matters within our family. We protect each other." Stephanie turned on her heels and walked to her vehicle.

"Who's protecting you? Raphael? The last time I checked, James is still sleeping in the same house as you," I yelled after her. Stephanie froze.

"Shut up, Levi. You have no fucking idea. You think I like the comments? The gawking? But I suck it up, I suck it up because that's what I have to do. Leave it. I can handle it; I always *fucking* have." Stephanie bristled. Her eyes on me, begging me to let it go, her face looked completely exhausted. I watched as she began to pick at where her jaw scar was hidden under makeup. She let out a whimper, suddenly seeming so fragile and helpless as her eyes darted from me to our audience. I reached forward, opening my mouth to comfort her, but the words stuck in my throat.

What could I possibly say?

All I knew, all my brain could comprehend was that I wanted to take it away. To grab her and shelter her from whatever hell kept filling her trances. But instead, all I could do was stand there, unable to get a word out, unable to even step forward and wrap my arms around her. I was stumped.

How do I help her?

Dad stepped toward her. "Stephanie, why don't we call the police? They can help you," dad voiced gently.

"Like the police have ever helped me," Stephanie murmured, her eyes still firmly on the audience before getting into her vehicle. I ran behind it, putting my hand on the back of it. I stood there, refusing to allow Stephanie to reverse out of the parking lot. I couldn't let her leave like this. I was terrified that this was it. I loved her.

I needed her.

I stood firm. None of our audience went in, intrigued for how this movie would end. How this would resolve itself. The only thing I knew was she wasn't leaving until we resolved this issue. After a few minutes, the Range Rover pulled up behind us. Eli jumped out of the passenger side.

"What the fuck is wrong with you, Levi?" Eli muttered as he walked by me. He tapped on Stephanie's window. "GO INSIDE! THIS ISN'T A FUCKING SHOW!" Eli bellowed at my family who were still standing outside watching this unfold. The crowd remained motionless, out of fear for Stephanie's safety or curiosity, I wasn't sure. But not a single muscle moved toward the door.

"Are you the guy?" dad demanded.

"No, this is Eli," I replied. Stephanie got out of her car and ran to the Rover.

"She needs to call the police," dad instructed.

"The police?" Eli cackled. I walked over to the vehicle and opened the door.

"Stephanie, please talk to me," I knelt down, staring at her intently. Stephanie barely looked up at me.

"How could you, Levi?" Stephanie whispered. "We trusted you." Stephanie picked at her scar, her pained eyes on me. Raphael got out of the driver's seat.

"I didn't mean to, I said the least amount of information possible," I blurted. Raphael pulled on my shirt to get me to stand up. I obeyed, bracing myself for a punch. Raphael shut the door.

"This won't happen again," Raphael stated. I nodded. "Stephanie just needs a bit to cool off, she'll be fine by midnight," Raphael assured. I nodded. "No police."

"No, never," I replied.

"Sort this out and she'll come back in," Raphael instructed. I nodded and walked back to dad. Raphael opened the door and knelt beside Stephanie.

"She's not safe there," dad said to Eli.

"Sir, respectfully, you don't know shit," Eli replied.

"Eli, back in the car," Raphael called walking over.

"No—" Eli started. Raphael raised a finger then gestured to the car. Eli nodded and obeyed. "Good afternoon, you must be Mr. Davis." Raphael extended his hand to my dad. Dad eyed it before returning his cold, unyielding gaze to Raphael's face. Not a muscle moved to shake his hand. Raphael lowered it, puffing out his chest for the pending fight of wills. "I think there's been a bit of miscommunication."

"I doubt that," dad retorted.

"We made a mistake not telling Levi the comment the guy made. He told her that Levi would love to share her with him and his friend. Disgusting, yes, not a threat though. It was taken care of and I can assure you that no comments like that will be made again. I also want to assure you that if anyone threatened Stephanie they certainly would not be in the same house as her nor would he have any ability to come close to her." Raphael met my dad's unmoving glare. Dad didn't shift, he didn't back down, he raised an eyebrow, challenging Raphael's story. "Levi, can you leave us for a second?" Raphael asked, his eye contact not breaking from my dad. I nodded. "Can you also bring everyone in? Stephanie doesn't like this kind of attention." Raphael looked at me. I went over to the crowd and escorted them into the house.

"That poor girl," my grandma murmured. "Beauty can truly be a curse."

"Your dad sometimes forgets that the police don't always protect everyone," my aunt stated. We stood there in silence, the moments ticking by. I walked to the living room to peer through the curtain.

"So she's really fucked up, that's how you landed her," Ben laughed.

"Can you repeat that?" Raphael purred, standing in the doorway to the living room. Ben turned sharply. Raphael cracked his knuckles, his icy glare digging into Ben as he stepped forward.

"No, uh, I didn't say anything," Ben trembled.

"That's what I thought," Raphael growled. Ben sheepishly scampered from the room. "Stephanie will be in shortly." Raphael stepped over and stood beside me, looking toward the party.

"I'm sorry," I blurted.

"Just be more careful." Raphael shrugged. My dad walked in and handed him a beer.

"I'm sorry for all this, we shouldn't have assumed," dad rubbed his face. His saddened gaze resting on Raphael as he shot him an apologetic smile.

"Don't apologize, I'm glad to see more people looking out for Stephanie. She's never had a proper family, I'm thrilled she's gaining one through Levi," Raphael stated.

"You've done well by her."

"No, I spent less than a year with her in foster care, who she's become is purely based on her own perseverance and grit. She's stronger than I'll ever be." Raphael murmured. Stephanie walked in, everyone turned and stared, their curiosity burning a hole in her.

I saw her shrink under their gaze, glancing yearningly at the door. A cold bottle pressed against my arm as Raphael shoved the beer into me. My fingers grasped it before he quickly let go. I stumbled slightly, trying to ensure the bottle didn't fall. That seemed to be the furthest thing from Raphael's mind as he walked over, using his body to shield her from their scrutiny. My instinctual sip from the bottle was met with a huff and my dad confiscating it.

Raphael leaned over, whispering something to her. Stephanie took a deep breath in and nodded. Raphael smiled, whispering something else before mockingly messing up her hair. Stephanie giggled and playfully shoved him. Her nerves gone. Raphael bowed and gestured to me; Stephanie regally patted his head before stepping over to me.

"Let's go to the basement," I stated. Stephanie nodded, following me as we retreated to privacy and sat on the couch, the silence burning into us.

"I, uh, I overreacted. I'm sorry," Stephanie breathed.

"These guys are bigger than me, they carry guns, they have these sadistic sides. I understand Raphael protects you, but he's not around all the time. I understand you can protect yourself, but you're smaller Stephanie," I whimpered. Stephanie shifted uncomfortably.

"I, uh…" Stephanie took a long pause. "I understand the dangers, but I can't do anything about that now. I am a target." Stephanie bit her nail. "A few more jobs and they may allow me to leave."

"We can leave," I gently cupped her face in my hands. "A few more jobs and *we* can leave, we can settle in a small house, live a quiet life," I whispered to her.

"You'd get bored." Stephanie shrugged.

"I will never get bored of this." I kissed her on the forehead. "We can get married, have a few kids, live a normal fucking life Stephanie, together, no danger, no gawking, no comments. A few more jobs and we run from them if they don't want you to leave." I pulled Stephanie into me, she gripped me tightly, like she was terrified I would start sprinting in the other direction. "I love you," I nuzzled her nose.

"I love you too," Stephanie choked, her eyes misty with tears.

"I imagine Raphael will be living in a cabin on our property."

"Probably," Stephanie giggled. "What did I do to deserve you?"

"Must have sold your soul," I winked. Stephanie nodded and laughed.

"I love you, Levi, I'm so sorry for bringing you into this." Stephanie sniffled.

"I am so glad you did," I kissed her hand. Stephanie leaned forward, locking our lips together, she pulled back slightly, watching my expression to tell her whether she should continue. I yanked her onto my lap, smothering her with desperate kisses as she undid my pants. She pulled them down slightly, grabbing my erection and positioning it as she moved her thong out of the way. I moaned softly as I went inside her. My whole body was on a high after having her come back to me. I had thought I lost her. I could feel every inch go in as Stephanie moved slowly along my shaft. She had one hand clutching my hair, the other on the back of the couch. I felt her breath on my ear. I tilted my head back in bliss as she took me all in again. I focused on her movements, the moment. Everything felt perfect.

"What are you two doing?" Dad's voice echoed through the basement. Stephanie buried her face in my chest. An ostrich reaction to danger.

"Nothing, uh, just kissing," I called.

"It's, uh, almost midnight," dad announced, he walked back toward the stairs. "I hope you're using protection," he muttered before continuing up the stairs. Stephanie giggled and brought her lips to my neck.

"We forgot protection," I mumbled.

"I'll take the morning-after pill." Stephanie returned to moving along me. I grabbed her hips stopping her.

"Maybe we shouldn't," I sighed. Stephanie nodded and went to get off. My body felt sore from the lack of completion. Physically, I needed her right now; mentally, I needed her right now. "Fuck it," I whispered. Stephanie giggled and kissed me as she returned to fucking me. I moaned with pleasure. Stephanie gently bit my ear.

"Fuck," Stephanie breathed into my ear. Both of her hands went to my hair as our tongues meshed, my fingers glided up her dress, I felt her smooth skin jilt under my touch. The unbelievable spark driving our fervor. My body swelled with pleasure, I grunted loudly as I finished inside her. Stephanie bit my nose playfully.

"I love you so fucking much," my lips glided along her jaw. Stephanie got up, repositioning her thong to cover herself again.

"Okay, let's go talk to your grandparents," Stephanie grinned. I did my pants up.

"To be able to do that to me, then go up and put this innocent persona on for my family, you are the perfect woman." I took her hand and we walked upstairs. "Where's Raphael?" I asked my dad as Stephanie went off to speak with Aidan and Lucas.

"Oh, he left after you and Stephanie went downstairs, he said he didn't want to intrude, just wanted to make sure Stephanie was comfortable. Good man," dad nodded.

"What did he say to you?" I demanded, intrigued by the change of attitude.

"Not my story to tell, son," dad said softly. "Just keep an eye on the situation and tell me if anything changes, something still doesn't sit well with me."

"Ya, of course," I replied. What story was he talking about? I looked over to see my grandma hugging Stephanie. My heart pounded in my chest in pure love. My grandma cooing as she stroked Stephanie's jaw lovingly. With that I felt our lives flash before my eyes, bringing the children up for family events, our lives calm and loud. A smile crept over my lips, doing a few jobs with her was the right decision. I would do anything to allow her to feel safe. A few jobs would be easy.

I stepped over to her, gliding my fingers along her spine. Stephanie leaned into my touch, shooting me a tender grin. What I wouldn't do to wake up to that smile every day.

"You have a good one," my grandpa said to me. "I can see that you two love each other very much, don't lose her."

"I don't plan on it," I laughed, putting my arm around her waist and kissing her on the cheek.

"We're so glad to have you in our family," my grandma took Stephanie's hand and looked at her gently. I looked over to see tears welling in Stephanie's eyes.

"I'm sorry," Stephanie whispered, wiping the tears away meekly.

"Oh, don't apologize," my grandma pushed me out of the way as she pulled Stephanie into her embrace.

"Let's leave them, my love." My grandpa nodded and took my grandma's hand to go talk to my parents.

"Are you okay?" I whispered.

"You have no idea how lucky you are," Stephanie took a deep breath in to compose herself.

"What's your New Year's resolution?" Lucas asked, swinging back to talk to us. Aidan followed. Stephanie sniffled, wiping the tears from her cheeks before returning to her typical demeanor.

"I'm perfect, I don't need to fix anything," Stephanie joked.

"What about making more money?" I grinned.

"That sounds so shallow," Stephanie replied.

"What about the generic 'workout more'?" Aidan proposed.

"She already works out two hours a day, I would rather if she didn't die," I laughed.

"What are yours?" Stephanie asked.

"To get a girlfriend," Lucas smiled.

"To have sex," Aidan whispered.

"To make more money," I winked at Stephanie playfully.

"Okay guys, ten seconds!" dad announced. We all gathered around the television and chanted down before all screaming "Happy New Year!" as my dad popped a bottle of champagne. He handed out glasses to the 'adults' at the party, the rest of us 'children' were given sparkling juice. We all stood in a circle. "What are everyone's New Years' resolutions?" dad queried. Everyone went around to say vague "have a successful year," "workout more" and "make more money" statements. The focus turned onto Stephanie who thought for a second.

"To follow my heart no matter my obligations," Stephanie stated.

"What a lovely resolution," mom commented. I pulled Stephanie into me and gave her a kiss on the head. The party shut down soon after.

"Raphael mentioned that they were hoping to take you on that vacation relatively soon. He suggested you leave tomorrow and take a few days off classes. If you feel confident that you won't miss too much, maybe this is a good time," dad said to me, I blinked in surprise.

"Ya, that sounds great," I nodded.

I woke up suddenly to mom shaking me. I grunted and tried to roll over to continue to sleep but my mom wasn't having it.

"Get up, Stephanie's here," mom announced. I sat up slowly. My mom left the room. I grabbed a few items and stuffed them into my bag walking sleepily down the stairs. Stephanie was standing at the doorway in a short pale green dress.

"Guess I'm not very motivating," Stephanie joked.

"Not one bit, no," I muttered.

"Our first stop will be coffee?" Stephanie offered.

"A little more motivating." I kissed Stephanie on the cheek. We left the house, waving, and got into her red car. We drove straight to a drive-through coffee place. "Get me like a caramel latte," I requested. Stephanie nodded.

"Can I get a large caramel latte and a large latte please," Stephanie ordered. We drove up to the window to pay.

"That's a lot of coffee, Stephanie. Are we fighting God today or something?" I demanded.

"I'm not dealing with grumpy Levi this whole drive," Stephanie retorted. I shrugged. They handed us the lattes and we began to drive off. "Can you get the pill from my purse? I wanted to take it in front of you for peace of mind."

"You know I trust you, right?" I riffled through her purse and found the box, taking out a small pill.

"I know, just this takes away the whole 'what if' question," Stephanie replied. I handed her the pill, she took it and chased it with coffee. "The pharmacist slut shamed me," Stephanie laughed.

"Did you punch them?" I joked.

"No, I told her we were married and she stopped." Stephanie

shrugged.

"Okay, I don't want to be an asshole or anything, but should you be on birth control?"

"Would you like me to be on birth control? Like, I've always just used condoms, the whole going to the doctor constantly thing doesn't really suit my lifestyle," Stephanie drummed the steering wheel.

"Fair enough."

"Are you sure?" Stephanie asked.

I nodded. "I mean we always have the morning-after pill if we get too caught up," I remarked.

Stephanie nodded. "Did your dad say anything about walking in on us?"

"My dad would hate any conversation like that, he's very awkward about sex, I managed to never get a sex talk," I boasted.

"My sex talk was having sex," Stephanie laughed.

"Who was your first?" I asked curiously.

"Uh, okay," Stephanie looked at me caught off guard. "I don't know his name," Stephanie murmured.

"Damn, Stephanie," I chuckled. "Mine was with a girl named Lily, it lasted a millisecond."

"So you lasted longer back then, odd," Stephanie joisted.

"Fuck off." I shook my head disapprovingly at her. "Is it someone you don't want me to know about?"

"No, it was at a party and, uh, he never introduced himself." Stephanie took a sip of her coffee.

"You sure it wasn't Barry?" I prodded.

"God, I wish it was, I bet he would be fantastic," Stephanie smiled at me mockingly.

"I agree, you think he'd be into a threesome?" I teased.

"I'd be there, so yes," Stephanie winked at me.

"Wow, rude. I thought he would be coming for me."

"He may switch from the Stephanie fan club to the Levi fan club, you may impress him."

"Okay, ew, I don't like this anymore." I groaned. Stephanie giggled. "Did you ever sleep with Barry?"

"No," Stephanie laughed. "He just had a little crush when I first arrived, nothing came of it. I never thought of him in that way."

"Have to say I'm relieved. Part of me was nervous when I heard you picked him up."

"You can tell me if you get jealous, we can talk about it. The guys poke and prod, don't let them make you think you can't just tell me how you're feeling." Stephanie commented.

"What like communicate? Ew," I joked.

"I'm serious," Stephanie frowned.

"You can't tell me that any of your other ex-boyfriends talked to you about this stuff." I shook my head.

"Keyword there is *ex*-boyfriends, why do you think you need to be like them? They didn't last."

"I don't feel like I need to be like them," I huffed.

"Okay." Stephanie nodded. "Just wanted to make sure. They're all dickheads."

"Jace isn't that bad," I muttered.

"Uh, what?" Stephanie stared at me, completely bewildered. "What did Jace say to you?"

"He didn't say anything, I'm not an idiot, he's constantly making comments," I snapped.

"I slept with Jace once, I was really mad and trying to hurt someone else. Not a boyfriend, was just sex, once," Stephanie clarified.

"Who were you trying to make mad?" I interrogated.

215

"It was a really fucked up time, can we not talk about it?" Stephanie pleaded.

"Why don't you tell me anything?" I whined. "Everything's a fucking secret."

"Not everything's a secret, I just don't want you to look at me differently," Stephanie's voice faltered.

"Have you slept with Eli?"

"We're not gonna do this, Levi," Stephanie murmured. "Stop being an asshole, why the fuck do you care so much?"

"Would it be easier for me to ask who you haven't slept with?" I snarled. The minute the words left my mouth I regretted them. My brain catching up in horror to what my mouth had decided to blurt. "Fuck, I'm so sorry Stephanie, I'm just grumpy."

"How many people do you think I've slept with? Do you understand how many people there are on this earth?" Stephanie joked, breaking the tension. I sighed in relief.

"You may be efficient," I pondered. Stephanie laughed.

"I know that it can be frustrating when I don't tell you certain things," Stephanie commented. "But in my history, things aren't as straightforward as yours. When I fucked Jace it was vindictive and vicious, and I regret it."

"Did it work in making that person mad?".

"Yes, too well," Stephanie's eyes stared blankly to the road. That look she had when her mind captured her was plastered on her face. This memory that imprisoned her, snagging her from me once again. I cleared my throat, wanting to bring her back to our reality. Our happy reality. Stephanie blinked before shooting me a smile. "One day I'll tell you everything in detail, just not yet," Stephanie vowed.

"Whenever you're ready, I shouldn't have pushed."

"I understand why you did." Stephanie squeezed my hand tightly.

"You are more than perfect, I would marry you right now if I could." I beamed at her.

The rest of the car ride was filled with karaoke and small talk. By the time we reached the treehouse, it was completely dark outside. Stephanie grabbed the key and we drove deep into the forest. We parked outside a massive treehouse.

"This is so fucking cool." I breathed.

"Let's go in." Stephanie grabbed her stuff and we walked up to the treehouse. They had ceiling to roof windows showing the dark green landscape that surrounded it.

"I need a shower, I feel yucky." Stephanie dropped her stuff and went looking for the shower. I looked around, the tree trunk went through the center of the room. It was magnificent. The living room held a fireplace and couch, the kitchen was a small kitchenette, the bedroom held a queen size bed with white bedding. I set both mine and Stephanie's bags in the bedroom.

I walked into the bathroom. I could see Stephanie's body through the textured glass. I was mesmerized. My eyes ran along her as she tilted her head back, allowing the water to cascade over her. She was everything I wanted. My dreams would never be so ambitious as to dream her up. She was a masterpiece, a complex abstract painting that had to be deciphered. The bright colors shadowed by complete darkness. I watched her longingly. Wanting to carry the brush to help her repaint some of the darkest areas. When would she let me? When would I get to see the reasons behind the coloring? Every movement she made; my eyes followed. I would figure her out. It was my personal project.

I stripped down slowly, my eyes never leaving her. I stepped into the shower. "Finally," Stephanie muttered. She locked our lips, pulling me into her embrace. The steaming hot water scalded my arm.

"Fuck, why is this so hot?" I recoiled eyeing the red mark on my arm from where the water hit.

"It's a normal temperature," Stephanie replied, confused by my reaction.

"Are you the fucking devil? How can a human like these temperatures?" I turned off the shower and passed Stephanie a towel. She dried her hair and wrapped herself up. I went to the bedroom, placing my bag on the bed. I took out a fresh change of clothing.

"The devil requests your company," Stephanie mused behind me. I turned around. She dropped her towel on the floor revealing that body that made me drool. I knocked my bag and clothing off the bed quickly sitting down, my arms extended to her. Stephanie came over to me, straddling me and holding herself above my erection as she pressed our lips together, her tongue flicking into my mouth.

"If we have sex now without a condom, do you think the pill from this morning will cover it?" I kissed her chest frantically.

"The condoms are right there." Stephanie gestured to her bag.

"Come on, it'll be fun." I looked up at her pleadingly. I circled my tongue around her nipple before taking it into my mouth, toying with it in my teeth. Stephanie moaned. I knew I had convinced her. She allowed me to push her over, my teeth bit hungrily at her neck. Stephanie positioned me correctly, I shoved myself into her completely. Stephanie groaned with pleasure, her hands going to my ass digging her nails into me as I thrust into her.

"Fuck," Stephanie breathed, one hand went to my back, her

nails beginning to dig in. I pulled her head to the side, kissing her neck then biting down. "Holy shit." Stephanie pressed her body into me. I began to pound into her violently. The entirety of my hard shaft thrusting into her bare flesh. My mouth moving between biting and kissing her neck. Her breath became unsteady, her eyes pleading as I continued.

"Fuck, fuck, fuck, fuck!" Stephanie screamed, her nails dragging along my back, scratching at me as she began to whimper. I didn't let up with my movements. Her breath returned as she locked our eyes, she looked hungry for me. Desperate for me. I collapsed my lips on her, feeling my body get closer to finishing. I bit her lip gently, my breath hitched as a wave of pleasure collapsed over my body.

"I'm gonna come," I announced. Stephanie arched her back and pulled me into her. I grunted as I climaxed, filling her completely. I rested there for a second before removing myself and lying beside her. Something primal in me felt success and ownership knowing I had finished inside her.

She was *mine*.

"That was fantastic," Stephanie murmured.

"Fucking phenomenal."

The next few days were bliss, our days were filled with sex, future plans, small talk, food and sex. We packed up and got into the car to go back to reality.

Stephanie seemed so free away from it, her personality became a more extreme version of what I knew, her laughs were louder, conversations less stifled, moans unhindered. I couldn't help but fall more in love with this freed version of her. I wanted so badly for us to get away from it all permanently. I watched her begin to drive, her body slightly stiffened knowing what she was

219

returning to. Almost like she was putting on her mask in preparation for returning home.

I was going to get her out.

A few more jobs, we make enough money and we run. I wanted our future to be this. I wanted her to never have to put that mask up again.

I wanted her to be *free*.

"What?" Stephanie giggled looking over, seeing me watching her.

"I, uh, I just really enjoyed this," I mumbled. "You're different when you're not around them."

"What, do you hate me now?" Stephanie joked.

"You just seem happier."

"It's because I am happier." Stephanie shrugged. "This may be hard to believe, but the guys and I are actually very close. Just whenever a man comes into my life it's like they forget I'm a human."

"Yes, we all sometimes forget our friends are human." I rolled my eyes.

"We aren't talking about typical people here, you need to remember that. How we feel doesn't necessarily translate for them. They love me, and none of them would hurt me, but for them sometimes something darker can slip through," Stephanie replied.

Right, they're killers.

"What about Eli?" I asked slowly. I had been curious about him. His threat terrified a man about three times his size. Stephanie took a deep breath and tapped on her steering wheel, debating.

"I really don't think you're ready to know that," Stephanie shifted.

"I know about James and Jace, can't be that bad."

"What Eli used to do is dark, Levi. What he used to do, that's not something you're ready to hear."

"Why is he with you guys?"

"Because I want him to be," Stephanie murmured. "Look, Eli will tell you when he's ready." Stephanie looked at me. I nodded. That was that. Nothing further was said about the topic. I knew I wasn't going to learn about it. I had to trust Stephanie's decision.

We drove the long rest of the way. I felt my heart drop as I saw my house. I didn't want to go back to normal life.

"I'll see you tomorrow morning." Stephanie kissed me. I got out of the vehicle. The house was dark, I went upstairs and went to sleep.

I rolled out of bed feeling miserable that I was waking up to my normal bedroom without Stephanie by my side. I threw on my clothing and went downstairs.

"How was the trip?" mom called.

"It was amazing," I replied. "I need to get going." I rushed out the door and walked to the university.

I entered the cafeteria and waved to Aidan, Lucas and Stephanie who were already seated. "I missed you this morning." I kissed Stephanie on the cheek.

"I missed you last night." Stephanie bit her lip slightly. Fuck.

"Are we invisible again?" Lucas rolled his eyes.

"The trip went well then?" Aidan prodded.

"Oh, it was phenomenal," I kissed Stephanie's neck, my body wanting her fiercely.

"Hello? Stop please," Lucas snipped, leaning forward and trying to pull us apart.

"Why can't I kiss my girlfriend?" I retorted.

"Because when you two kiss you don't kiss normally, it's always like you're about to have sex, it's disgusting," Lucas muttered.

"I mean, if you want to watch," I joked and went to kiss Stephanie. Stephanie laughed and pushed me away.

"Guys, we have a party to plan," Aidan announced. "So this Saturday, I've already spread the word. Who's on alcohol?"

"Raphael is on alcohol," Stephanie stated.

"I am so close to fucking your brother, I hope you know that," Aidan winked.

"Foster brother," I corrected. Aidan rolled his eyes.

Chapter 11

"I'm not sure I understand why Stephanie couldn't leave?" the green-eyed lady said slowly.

"They were dangerous people, dangerous people that she loved. You could always see her fighting with herself when she talked about leaving. She knew she had to, part of her was scared, part of her didn't want to lose them, but mostly she was just waiting for Raphael," I replied.

"Did that ever concern you that she felt such loyalty to Raphael?" the brown-haired lady questioned.

"Yes, of course. It would concern anyone, I think. But I knew Stephanie loved me and saying goodbye permanently to the only consistent person in your life would be more difficult than I can imagine. I knew once I stayed and never left her, she would let him go, I think he knew that too." I paused picking at my thumb trying to stop the tears. I rubbed my face feeling utterly exhausted. My emotions a mix of numbness, hatred and pure sadness.

***

The week passed quickly in a barrage of demands from Aidan and Lucas to make this party perfect. As Stephanie's cottage was far, I had no expectation people would drive all that way for free alcohol. But Aidan's idea was different.

Aidan, Lucas and I waited around Aidan's car waiting for

Stephanie to arrive.

The familiar red Toyota pulled up beside us. I got into her car. Aidan was beaming and got into his truck. We began the route to the cottage.

"Raphael has stocked up on alcohol, James stocked up on weed, Jace stocked up on snacks," Stephanie listed.

"Thank God James didn't stock up on snacks. The house would stink of sardines," I joked.

"Have you seen him eat them yet? He takes them and swallows them like a pigeon. Disgusting." Stephanie made a shiver movement. I laughed. "What have you told them about the family?"

"Literally nothing but the fact Raphael is relaxed and not like a parent."

"I'm getting nervous, what if Raphael scares them too? He scared you at first." Stephanie nervously rubbed the steering wheel.

"He scared me because I showed up unannounced and the next morning he offered to take me on a 'hike' with a handgun," I chuckled. "As long as he doesn't do those things, I think we'll be okay."

"God, you must really love me," Stephanie giggled.

"That I do." I looked in the rearview mirror, seeing Aidan's car following closely. We made our way across the jagged roads, then across the dirt roads. We finally pulled into Stephanie's driveway.

"No one is going to make that drive," Stephanie smiled at me, undoing her seatbelt and getting out of the car. Raphael was standing at the doorway looking on as Aidan's vehicle pulled into the driveway. His looming figure accentuated by his long, dark, coat. He turned on his heels and marched into the cottage.

Stephanie and I entered the cottage, followed nervously by Aidan and Lucas.

"Lucas and Aidan," Raphael smiled, tilting his head slightly. "I have heard so much about you."

"I have heard nothing about you," Aidan breathed a laugh.

"The way I like it." Raphael extended his hand.

"This is Raphael, Stephanie's foster brother," I introduced. Aidan and Lucas shook his hand.

"That is James, Eli and Jace." I pointed to each of the men who stood dauntingly by the entrance. Lucas and Aidan waved.

"Who's ready for a party?" Jace yelled. "We have weed, alcohol, do you boys need any condoms?"

"Jace," Raphael shook his head. Jace sighed and walked away to the hangout room. "Make yourself at home," Raphael nodded toward Aidan and Lucas.

"We're going to be over there, if you need anything, give a shout," Eli said to Stephanie and me and left to the hangout room with James.

"I'm going to get changed," Stephanie announced. We all nodded. Raphael watched as she walked away.

"If you would excuse me," Raphael immediately followed her.

"This is going to be sick," Aidan stated.

"Yep," I replied then stepped in Raphael's footprints in curiosity.

"I can literally cancel it right now," Raphael said in a hushed tone. "Are you sure about this?"

"Yes, I'm fine, I promise I'm fine. It's been a while." Stephanie whispered.

"Come get me if you need anything," Raphael murmured. I looked in. Raphael gently lifted Stephanie's chin so her eye contact was meeting his. "Anything," Raphael breathed. I shifted slightly, trying to get a better look at the stares they were giving each other. Raphael's gaze fluttered over to the movement, blinking as he saw me. He stepped back surprised and left through the doorway. "Keep an eye on her." He ordered. I nodded.

"So I was thinking this?" Stephanie held up a black lace bodysuit. "And shorts of course."

"You'll look amazing," I remarked, stepping closer to her. "What was that about?" I gestured to the doorway where Raphael had left.

"Just Raphael being overprotective," she sighed. "Can you close the door? I want to get changed."

There was a knock on the front door. Our first guest. Aidan opened it excitedly, a few people stumbled in. They all immediately went to the kitchen where the drinks were all laid out. Soon enough the cottage was packed full of people.

"I don't get how people find these things enjoyable," Raphael muttered, lighting up a joint. I shrugged.

"Are we supposed to be more involved in it?" Stephanie asked, taking a sip of beer.

"Yes, you two, go have fun." Raphael motioned to the horde. Stephanie pointed across the party to Aidan and Lucas dancing energetically to the music. She grabbed my hands and led me to them. We broke out dancing terribly, losing ourselves in the music and our surroundings. This is why people like parties.

Song after song went by. Stephanie grabbed my arm. Everyone was stumbling drunk. "Do you want to go to our bedroom?" Stephanie whispered loudly. I turned to Aidan and Lucas who gestured for us to go. She grabbed my arm determined

226

to bring me to the bedroom. We opened the door to see a couple already on the bed.

"Let's go," I urged, trying to pull her away from the bedroom. She didn't budge.

"St…" the girl underneath muttered.

"Shh, it's okay," the guy said, undoing his belt while kissing her. I tried to pull Stephanie away again. Stephanie shook me off and moved closer to the bed.

"Get off her," Stephanie hissed.

"Give us some privacy please," the man growled.

"Get off her," Stephanie repeated, trying to push him off.

"Quit it, you bitch. Give us some privacy." The man shoved Stephanie. She immediately reached under her bed.

"Get the fuck off her," Stephanie repeated, putting a handgun to the man's head. I rushed toward her.

"Jesus fuck, I'm going, she wanted this. Fucking psycho," the man huffed as he rushed out of the bedroom.

"Thank you," the girl murmured, her eyes barely opening.

"Hey sweety, did you come here with anyone that can take you home safely?" Stephanie crawled up beside her. The girl curled up into Stephanie.

"L…" She began to speak. She swallowed hard. "Leah."

"Okay, Levi is going to find Leah and bring her here. What is your name?" Stephanie stroked her hair softly.

"Cassandra," the girl whispered. Stephanie nodded toward me. I instinctively left the room and desperately went to the first girl I saw.

"Is your name Leah?" I demanded. She shook her head. "Do you know a Leah?" I asked. She shook her head again. I went to the next girl. "Are you Leah?" She shook her head. "Do you know Leah?" She shook her head again. I felt a hand on my arm

227

and turned around determined to keep searching. Jace stood there.

"We're looking for a Leah?" he questioned.

"That came with a Cassandra," I clarified. He nodded and spread the news to the other guys. I saw Raphael push his way through the party to Stephanie's bedroom. "Are you Leah?" I queried the next woman. She shook her head. "Do you know Leah?" The woman nodded. I sighed in relief. "Can you bring me to her?" I requested. The woman nodded and led me to a girl holding a bottle of water. She looked at me confused. "Are you Leah?" She nodded. "Did you come with a Cassandra?" She nodded.

"Is everything okay?" Leah asked.

"Come with me," I urged. I saw Raphael standing in the kitchen. I nodded to him.

"Everyone get out of my fucking house!" Raphael screamed. I gestured for Leah to continue following me. I led her to Stephanie's bedroom. Leah went in and knelt by the bed. I stood there a few seconds, then decided I would be of more use in crowd control. Most people had already left, leaving Aidan and Lucas looking at Raphael. I walked over. "If you're not my family, you need to fucking leave now," Raphael ordered viciously.

Aidan and Lucas nodded then gestured for me to come with them. Raphael put his arm out to prevent me from leaving. "I said family stays." He looked at me. Aidan and Lucas exchanged a bewildered expression before leaving. Raphael took a deep breath in.

"Are you her brother?" The man who was on top Cassandra growled. Raphael turned around confused. The man took that as a yes. "You need to control that cunt, she just put a gun to my

228

head!" He yelled at Raphael. Raphael took a drag off his joint. Jace, Eli and James stood around this interaction ready to jump in. Raphael got closer to him. "There was no reason for it, put that bitch on a fucking leash." The man turned sharply to leave. Raphael grabbed his arm and spun him back to face him.

"I welcome you to call the police," Raphael voiced calmly. "But I don't think you will, because somewhere in that fucked-up brain of yours you realize that you did something wrong," Raphael hissed, his face inches from the man.

"She wanted me to do it," the man protested.

Raphael stayed silent for a second, taking a long drag on the joint. His glare burning in the man as he exhaled the smoke in his face. Raphael suddenly took the joint and put it out on the man's neck. The man shrieked in agony. "What the fuck," he yelped.

"Did you see anything Jace?" Raphael inquired, not breaking eye contact with the man.

"I saw him asking for it," Jace replied.

"That's what I saw too," Raphael took his gun out of his back pocket. "If I hear any word of you telling what happened just now, or if I hear that you told people anything but the truth that you can't get a woman to fuck you in her sane mind..." Raphael dug his gun into the man's head. "I will blow your fucking head off. Kapeesh?" Raphael snarled. The man nodded. Raphael stepped back. The man quickly sprinted away crying. Raphael rubbed his face.

"FUCK!" he shouted. "Can someone check if the girl is still here?" Raphael rasped. Eli nodded and went off. Raphael fell to his knees looking exasperated. He threw his gun down.

"She left with her friend," Eli announced. Raphael slowly stood up and walked to Stephanie's room. We stood there in silence, before I left to her room. I stood in the doorway looking at Raphael holding her protectively. His eyes closed; his fingers clutched onto her like he was terrified she would collapse. Jace came over and shut the door in front of me.

"Leave it," he whispered to me. Jace began to walk away. I followed him.

"I should be in there with her!" I yelled. Jace turned around and shook his head.

"Leave it," Jace snipped. I followed Jace as he walked back to the living room, he picked up Raphael's gun and placed it on the kitchen counter.

"What was all that?" I demanded, desperately attempting to connect the dots.

"That's a question for Raphael. After." Jace walked upstairs.

I paused in the empty room that had so recently been full of people. I made my way slowly to the hangout room and waited, staring at the turned-off television. It felt wrong to distract myself when she was in her room possibly breaking. I sat there for what felt like hours.

"Come for a walk with me," Raphael commanded. I stood up instantly and we went outside walking out into the forest. A few minutes went by in silence as our feet trampled on the terrain. The sticks cracked and filled the eerie quietness.

"She's sleeping in Eli's room tonight, I'll wash the sheets from her bed," Raphael said quietly.

"What just happened?" I questioned.

"What are you confused by? The fact a man tried to rape a girl in Stephanie's bedroom or the fact a woman would have a strong reaction to it?" Raphael hissed.

He paused.

His expression wavered from anger to sadness before he pulled a joint from his pocket and stopped to light it. "I'm sorry, that was uncalled for." Raphael looked away from me, tears visibly in his eyes. He took a long drag of the joint. Like a man breathing after being suffocated.

"It was a stupid question," I admitted. Raphael nodded. We walked further.

"Fuck," Raphael whimpered wiping a tear from his cheek.

"Are you okay?" I asked, somewhat bewildered by this reaction. The conflict was avoided. No one was harmed.

"Ya, I'm fine." He choked and took another long drag of his joint. He shook his arms trying to compose himself.

"Why…" I started asking. I hesitated but continued despite my mind screaming for me to stop. "Why are you reacting like this?"

"Just always hard seeing her relive it." Raphael stared intently at his joint.

"Relive what?" I demanded.

"Stephanie…" Raphael took a wavering breath in. "I didn't get to her in time," Raphael whispered, like the reality of what happened would be shielded if the trees couldn't hear. My heart sank as I realized what had happened. "I pulled him off her." Raphael faltered. "I swore I would come back to get her; I swore I would protect her."

"She's safe, you did come back for her." I put my hand gently on Raphael's shoulder.

"I should've gotten there sooner." Raphael's voice wavered. "After the hospital, I forced her to go to the police, I sat there and waited as they interrogated her alone like *she* was the criminal. They didn't do shit." Raphael sniveled. "He was the first person I killed. Screamed like a little fucking girl." Raphael's voice became calm, his face turned blank. "The men will drive you home tomorrow morning. They're going to stay at the house until

Stephanie feels okay." Raphael stated.

"Ya, of course," I murmured.

"We should probably head back, can you help me change the sheets?" Raphael asked.

"Yes," I said. We continued to walk in silence until we reached the cottage and immediately stripped the sheets and dressed the bed with visibly different sheets. Raphael said it would be easier that way.

"I'm, uh, I'm sorry about your friends," Raphael gestured to the entrance.

"I'm sure they understood," I replied. Raphael disappeared into the now dark hallway. I looked around her room, then got up and went to the couch to sleep. Eli was on the other side. Neither of us were asleep but we didn't say a word to each other.

I lay there looking at the ceiling until sunlight poured into the cottage. I heard movement as everyone got ready to leave. Eli picked up his bag from beside the couch and walked to the entrance. I pulled myself up and grabbed my bag from the bedroom and proceeded to the door. We all looked at each other and left. We packed into the van without saying anything.

"Did anyone sleep last night?" Jace asked as he drove the vehicle. Everyone mumbled a no. "Neither did I," Jace said, watching the road. "Did anyone have any solid interactions with Raphael? He only came in to tell me I was leaving in the morning," Jace muttered. Everyone mumbled the same. I hesitated.

"We spoke," I announced. Everyone turned and stared at me.

"How was he?" Jace queried.

"Not great."

"Did you get the answers you were looking for?" Jace looked at me in the rearview mirror.

"I did," I looked down at my hands, ashamed I had been pushing for them.

"How are you feeling?" James turned around.

"I'm fine." I looked up.

"You're not fine, none of us are. We all love her and it hurts to see her like that," Jace rubbed his face. We continued on in silence until we reached my house. I got out and waved.

"Aidan called last night worried about you, he said there was an incident last night," mom said, worried.

"Ya, a pretty major one," I replied tiredly. My mom and dad stared at me. "A girl was nearly raped. Stephanie stopped it."

"So no one was hurt?" mom clarified.

"Well not technically," I murmured.

"Then that's good," mom dismissed as she left the room.

"How is Stephanie with this?" dad questioned, softly.

"Raphael told you?" I demanded. Dad nodded. "She's not good." Tears welled in my eyes. My heart clenching as I finally had a second to process. Dad picked up his chair and placed it next to mine, taking me into his arms.

"It's never easy to see someone you love to relive something so horrific," dad stated, stroking my back.

"I just wish I could take it away," I whimpered.

"I know, son," dad squeezed me tightly.

Chapter 12

"So he admitted without alluding to you that he had previously killed someone?" the green-eyed lady asked.

"I mean, yes, but I wouldn't count that as a human," I retorted.

"And he threatened someone in front of you," the brown-haired lady stated.

"Ya, I guess, but he's not the one in the wrong." I snapped. Both ladies stopped writing and looked up at me.

"You came in here saying that he did this, but whenever we draw conclusions that he may be capable of killing someone, you defend him," the green-eyed lady sighed.

"You're right, I'm sorry." I looked down at the plain table.

***

Friday rolled around and there was still no contact from Stephanie. Aidan and Lucas completely ignored the events of the last weekend. The lack of confirmation and speaking about this monumental event made me start to feel like it had never happened. That I had taken some drug and hallucinated the entire thing. There was a firm knock on the door. My mother went to open it as I remained at the kitchen table staring at my dinner.

"Hi, I'm Eli." Eli's voice rang through my home. My head perked up with confusion. I made my way to the door. Eli stood there in his workout gear. "We thought maybe you'd want to train with us."

"Oh, well, we were just having dinner," mom explained.

"I'll be out in a second." I nodded to Eli. Mom shut the door abruptly.

"Who's Eli?" mom demanded.

I ran upstairs.

"He's a friend of Stephanie and Raphael," I called back. I went into my room to change into my workout gear.

"We're eating dinner!" mom protested. I pulled on my workout gear and left my room.

"If Raphael's friends say I should train with them, I'm going to train with them." I looked my mother in her eyes. She recoiled in shock. I could not think of the last time I talked back to my mom. I ran down the stairs.

"Come back and finish your dinner!" dad yelled. I shut the door behind me. Eli and I walked out to the Rover.

"We thought we would send the least intimidating of us," Jace smiled standing at the open driver's door. We all piled into the vehicle and drove a few minutes to a large field.

"Have we heard anything?" I asked.

"Yes, we're heading back up this weekend. Raphael wants you to come." Eli began jogging beside me. I joined, keeping pace with him.

"Is Stephanie okay?"

Eli nodded. "Each time she jumps back quicker," Eli explained. "We lay low and wait for Raphael's signal."

"Okay," I replied. I slowed my pace slightly, beginning to feel out of breath. Eli slowed too.

"Ah, there he goes." Eli gestured to Jace who was running off the field to some young women. "He's enjoying not being in the middle of nowhere." Eli winked at me. I laughed. "Do you have to ask your parents to come up?"

"Ya, I guess."

"Maybe I should have brought a pie or something," Eli muttered to himself.

"I'm sure it'll be fine.".

Jace didn't return for the entire workout. By the end, we were all gasping for breath and covered in sweat.

"Let's get you home, we'll pick you up at seven," James patted me on the arm. At seven? In the morning?

"What about Jace?" I looked around for him, he was nowhere to be seen.

"He can jog back to the house." Eli shrugged, getting in the driver's seat. I understood why Jace always drove. The drive that was supposed to take a few minutes took a few seconds. It was pure mania. I took a breath before entering my house.

"I'm going up to the cottage tomorrow," I shouted from the hallway.

"Again?" mom called after me.

"Yes!" I yelled back from the kitchen as I opened the fridge. I pulled out my carton of eggs and pulled a cup from the cupboard. I cracked the four eggs into the glass. I looked down at the gooey mess and took a deep breath in. It was getting easier, but it was still remarkably unpleasant. I chugged it down as quickly as I could, gagging. I shook my head, put the eggs back in the fridge and went up to sleep.

My alarm went off at seven, I rolled out of bed, threw my clothes on and quickly grabbed my bag. I ran downstairs.

"Breakfast?" dad hollered.

"I'm late!" I responded, sprinting out of the house to see the Rover already there.

"Ah good, we thought we would have to break you out," James mused. We got into the vehicle and drove to the cottage.

Raphael stood at the doorway staring, looming over us. We all got out of the vehicle. Raphael gestured for us to come in. We all stepped around him and into the cottage. My heart pummeled in my chest eager to see Stephanie after what felt like an eternity away from each other. Stephanie walked toward us. Jace picked up Stephanie and spun her around. She wore a loose black crop top and shorts. Jace let her down and she turned to me.

"Hey sexy," she smiled. We embraced. It was nice to feel her warmth again. "I want to go shooting," Stephanie announced, turning to everyone.

"Oh damn, been a bit since we all went out together," Jace grinned, ruffling Stephanie's hair playfully. We all quickly put our stuff back in our rooms and met outside. Raphael and Stephanie were waiting outside whispering to each other. I walked up to them.

"Ah, speak of the devil," Stephanie winked at me jokingly. She kissed me on the lips then looked over my shoulder and darted off. I turned around, seeing Eli carrying a case.

"He's our shooter," Raphael gestured to Eli. Eli said something to Stephanie. Stephanie giggled and pushed him.

"How is she?" I questioned.

"She's great, if she had it her way, you guys would've come back the day after. Thought it was safer for there to be distance for longer," Raphael stated. "Uh, about that night, I shouldn't have taken you on that walk, that was too much to put on you." Raphael began to follow the rest of the family along the trail. Jace had Stephanie on his back now as we began the route.

"Raphael, it's fine, we're family," I commented. Raphael smiled slightly and nodded.

"Raph?" Jace called, turning around and walking toward us with Stephanie still on his back. He began walking backward in front of Raphael and me. "Stephanie was saying you haven't been able to figure out the pharma situation," Jace stumbled slightly.

"The only way I can find is to hack, and none of us are hackers." Raphael gestured to the group.

"Fuck, is this how it feels like to age out of a profession?" Jace joked.

"With the kind of money this job would give, easy retirement if you wanted it," Stephanie said into Jace's ear.

"No way we can do it?" Jace frowned.

"No, we know no one on the inside and I don't know anything about electronics," Raphael responded. Jace shook his head, disappointed.

"We are destined to live a life of poverty, Stephanie," Jace sighed dramatically, placing Stephanie down. "The boy won't get his first billion dollar cut."

"Uh, what corporation is it?" I asked, stopping. Something in my head suddenly clicked.

"Something about birds." Raphael shrugged.

"New Bird Medical Corporation?" I beamed with excitement. Everyone looked at me with confused expressions plastered on their faces. "My uncle works there, in IT."

"No fucking way," Raphael laughed joyously. Jace picked me up and twirled me around.

"My man!" Jace yelled, putting me back down. The other guys came over to investigate. "He gave us an in!" Jace shouted to them.

"I'll call my guy now," Raphael grinned and walked back up the trail a bit.

"Billions?" I asked Stephanie. She nodded. "Yes!" I screamed. I grabbed Stephanie, wrapping my arms tightly around her.

"We're gonna be billionaires," she giggled, doing a little happy dance.

"Ya we are!" Jace shrieked. All the men were hugging each other and giving high fives. Stephanie was just looking in my eyes. Her hand gently caressed my face.

"Give this man a reward tonight Stephanie!" Jace shouted abruptly, hitting my arm. It broke Stephanie's trance with me as she rolled her eyes.

"Go." Raphael looked at the group and gestured for them to leave us. Everyone immediately obeyed. "We split everything we get equally, no one gets hurt, no one gets caught. You eat, breathe and fuck thinking about this job. This comes first."

"I don't think Stephanie will like that very much," I joked.

"She'll be doing the same," Raphael stated, unimpressed. I nodded looking forward. We reached the clearing and everyone spread out. Eli set himself up excitedly. Within seconds the noise became deafening. Stephanie passed me her handgun. She stood beside me and watched me shoot.

"You're tilting to the right, keep everything straight." She straightened my hand. I shot a few more times. I hit the target all in the same place but very off-centered. She looked over my right shoulder and readjusted my stance gently. She nodded to me. I shot again, hitting the target straight on. "Straight feet, straight hips, straight arms, straight hands," she reminded. I glanced over at her. Her body was so close. I dropped my arms and kissed her, wrapping my free arm around her. She melted into me instantly. I heard a click and felt something at the back of my head. I released her and slowly put my arms up.

"Shoot," Raphael ordered.

"Put the gun down, Raphael, it's not funny," Stephanie urged.

"Shoot!" Raphael bellowed. My heart raced. I tried to steady my breath as I raised my arms to shoot. They shook as I released the safety. I shot a few times. Nothing hit the target. "Focus on shooting until panic doesn't affect you," Raphael spat in my ear. Stephanie grabbed the gun and pointed it at Raphael.

"Shoot," she ordered. Raphael looked at her, then raised his left arm and shot three times. All of them hit the target in the center.

"Where's my kiss?" Raphael snarled mockingly. He walked off to Eli. Stephanie shot the target multiple times out of frustration. They all hit dead center, all going into the same small hole.

"Let's go back to the cottage," Stephanie grumbled.

"No, I want to practice," I replied. Everyone gradually headed back. I continued until darkness enveloped me.

"You're going to use up all our bullets," Eli joked. I turned in shock, I thought everyone had left. Eli put his hands up. "Please don't point that at me," Eli muttered, grabbing the gun from my hand and putting the safety on. He placed it in his back pocket.

"Sorry," I muttered.

"Use this, it's better," Eli passed me another gun. "It'll have a different feel."

"Thanks." I took off the safety and shot, my bullet didn't hit the target. I shot a few more times.

"Slow down," Eli chuckled. I looked over. "Watch where the bullets go and correct. It's not about getting it right the first time, it's about knowing how to correct," Eli instructed.

I nodded. I shot and altered it slightly and shot again. The bullet hit the edge of the target. I looked over, excited. I returned my focus to the target and lost it.

Eli laughed. "Man, relax." Eli took the gun from my hands. "Shake yourself out. You're too stiff, you're not allowing yourself to be comfortable. Harder for your body to learn when your mind is controlling it. Shake." Eli placed the gun in his pocket and shook out his arms jumping up and down. I followed suit. Eli passed me the gun back. I shot at the target, then altered and shot again. I hit the side of the target. I smiled at Eli and turned back to the target, shooting again. It hit close to the center. I shot again. It hit dead center. I laughed joyously. "There we are." Eli patted me on the back. I shot again, dead center. "Now you know how to correct," Eli announced.

"Holy shit, thanks." I put on the safety and passed it back to Eli, quickly wiping down my fingerprints. I looked down, noticing he was wearing gloves.

"What I do." Eli took the gun from me and placed it in his back pocket. We turned and began to walk back.

"Raphael said you were the shooter of the group," I commented.

"That I am."

"Can I ask you a question?" I asked. Eli nodded. "They call you the puppy because you barely talk to anyone but Stephanie. Why are you here?"

"Why am I a part of the family if I'm not a fan of everyone in it?" Eli clarified.

"Ya."

"I joined for Stephanie, have to put up with the others to be around her." Eli shrugged.

"I thought you weren't interested in her?" I muttered,

attempting to hide my nerves.

"Doesn't mean I wouldn't give everything to protect her."
Eli looked over at me.

"Protect her?" I stopped.

"There's a lot to hurt you in this profession," Eli laughed.

"Ya," I sighed. We continued to walk back to the cottage, filling the silence with small talk. I walked into the house. Raphael instantly walked to me. Eli disappeared to his room.

"You need to tell your parents you're thinking of going into IT, make it their idea to visit your uncle's work. We don't have much time, so we need to be careful," Raphael instructed. "Your job is to get us in the building, the rest will be up to us."

"My uncle won't be killed, right?"

"No, we'll bring in guns, but they'll be used as a defense if any security guards or police come by. Your uncle won't be harmed." Raphael looked me in the eyes. "You have my word."

"Okay," I nodded. "Please stop putting guns to my head."

"It's too fun," Raphael chuckled. I walked over to Stephanie who leaned on the counter in the kitchen drinking a beer. I pulled her into me, locking our lips together as I shoved my tongue in her mouth. Stephanie pulled away and set her beer down.

"Let's go to our room," she breathed. I followed her obediently. We walked into her room, she closed the door gently behind her.

Stephanie removed her clothing and laid down on the bed. My eyes followed her, gliding over her body. My heart quickened, completely entranced and my blood rushing to my growing erection. She looked at me and moved one hand to her breast, the other one continued lower, her fingers beginning to massage herself. My breath caught as I watched her, our eyes locked. It was impossible to break her intoxicating eye contact. I

242

took off my clothing, my stare unwavering. I stepped until I could see in between her legs.

I dropped to my knees, my mouth gliding up her thigh until I reached her. I gave her a quick peck, Stephanie groaned in frustration. I chuckled before quickly darting my tongue between her cleanly shaven lips. Her wetness coating my tongue as I continued the same movements she made with her fingers. Breaking it up by adding light suction. I shoved my middle finger into her without warning. Stephanie gasped with pleasure as her body melted into me, her body shivering at the unexpected intrusion. I stroked her slowly and deeply, my tongue not letting up from its attack on her clit. . She squirmed with pleasure. It didn't take long before she moaned loudly and her body convulsed as she climaxed. I licked her one final time, pulling out my finger.

I put on the condom quickly and got on top of her. Pushing into her inch by inch, watching her eyes plead for it. Her hips moving to take more of me. I paused, enjoying her desperation. Stephanie impatiently grabbed my ass, yanking me until the entirety of my length was inside her. Her eyes rolled back in ecstasy. I began to pound into her with fury, my confidence at an all-time high.

"Fuck," she whimpered. I grabbed her ass with my left hand, holding her slightly up. Stephanie's moans increased. Her chest heaved, her eyes firmly on me, begging for me to continue. I was completely at her mercy, focusing my movements to give her the release she needed, the release she was pleading for. Stephanie clutched onto me. "Fuck, fuck, fuck, fuck," Stephanie gasped as she climaxed, her nails completely tearing into me. The slight pain sent me over the edge. I grunted loudly as I finished, pounding her deeply.

I lay beside her. "That was amazing," she muttered.

"It was," I panted.

"Where do you want to go with our billions of dollars?" Stephanie rolled over to face me, her fingers gliding along my chest.

"Antarctica," I replied.

Stephanie laughed. "Too cold," she smiled. I loved that smile.

"Cuba?" I offered.

"Too hot."

"Okay, Ms. Picky." I trailed my fingers along the side of her face. "What about Denmark?" I pushed her hair behind her ear. "We get a little colorful house on the coastline, maybe get some sheep..." I began, watching her reaction closely. "Maybe have some kids, grow old."

"You're so cheesy," Stephanie giggled. "It's perfect." She curled up next to me. "I want to have dinner with your parents," she whispered. I nodded. "Did you enjoy your extra shooting?"

"Ya, Eli gave me some pointers. Hit the target dead center," I smiled proudly at her. Stephanie sat up on her elbow and looked at me in surprise.

"Eli taught you how to shoot?" Stephanie demanded.

"Ya, why?"

"He hates teaching people how to shoot." Stephanie lay back down.

"Guess I'm special," I smirked at her.

"I fucking guess," Stephanie smiled at me. "He doesn't like many people. But I guess you're very likable." Stephanie grinned, kissing my fingers lovingly.

I woke up to light coming into the room. I smiled to see Stephanie still asleep. I stroked her arm gently and kissed it, cuddling her tightly. She groaned slightly and scooched her body back closer to me. I saw a smile form on her face. She fell soundly back asleep. I lay there enjoying this moment.

There was suddenly a piercing bang. I jumped up. Stephanie ran and grabbed a robe and her gun. I put on my pants and ran out. Eli was standing there with a gun in his hand, a silencer elongated the barrel. It was pointed to the kitchen table which was on its side. He shook his head. Jace passed him another gun.

"What the fuck is going on?" Raphael ran in behind us, in nothing but his briefs, holding his handgun.

"It's going to happen inside, I want a quiet gun," Eli explained. He shot the next gun, a splitting bang echoed through the room as the bullet hit the table. He shook his head. Jace passed him the next one.

"Why the fuck are you doing it at six in the morning?" Raphael snarled.

"Quieter." Eli shrugged.

"That's how it's meant to be!" Raphael yelled. Eli shot his next gun and nodded. Eli paid no attention to Raphael. He was with his one true love, his gun. "A bunch of fucking lunatics." Raphael stormed off back to his room. Stephanie giggled.

"I thought the guns were just for defense," I whispered to Stephanie, wrapping my arms around her from behind.

"We don't want our defense to alert every human in the city," she replied, leaning her head against me. I nodded and kissed her gently on the neck.

"I love you," I whispered to her.

"I love you, too," she replied, pulling my arms tighter.

"Do you think they know that those bullets are just going through the kitchen table?"

"I do, yes," she laughed. "They'll fix any damage." She

pulled away to start coffee. Eli shot again.

"We have the winner, good weight, better sound." Eli tossed it back and forth from one hand to the other.

"Either that or you've gone deaf," I smiled. Eli grinned and gave me the finger.

"I'm going to get dressed," Stephanie said to me and walked down the hallway.

"You sure?" Jace shouted out after her. Stephanie turned around and gave him the finger.

"Today's a big day for you." Raphael came out of the hallway, putting his shirt on.

"Are you going to take his virginity?" James joked, coming into the room. Eli and Jace laughed. Raphael put his finger up without breaking eye contact with me. The room silenced.

"You're going to get us in," Raphael stated. He broke eye contact and went to the coffee machine.

"What? Today, today?" I demanded, turning toward him. There was no way.

"The robbery isn't today." Raphael poured his coffee. "You're going to get in with your uncle. By the end of this week, I expect an answer to all of these questions." Raphael passed me a folded piece of paper. I opened it up.

"What if he doesn't want to answer some of these?" I murmured, looking at the daunting list.

"He needs to." Raphael took a sip of coffee. I nodded slowly, putting the questions into my back pocket.

Chapter 13

"Okay, can you speak more on how your relationship was with Raphael at this point?" the green-eyed lady asked.

"We were family," I responded.

"He put a gun to your head," the brown-haired lady commented.

"Whenever he was aggressive, I felt like I needed to prove myself to him," I replied.

"And how was your relationship with Stephanie?" the green-eyed lady clarified.

"Perfect." I smiled to myself.

***

Stephanie and I pulled into my driveway. She put the car in park and smiled at me. "Are you nervous?"

"Kind of," I responded.

"Just keep your eyes on the prize." She undid her seatbelt and set her hand gently on my face. "You and me, never having to work, just together." She beamed at me.

"How could I forget that prize?" I laughed and kissed her, my hand running through her hair. I undid my seatbelt and leaned in further, my fingers gliding up her body. There was a loud bang at the driver's side window. I jumped and Stephanie instinctively reached for her gun. I grabbed her hand, preventing her from pulling it out as I looked up seeing my dad hovering over the window. Stephanie took a breath in and slowly released it. She unrolled her window.

"Hello, Mr. Davis," Stephanie smiled politely at him.

"Hello, Stephanie, I didn't mean to scare you two.Just thought I would come out and ask when you would like to come over for dinner with us. We thought as you're getting..." dad paused gesturing to the vehicle "...closer to my son, that we should get closer to you," dad laughed awkwardly then his smile faded. "Not in the same way, of course."

"Ya, of course. What about Thursday?" she smiled.

"Thursday it is, let's say six?" dad suggested. Stephanie nodded in agreement. Dad slowly walked away.

"Oh my God, that was so embarrassing, I'm so sorry." I put my face in my hands.

"No, it's sweet," Stephanie said reassuringly. "Always nice to know your boyfriend's parents don't want to fuck you."

"Shut up, please," I groaned.

"Tell me how tonight goes." She grinned and kissed me on the cheek. I got out of the vehicle and went into my house.

"I hear Stephanie's coming over on Thursday," mom called over from the kitchen table. I walked in, my dad sat there eating lunch. "It will be nice to know more about this young lady."

"Ya, she's excited to come over," I grabbed a bag of chips and sat down at the table.

"When do you think her brother can come over?" dad asked.

"Foster brother," I clarified. "Raphael likes that distinction."

"Why?" dad gave me a confused look.

"I don't know, they didn't grow up together or anything. Probably doesn't want to lump her in with his actual family. He didn't like them much." I shrugged.

"Okay, when do you think her foster brother would like to

248

come over?" dad asked.

"I don't know, like Stephanie said, he's not really the 'dinner' type." I ate a few chips.

"Your dad and I are worried, you've been spending a lot of time with him and Stephanie and, frankly, his friends look and seem dangerous. We don't want you hanging out with the wrong crowd," mom said as she reached out her hand and put it on mine.

"Okay, I'll ask him," I promised. My mother nodded, pleased with herself.

"Are you using protection with Stephanie?" dad blurted.

"Oh my God! Stop!" I groaned, leaning back into my chair, covering my face.

"Sweetheart, being sexually active isn't a bad thing," mom smiled.

"You can always come to us if you have any questions." Dad took mom's hand in his.

"I don't have any questions." I felt like shriveling up.

"Do you need us to buy condoms for you?" dad offered. Make this stop.

"No, we're using protection. I am able to buy condoms on my own," I stated.

"If you feel embarrassed asking us, your dad puts them—" mom started.

"No. Stop this," I whined, shaking my head. "Can we please change the topic?" I asked. My parents nodded. "I've been thinking of majors."

"And what are you thinking of changing it to?" My mom asked sweetly.

"Something with computers, I think I would enjoy it and there's a lot of money in it." I rubbed the back of my neck, nervous about whether they would take the bait.

"Oh well, your uncle's an engineer, do you want me to call him?" mom jumped up, excitedly. "I always thought you had a mind for computers."

"I'm happy you're thinking of future careers," dad said sincerely.

"I would love it if you called him, maybe he can give me some insight." I nodded. My mom overjoyed, sprung to action dialing his number. She left to the other room.

"What if you brought him to your work?" I overheard her saying. "Thursday could work, we do have a guest coming over... ya, Levi's girlfriend... it seems pretty serious, he seems to spend every waking minute with her... ya, she can pick him up after... we're still trying to get the brother to come over, they keep saying he's not a dinner person..." My mom laughed. "I'll keep that in mind... ya, okay, I'll tell Levi... yes, five thirty on Thursday, I got it. Okay, great, bye." My mom walked back over to the kitchen table. "Thursday at five thirty, Stephanie can pick you up after and you guys can come back here," mom beamed.

"That's great, thanks mom," I stood up and hugged her tightly.

"How was your weekend, guys?" Stephanie and I sat down with Aidan and Lucas. Aidan and Lucas looked at each other surprised.

"You're back," Lucas said nervously.

"I bet your weekend was better than mine, my parents gave me a sex talk." I quickly changed the topic. Lucas and Aidan laughed.

"Oh, I'm jealous, I never got a sex talk," Stephanie pouted.

"Okay, Stephanie," Aidan reached out his hands. Stephanie looked at me confused then held his hands. "Sex is when a human being and another human being love each other very much."

"Okay, I'm out," Stephanie laughed. "Did you tell them we're waiting until marriage, I don't want them to think I'm a whore," Stephanie joked.

"I think you waved that goodbye when we made out in my driveway and my mother said, and I quote, 'that was quite the kiss,'" I mocked.

"Why do parents feel the need to comment on that stuff," Aidan said, disgusted.

"My parents gave me a book." Lucas shrugged. "It was actually useful."

"Wait, was I your first? Does Lily not exist?" Stephanie blurted.

"No, they're years too late," I laughed.

"You were my first, now you have to marry me," Stephanie said, holding in a laugh.

"I know that's a lie and I will, but not under false pretenses." I leaned toward her and began tickling her.

"Okay, it's a lie, it's a lie!" she shrieked with laughter.

"My parents sat me down for like an hour and went through everything in excruciating detail. Even used themselves as examples," Aidan voiced pitifully. We all faked gagging.

"What's everyone's number?" I asked at the table. Watching Stephanie closely.

"One," Lucas announced proudly. Aidan held up a zero.

"Three-hundred and thirty-two," Stephanie joked.

"You whore!" I gasped playfully.

"Does sex where the guy really sucked count? Cause I don't think it should," Stephanie giggled.

"It counts or I have none," Lucas replied. Stephanie nodded.

"Okay, um fourteen."

"Well done," Aidan gave her a high five.

"Have you made anyone cry while having sex with them?" I asked.

"No?"

"I was just checking to see if it was a family trait," I laughed. "Her foster brother made a girl cry during sex."

"No way!" Aidan murmured.

"Oh, Jace told me about that, he told her she was 'too ugly to finish to.' Jace apparently was quite traumatized," Stephanie giggled.

"Your brother is so cool," Lucas praised.

"Jace told you? You weren't there?" I clarified.

"No, uh, Raphael kicked me out for a bit," Stephanie nodded slowly. "Anyway, what's your number, mystery man?" Stephanie nudged my arm.

"Three," I replied.

"Oh, you player!" she mocked.

"Well I plan on not increasing it, so you'll have to live with a three." I leaned in to kiss her.

"Ew," Aidan complained. I put up my finger toward them and pressed my lips against hers.

"I have to get to class," Stephanie pulled away and whispered. I nodded.

"Bye, Stephanie!" Lucas yelled. Stephanie waved and left.

"You guys seem serious," Aidan stated cautiously.

"We are," I smiled.

"You and her brother seem close," Aidan continued.

"Foster brother," I corrected.

"We've just noticed you've changed a lot, you haven't been hanging out with us, you've been working out constantly…" Aidan started.

"I'm sorry I haven't been hanging out with you guys that much, I've just been spending a lot of time with Stephanie," I replied.

"There's nothing wrong with that, it's just odd, her brother—" Aidan began.

"Foster brother," I corrected again.

"Her foster brother called you family," Aidan observed.

"You're even starting to dress like him," Lucas added.

"Have you joined a gang? I mean, we'll support you, we just want to know if this is… dangerous," Aidan uttered.

"I'm not part of a gang," I laughed.

"No, you've just joined a group of strong men, and Stephanie, who live in a mansion of a cottage in the middle of nowhere. You know about his sex life. The first time we were there we found a grate—" Lucas listed.

"The grate has been taken care of," I interrupted.

"It was still there," Lucas snapped. I nodded. "We just want to know you're safe."

"I am, it's just some people who don't have parents who have made their own family," I explained.

"But you do have a family and you have us," Aidan contended.

"I know, I promise it's not like that, I am not part of any gang or mafia or whatever," I promised.

"Okay," Aidan affirmed. "You know you can call us, literally whenever," Aidan concluded. I nodded. "Good," Aidan smiled.

"Why don't we go to my house tonight and chill," I offered. Aidan and Lucas agreed.

We all met up at the end of the day and walked back to my house.

"How are your classes going?" I asked.

"Range from boring to hell," Lucas whined.

"Same, I hate them all," Aidan replied.

"Why don't you change majors?" I queried. They looked at me.

"What will that do? We'll end up in the same career anyway," Lucas stated pessimistically. I shrugged.

"Are you changing majors?" Aidan demanded. I shook my head. I stopped. In my driveway, there was a black Maserati. My heart started beating quickly. Did someone find out? "Did you get a new car? It's so fucking cool!" Aidan exclaimed, excitedly. I shook my head slowly.

"There you are, I've been waiting for a while," Raphael frowned, stepping out of the car. "We're going for a drive."

"I already have plans, Raphael," I smiled.

"Yes, plans to go for a drive with me," he retorted. "Get in, I can drop your friends off." Raphael got in the car. I sighed. Aidan and Lucas looked at me disappointed. I gestured to get in the car.

"Is this new?" Aidan questioned, getting into the back seat. I got into the passenger seat and Lucas went to the back.

"New to me, in great shape though," Raphael responded. Raphael wore leather gloves, sunglasses and his typical long coat.

"Sick man, when did you get it?" Lucas slowly stroked the seats and looked carefully at the interior.

"This morning," Raphael grinned looking in the rearview mirror. "Put one of their addresses in." Raphael turned on the car and pulled out of the driveway. He reached in his pocket, pulling out his iPhone.

"What's your password?" I asked.

"Just point it at me," Raphael replied. I did so. He looked at the phone and unlocked it.

"I now have complete control over your life," I joked, gesturing to the unlocked phone. "I can fuck it all up."

"Would be thrilled to see you try," Raphael laughed. "You've been keeping up with your exercises?"

"He's been working out consistently," Lucas put in. Raphael nodded approvingly.

"How have you boys been finding school?" Raphael inquired, sounding like he was talking to toddlers.

"We're fine," Aidan retorted.

"I hope there are no hard feelings for the party," Raphael voiced.

"No, we get it," Lucas replied.

"If I can do anything to make it better, I can get you anything you want, weed, cocaine, condoms," Raphael smiled.

"Jesus fucking Christ, Raphael, please don't offer them illegal drugs," I scolded. "He's not a drug dealer."

"No, but I know many," Raphael put in quickly.

"They don't want cocaine. You don't even do cocaine!" I argued.

"Ya, I don't need anything to make me more energetic, I'm an Energizer bunny," Raphael joked.

"Okay, stop," I groaned.

"Your friends are cooler than you," Raphael sighed. "Come on boys, anything you want?" He looked in the rearview mirror encouragingly. Raphael's phone began to buzz, I looked down to see Stephanie's name.

"Stephanie's calling." I showed him the phone.

"Ignore it, she knows I'm with you. Probably why she's calling," Raphael stated. Aidan and Lucas spoke among themselves.

"Can we ask you a few questions?" Aidan announced.

"I am an open book," Raphael responded.

"How do you get women to have sex with you?" Aidan demanded. I threw my hands up in disbelief.

"He's not the one you should be asking that!" I turned around to look at my friends.

"I have an answer lined up, but would you rather take this one Aphrodite?" Raphael mocked.

"Shut up Levi, let him answer," Lucas begged.

"First of all, you don't get women to sleep with you. You want women to be *trying* to sleep with you, not something you have to conquer." Raphael raised his first finger. "Confidence speaks louder than looks, but that doesn't mean be an asshole. Just stand up straight, confidence works best when you're not demeaning. Last but not least, my words to live by, don't have sex with people unless you want to. Don't let other people get in your head about it, it won't end well."

"Is that when you made a girl cry?" Aidan questioned.

"Did you tell him that?" Raphael mused. I nodded. "Yes, I was not over someone, my friends kept telling me to move on and fuck someone else. I tried to, I was an asshole and made her cry."

"Why did you kick Stephanie out?" Lucas demanded. Raphael's smile quickly faded.

"Now that's a question to ask me when I'm high or drunk," Raphael murmured. He stretched out uncomfortably. "Uh, the long and short of it is we had a terrible fight. I was an asshole and said some really shitty things to her. She in return did something shitty to me. I couldn't handle it, so I kicked her out. It took me a while to get her forgiveness. We were younger, a bit too much freedom and a bit too dramatic." Raphael nodded to himself satisfied with his answer. He pulled the car up to the curb beside Lucas's driveway. "Do you want to try to drive the car?" Raphael turned to Lucas.

"No fucking way," Lucas exclaimed, pure excitement on his face. Raphael nodded. Lucas got out of the car at lightning speed. Raphael got out and walked to the passenger side. I got out of the car.

"Stephanie will have the same answer as me," Raphael asserted quietly to me as we stood outside the passenger side. "No need to bring back those emotions." Raphael shook his head. I nodded. "Good." He sat in the passenger side and I retreated to the back seat. "Do you know how to drive?"

"Yes?" Lucas replied, unsure.

"Okay, do you know which one is the gas, and which one is the brake?" Raphael asked. Lucas nodded. "Okay, press on the brake and put the car in drive." Raphael gestured to the gear shift. Lucas nodded and did it. "Okay, now release the brake," Raphael instructed gently. Lucas did so.

"Wow! Guys, are you seeing this? I'm driving a Maserati!" Lucas screamed in delight as we went about two miles an hour.

"Lucas, slow down before you get a speeding ticket," Aidan laughed. Lucas continued on for a while.

"Okay, now press the brake," Raphael instructed. The car abruptly halted. "Put it in park." Raphael ordered. Lucas obeyed. We all got out of the car. "I can swing around and drop you back," Raphael offered. We all turned to see Lucas's house not far away.

"I think we're good," Aidan replied.

"Am I not dropping you back?" Raphael clarified.

"No, I'll just stay here," Aidan responded. Aidan and Lucas

began walking back to Lucas's house. I got in the passenger side again.

"Where are we going?" I turned and asked.

"To our target," Raphael grinned at me, closing his door. Raphael's phone went off again.

"It's Stephanie." I showed Raphael his phone again.

"Ignore it," Raphael responded, focusing on the road. "How did the conversation go?"

"I am meeting my uncle at work on Thursday, Stephanie is going to pick me up," I replied.

"Did you make it their idea?" Raphael looked over at me. I nodded. "Excellent, well done. We don't have long to pull this off. Are you ready?"

"I am," I affirmed. Raphael nodded. "My mom and dad want to have you over for dinner."

"No fucking way," Raphael laughed.

"They're scared I'm falling into a bad crowd."

"No, you're falling into your rightful family," Raphael scoffed. I smiled. "Wait, actually…"

"What, I've been kicked out of the family?"

"No, that's a good alibi. Ya, we'll organize it."

"Okay, they'll be thrilled. Just uh, no guns."

"Well, there goes my dinner game of Russian roulette." Raphael rolled his eyes. He pulled into the parking lot of the building. "So this is it." Raphael sighed.

"This is it."

"Okay, when you go in I want you to—" Raphael started. Raphael's phone began ringing. I showed him that it was Stephanie. "Put it on speaker."

"Jesus fucking Christ, Raphael, why were you ignoring my calls?" Stephanie yelled angrily through the phone.

"We were with Levi's friends," Raphael explained.

"I think he won Lucas over," I announced.

"Oh and how is that?" Stephanie asked, irritation running through her voice.

"He let him drive the Maserati," I laughed. There was a long pause.

"Raphael, wipe his fingerprints off, it's not funny," Stephanie scolded. I looked at Raphael confused.

"Urg, you're no fun," Raphael frowned. He lifted up his shirt and began to wipe the steering wheel.

"Is he doing it?" Stephanie asked.

"Yes," I responded. "Did you steal this car?"

"Well, I'm not gonna drive my own car to stake the place we're going to hit." Raphael began rubbing the gear shift and sat back up straight. "I'm bringing it back, they probably won't even notice," Raphael muttered. "Okay, we have a normal entrance, looks like two swinging doors to get in. There's another set after so I'm thinking there's a buzzer. Five cameras, only one pointing at the door, two pointing away and two at the corners of the building. The lights are still on up on the sixth floor and a few on the fourth," Raphael listed. He paused and leaned back thinking.

"Is that all?" Stephanie asked unimpressed.

"Well I can't really crash the car into the building to get information now can I?" Raphael retorted. "If there's security, you better be banking that they enjoy a show."

"I don't think Levi would be too thrilled with that," Stephanie replied.

"You and Levi of course," he responded. "Just something to distract them from the cameras."

"What do you mean?" I asked.

"He wants us to have public sex in front of the cameras,"

Stephanie explained.

"It's effective." Raphael shrugged. "Okay, we have someone leaving. They use their pass to get out. The doors will need to be propped open for the entirety of it."

"And how should we do that?" Stephanie probed.

"That's for Levi to figure out." Raphael looked at me. "He'll get a better look at the door. Oh, look at that." Raphael chuckled.

"What?" Stephanie asked.

"A drug dealer is coming to the building." Raphael pointed to a man getting off his bike.

"How do you know he's a drug dealer?" I queried.

"Tattoos, backpack and on a bike," Raphael muttered, intrigued with what was unfolding in front of him. A man came out of the building, propping the door open with his foot. He and the drug dealer looked both ways before completing their transaction. "There's no security."

"How do you know that?" I asked.

"He's literally standing right under a camera. Pay attention." Raphael shook his head at me.

"It's his first time, relax," Stephanie sighed.

"I wasn't this stupid on my first time," Raphael replied.

"You chose to take him, I asked to go," Stephanie commented. He wanted to take me? I smiled proud of myself.

"Oh wipe that smile off your face, it's only because you're going in on Thursday."

"If that were the reason you could have still taken me," Stephanie pointed out.

"And deal with two people who don't know how to shut up? No thank you." Raphael abruptly opened the door. "Hey!" he screamed. The drug dealer began to run away. "Come here!" Raphael shouted. The man looked over. Raphael gestured for him to come over. The drug dealer did this slowly, not sure if he was being set up. He reached in his bag. "Me and my, uh, boyfriend are looking for a good time, what do you have?"

The drug dealer looked into the vehicle. "You're together?" The drug dealer asked.

"Ya, I know he's out of my league." I shrugged. The drug dealer nodded.

"What do you have?" Raphael repeated.

"I have some weed?" The drug dealer offered.

"No, come on, I have weed at home, any cocaine, ecstasy?" Raphael questioned. "Meth?"

"Ya, I have meth and cocaine." The drug dealer replied.

"Okay, how much?" Raphael asked.

"Two fifty for an ounce," the drug dealer replied.

"Okay, an ounce of each. Sweety, could you hand me the wallet in the glove compartment?" Raphael asked. The drug dealer looked around unsteadily. I opened the glove compartment to find a massive stack of one hundred dollar bills. I leaned out and passed it to him. The drug dealer's eyes opened wide. "How much to know how often you come and sell to that man?"

"What's that to you?" The drug dealer grumbled.

"We're uh—" Raphael hesitated as he thought.

"We're looking for a third," I called out. "He's exactly our type."

"Ya, uh, we were hoping you could make an introduction next time we're around. So is it like, a weekly thing or a daily thing?" Raphael demanded.

"I'm not going to tell you that," the drug dealer scoffed.

"What if I bought you out of everything you have on you," Raphael suggested.

"Okay," the drug dealer nodded.

"How much?"

"Five grand," the drug dealer responded. Raphael began counting out the money. "Or maybe you give me everything you have and I keep my stuff." The drug dealer pulled out a knife. Raphael gave him an unimpressed glare. He grabbed the drug dealer's hand that held his knife and pulled him closer, using his right palm to hit him on the nose.

"I was trying to be nice," Raphael sighed. The drug dealer stood back holding his bleeding nose. Raphael took his gun out. "You tell me how many times you come here, you give me that bag and, because I'm feeling generous, I'll still give you the five grand and I'll let you live."

"I come here every day," the drug dealer whimpered. Raphael nodded, grabbing the drug dealer's backpack and tossing it to me. Raphael finished counting out the five grand.

"Pleasure doing business with you." Raphael passed him the cash and got in the car.

"Your boyfriend's a psycho!" The drug dealer yelled.

"I know!" I shouted back. Raphael shut the door, turned the vehicle on and drove off.

"So now that you've dated both of us, who is better, me or Raphael?" Stephanie's voice rang out. I jumped, having forgotten she was on the phone.

"Obviously me, I just bought him five grand worth of drugs," Raphael joked. "He was such an asshole!" Raphael complained.

"Why did you give him the five grand?" I chuckled.

"We want him alive. If he's a runner and he loses five grand worth of drugs, he's not going to be running very fast anymore." Raphael turned to me. "What's in the goody bag?" Raphael gestured to the bag. I unzipped it and found bags of various items.

"I literally have no idea," I replied. "A lot of white, oh there's weed."

"I'm thinking of a pre-heist drug fest," Stephanie joked.

"That is the worst idea I've ever heard come out of your mouth."

"Where am I picking you up from, Raphael? Same place?" Stephanie asked.

"Yes, I'll call you closer to the time," Raphael answered. The phone hung up. Raphael took the phone from me and put it in his coat. We drove back to my house. Raphael pulled into the driveway and got out of the car with me.

"What are you doing?" I demanded.

"I think it's time for me to properly introduce myself." Raphael shrugged. We walked up to the door. Raphael knocked politely. Mom opened the door in her dressing gown. "Hello, Mrs. Davis, I'm sorry for disturbing you. I'm just bringing your son back."

"Oh, Stephanie's brother?" mom asked, confused. My dad stepped behind her.

"Foster brother. I wanted to properly introduce myself, my name is Raphael Carter." Raphael stuck out his hand. Both my parents shook it slowly.

"Oh, I'm sorry, Levi did tell me you preferred that. Come on in!" Mom and dad stood off to the side. Raphael entered slowly, looking around the house.

"You have a beautiful home," Raphael charmed. Mom gestured to the kitchen table. Raphael sat down.

"Do you want a beer?" Dad asked.

"I would love one," Raphael cooed. Dad went to the fridge and passed one to Raphael. "So, Stephanie and Levi seem quite taken with each other," Raphael gestured to me. I slowly sat down next to him, somewhat taken aback by the 'father of the year' act he was putting on.

"Yes, they certainly are," dad chuckled.

"You don't seem much older than Stephanie," mom stated.

"No, there's not much of an age difference. We met a year before I aged out of foster care. I promised her I would come back and we would be our own family. So that's what happened," Raphael explained. My parents nodded slowly.

"And what do you do?" dad asked.

"I'm a contract worker, mostly construction," Raphael lied without even a flinch.

"Honest work," My dad nodded respectfully.

"It pays the bills," Raphael smiled.

"So are Stephanie and Levi in the same year? He doesn't tell us anything," mom leaned forward, eager to hear all of the gossip.

"No, Stephanie's actually in first year, she took a few years to decide what she wanted to do. Originally, she thought she would work with me, but then she fell in love with history." Raphael shrugged.

"Well Levi may be beginning again, he's been thinking of going into something with computers." Dad gestured to me.

"Well, I selfishly would be glad of that, he has been such a great influence on Stephanie," Raphael patted my shoulder.

"He has?" mom asked with a bewildered expression plastered on her face. Thanks, Mom.

"Oh yes, they're always studying. I'm always trying to get them to go for walks, or out to dinner, to have fun, but they just keep studying." Raphael shot my mom a smile. My mom beamed with pride. "I'm just happy she has a consistent person in her life, nice to see her opening up to someone."

"That is great news," my dad nodded.

"I keep telling Stephanie that we should have a big family dinner." Raphael sighed.

"We have been saying the same thing!" Mom exclaimed. "What about this Thursday?"

"Oh, I can't this Thursday, I have a work thing," Raphael responded. "What about next Thursday?"

"Well that sounds wonderful, I insist you and Stephanie must come here. Let's say six p.m.?" mom suggested.

"That sounds perfect," Raphael grinned. "I have taken enough of your time, it was very nice formally meeting you," Raphael said sincerely. He shook my mom and dad's hands then left, the door shutting behind him.

"He seems lovely, what do you mean he's not the dinner type?" Mom glared at me.

"Stephanie told me he wasn't." I shrugged, passing the blame.

"So what were you up to tonight?" mom asked.

"Raphael just wanted to take my friends and I out in his new car." I got up.

"That's very nice of him," dad commented.

"He's a nice guy," I replied, heading up the stairs to my room.

Chapter 14

"So Raphael didn't give you a choice about going with him?" the brown-haired lady clarified.

"No, giving people a choice isn't his style. In his eyes he was the leader, so people should obey his every whim," I sighed.

"And in your eyes?" the brown-haired lady asked.

"What?" I murmured, rubbing my face, exhausted.

"Was he the leader in your eyes?" the brown-haired lady clarified.

"Yes," I replied.

***

"Are you okay?" Stephanie demanded. We waited outside the building in her car. "Okay relax, you're going to have an aneurysm."

"This is my first time, I'm sorry I'm nervous," I growled.

"You mean I get to take your virginity?" she joked, nudging my arm.

"Let me focus," I snapped at her.

Stephanie took a deep breath in. "Do you want to go over the list?"

"No, I know what I have to do, just how the fuck am I supposed to ask my uncle how to delete research without being fucking suspicious," I hissed.

"Look at me," Stephanie murmured. I shook my head, my

eyes focused on the building ahead of me. "Look at me!" she yelled. I curled back in shock. I had never had her yell at me before. I turned to look at her, irritated.

"What?"

"Denmark."

"Okay fine, I'll stop being an asshole." I breathed a laugh.

"There he is," Stephanie patted my cheek. She looked down at the clock. "Showtime," she whispered. I nodded and got out of the vehicle, walking over to the doors and phoned my uncle.

"Hello?" My uncle's voice rang through the telephone.

"I'm downstairs."

"Okay, I'll be right down," my uncle said, I waited by the doors. He waved me in the first set of doors, then pressed his pass against a pad next to the door and opened the second. I walked in.

"Do those first doors not lock?" I clarified.

"Not until I'm long gone," my uncle opened his arms for a hug. I walked into them, embracing him tightly. "It has been too long since I've seen you," my uncle patted me gently on the face then turned. "This is where I work, the lab is to the right." My uncle gestured to a door to the right. A pad similar to the one at the front was next to it.

"Can we see inside?" I asked.

"Oh no, I don't have access to that." My uncle led me straight to the elevator.

"Do you work late often?" I scanned the elevator, there was one camera.

"Every Thursday, I like to do security checks on Thursday."

"That's cool," I nodded watching the levels go up.

"So, how is Stephanie?" My uncle grinned at me eagerly. We arrived at our floor. Seven.

"Good," I replied. I followed my uncle out of the elevator.

"You know, I met my wife when I was in university," my uncle gleamed. He walked over to his office. "I know that must be hard to imagine now that our kids are in university," my uncle laughed.

"Not hard to imagine at all," I chuckled. I looked around the room. It was set up like a typical office with dividers. Two cameras watched the entire space. I walked over to his office. It had glass doors and sat against a window.

"So this is where I work," my uncle gestured to the room.

"Very cool, how does this all work?" I gestured to the building.

"I make this all work," my uncle declared proudly.

"Have you accidentally deleted research by accident?" I blurted. My uncle looked up confused. "That's what I would be scared to do."

"Well, I guess it's possible if you deleted it and the servers caught fire," my uncle laughed.

"So not a valid fear then," I smiled. My uncle shook his head.

"Here, take a look at this." My uncle gestured for me to sit in his chair. I looked at his computer. A barrage of numbers and letters were in front of me. "This is what makes it work. Everything has to be encrypted."

"And you control that?".

"I control everything," my uncle bragged.

"You're pretty impressive." I looked up at him. My uncle puffed out his chest slightly.

"I'm so excited that you're thinking of going into this field. I can finally talk to someone about all this." He gestured to the computer. "I can get you a job at this company, the pay is excellent and hours are predictable, perfect for raising a family."

"That sounds fantastic," I grinned. "How do you send information?"

"Well, we encrypt our messages."

"So you can't use USB sticks or anything?"

"I mean you could, but if that information got into the wrong hands, you would probably be fired," my uncle chuckled.

"Okay, noted."

"You have to get back, Stephanie's probably waiting for you." My uncle began moving toward his office door.

"Can you show me the servers? I've never seen any before," I requested. My uncle smiled excitedly and gestured for me to follow him. I stood up and followed him out of his office. Immediately to the left was a door. My uncle opened it and turned on the lights.

"This is where the magic happens," he remarked. I walked in. The room was almost full of black boxes. The lights flickered on them. I looked around. No cameras.

"Very neat," I nodded toward him and walked out of the room. He closed and locked the door behind me. We walked to the elevator.

"Please feel free to come back whenever," my uncle insisted as we waited for the elevator to get to the ground floor.

"Of course." The elevator reached the ground floor. My uncle and I walked out. "Thank you for doing this."

"I mean it, whenever," my uncle asserted, buzzing me out. I waved as I left. I stepped over to Stephanie's vehicle. My heart is still pounding.

"I feel like the fucking man," I purred getting in. "Let's fuck, now." I leaned in to kiss her. She put up her finger.

"Please don't," Eli's voice rang out through the phone.

"Tell us everything while your mind's still fresh," Raphael

ordered. My face flushed in embarrassment.

"Is everyone on this phone call?" I mumbled.

"Yes," James responded.

"Okay," I rubbed my face. "Uh, first set of doors don't lock until after my uncle leaves, second is accessible by key card. To the right, there's a lab accessible by key card. My uncle does not have access to that. One camera in the elevator. Two cameras on the seventh floor. My uncle has the only office on the seventh floor. He works late every Thursday. Information is encrypted but can be downloaded onto a USB stick. Information has to be deleted and the servers need to be destroyed. The room that holds the servers is the door directly to the left coming out of my uncle's office. He has the key to the door. You need a key card to come out."

"Great, next Thursday it is," Raphael announced.

"Will we be ready? That's a week," I scoffed.

"We'll make sure we're ready," Raphael hung up the phone.

"Abrupt," I commented.

"He's in planning mode." Stephanie shrugged. "You are the man." Stephanie leaned into me.

"I'm not in the mood anymore, kind of got ruined," I muttered.

"But you are such a man," Stephanie glided her fingers along the inseam of my pants, biting my ear softly.

"Fuck, mood back on," I allowed my head to roll back as the blood rushed to my erection.

Stephanie undid my belt and pants. I watched her as she carefully took my shaft in her hand and began to suckle on my tip. "Fuck," I moaned. My phone rang loudly. "It's my mom." I sighed. Stephanie sat up grumpily. "Hello?" I picked up the phone covering myself up and doing up my pants.

"Hello, we were just wondering if you guys are coming back?" mom questioned.

"Ya, we're on our way," I replied. Stephanie started up the vehicle and began to drive.

"How was your uncle?" mom asked.

"He was great, we'll be home soon, I love you," I dismissed.

"I love you too, see you soon," mom responded. I hung up.

"Your parents are cockblockers," Stephanie grumbled.

"I think that's what parents are meant to be," I replied.

"How was it with your uncle?"

"Exhilarating. I get it. I felt like God."

"Wait until you put a gun to someone's head, that power, nothing like it," Stephanie murmured.

"That was a psychopathic thing to say," I retorted. Stephanie shrugged.

"I'm not saying you should do it…"

"Yes, just *when* I do it."

"It comes with the territory!" she protested.

"Have you killed someone?" I demanded. I never thought of the fact she probably has. She looked at me for a few seconds. "Stephanie, have you killed someone?" I yelled.

"Not directly," Stephanie tapped the steering wheel.

"What does that mean?" I turned to her abruptly.

"I've set people up to be… taken out," Stephanie shifted.

"What?" I looked at her confused.

"I've worked some jobs that I, uh, I draw them in and get the people in an easy position for them to—"

"What the fuck, Stephanie?" I bit out.

"What did you expect, Levi?" Stephanie quipped.

"For you to have some sort of innocence or empathy? For you to not have murdered people? For an ounce of normality in our conversations?" I shrieked. Stephanie pulled over. She took a deep breath. The silence between us was deafening. Stephanie looked over at me, her eyes gliding over my face, evaluating me.

"What do you want me to say to that?" Stephanie squeaked. I was taken aback. Her expression was calm, no anger crossed her face. Her eyes were on me. I realized she was actively trying to figure out what I wanted.

"I don't know, Stephanie," I muttered, rubbing my face. "This is fucked up, you know that right?"

"You didn't blink when the guys said what they've done." Stephanie stared at the steering wheel.

"I'm not fucking them, Stephanie!" I seethed.

"Wow." Stephanie didn't look up from the steering wheel. She passed me her keys and got out.

"What?" I demanded. I got out of the vehicle, slamming the door behind me. Stephane continued walking away. My heart pounded. Fuck. "Where are you going, Steph?" I croaked, pure panic racing through my veins. Stephanie stopped. She turned around and stared at me. My heart broke as she stood there, I could see tears running down her face as she bit her nail. I stepped forward, my eyes pleading for her to talk to me. I saw her take a few deep breaths before walking back.

"I'm sorry," Stephanie cried. I pulled her into me, holding her tight and kissing the top of her head.

"Please, never walk away," I clutched onto her. "It just caught me off guard."

"You think you can still love me?" Stephanie murmured. I pulled away from her, staring at her in surprise.

"Stephanie, I will always love you," I vowed.

"I'm not just a good fuck?" Stephanie looked up at me.

"No, you are a fantastic fuck," I joked. Stephanie hit my arm gently and giggled. "I love you." I pulled her into me and laughed.

"You're an asshole," Stephanie stated.

"I'm your asshole." I kissed her forehead. "Okay, let's get going, my mom has probably called me fifty times." I pulled away and passed her the keys.

"She's going to hate me," Stephanie whined. We walked back to the vehicle.

"My mom already loves you, you can do no wrong in her eyes," I chuckled.

We drove to my house and pulled into my driveway. Stephanie picked at her arm scars. "Are you okay? Relax, you're going to have an aneurysm," I mocked. Stephanie pushed me playfully. She turned the car off and we walked up to the door.

"Oh, welcome!" mom ushered Stephanie into our house. "I'm so glad you could make it."

"I am so glad that you invited me," Stephanie replied. My mom pointed to a spot at the kitchen table. Stephanie sat down.

"We formally met your brother – sorry, foster brother – a few days ago. He seems like a lovely man. He scheduled a big dinner with us!" mom announced gleefully. I sat down beside Stephanie.

"You guys must have made quite the impression on him. He does not make dinner plans lightly," Stephanie grinned. Mom and dad looked at each other, proud. Stephanie's eyes bulged as mom plopped a massive piece of lasagna on her plate. "Thank you."

"So Raphael said you're in first year?" dad clarified. Stephanie nodded. "What prompted the change from working with Raphael?"

"Oh, uh, just didn't love the career Raphael's in." Stephanie shrugged. "Eli, I think you've met him, is a massive history buff and kind of introduced me to it and I fell in love with it."

"What do you plan to do with it?" mom asked. The question everyone dreads, yet people still feel the need to ask.

"I would love to be a curator and maybe one day own a museum," Stephanie said, taking her first bite. "This is really good."

"Well, thank you," mom cooed. "I'm sure Levi told you he's thinking of switching to something with computers."

"He did," Stephanie nodded.

"What do you think of that?" dad asked.

"Whatever he wants to do, I'll be supportive, I just want him to be happy," Stephanie shot me a loving glance.

"Very diplomatic." Dad leaned back slightly. "I'm assuming you're going to their cottage again this weekend?" dad turned to me.

"If I could steal him on Friday, I kind of have a surprise for him," Stephanie smiled at my dad.

"We would like to have your number in case something happens," dad reasoned. "Will your foster brother be there for this surprise?"

"Oh, of course, he's very protective," Stephanie affirmed. Dad looked at mom and shrugged.

"Of course, sweety, we'll expect him back Sunday night," mom stated. "How was the visit with your uncle?"

"Oh, it was great, it was so cool. Did you know he controls everything?" I asked, eating my lasagna.

"No, he stopped trying to explain his career years ago," mom chuckled.

"Is it something you see yourself doing?" dad queried.

"Oh definitely, I think I'll meet with the university on

Monday and discuss changing degrees," I grinned.

"I'm so happy about this, I was so concerned with your English degree, there's not many jobs in it," dad commented finishing off his lasagna.

"I mean, I could've written a book." I shrugged.

"I doubt you would've done that," mom dismissed, smiling. I shrugged again. "Would you like any more, sweety?" mom turned to Stephanie.

"No, I am stuffed. It was delicious," Stephanie cooed. My mom stood up and gathered the plates.

"I've made a cherry pie for dessert," mom announced. Dad and I cheered. Stephanie giggled. My mom cut and handed out slices to everyone. Stephanie took a bite.

"Oh my God, this is amazing." Stephanie's eyes grew big. We all laughed and nodded.

"The recipe is top secret," mom mused.

"You are so lucky," Stephanie shot me a envious look. "To have a professional baker as your mom, I am so jealous."

"She is pretty cool," I laughed.

"I like this girl," mom cooed. The slices of pie quickly vanished from everyone's plates.

"I better be off," Stephanie announced. "Thank you so much for having me."

"It was a pleasure having you over, feel free to come by anytime." Mom and dad both gave her a tight hug.

"I'll pick you up at seven a.m.," Stephanie looked at me.

"Good luck with that," dad cackled. Stephanie giggled and gave me a hug.

"Wear your bathing suit," she whispered in my ear. I nodded. She pulled away and left.

My alarm abruptly interrupted my sweet sleep. I looked at the time. Quarter past six. I have time. Snooze. The alarm went off again. Six thirty. I have time. Snooze. My alarm went off. Six forty-five. I'll start getting up soon. Snooze. My alarm goes off. Seven. Fuck, I was late. I sat up straight, pulled on my clothing I had laid out and grabbed the bag I had packed the night before. I ran down the stairs and outside.

"You're almost on time!" Stephanie mocked. I stuck my finger up at her as I got in the car, placing my bag at my feet. "Are you wearing your bathing suit?"

"I am, are you?"

"I am," Stephanie smiled. She was wearing a long baggy shirt that covered her shorts. She had sunglasses on, her hair in a messy ponytail. She pulled out of the driveway and we began our journey.

"Are we, like, swimming for our workout?"

"Something like that." Stephanie winked at me. "How did you sleep?"

"Meh, not great."

"Anything on your mind?"

"Well, I mean, next week." I shrugged.

"Are you worried about something in particular?" she inquired.

"Raphael hasn't told me any sort of plan."

"He will tomorrow night, then we open our bag of drugs and see if we can expand on it," Stephanie laughed.

"Why tomorrow night? Are they not meeting us?"

"They aren't, I am kidnapping to have you all to myself," Stephanie beamed.

"You lied to my parents?" I chuckled. She nodded. "You're going to hell," I mused.

Stephanie roared with laughter. "I had to, they wouldn't have allowed you to come."

"I am so disappointed in you, young missy," I joked.

"Would you rather not come on a full day and night trip just with me?" She leaned back and gave me an "I know you" look. I paused for a second.

"Hell here I come!" I shouted. Stephanie giggled and merged onto the highway. "Where are you kidnapping me to?"

"It's a surprise, do you ever listen to me?" Stephanie sighed. I shook my head. "I have two of those canned iced coffee things for us in my bag." She gestured to the back. I grabbed it, opened it up and took out the two iced coffees.

"Did you bring an entire box of condoms?" I queried, picking up the box.

"I like being prepared," Stephanie grinned.

"Did you pack any clothes? I see alcohol and condoms, that's it."

"I only brought the necessities." She smiled at me. "I have a change of underwear."

"Okay, I'm glad about that," I replied, still looking through her bag. "Is this bubble bath?"

"Yes, look, it says sensual."

"One, where the fuck are you taking me and two, you're an absolute weirdo."

"One, it's still a surprise and two, you're the one who fell in love with me, so who's the actual weirdo?" Stephanie pointed at me.

"You have raised a fair point," I nodded in my defeat.

We drove for over two hours before Stephanie pulled the car into the parking lot. I looked around seeing we were at a boardwalk.

"Our first stop," Stephanie announced and got out of the vehicle. I followed. She held my hand as we walked out to the boardwalk. "I'm hungry," she said and ran toward a hotdog stand. She ordered one for each of us, a big smile on her face. She handed me a hot dog. I put ketchup, mustard, relish and onions on mine. Stephanie took a big bite of her plain hotdog.

"No, please don't tell me you eat them plain," I begged, determined to have a somewhat normal girlfriend. The black coffee was enough of a red flag.

"I don't, you're just taking forever." Stephanie pushed me gently to the side and put ketchup and onions on hers. Better than plain. Stephanie took another bite of her hotdog as we continued to walk on the boardwalk. I looked over and saw ketchup around her mouth.

"I have never seen you more attractive," I joked. Stephanie cleaned off her face laughing. I was hungry from the long car ride and we both finished off the hotdogs quickly.

The hot day burned at my skin but Stephanie seemed unperturbed. She skipped along as we walked hand in hand along the long boardwalk. Like any normal couple, living a normal life. Is this what she wanted? Is this why she brought me here? To show me the life she wants? I had to admit this was tempting, these pure moments as she clutched onto my hand like she was afraid of losing me in the limited crowd. Stephanie pointed to every person rollerblading like it was a circus show.

"They're just rollerblading, you can do it if you'd like," I chuckled, trying to work out her fascination with them.

"I don't want to die, thank you, it's neat."

"Hey!" I shouted at a man rollerblading by. He started skating in place. "Where can you buy Rollerblades?" I asked. He shrugged and skated away.

"Your plan is foiled Mr. Davis, I get to live another day," Stephanie mocked.

"If we see a place to buy them, without me asking anyone, we're getting you some," I stated.

"No."

"What if I buy you one of those fruit juice things?" I pointed to a stand not too far away which made a smoothie out of the fruit on the inside and poured it back into the peel. Stephanie nodded. "Jesus, you are too easy," I laughed. We walked up to the stand. "What would you like?"

"A mango please," Stephanie beamed at the vendor. I reached into my wallet and paid. The vendor gave Stephanie her mango. Stephanie did a little happy dance. I took her hand and we continued walking.

"Do you believe in psychics?" I smiled pointing to a psychic booth. Stephanie shook her head. "Come on, it'll be fun," I dragged her over.

"I don't want to know anything bad though," Stephanie groaned.

"Ladies first," I said to her, paying for her tarot card reading.

"Hold my mango," Stephanie grumbled, jutting it into my hands. She sat down in front of the psychic. "Can I ask that you only tell me the good parts?"

"No," the psychic replied. "Do you have any specific questions?"

"No," Stephanie bit her nail. I watched as her anxiety increased as she sat in front of the woman. Maybe this wasn't a good idea.

"Let's do a general reading then. Let's flip three cards," the psychic replied gently. "Three of Swords. This typically shows that you will go through some sort of emotional grief. The Sun.

Typically resembles some type of success that radiates good energy throughout your life. And the last card is The Empress." The psychic shot me an excited grin.

"What?" I voiced nervously.

"Well, typically The Empress and The Sun together can indicate a pregnancy." The psychic smirked.

"So, I'm going to get pregnant but I'll be emotionally distressed by this," Stephanie said slowly.

"Could be, but could indicate another moment of emotional distress or heartbreak," the psychic patted Stephanie's hand gently. Stephanie nodded.

"Does the success stand by itself?" Stephanie clarified.

"Could mean a success, or could just be in relation to The Empress," the psychic replied. Stephanie nodded again.

"Okay, great," Stephanie stood up abruptly.

"Do you want a reading?" the psychic turned to me. I shook my head grabbing Stephanie's hand as we walked away from the booth.

"Guess I'm going to have your babies," Stephanie laughed.

"How dare you be emotionally distressed by that," I winked. Stephanie grabbed the mango from me and drank the rest, throwing it away at the next garbage can. "Let's go swim." I pointed to the stairs that headed down to the beach area. Stephanie ran toward them, I ran after her. We raced until the shoreline. Stephanie, of course, won.

"I am the man!" she announced, dancing. I took off my shirt and grabbed her, throwing her over my shoulder. I walked into the water. It was cold. "Take my phone out of my pocket," she requested. "And my wallet," she added. I walked out of the water.

"Okay, just take your shorts off," I sighed. She took off her shorts and shirt revealing a simple black bikini. I picked her up again and walked back into the water. "Let's try this again," I walked until Stephanie's legs were just touching.

"No, it's cold," she complained. "Let's not go swimming."

"We're going swimming," I replied. It was cold. Very cold. But now I had to go through with it.

"No, I think it's okay not to," Stephanie insisted. I tossed her into the water. She went completely under before surfacing with an angry expression on her face. I began to run to shore. I was no match for her. She ran and grabbed me, toppling me into the frigid waters.

"How dare you!" I joked. Stephanie smiled mischievously and splashed me in the face. I ran toward her grabbing her out of the water then spinning her around. I set her down and kissed her. She leaned into my ear.

"I want donuts," Stephanie whispered. I laughed. We walked out of the water and got dressed. The sand getting stuck everywhere. We walked back up to the boardwalk. Stephanie gleefully pointed at a donut stand. She skipped forward and got us five. They were still warm. Stephanie immediately grabbed one taking a bite. "Mmm," she moaned gleefully.

"I am so in love with you," I murmured. Stephanie gave me the finger. "No, I'm serious. I am so in love with you."

"I love you too," she said, covering her still full mouth. She swallowed. "We should start heading to the last location." She smiled at me, handing me a donut. I nodded as we began to trek over to the vehicle. The donuts were amazing. She was right to crave them. We ate the last few and threw out the bag.

"Where's the second location?" I asked, getting in the car. Stephanie tossed her wallet and phone into her bag.

"You will see soon, patience," Stephanie giggled while reversing the car. We drove a few minutes before pulling into the parking lot of a massive tower. Stephanie grabbed her bag, putting the sunglasses on top of her head. I grabbed my bag and followed her inside. The resort was massive. We walked to the check-in counter. "Checking in for Stephanie Gibson," Stephanie passed her credit card and ID.

"Oh welcome back, Ms. Gibson. Is it just the two of you today?" The clerk smiled at her.

"It is," Stephanie replied. An elderly bald man walked out.

"Excellent, everything has been paid in full." The clerk put the hotel key on the counter.

"Ah Stephanie, I was so excited to see your name on our bookings." The bald man embraced Stephanie. "And who is this young man?" The bald man turned toward me.

"This is Levi, my boyfriend," Stephanie introduced me.

"Welcome to our hotel," the man shook my hand. I nodded. "Well, call down if you need anything. Enjoy your stay," the bald man grinned at Stephanie. Stephanie nodded, taking the hotel room key from the clerk. She smiled and waved as we left for the elevator.

"How often do you come here?" I asked.

"A lot," Stephanie smiled. "We don't get a lot of continuity and they're loyal here. So we like to come back."

"What, they'll lie if the police come asking for you?" I joked.

"Exactly. We pay them extra to do so. They turn their cameras off when we arrive." Stephanie clarified.

I wasn't expecting that.

"How much do you pay them?" I demanded.

"That doesn't matter." Stephanie winked. The elevator stopped at our floor. We walked to our room. Stephanie unlocked the door and opened it. The room was massive.

"What the fuck. How rich are you?" I questioned, looking

around at the suite. To the right, there was a bar, and straight on was a billiard table.

"Very." Stephanie shrugged. "We're good at what we do." Stephanie took off her flip-flops and went into the room. I took off my shoes and walked to the massive window that looked over the water. To the right of the billiard table, separated by a small wall, sat a couch and television. Stephanie walked toward me and leaned against my shoulder. "I thought it might be good to show you our future." Stephanie cooed, leaning in. She kissed me gently on the lips.

"Is that a bottle of champagne?" I looked over at the coffee table in front of the large couch. There was a bucket of ice with champagne sticking out and two champagne glasses sitting next to it. I walked over. It was a bottle of Dom Perignon. A note was next to it. I picked it up. "Have fun – Raphael."

"My favorite," Stephanie said, pulling the bottle out of the ice. "Open it, I'm going to put the beer in the fridge." She passed me the bottle and went to her bag.

"Let me get this straight, we pull up to this resort, we have a massive suite at this resort, we were personally greeted by the manager, Raphael sent us a bottle of Dom and you brought beer from home?" I laughed. Stephanie shrugged, unloading the cans into the fridge.

"This is just to get us started," Stephanie gestured to the beer in the fridge. "We'll order other things." Stephanie walked over as I popped the cork. I filled up the two champagne glasses.

"To our future," I exclaimed. We clinked our glasses as I beamed at Stephanie.

"Let me show you my favorite part." Stephanie indicated for me to follow her. She led me through the door to the right of the television, past the bedroom and into the washroom. Straight on there was a large bathtub. The stand looked like it was made of marble. On the wall behind the tub hung a massive mirror. Stephanie smiled at me. She then proceeded to point to a shower. "They have a rainfall shower," she whispered excitedly.

"I literally just saw that we have a billiard table in our room and you're excited about a rainfall shower?" I mocked.

"It's the best type of shower," she protested. I pulled her into my arms and quickly tickled her. She laughed and pulled away. "You'll see!"

"Okay." I shrugged. Stephanie stripped down and put her sunglasses on the bathtub stand. "I will never get used to seeing you naked," I murmured in awe.

"Shut up, strip," Stephanie ordered.

"Yes, ma'am," I said obediently. I stripped down as Stephanie turned on the water. She kept her hand under it until she was satisfied with the temperature. She stepped forward, wetting her hair. Her head tilted up. I watched the water glide across her face down her body, gliding over every curve. I felt weak looking at her. She stepped back, motioning for me to join her. I stepped in and jumped back. "Jesus fuck Stephanie, turn the temperature down."

"You're weak," she muttered, reaching for the faucet and turning it down to a manageable temperature. I nodded, testing it with my hand. She stood back directly in the water, putting her hands up and letting it wash away the sand. She stepped forward, kissing me deeply. She turned so I was in the water. I understood what she meant. The water was the perfect pressure. The perfect shower. I rinsed off the sand, enjoying this phenomenal feeling. My eyes peeled open, and I saw Stephanie staring intently at me.

"What?" I asked. She smiled sweetly, biting her lip.

"I love you," she breathed before blinking and swiftly

getting out of the shower grabbing a towel to dry off. I rested there for a few seconds, taking in the last bit of the warmth before turning the water off.

"Want to lose at a game of pool?" Stephanie quickly ran and got the hotel robes, handing me one.

"Oh sweety, I don't think you know this about me. But I am the pool champion." I approached her and pulled her into me.

"Shall we make it interesting then?" Stephanie smirked.

"What do you want if you win?" I asked.

"I want you to remind me what that tongue can do," she placed her hand on the side of my face, stroking her thumb over my lips. I nodded. "What do you want?"

I paused. "I want to get a bottle of Patron tequila," I requested. Stephanie giggled and nodded. We walked over to the table.

"I'll break," Stephanie announced, grabbing a cue. The balls were already set up. She split them perfectly, sending a solid into the right hole.

"Great, I'm stripes," I smiled. We were evenly matched. We were soon both going after the eight-ball. "Ha, you fucked up, I'm set up now," I mocked. Stephanie positioned herself on the other side of the table. I drew my cue back as she undid her robe. The cue ball went past the eight-ball, hitting nothing. "Fuck! No! You are such a cheat."

"No," she smirked, grabbing the cue ball and putting it in place for the perfect shot. The eight-ball went in effortlessly. "I am a winner," she boasted. She sat up on the table leaning back. I obediently got down on my knees in front of her. Her legs went over my shoulders as I gently bit her inner thighs. She squirmed in anticipation. I brought my mouth to her, kissing her gently, enjoying her trembling with lust. I began licking her tenderly.

She moaned loudly. I continued licking and gently sucking until she became putty in my hands.

"Fuck!"

She arched her back and convulsed as she finished. She threw the cue ball in the hole and grabbed me gently, pulling me onto the table with her.

"I'll grab the condom," I whispered to her, before quickly grabbing the box of condoms and tore it open, taking one. She scooted back and lay down, pulling me closer with her legs. I ripped open the packet and put the condom on. She positioned me correctly. I pushed forward. "Baby," I whimpered as I entered her. I wrapped my left arm around her, holding her body in place, grabbing the raised part of the pool table with my right hand, pulling and pushing myself into her. Stephanie gasped, gripping my back in pleasure. Her nails dug into me.

"Yes," Stephanie groaned biting her lip. I didn't relent, continuing to shove myself into her. She moaned loudly, pressing herself against me. "Fuck yes!" she screamed. "Fuck, fuck, fuck, fuck." She let out a loud gasp then a loud moan.

"Stephanie," I grunted, thrusting into her as I climaxed. Panting, I pulled out and hopped off the table, taking off the condom and going into the bathroom to throw it out.

I heard voices outside. I grabbed a towel to cover myself and went to investigate. Stephanie was rifling through her bag pulling out her wallet. My eyes looked over her for a second, she didn't seem panicked or worried. I stepped closer, peering at the door. The room attendant stared at me, biting his cheek as he tried to keep from laughing. I backed away slowly. Stephanie passed him five hundred dollar bills.

"I do hope I didn't interrupt anything," the waiter smirked, taking the money.

"Food is never an interruption, have a great day," Stephanie pulled the cart in. The waiter nodded and left as Stephanie shut the door.

"Did you just buy a five hundred dollar meal?" I questioned in shock, putting my robe back on.

"No," Stephanie giggled. "That was the tip."

"What the fuck did you get?" I asked, walking over to the trays curiously.

"The usual," Stephanie unveiled the trays. "Two club sandwiches and fries." Stephanie grabbed her plate and walked to the couch. I grabbed my plate and followed her.

"Have I told you you're weird?" I commented, sitting next to her. She did a happy dance when she ate one of her fries.

"It's good!" she insisted. I took a bite. She was right. I had never had a better sandwich in my life. "So?"

"Okay, fine," I muttered. She laughed.

"What do you think will be the first thing you buy?" Stephanie rested her head on her hand, looking up at me as she batted her thick eyelashes.

"The first thing I'll buy are roller-skates for you," I laughed. Stephanie threw a fry at me.

"I'm serious!" she grinned, taking a bite of the club sandwich.

"I am!" I retorted, throwing a fry back at her. "It's not like I can buy a house or a car without anyone getting suspicious."

"What if we left?" Stephanie shrugged. "We can come back to visit your family and your friends. May be less risky."

"I thought you wanted to finish your degree here," I replied, surprised by this line of questioning.

"I do, if you want to. But we also have the option of leaving. Raphael got us all fake identities just in case something goes wrong. We want it to be your decision if you want to go," Stephanie said gently.

"I'd be able to see my parents and call them? And same with Aidan and Lucas?"

"Yes, of course, just calls at first, but after a while, people stop asking questions, you can return whenever you like, no one will ever get in the way of you doing that."

"Why the change?"

"With the server needing to be destroyed, we're concerned that this will turn into more of a big deal. With the amount of property damage and how they'll have to do it."

"Where are they thinking of going?"

"They're waiting until they hear what you want to do," Stephanie replied. I nodded slowly. I paused for a few seconds debating in my head.

"I want to leave."

"You don't have to decide now," Stephanie uttered. "I just wanted to let you know."

"No, I want to leave," I asserted. "This is the first time I've felt like I was living. I want to do this." I grabbed Stephanie's hand excitedly. "We can continue this career until we're ready to retire. Then we go to Denmark, buy a museum and live."

"Are you sure?" Stephanie murmured.

"I've never been so sure of anything in my sad little life," I affirmed. I put my plate on the coffee table. I grabbed her and put hers on the coffee table too. Stephanie put her champagne glass down. I moved closer to her, sitting facing her and stared into her eyes for a few moments. Those blue eyes that made everything else disappear. I cupped her chin. "Let's live like a king and queen, we can control this world together."

"There's no going back."

"Now, why would I possibly want to go back?"

"You're absolutely sure?" A smile began to cross her delicate lips.

"I am absolutely sure." I breathed. Stephanie giggled and lay down. I kissed her neck gently. "I am so addicted to you.".

"Grab a condom," Stephanie ordered. I obeyed. I returned to an empty couch. My eyes glided around confused before I walked into the bedroom. She sat on the bed staring at me. Her robe on the ground beside the bed. I dropped my robe quickly. "Lay down," she commanded. I flopped down, my eyes on her. She took the condom from me and put it beside me. "Close your eyes," her fingers glided over my face, her thumbs gently closing my eyes. I laughed, not really sure what to expect. Her bare feet pattered on the floor as she left then returned. Suddenly I felt a freezing cold substance on my chest. My eyes flew opened as I yelped. A piece of ice lay on my body. "Eyes closed." Stephanie shook her head at me disapprovingly.

"Why is there ice?"

"Close your eyes."

I suspiciously obeyed. The ice was removed from the center of my chest before I felt it be pressed against my nipple. I took a sharp breath in. Her mouth collapsed around my now freezing nipple. I gasped in pleasure. The cold followed by the heat allowing me to feel every subtle movement as she flicked it with her tongue.

"Oh, baby," I groaned. The ice moved to my other nipple before she took it in her mouth. "Oh." Pleasure hit me in waves as she began to nibble and pinch at them, the ice freezing them before she warmed it with her sensual touch. The coldness was removed, her warm body moving on top of me. I felt her lips press against mine; the cold ice polarized by the heat emanating from our passionate interlocking. "You're cold," I joked.

"You have no idea." Stephanie giggled, nuzzling our noses. She locked our lips again before kissing down my body. The chilly ice tightening my abs as she moved lower. Her body moved off of me. An abrupt drip of freezing cold water hit my erection. I jerked forward, wheezing slightly in shock. I felt her fingers delicately move along me as it twitched. She pulled down my foreskin, the iced water hitting my sensitive tip.

I gasped, the glacial liquid shooting pain through my veins. Her lips suddenly collapsed around me, the coldness heightening the sensation of her suckle. I gripped onto the blanket as pure ecstasy consumed me. A whimper escaped my lips.

"Don't come," Stephanie pulled back, pressing the ice against the base of my length. My pending climax retreated immediately with the jolt of pain. Her lips returned to me, the ice and her mouth moving along my rock-hard shaft. I squirmed, the delight and distress driving me insane. The ice was removed, her mouth gliding to the base, taking every inch of me. I felt her throat contract as she began to move along me deeply. A frosty drip hit my aching balls.

"Urg," I jolted, the chilly water continuing it's attack as her warm and inviting mouth comforted my erection. My body was in a state of extreme need. My balls heavy, my erection pulsating with every touch and lick. The steady and unyielding sudden shot of that sharp drip piercing my ability to climax. This limbo of ecstasy and pain holding me captive. The ice was abruptly clutched to my balls. I let out a shriek at the precipitated affliction of agony. My body convulsed, attempting to withdraw from this torture. Her mouth was removed. I let out a whimper.

"I'm going to fuck you," Stephanie informed.

"Please," I begged, my voice was hoarse. The consuming

lust jumping at the idea that perhaps she was done her toying. The ice was removed. I felt her body lower onto me, my throbbing erection penetrating her warm, bare, flesh. She stopped halfway. "Fuck me," I pleaded. Stephanie glided the ice along my lips, my tongue reached out, gliding over this instrument of tantalizing torture.

"Hold it with your lips." She ordered. I clutched the freezing material between my lips, desperate to do whatever she ordained. I needed release, the kind only she could give me.

I reached for her hips, wanting to urge her down my length. Stephanie quickly grabbed my arms and pinned them above my head. She kissed my neck gently, then bit my neck hard. I took a sharp breath in with the pain. The cold from the ice hurting my teeth. Immediately she pressed down, my erection entering completely.

I groaned, my body filling with pleasure after the sudden pain. My brain occupied with trying to hold the ice between my numb lips. She leaned forward, placing all her weight on a hand on my chest restricting my breath. My pulse quickening. I was hers. Completely hers. She could do whatever she wanted to me. I moaned loudly at the thought. Her body moved along my pulsating member rapidly, restricting my breath as she raised herself, pleasure tearing through my veins when she lowered herself. I could feel I was on the brink. The frigid ice dissipating in my mouth. My lips tired, my body withering in hedonistic gratification. Stephanie leaned forward biting down on my neck hard. Combined with the indulgent impaling, it was just too much. My body shuddered as I climaxed, my erection shamelessly jerking as it injected into her.

I bit down on the ice, swallowing it. My breath uneasy as I stared at her in complete amazement. Stephanie rocked her hips, milking me as she groaned. "Oh, yes, baby," I breathed, clutching onto her. Watching her frenzied for me was a different level of satisfaction. I sat forward, wrapping my arms around her as I collapsed my lips on hers. A moment of pure bliss as we came down from our high.

"We should have a bath," Stephanie murmured.

"Put that bubble bath to work." I winked. "Stay here," I instructed, rolling over and giving her a sensual kiss, I sat up, her eyes closed as she took everything in.

My eyes leapt to the unused condom laying on the bed. Had she not noticed and got wrapped up in the moment? A hopeful thought clung to me as I quickly snatched the unused condom, hiding it in my hand as I darted to the washroom. I ripped it open, tossing the wrapper and condom separately in the trash before I started the water for the bath. If she hadn't noticed maybe this was our chance to get away, an added reason for her to run away with me.

I stepped out of the washroom to grab the bubble bath. Stephanie was still laying there in all of her perfection. Her body on full display, her eyes still closed as she stroked the center of her chest, a delicate smile on her lips. I rested there for a moment, taking her in. There was nothing I was more certain of. I wanted her forever. I wanted the house full of screaming toddlers, the early mornings dealing with the kids, the late nights and fights with each other. Our future life shot through my head as I grinned, the pregnancy cravings I'd have to get up in the early hours to get, the complaints, the foot rubs and massages to reduce the discomfort. There was nothing I wanted more.

Her eyes flew open, sensing a watching eye. "What?" Stephanie giggled.

"I love you," I murmured. A giddy smile crossed her face,

her eyes giving me a look I hadn't seen before. A look that made my heart stop, my breath hitch, and a whole host of butterflies burst in my stomach. A look of love. That look people fight their whole lives to get. The look my mom and dad shared.

"I love you," she whispered, like it was a secret no one could know. I crawled onto the bed, wrapping her in my arms. I was going to sustain that look.

Whatever I had to do.

"You're going to flood the washroom." Stephanie breathed a laugh.

"I need to grab the bubbles or we'll have a bubbleless bath." I bit her nose gently.

"A bubbleless bath is no bath to have." Stephanie grinned playfully. I tore myself away from her, going to the bag and grabbing the bubble bath before dumping a whole bunch in the running water. I darted and grabbed the bottle of champagne, setting it to the side.

"It's ready," I announced. I heard her bare feet on the floor before she entered. I hopped in the bath first, she got in and sat in between my legs, leaning against me.

"Would you want me to take your name?" Stephanie asked.

"I would love that," I replied.

"Stephanie Anna Davis," she said out loud.

"I love the sound of that." I kissed her on the cheek. "Would you want to take my last name?"

"I would, I never liked my last name," Stephanie sighed.

"Then Stephanie Anna Davis it is," I smiled to myself. "Aren't we changing names though?"

"Ya, but one day," Stephanie grinned. I wrapped my arms around her. Stephanie took a swig from the bottle of champagne and handed it to me. I took a long gulp. "This is perfect,"

Stephanie said quietly. We lay there saying nothing to each other. Just enjoying each other's company.

"We should go to bed," I whispered to Stephanie.

"No," she whined.

"It's late," I laughed. She sat up and got out of the bath. I got out, taking the plug out of the bottom. I lay in bed under the covers, wrapping Stephanie tightly like I could shield her from the world with this blanket. She curled up against me. I gently trailed my fingers along her arm. There was nothing I wouldn't do for her. There was nothing I wouldn't do to make sure she was *mine*.

The sun poured through the large windows. I opened my eyes and looked down seeing Stephanie still gently curled up at my side. I smiled to myself in pure happiness. Stephanie's phone began to ring on the bedside table. I sat up to see who was calling. It was Raphael. I leaned over and grabbed it.

"Hello?" I asked into the phone.

"Ya, just me. I wanted to check in to make sure you were on your way back soon," Raphael voiced.

"What time is it?" I asked.

"Eleven, I would like you here prior to nightfall," Raphael ordered.

"Ya, we'll head out now," I stated.

"Are you just waking up?" Raphael asked.

"Yep," I replied.

"Big night then," Raphael laughed. "Okay, see you guys soon." Raphael hung up the phone. I gently shook Stephanie.

"I'm up," she muttered, stretching out and slowly coming to life. She rolled out of bed and went to her bag. Stephanie returned fully dressed and tossed my bag to me. She went to the bathroom to do her makeup. I got dressed. "Okay, let's go," Stephanie frowned. "Um, did we use protection last night?"

"Ya," I lied.

"I figured, just couldn't quite remember." Stephanie giggled.

"We were completely responsible." I embraced her tightly, kissing her neck tenderly. We grabbed our stuff and left the room. "Checking out for Gibson," Stephanie requested at the checkout counter. She reached into her bag and pulled out a large envelope. "For your team," Stephanie grinned. The clerk gleamed as she checked the envelope.

"Leaving already, Ms. Gibson?" the bald man came out and grabbed her hand gently.

"Yes, unfortunately we have to get back," Stephanie grimaced.

"Please come back and stay with us soon," the bald man gently kissed her hand.

"Of course," Stephanie nodded. She waved at the clerk, and we left.

The drive back felt excruciatingly long. The sadness of leaving our bubble, paired with the extra time to get to the cottage, made it almost unbearable. We pulled up in the driveway in the late afternoon. We grabbed our stuff and headed into the cottage, quickly putting the stuff in Stephanie's room prior to coming out to the men. Raphael was holding a beer standing in the kitchen waiting for us to come out.

"There you are, we were thinking we would have to make a search party," Raphael joked. James and Jace came into the room.

"How was it?" Jace called to me.

"It was great," I beamed.

"I guess now we know who the bitch is," Raphael mocked, gesturing to my hickeys.

"Oh, shut up Raphael," Stephanie rolled her eyes, grabbing a beer from the fridge.

"I'm the bitch for having a girl ride my dick? I'll take it," I snapped back. James and Jace broke out in hysterical laughter.

"Guess you got me there," Raphael chuckled.

"I'm glad she didn't kill you," Jace laughed.

"Can everyone shut up about our sex life?" Stephanie grumbled.

"Okay, so we have a plan to go over, all minds at full capacity, please. We have cocaine, meth, weed and alcohol. Please take whatever will help," Raphael announced. I felt like I was in a bizarre group project as Jace pulled out the backpack that we took from the drug dealer. Stephanie walked away. "James, can you roll a few joints for the table?" Raphael asked. James nodded. Raphael followed Stephanie into the hangout room.

"Here," Jace grabbed my hand and poured a white line of powder along the back of my hand.

"What is it?" I muttered.

"Cocaine," Jace replied, pouring a longer line on his own. He pressed his right nostril closed and breathed in hard through his left nostril until the line was gone. He gestured for me to do the same.

"You don't have to," James commented.

"Oh, shit sorry, ya, you don't have to, assumed you would want to try," Jace remarked, reaching for my hand to wipe it off.

"No, I want to try it," I snorted the line.

"It's gonna be a party now," Jace shouted excitedly. James snorted his line and grabbed a bag of weed bringing it to the table to roll the joints. Jace and I followed to the table.

"Okay, so Eli is away buying us new suppressors because ours aren't 'good enough,'" Raphael sighed. There was a standing pad of paper next to where Raphael was standing. James began grinding the weed up.

"What did you take?" Stephanie asked gently.

"Cocaine," I replied.

Stephanie nodded.

"Make sure you drink water," she smiled sweetly at me. I nodded.

"Focus, please," Raphael grunted. Stephanie turned back and nodded to him. "I will break the cameras outside an hour before we go in. Eli and I will go in. The drug dealer shows up and we walk on in. We will have black spray paint and will cover every camera, go to the seventh floor and get Levi's uncle to download the information we want on this stick." Raphael held up a small USB stick. Raphael grabbed a joint and lit it, taking a long puff.

James passed me a joint. I took it and lit it. Stephanie looked over at me but turned back to Raphael when he continued to speak.

"The uncle is not to be hurt. We take the keys and go down to the front door. We will let James in. I will leave and meet Levi and Stephanie at Levi's parent's house. Eli will leave with Jace to do the drop. James will hook up explosives in the server room, surrounding the lab and surrounding the base of the building. He will pull the fire alarm, allowing everyone remaining to leave the building. He will then get in his car ready for a getaway before promptly blowing up the building. James will switch cars a few times, before being picked up by Jace and Eli on the way back. They will come to the cottage and pack up. Stephanie and I will finish up at Levi's. We will return to the cottage. It is important that you do not seem suspicious that first night. We need the suspicion to be thrown off. We will pick Levi up in the morning and head to the next location." Raphael finished. "Any questions?"

"Do we know where we're moving to?" Jace questioned.

"Putting out some feelers, probably won't know until the day." Raphael stated. Jace nodded. "How are the explosives going?" Raphael turned to James.

"I have my seller lined up for Monday, he's going to demonstrate a few and I'll choose," James replied.

"What does he take, cash or gold?" Raphael queried.

"Cash," James leaned back.

"Give me the number and I'll get it." Raphael shrugged. "Jace, Levi? Any questions?"

"I'm assuming we'll get the drop coordinates closer to the date," Jace remarked.

Raphael nodded. "They have requested no weapons. But wait and watch them before leaving the weapons," Raphael ordered. "Levi, any questions?" Raphael turned to me. I shook my head. "Then I think we have a plan," Raphael declared.

"We need a backup plan if the drug dealer doesn't show up. He didn't show when Levi was getting a tour," Stephanie strummed at the table.

"Don't like my plan dear sister of mine?" Raphael chuckled. Jace and James got up. Jace grabbed my shoulder and gestured for me to follow him. I looked at Stephanie whose eyes were on Raphael, her fingers anxiously picking at her jaw. Raphael was smirking, he took another long drag on his joint. I slowly got up and left with the guys. James and Jace took me outside. We walked to the tree line and sat down.

"Just like the good old days," Jace joked looking at James.

"Almost forgot," James murmured.

I looked over at them. "What?" I demanded. They both looked over like they had forgotten I was here. We sat there in silence listening to the loud forest and smoking. "Can I ask a question?"

"Ya man, what do you want to know?" Jace huffed.

"Why did Raphael kick Stephanie out?" I asked. Jace looked at me, he turned to James who shrugged.

"I guess someone has to tell you." Jace looked down at his joint. My mind began to race. "You are as high as a fucking kite; do you want to hear this now?"

"I don't really know what you're going to tell me," I commented.

"Are you able to hear any stories at the moment?" James leaned forward and looked at me, inspecting my eyes. I nodded.

"Okay," Jace sighed. "Uh, where do I start?"

"The banker," James put in.

Jace nodded. "When Stephanie first started with us, Raphael wasn't great with her. We all went from small level shit to... where the money is," Jace explained. "We had a major offer on this bank security system. Stephanie's a beautiful girl and Raph couldn't figure out any other way to get in. So, he told her to fuck the security plan designer. She did. The plan was perfectly executed, we got a couple million dollars. But when she came back, Raphael was vicious," Jace began. "We always had an idea that it was happening, the fights, the loud sex—"

"They were fucking?" I clarified.

"They were in love with each other," James stated.

"Ya, anyway, Stephanie came back from this job and Raphael couldn't live with it. Every chance he got he would make her life a living hell. Constantly high or drunk and ripping into her. It was terrible. She was constantly in tears. He never let her sleep," Jace continued.

"Why didn't she leave?" I asked.

"She thought it was her fault," James breathed a laugh, shaking his head. "We should have stepped in. But we didn't know what to do, you know? We knew Raphael was troubled but this was a different level and we were lost on how to deal with it."

"But he had asked her to do it," My eyebrows furrowed in confusion. They both nodded.

"What makes it so fucked up," Jace murmured. "This one fight was terrible. You could hear Raphael shouting, but Stephanie wasn't bothering to fight back anymore. Then Stephanie comes out. She had never left mid-fight. And she comes up to me and presses into me with a smile on her face like nothing had just happened. She looked at me and told me to fuck her. I hesitated and she leaned and whispered that she knew I wanted it. Bit my ear. I shouldn't have done it. I knew she was upset. But she looks magnificent and I always wanted to, but she had always been Raphael's precious object."

"Like an expensive painting, he loved when you looked, but God fucking forbid you touched it," James muttered.

"Ya, so anyway, we uh, we went to my room and fucked. Raphael came in after. I went to grab my gun, thinking he was going to kill us. But he just walked over to her. He spat on her and told her to leave in his shirt and a thong in the dead of winter. He didn't allow her to bring anything. No phone, no shoes, it's a miracle she fucking survived." Jace rubbed his face.

"Why weren't you kicked out?" I grumbled.

"I don't know." Jace shrugged. "I guess because, in

Raphael's mind, I was the tool, not the person who hurt him. Anyway, Raphael lost it after she left. He wasn't sober, ever. It was obvious Stephanie was the one making the plans, none of his work. Ever. We both stayed in communication with Stephanie. She thrived when she wasn't under Raphael's control. She met Eli and they were doing their own stuff."

"Were they together?" I questioned.

"No, they've always just been friends," Jace smiled faintly. "It took us forever to convince Raphael to get over it and bring her back."

"We were nervous when you came into the picture. But Raphael took a shine to you," James stated. "I mean, he's obviously still pissed that she's with someone else," James gestured to the house, "but not to the same degree."

"He's still in love with her," I breathed, my mind finally clamoring its way to that conclusion. Jace and James both nodded. "Can I tell you something?" I fidgeted. Jace and James turned in surprise. "When I was first here, with my friends, one of them found a grate that looked from Raphael's room into Stephanie's. He had that painting blocking it from Stephanie's side."

"Did you tell Stephanie?" James demanded.

"No, I put a different painting in front."

"Did he say anything about that?"

"The next morning. He took me for a walk, put a gun to my head and said I was just as much at fault because I covered it without telling her."

"Fucking hell," Jace muttered.

"What the fuck, Raphael?" James murmured.

"You guys didn't know?" I asked. I had hoped that others had knowledge of it.

"No clue about it," Jace mumbled, his face completely exhausted.

"I have to go," I whimpered. Jace pulled out his gun and passed it to me. I took it, tucking it in my back pocket as I walked back to the house. I took a deep breath in before opening the door. Stephanie was sitting with her face in her hands.

"Mouse," Raphael muttered, he removed her hands from her face. Stephanie looked at me and smiled faintly. Raphael turned around abruptly, opening his mouth in vexation.

"Why didn't you tell me?" I demanded. Stephanie slowly got up.

"Tell you what?" Raphael mused. Stephanie shot him a dirty look and walked to me.

"That you two fucked!" I yelled.

"I'm so sorry," Stephanie whispered.

"You never asked." Raphael shrugged.

"Oh, yes, I'm sorry for assuming that the man she called brother never fucked her," I hissed.

"Foster," Raphael rolled his eyes.

"Raphael, shut the fuck up," Stephanie snapped. "Levi, look at me, I'm so sorry."

"Stop apologizing, Stephanie. If he was pissed at us for fucking, he wouldn't have just started an argument with you and me. I think there's someone else that should be here," Raphael chuckled.

"Raphael, shut the fuck up," Stephanie implored.

"Jace isn't still in love with her," I retorted.

"This is bullshit," Raphael laughed, stood up and started to leave. I pulled the gun on him. "You have a terrible shot," Raphael smirked.

"That doesn't mean the bullet won't hit you," I stated. "He's in love with you," I murmured to Stephanie.

"Why does that matter? I chose you. I'm in love with you." She begged, pressing herself against me, looking at me intently. Her cheeks were wet with tears, her voice no more than a desperate whisper full of agony. The pleas didn't cut through the burning fury I was engulfing in.

"I don't think he understands that," I growled. "Prove it to him," I ordered, undoing my belt. She swallowed hard then nodded. Stephanie slowly got down on her knees, undoing my pants.

"Stephanie—" Raphael began. Stephanie stuck up a finger. Raphael immediately fell silent. She took out my penis and wrapped her lips around it.

"Fuck," I moaned, putting my gun down. Raphael's jaw hardened. He glared at me. The type of glare that purely demonstrated an insatiable hatred. I smirked as my fingers intertwined with her hair, urging her mouth deeper. I saw the look of pure pain in Raphael's eyes before he darted off. I won. "Let's go fuck." I looked down at Stephanie. She nodded. I did my pants back up and wiped down the gun, placing it on the table.

We proceeded to the bedroom. I left the door open, determined to rub my victory in Raphael's pretentious face.

She was mine.

Not his.

Mine.

We stripped down. I pointed to the bed. She obediently lay down. I crawled on top of her, positioning myself. I rammed myself into her, using the headboard as leverage as I began to pound her mercilessly. I leaned forward, biting her neck viciously.

"Holy fuck," Stephanie moaned pulling me into her. Her nails sank into me. That egged me on, my primal instincts kicking in as I shoved myself into her. My left hand went to her hip, my fingers digging into her. The mix between the cocaine and anger running through my veins allowed me to pummel her in a complete animalistic need. "Fuck, fuck, fuck, fuck!" Stephanie yelled, her nails tearing into me harder as she climaxed. I continued to pound her mercilessly. I bit her neck hard, grunting loudly as I finished. I lay there staring at the ceiling until I crashed.

Chapter 15

"That was a lot of information for you to take in, especially when you were high," the green-eyed lady remarked.

I chuckled. "Yes, it was. Looking back, I should have known. Raphael wasn't subtle in his hatred of our relationship. I just thought it was a fucked up brother thing, not a fucked-up ex-boyfriend thing," I replied.

"With what you know now, who do you think decided to introduce him under the label of foster brother, Raphael or Stephanie?" the green-eyed lady asked.

I thought for a few seconds. "Stephanie. Their break up was still sore, she probably thought it would be easier for her and Raphael to just not answer questions," I stated.

"Do you think there's any chance that Stephanie reciprocated the feelings Raphael had?" the brown-haired lady queried.

I laughed. "No, she was friendly with him, but I never had a serious fear of her wanting him."

"When you threatened Raphael with the gun, was there a chance you would've pulled that trigger?" the brown-haired lady questioned.

"No, it was an empty threat at the time. But if I could go back, I wouldn't hesitate. Would've saved a lot of heartache," I mused. The two ladies sat back and gave me a frustrated look.

***

I woke up with an unbelievable headache. Stephanie rounded the corner in her robe, shutting the door behind her. She approached the bed with a glass of water.

"God, I love you," I whispered, grabbing the water from her hand. She passed me ibuprofen. I took it and chugged down the glass of water. The events of last night hit me hard. "Fuck," I muttered trying to make sense of it all.

"How much do you remember of last night?" Stephanie asked quietly.

"Everything," I replied. "I'm sorry, that was a terrible thing for me to have done to you," I muttered.

"I should have told you," Stephanie replied.

"Why didn't you?"

"I, uh… I thought you would think less of me and I really love you," Stephanie looked down at her hands.

"Hey," I gently took her face in my hands. "You could've fucked everyone in the country of Russia and I wouldn't think less of you," I murmured. Stephanie giggled. "Just, don't do that now. I expect to be the only person fucking you now, in case that wasn't clear." I winked at her.

"You're the only person fucking me now," she confirmed.

"Then I am perfectly fine," I kissed her gently on the forehead. "No one should treat you the way I treated you last night."

"You were high on cocaine, Jace shouldn't have given you a gun."

"No, probably not, but I'm sorry," I stared into her eyes sincerely.

"It's okay," Stephanie smiled.

"Is Raphael going to kill me?"

"No, uh, I talked to him this morning, he thinks after this robbery, you and I should split off from the group for a bit. He thinks you and him just need some time apart." Stephanie turned toward me. "But that's fine, it'll be just us for a bit."

"I can't complain about that outcome."

"Good morning!" Jace yelled walking into our room. I grabbed my head in pain. "Raphael has left, so you guys can come out of prison."

"Raphael left?"

"Yup, he took one look at the hickeys on Stephanie's neck and he said, 'Levi has to go' and Stephanie said, 'you have to go.'" Jace gleefully sat on the bed with us. I looked toward Stephanie. My heart swelled knowing she had forced him out. She chose me.

"God, I love you," I looked at her completely mesmerized.

"I hear you did something very stupid last night," Eli walked into the room, sitting on the bed, his eyes were on me, irritated.

"You mean something completely fucking cool. Balls of fucking steal," James praised, walking in and sitting on the bed too.

"Hey, Stephanie, is this the most amount of men you've had on your bed at one time," Jace winked.

"The most amount of men I've had on my bed that I don't want to be here, yes," Stephanie retorted.

"Sassy," Jace chuckled.

"How are you feeling?" James asked me.

"Headache, but other than that, feeling stupid and kind of great," I replied.

"They're kind of excited that you put Raphael in his place. No one has really done it," Stephanie explained.

"Except the great Stephanie Gibson who smacks him down

a couple of notches every now and then," Jace teased. Stephanie took a little bow. "But you man, you knew what would hurt and you fucking leaned in."

"I am very impressive." I laughed. "How did the buying of the silencers go?" I turned to Eli.

"Fine," Eli answered coldly.

"How was the fueled-up cocaine and rage sex?" Jace prodded.

"Please learn boundaries," Stephanie muttered.

"How was the cocaine and rage-fueled sex?" Jace turned and questioned me.

"Pretty fucking great," I commented.

"I'm gonna assume you enjoyed it too, as I have ears. And your neck." Jace gestured to the bruises that covered her. Stephanie hit him with a pillow. "Stop hitting on me, your boyfriend is right there," Jace laughed.

"Okay, we need to get dressed," I announced to the guys. Eli got up and left. Jace and James remained.

"We shouldn't have told you last night," James admitted.

"And I shouldn't have given you a gun, we were high and not thinking clearly," Jace stated. Stephanie got up and went to her closet to pick out her outfit.

"A lesson to never mix drugs," James laughed.

"Jace, don't turn around," Stephanie ordered.

"Nothing I haven't seen before," Jace called back.

"You haven't seen her new tattoo," I joked, winking at Jace. Jace began to turn around. I hit him hard with a pillow.

"Ow, what is with you two this morning?" Jace whined.

"Can you pass me some underwear?" I called to Stephanie. Stephanie walked over in her underwear to my backpack and tossed me a pair of boxers. "Close your eyes, both of you," I ordered. James closed his eyes.

"Nothing I haven't seen before." Jace shrugged. I rolled my eyes hopping out of bed and quickly pulling on the boxers. "I have seen both of you naked!" Jace announced triumphantly.

"Because you're a pervert," Stephanie rolled her eyes. She had pulled on her light blue crop top and shorts.

"Maybe. But I can confirm when your children grow up, they'll be sexy as fuck," Jace laughed.

"What every mother wants to know. That her children will be sexy," Stephanie mumbled. I pulled on my pants, walking over to Stephanie, wrapping my arms around her.

"Just means they'll always have the option of being famous porn stars," I hugged her tightly.

"Music to my ears," Stephanie muttered.

"Every parent's dream," James laughed. "Hey, Levi, give us a flex," James instructed. I obeyed, striking a pose.

"That's the work of the eggs," Jace declared. I looked at Stephanie.

"You do look really hot," Stephanie ran her fingers over my chest. I puffed out my chest with pride.

"Steph, shall we make breakfast?" Eli asked, walking in.

"We can have, like a fivesome right now," Jace said.

"Ya we can," James winked at Jace.

"Ew," Eli whined.

"I'm in," I joked, kissing Stephanie on the cheek.

"Well, you three have fun," Stephanie patted me gently on the arm and walked out of the room.

"We will!" Jace shouted after her. Eli followed Stephanie out. "Urg, it's been so long since I've hooked up with someone." Jace complained, sticking his head in a pillow.

"Same," James muttered.

"Oh, shut up, you fuck the pizza man like every week. It's the closest thing I've seen to you being in a committed relationship," Jace replied.

"You go every day looking at one unattainable woman. I go every day looking at three men, four when Levi's here." James shoved Jace.

"Who says I'm unattainable?" I winked at James.

"Don't play with me like that," James raised both his middle fingers at me.

"What if we all went out tonight?" I grabbed my shirt, pulling it over my head. "Raphael's not here."

"Boy's got a point." James shrugged.

"Stephanie!" Jace yelled. Stephanie's footsteps echoed through the hallway. She appeared in the doorway. "We're going out tonight!" Jace announced.

"Okay? It's Sunday, I can't imagine it being very fun," Stephanie voiced.

"Oh, it'll be fun. This is the first time we've been able to do something like this for months," Jace stated.

"Months," James repeated.

"Eli!" Stephanie shouted. Eli joined her at the doorway. "They want to go out tonight."

"It's Sunday, will anywhere be open?" Eli pondered.

"We'll find somewhere that is," I said.

"Thank you, Levi," Jace smiled. "Eli, I can be your wingman."

"No thank you, I will come out if you don't do that," Eli suggested.

"I will take it," Jace laughed. "So, Stephanie, what will it be? Your boyfriend is coming with us."

"I mean, I'm obviously coming, I just want you guys to have

realistic expectations," Stephanie smirked.

"Our expectation is that we're gonna get fucked," Jace gave James a high five.

"Okay, cool," Stephanie laughed. "You guys sort out your plan for that." Stephanie nodded at us before leaving with Eli. James got up and shut the door before pointing to the painting hanging on the wall. I had forgotten I told them about the grate. I nodded. "I'm going to grab something for you to wear from Raphael's closet," James said loudly. He left the room, shutting the door behind him. Jace stood up and took the painting down. Turning it around.

"What the fuck?" I hissed. "I covered the back with insulation." I grabbed it from Jace's hands.

"Looks like he ripped it out." Jace pointed to the edges that still held pink residue.

"Okay, so this is fucked up," James said from behind the grate.

"I just want to make sure nothing is visible at the moment." Jace placed the painting back up. James came back inside the room.

"I can't see anything from that side with the painting up." James passed me a stack of clothing. "I would say we should board it up, but Stephanie's leaving before he comes back, then we're moving. I don't think it's worth it."

"I'm glad you and Stephanie are leaving for a bit. We'll sort Raphael before you guys join back up," Jace nodded toward me.

"Should we tell Stephanie?" I picked at the clothing in my hand.

"No, let us sort this out," James instructed.

"Stephanie will forgive Raphael and he'll end up feeling validated in his sick obsession," Jace muttered, frustrated. "Not our first rodeo."

"We'll not ask you guys to rejoin until we know it's okay," James put his hand on my shoulder sincerely.

"I'll miss you guys," I frowned.

"We'll miss you too," Jace grimaced. "Good luck trying to shake Eli off Stephanie though, he may be coming with you guys," Jace laughed.

"What if you guys came with us too? Leave Raphael," I stated hopefully. James and Jace looked at each other.

"You know we can't do that. He's family," Jace murmured. I nodded.

"I know, just being stupid," I breathed a laugh.

"No, you're making more sense than us," James sighed. "Just the undying loyalty of the streets."

"Breakfast is ready," Stephanie opened the door. "Is there a funeral I don't know about?" Stephanie looked at us confused by our somber expressions.

"We're just saying we're gonna miss you guys," Jace replied. Stephanie nodded slowly, stepping into the room.

"It probably won't be too long," Stephanie replied.

"Ya, probably," James muttered.

"Just don't pick up any more strays please," Jace laughed. "We've got our hands full taking care of Eli."

"So, there's a bar that's open until late about an hour away. Thought it may help your game if we took Raph's vehicle," Stephanie held up the keys, a wide grin on her face.

"No fucking way, he didn't take it?" Jace beamed.

"He took my car, I thought I deserved a few days of luxury," Stephanie giggled.

"I could fuck you right now," Jace walked forward in amazement.

"Hey, relax," I said, putting my hand out. Jace grabbed the keys from Stephanie.

"Can I drive?" Jace questioned.

"There, but I'm driving back," Stephanie replied.

"Oh, I don't plan on returning with you guys anyway," Jace smiled. We all made our way to the kitchen. Eli was happily eating his eggs at the counter looking at his phone.

"Excited about the car?" Eli looked up.

Jace nodded. "Hell fucking ya, I can't believe Raphael left his car. His rich person car."

"It's not Raphael's car," James grinned. "I can't believe you guys don't remember. The Rolls was a present for Stephanie."

"Your ex-boyfriend bought you a Rolls? Why are you even with me?" I joked while hugging Stephanie from behind.

"I don't have any memory of that," Stephanie laughed.

"She then rejected it and bought that crappy red Toyota the next day," James chuckled. "The stupidest 'fuck you' that ever happened. So technically it is actually Stephanie's Rolls."

"I remember it," Eli smiled. "Raphael tried to slice the tires of the red Toyota after. But Stephanie threatened to do the same to the Rolls and he quickly stopped."

"You're such a badass," I praised. "Can we take the Rolls with us when we leave?"

"I mean it is mine." Stephanie shrugged.

"No, gift it to me," Jace pleaded.

"If Levi wants to learn to drive, we'll take the Rolls," Stephanie glanced over at me.

"Levi, you never want to drive, it's dangerous, stressful and time-consuming. Stephanie won't love you if you know how to drive," Jace stared at me intently.

"For a Rolls, I will learn to drive," I grinned.

313

"There you have it, we're taking the Rolls," Stephanie announced. Jace groaned.

"Zip me up?" Stephanie asked. She moved her hair over her right shoulder. I walked over and slowly zipped her skin-tight, black dress up. Her hair was in loose waves, and she had a red lip. We walked out of our room. James whistled. Stephanie did a little twirl. I wore black pants and a black T-shirt that James had pulled from Raphael's closet. Raphael's shirt fit tighter on me than normal. Stephanie walked over to me.

"You look like a goddess," I whispered in her ear. Stephanie bit her lip gently.

"We don't have time for that, it's time to go." Jace stepped uncomfortably close to us. Stephanie rolled her eyes and stepped back from me. Jace wore a pair of jeans and a tight white T-shirt.

"Let's get going!" James said excitedly, wearing ripped jeans and a white collared shirt slightly unbuttoned. Eli wore a blue T-shirt and black jeans. He led the way outside. Jace got in the driver's seat, Stephanie in the passenger. Eli, James and me scrunched into the back seats. The seats were a beige leather with mahogany wood finishes. It was exquisite. Jace started the vehicle and nodded at Stephanie putting it in drive.

"Fuck, listen to that engine." Jace rubbed the dashboard.

"Please don't fuck the car," Stephanie laughed.

"Oh, I would if I could," Jace replied.

"Probably the only way he's going to get laid tonight," Eli prodded.

"So, what's the plan if one of you guys pick someone up?" I queried.

"Jace and I will find our way home, don't you worry," James winked. We drove to the bar; the cramped back seat was getting stuffy as we pulled into the surprisingly full parking lot. We all got out. Jace handed the keys to Stephanie as we walked into the bar. The host quickly escorted us to our table.

"Can we get a bottle of Patron tequila?" Stephanie requested.

"What are we celebrating?" Jace mused.

"Levi wants to try it. It also may help to attract gold diggers." She winked at Jace. The waiter brought back the bottle and five shot glasses. "Thank you," Stephanie smiled, handing him a couple hundred dollars.

"Okay, let's see if you like it," Eli said, opening the bottle and pouring out four shots.

"To Levi's balls of steal!" Jace raised his shot glass. We all clinked the glasses, except Stephanie, and took a shot. It went down with a nice bite.

"Do you like it?" Stephanie questioned.

"It's really good," I nodded, pleased, placing my shot glass in the center of the table. Eli refilled the glasses.

"To my family!" I raised my shot glass. We all clinked and took the shot.

"She's kind of hot," James pointed subtly to a brown-haired girl on the other side of the room with her friends. Jace nodded.

"I'll be back," Jace got up and walked to the bar. He spoke to the bartender who nodded. Jace handed him some cash. He turned and walked back to our table. "Now we wait."

"What did you send her?" Eli asked.

"A bottle of Patron, inspired by Levi." Jace's eyes were transfixed with the table. The waiter walked over with the bottle of tequila and gestured to us, setting it in front of a blond-haired woman. He set down three shot glasses for her and her friends. All the women turned and looked over at our table. Jace waved.

"That's not the girl I pointed to," James commented.

"Bartender said she had a wedding ring on, so I changed my focus," Jace laughed. The blond-haired woman gestured for Jace to come over. "See you guys tomorrow," Jace stood up and walked over to their table. He sat next to the blond-haired woman.

"That was quick," I remarked.

"He still has to close," James leaned back scanning the room.

"So, when did you get home?" I asked Eli.

"Early in the morning, it was pretty far away." Eli shrugged. "How did you enjoy the resort?"

"It was phenomenal," I replied.

"Did you get to the casino?" Eli questioned.

"No, uh, we were preoccupied," I smirked.

"Cool," Eli twirled the shot glass in his fingers, an unimpressed expression plastered on his face.

"This drink was sent over by that young lady over there." The waiter placed a shot of a clear liquid in front of Eli. Eli waved to the woman politely.

"Can you send her an expensive bottle of Scotch and politely tell her I'm not interested." Eli smiled at the waiter. He reached in his wallet and pulled out about a grand in one-hundred-dollar bills. "Any extra keep as a tip," Eli instructed. The waiter smiled and nodded.

"Okay guys, bye," James abruptly stood up and walked over to a young man standing at the bar. We watched as the waiter brought over the bottle of whiskey to the young lady that hit on Eli. The waiter spoke to her for a few seconds, she nodded and thanked him, waving sweetly at Eli. Eli gave her a thumbs up. The lady went back to speaking with her friends.

"Damn, she took that like a champ," Stephanie commented.

"Rejection is easier to swallow with an expensive gift." Eli shrugged. James waved to us as he left with the young man.

"Well done, James," I murmured.

"Jace is still working on the woman," Stephanie gestured over to their table. The waiter returned with a martini and placed it in front of Stephanie.

"From the young man over there." The waiter gestured to a young man standing at the edge of the bar. He waved at her.

"Uh, can you do the same thing that you did for Eli?" Stephanie requested, gesturing to Eli. "But tell him I'm taken." Stephanie pulled out a grand and gave it to the waiter. "Keep the rest as a tip," Stephanie smiled gently. The waiter nodded and headed back.

"That poor waiter's job is basically coming on to people and rejecting them," Eli said sympathetically.

"I wonder if that's typical or if we're just lazy," Stephanie laughed.

"At least we tip well." Eli shrugged. Jace got up with the young lady and left, flashing us a smile. Eli stiffened. Another martini was placed in front of Stephanie.

"I thought I should introduce myself." The young man at the bar grabbed a seat and sat down beside Stephanie.

"Oh, I'm taken," Stephanie uttered. I waved uncomfortably.

"And he doesn't like competition?" the man smirked.

"I don't see competition, I see a pathetic man who can't take no as an answer," Stephanie retorted. I slowly grabbed Stephanie's purse, putting it on my lap.

"Calm down, with a mood like that I doubt he's fucking you well enough," the man leaned forward. Stephanie laughed angrily.

"Please don't touch me," Stephanie smiled aggressively. I looked down to see the man's hand on her thigh. The man moved

317

his hand up slightly. Stephanie stood up. I stood up too, pulling the chairs away. Stephanie turned to walk out of the bar. The man grabbed her arm.

"I can show you a good time," the man insisted. Stephanie punched him directly in the nose and left. Eli nodded toward me. "That bitch. I'm calling the police," the man whined holding his now bleeding nose. I sat down where Stephanie was sitting, reaching into her purse and pulling out her gun.

"You call the police, we'll kill you," I whispered, leaning in and placing the barrel of the gun against his penis. The man's eyes grew big. "We'll find you, kapeesh?" I hissed. The man nodded eagerly. I put the gun away and stood up, looking around. No one seemed to notice the events that had just unfolded.

"Pathetic," Eli spat on him and walked to the bar. I grabbed the bottle of Patron on the table. "Sorry about the mess." Eli gestured to the man holding his nose passing the bartender another grand.

"I am honored to clean up that mess," the waiter gleamed. He handed Eli the expensive bottle of whiskey Stephanie had bought for the man. "I don't think he'll have much use for this," the waiter laughed.

"Thank you," Eli smiled and grabbed the bottle of whiskey. We walked out of the bar. Stephanie was already sitting in the vehicle. I got in the passenger seat.

"I'm sorry guys," Stephanie murmured.

"You're kidding me, right?" I chortled. "That was literally the best thing I've ever seen."

"The waiter was so impressed he gave us the expensive bottle of whiskey you bought for him," Eli lifted up the bottle of whiskey.

"What an asshole," Stephanie shook her head.

"Understatement of the year," I exclaimed. "Maybe we taught him a lesson."

"We are vigilantes," Eli voiced dramatically. "Can we get ice cream?"

"It's eleven," Stephanie replied. "There are no ice cream places open."

"Gas station ice cream?" I suggested.

"That will do," Eli opened the expensive bottle of whiskey and took a gulp. He passed it to me. I took a swig; it went down smoothly.

"Damn, rich people alcohol is so much better," I muttered.

"You'll never have to go back," Stephanie giggled. We pulled up to a gas station in the Rolls-Royce. Eli ran in.

"Are you okay?" I asked Stephanie.

"Oh ya, I'm used to that. Assholes are everywhere," Stephanie sighed. I nodded. Eli came out, raising his arms victoriously with ice cream sandwiches in his hand. Eli got in the vehicle handing them out. We ate the sandwiches; Eli and I took turns sipping the alcohol. "We need to get you home; your parents are probably worried."

"Oh ya, probably." I shrugged. Stephanie turned the car on, and we began our drive back.

We pulled into my driveway. My dad came out and stood at the doorway. Stephanie turned off the vehicle.

"Fuck, we forgot your bag," Stephanie leaned her head back.

"That's okay, you can give it to me later." I reached over to give Eli the bottle of Patron. Stephanie stopped me.

"It's yours," she stated. We kissed quickly before I got out of the vehicle. Eli jumped into the passenger seat. They turned the car on and left. I walked into my house. Mom was standing there in her robe, dad beside her.

"Is that Patron tequila?" Dad pointed at the bottle in my hand. "You can't afford that and how is your girlfriend dropping you off in a Rolls-Royce?"

"Eli's rich," I replied.

"Are those hickeys?" mom demanded, turning my head.

"Should have seen the other girl," I joked. My parents did not laugh. I thought it was pretty funny.

"Are you drunk?" dad interrogated. I shook my head then laughed. "It's midnight on a Sunday, you have classes tomorrow."

"I'll be up on time," I chuckled. Mom and dad looked at each other. I walked past them to my room and went to sleep.

The sunlight woke me up early. The pain in my head was vicious, though not nearly as bad as the hangover yesterday. I pulled on my clothing and walked downstairs. I went into the kitchen and sat down at the table.

"Do you have a hangover?" dad yelled. I put my face in my hands and nodded. "Good, at least there's a natural consequence to your actions."

"Why are you mad?" I groaned.

"Well, our son pulls up at midnight, drunk, holding a bottle of alcohol with hickeys on his neck. On a Sunday," dad growled. Mom placed a glass of water in front of me. I took a sip.

"I admit, that's not a great look," I relented.

"That's an understatement," dad hissed. "Are you on drugs?"

"No, I am not on drugs," I insisted.

"Then why did that happen?" dad demanded.

"Uh, I was drunk because I was hanging out with the guys, I was late because Eli wanted ice cream and the hickeys are because…" I paused. Dad looked at me to keep going. "Stephanie's kinky?" I shrugged.

"Ew, don't tell us that," mom whined.

"What, how do you think hickeys happen? Why do I need to explain that?" I protested.

"Had sex would have been a sufficient answer," dad muttered.

"We've been having sex, that's not new. Why does it matter? I'm an adult. I got drunk but we had a designated driver; I was late, but I was safe; and I came home; Stephanie and I are having sex but we're using protection. The bottle of Patron was a gift. I'm doing everything right," I huffed.

My dad sat back surprised. "We'll be talking to Raphael about this on Thursday."

"Be my guest." I stood up and left, slamming the door behind me.

"Need a ride?" A voice called out of the familiar red Toyota. I walked closer. Raphael was leaning over toward me. I got in. We pulled out of the driveway and headed to school. "I wanted to give you this." Raphael tossed me a burner phone. My eyes zeroed in on a tattoo on his left arm, it was of a mouse holding a crown in its mouth and looking back at him. Fuck, how did I not notice it sooner? I'm a fucking idiot.

"Thank you," I muttered, putting it in my pocket.

"Trouble with the parents?" Raphael mused.

"We're not doing this," I snarled.

Raphael took a deep breath. "Look, I'm sorry for not telling you Stephanie and I slept together, I just don't understand why that was so important."

"Because you've been watching her!" I shrieked. "You've been listening and watching her. Why?" I growled.

"We've had this discussion before. Tell yourself what you fucking need to," Raphael hissed.

"You need to sort your shit out before Stephanie, and I come back."

"Look at you being protective," Raphael laughed. We pulled up at the university. "When I come calling, she'll come crawling back. You either come with her or fucking leave."

"She hasn't come crawling back to you yet, I'm feeling pretty fucking confident," I got out of the vehicle and slammed the door. I heard the squeal of the tires as he quickly pulled away.

I walked to the cafeteria. My hands rubbed my face as the loud noise punctured my head with pain. Stephanie, Aidan and Lucas sat at our usual table. I plunked myself down.

"Rough morning?" Stephanie joked, rubbing my back.

"You can say that. My parents bitched me out when I woke up, then Raphael picked me up like the good man he is and dropped me off here," I grumbled.

"Are you okay? What did he say?" Stephanie pouted empathetically.

"That you'll leave me," I put my head on the table.

"I thought you and Raphael got along?" Aidan asked.

"They had a pretty major fight on Saturday," Stephanie commented.

"Why?" Aidan queried.

"Because I was high on cocaine and I told Stephanie to suck my dick in front of him," I muttered. I banged my head against the table gently. Aidan and Lucas laughed. I sat back up. Stephanie shook her head at them.

"Holy shit, you're not joking?" Aidan's eyes widened.

"Did you?" Lucas questioned.

"She did, yes," I interjected.

"Why were you on cocaine?" Aidan pinched the bridge of his nose.

"It was offered to me, and I thought 'why not?'" I replied. "Now I know why not."

"That's a lot. So, I'm guessing you guys didn't have a good weekend?" Lucas clarified.

"No, it was actually amazing, besides that. We went to a resort, just the two of us. It was brilliant." Stephanie put her head against my shoulder. I put my arm around her squeezing tightly. I kissed her lovingly on the cheek.

"Okay, why were your parents mad at you?" Lucas wondered.

"I came home at midnight, drunk, with a bottle of alcohol. Oh and—" I turned my head revealing the hickeys.

"Ah, yes, okay, makes sense. Is Raphael mad at your set?" Aidan turned to Stephanie. Stephanie nodded. "So, we have an idea what you did at this resort," Aidan joked.

"Her set is from the cocaine and rage sex, mine are from the resort," I over-explained.

"Okay, fun. Uh, Lucas, how was your weekend?" Aidan changed the topic uncomfortably.

"Not as exciting that's for sure," Lucas mumbled.

We sat in the Rolls-Royce. Stephanie looked at me intently. My heart was beating at a record speed. I looked around, not sure if I wanted to do this anymore.

"Are you okay?" Stephanie asked gently.

"Ya," I said in a panic.

"Hurry up man, it's not that bad," Aidan complained in the back seat.

"What did you ask me to do?" I turned to Stephanie.

"I told you to put the car in drive," Stephanie smiled, holding back a laugh. I nodded to myself.

"Okay, okay, okay," I whispered, pressing firmly down on the brake. I moved the shift to drive and quickly looked back up.

"Now you can slowly release the brake," I inched my foot off the brake, my knuckles white, my hands sweaty. I looked around the empty parking lot.

"There we are, see you're driving!" Stephanie announced, clapping excitedly.

"I am," I voiced, barely audible through my terrified breathing. My head was firmly against the seat as I stared forward.

"Now you can press on the gas," Stephanie instructed. I shook my head profusely. "Okay, we can work on that next time."

"When you said you would take us out in a Rolls-Royce, I didn't think you meant this," Lucas whined.

"Okay, you can slowly start pressing the brake. Stephanie directed. I slammed on the brake. Everyone lurched forward. "Okay, now put it in park," Stephanie advised. I obeyed instantly. "There, see? That wasn't that bad."

"It was kind of fun," I smiled, undoing my seatbelt and getting out, switching sides with Stephanie. Stephanie leaned over and kissed me.

"Ew, stop it," Aidan said. "Are we going actually go out in it now?"

"I mean, sure, you asked for it. I know a place," Stephanie laughed, putting it in drive. We drove for a while before coming to Stephanie's selected location. It was a large raceway. She pulled up to the gate. An attendant walked out.

"Ms. Gibson, Raphael didn't tell me you were also stopping

by," the attendant smiled.

"Raphael's in there?" Stephanie queried.

"Yes, he is driving one of our Jaguars." The attendant looked down at his sheet. Stephanie looked over to me looking to see if I was okay with that. I nodded.

"Excellent, we will be driving this," Stephanie leaned over me and pulled out a large envelope of cash from the compartment. She counted out around ten grand and passed it to the attendant.

"Raphael has already paid for the court." The attendant refused the money.

"A tip," Stephanie handed him the money again.

"Thank you. You're always so generous to us," the attendant grinned. He gestured for the gates to open. I looked back at Aidan and Lucas who were obliviously looking out the window. Stephanie drove in.

"You must have really pissed Raphael off this morning," Stephanie murmured.

"What is this place?" I asked, looking around in amazement.

"An old race track. They filled in the center and now it's for people practicing their driving," Stephanie explained. We watched as a black Jaguar drove by quickly. Stephanie drove the Rolls to the center and parked it.

"This place is for me," I smiled at Stephanie.

"Not that type of driving," Stephanie stepped out of the Rolls. The Jaguar turned sharply, its tires gliding further before straightening. It sped toward Stephanie.

"Stephanie, get in," I opened my door and yelled. Stephanie put her hand up toward me and shook her head. The Jaguar continued to speed toward her. It spun to the side and glided to a stop inches before hitting her. Raphael got out and slammed the door. Not wanting Aidan or Lucas to hear the discussion between Raphael and Stephanie, I quickly got in the car and shut the door. Stephanie pointed at the vehicle instantly. Raphael said something then came over to the Rolls. He opened the back door.

"Ah, okay," Raphael mumbled, looking at Aidan and Lucas, shutting the door again. He pointed to the other side of the track. They walked over to the side. Stephanie was saying something pointing at the vehicle. He shrugged. She rubbed her forehead and shook her head. Raphael hit his heart with his hand. Stephanie put her hands up by her head.

"I wonder what they're saying," Aidan pondered. Stephanie pointed to the vehicle again.

"I think I have an idea," I replied. Stephanie pointed to herself. Raphael pointed to the car. Stephanie shook her head. She said something this time, looking calm. Raphael grabbed her hand and stepped closer.

"Are you going to share with the class?" Aidan asked. Raphael put his hand gently on the side of her face. Stephanie shook her head saying something. Raphael shook his head and gently kissed her forehead. Stephanie looked up at him. She said something, squeezing his hand. Raphael pulled her closer and whispered something in her ear.

"No," I replied.

"Fine," Aidan muttered. Raphael pulled back slightly, using the hand on the side of her face to tilt her face up. He went in for a kiss. Stephanie turned her head. She said one more thing, breaking away from him. She began to walk back to the car.

"Did he just try to kiss her?" Lucas demanded.

"I think so," Aidan uttered. "Did you know about that?" Aidan questioned me.

"Yes," I replied. Raphael ran after her. I got out of the car.

Raphael began walking backward, raising his arms up. Stephanie laughed.

"I'm gonna kick your ass," Stephanie prodded, smirking at Raphael. He shook his head. I walked to Stephanie. Wrapping my arms tightly around her and locking our lips together. I heard Raphael's car door slam. Stephanie pulled away from the kiss looking at me.

"I love you," I murmured, my hand caressing the side of her face. The Jaguar started behind us.

"I love you," Stephanie pressed our lips together. My right hand wandered down and squeezed her ass, pulling her into me. The Jaguar honked. I ignored it, my tongue thrusting into her mouth. My right hand moved up her shirt. I heard the Jaguar begin to drive backward and stop abruptly. I pulled away from our kiss. We began to walk back to the Rolls. I glared at the Jaguar. "He challenged us to a race," Stephanie advised.

"Good," I replied.

"Are you okay?" Stephanie questioned.

I smiled at her. "I feel on top of the world." I turned and grabbed her, lifting her up. Stephanie giggled and wrapped her legs around me.

"I want to fuck you," Stephanie whispered into my ear.

"I want to fuck you too, but perhaps let's wait for less of an audience," I laughed, putting her down. Stephanie slapped my ass, cackling as she ran back to the Rolls and got in. I sat in the passenger seat. "That was rude."

"I don't know what you're talking about," Stephanie winked at me.

"Are we allowed to ask questions about what just happened?" Lucas queried.

"No," I retorted.

Stephanie turned on the vehicle. Raphael spun the Jaguar around and stopped beside the Rolls. Stephanie rolled down her window.

"Are you ready?" Raphael asked impatiently. "Your driving gloves are in the glove box."

"Born ready." Stephanie leaned over me and grabbed a pair of leather gloves from the compartment.

"I'm gonna make you my bitch," Raphael winked and rolled up his window. He spun the Jaguar again, lining up the cars. Stephanie rolled up her window, rolling her eyes.

"Beat his fucking ass," I instructed.

Stephanie nodded and revved the engine. Raphael honked loudly. Stephanie honked back. Raphael honked again. Stephanie tapped her finger at the same time. Raphael honked again. Stephanie tapped her finger. Putting the car in drive and tightened her grip.

"Hold on," Stephanie yelled. Raphael honked again. Both cars took off with a loud squeal. Stephanie quickly turned to the left to get out of the center. Raphael's Jaguar rounded the turn easier and quicker, putting him in the lead. Stephanie's eyes zeroed in. She pulled in directly behind his vehicle. Stepping on the gas and nudging the back. She did this one more time before swerving the car slightly to the left and hitting Raphael's car on the back left. She quickly diverted to the left and continued on as Raphael's back wheels slid to the right. He swerved slightly, getting back in control. By the time he was going straight, Stephanie had passed him. Stephanie slid the car through the corner and continued on to the next lap.

"Well done," I muttered. Stephanie smiled. I turned to see Aidan and Lucas wide-eyed and clutching the seats tightly. Raphael approached from the center. He positioned his car next to ours pressing us into the wall. Sparks flew next to me. Stephanie giggled. She slammed on the breaks allowing the Jaguar to fly straight into the wall. Stephanie rammed into the back of the Jaguar pressing on gas, dragging his car against the concrete. Raphael jerked the car slightly to the left, breaking the hold the Rolls had on it. He pressed on his breaks suddenly. Stephanie swerved and managed to avoid the Jaguar. Raphael hit the right wheel of the Rolls with force as we passed. The Rolls spun. Stephanie leaned into it and threw the car in reverse, straightening it that way. We were face to face with Raphael. I gave him the finger. Aidan and Lucas joined in. Stephanie laughed as she swung the car to the left, tossing the car into drive and continuing on past the corner.

"Final lap," Stephanie announced. We were in the lead. Raphael rammed into the back of our vehicle. Stephanie smiled. Flooring the gas pedal to get some leverage before slamming on the brakes. Raphael swerved to avoid the car but wasn't quick enough and hit the car in the rear. Stephanie pressed on the gas flying through the turn and finishing the lap. Raphael stood no chance. Stephanie stopped the car and put it in park. Everyone got out.

Raphael parked beside us. "So, the student has become the master," Raphael shouted getting out of the Jaguar.

"I think we made you our bitch," Stephanie yelled back.

Raphael walked over, eyeing his precious car. "You absolutely demolished the Rolls," Raphael laughed.

"I think you did that when you slammed the vehicle," I retorted.

"We'll see what they have here," Raphael smiled gently at Stephanie. "How did you like it, boys?" Raphael asked Aidan and Lucas.

"That was so cool," Lucas grinned. Raphael nodded. He gestured to an attendant to come meet us. The attendant walked over.

"Is he going to be mad?" Aidan queried.

"No, Raphael buys the cars out before he takes them out, this is his anger management." Stephanie shrugged. I wrapped my arms around Stephanie.

"You did so well," I kissed her multiple times on the cheek and neck.

"What can I do for you, sir?" the attendant asked.

"We need two new cars," Raphael gestured to the crash. The attendant nodded. "What do you want, Stephanie?"

"I have my Toyota," Stephanie rocked on her heels.

"Lucas, choose for her," Raphael instructed.

"Aston Martin?" Lucas suggested.

"We have one Aston Martin DB11," the attendant stated.

"We'll take it, the usual type of deal," Raphael ordered. "Do you have any Bentleys?"

"We have one Continental and one Flying Spur," the attendant listed.

"Do either come in black?" Raphael asked.

"The Flying Spur," the attendant replied.

"We'll take that one too. Usual type of deal. Bring them out," Raphael commanded. The attendant nodded and left.

"Where's the Toyota?" Stephanie demanded.

"Smashed it before you got here, you're welcome," Raphael said.

"I loved that car," Stephanie whined.

"You loved that car because it pissed me off," Raphael mused. "Empty out the Rolls," Raphael instructed. Stephanie nodded and grabbed her stuff. Raphael grabbed his bag out of the

Jaguar. The cars appeared at the end of the track. They drove to the center and parked them. Raphael walked over, handing them a few envelopes of cash. The first attendant nodded to the second and they handed Raphael the keys.

"I need the Bentley this time," Stephanie called.

"Why?" Raphael questioned. Stephanie gestured to Aidan and Lucas. "I can drop them back."

"No, I'll do it," Stephanie smiled, putting her hand out for the keys.

"Okay," Raphael handed her the keys.

We all got into the new car. Raphael knocked on the window. Stephanie turned the car on and rolled down the window. "Just wanted to tell you how exquisite you look in a luxury car." Raphael leaned on the windowsill and winked at Stephanie.

"I'll see you at home, Raph," Stephanie replied.

"Nice choice of car, Lucas," Raphael pointed at Lucas and went to the Aston Martin. Stephanie rolled up her window.

"Do we want to know how Raphael was able to pay for two luxury cars in cash?" Lucas queried from the back.

"No," I laughed.

"Okay, cool," Lucas said slowly.

We dropped Aidan and Lucas off at their houses. "So much for not being suspicious with money," I muttered. "Two luxury cars in cash in front of my friends," I shook my head.

"Pretty fucking stupid," Stephanie agreed. "I'm sure Aidan and Lucas won't say anything though."

"You and I know they won't, he doesn't. He's jeopardizing Thursday."

"He'll pull through, he always does," Stephanie nodded to

me as she pulled into my driveway. "I love you," she nudged my chin.

"I love you too." I kissed her on the tip of her nose and went into my house and straight to my room.

Chapter 16

"Raphael is pretty reckless it seems," the brown-haired lady said. "Seems a far stretch from the mastermind behind this."

"He pulled through, I guess." I shrugged.

***

Tuesday and Wednesday went by painfully slow. We had to continue on like everything was perfectly normal. But as every second passed and Thursday approached, my anxiety grew. I sat at the kitchen table, playing cards with my dad. I had told him I had a big test tomorrow and needed to get my mind off it. There was a knock at the door. I opened it. Stephanie stood there in a yellow sundress.

"Can I spend the night here?" she fidgeted.

I nodded, opening the door wider for her to come in.

"Stephanie's spending the night," I called to my parents. Stephanie followed me upstairs to my room. "Are you okay?"

"Oh ya, I'm fine. Just Raph is being a bit of a dick, I went driving and flipped a car and I'm just—" Stephanie rubbed her face. I gently took her chin in my hand and tilted her head. She had redness on her jaw and her arms.

"What the fuck?" I muttered, my fingers gliding along the forming bruises on her jawline.

"Ya, the airbag got me," Stephanie grimaced.

"Son, can I speak to you for a second?" Dad popped his head

through the doorway. I stepped out, closing the door behind me. "Uh, okay, Stephanie's going to stay the night?"

"Ya, uh, she's just having a hard time right now. One of the guys isn't being very nice," I murmured.

"Is it the same guy?" Dad leaned forward.

"No, a different one," I replied.

"She can stay, anytime," dad nodded worriedly. He turned to leave then paused. "There's an Aston Martin in the driveway," dad commented.

"Oh ya, Eli crashed the Rolls-Royce. Stephanie's just borrowing it to get away from the guy," I replied.

"Oh, okay," dad left. I returned to my room. Stephanie was rifling through my notebook.

"Don't go through that," I grabbed it from her.

"What is it?" Stephanie asked, her eyes lit up with excitement.

"Just scribbles," I mumbled.

"Well, I am a big fan of your scribbles," Stephanie sat down on my single bed. "They're really good. I particularly like this one." Stephanie grabbed my notebook from my hands. She flipped through the pages. "I met her on a day the sky never awakened. The gray clouds echoed outside as they did in my head. With that smile, she lit up the sky and I was awakened."

"It's not good," I sighed, trying to take the notebook back.

"I love it. It is good." Stephanie looked into my eyes sincerely.

"It's about you," I rocked on my heels.

"In which case, I want this tattooed on me," Stephanie grinned. I laughed. "No, I'm serious. Whenever I see it, it would remind me of us. It's beautiful."

"Wouldn't that be narcissistic? It's about you," I prodded.

"One, I am a narcissist. Two, fine, but you need to write me a tattoo then," Stephanie handed me back the notebook.

"What, now?" I demanded. Stephanie nodded. "What about 'I am a narcissist'?" I chuckled. Stephanie gently pushed me. "Okay." I looked down at the blank piece of paper. A few minutes passed. "Okay, what about this? I am more than my broken pieces; I am the person who makes them whole again." I looked up at Stephanie. "No, it's stupid."

"I love it, it's going to be my tattoo." She held out her hand. I ripped the page out of the book and handed it to her. She stood up and tucked it into her bag.

"I'm glad you came by," I smiled. "I was kind of freaking out about that test tomorrow."

"Well, why don't we take your mind off that test," Stephanie smiled and straddled me. "Do you have any condoms? I keep them in my purse and Raphael took it hostage. We don't have time to get the pill tomorrow."

"No. Fuck, I cut my parents off when they were going to tell me where they keep them," I muttered, putting my head on her chest.

"Ask them where they keep them," Stephanie urged.

"No, no fucking way, that's so weird, Stephanie." I shook my head.

"It's that or we can't fuck," Stephanie leaned forward, biting my ear gently. She then softly kissed my neck.

"Fuck, fine. But this better be the greatest sex of my life," I scoffed.

"I will endeavor to make that the case," Stephanie smiled getting off my lap. I got up and went for the door. "Uh—" Stephanie pointed at my erection. I repositioned it, gave her the finger and walked downstairs. Dad and mom sat at the table, drinking tea together.

"I, uh," I started. "Stephanie, uh, I, um... can I get a condom?" I questioned.

"Upstairs, top drawer in my bedside table," dad instructed. I nodded and walked upstairs. I riffled through the drawer until I found an unopened box of condoms. I ripped it open and grabbed a few stuffing them into my pocket. I hurried back to my room.

"Did you get one?" Stephanie demanded.

"I got a few, just in case." I shrugged. "Now, where is my reward?" I joked. Stephanie gestured for me to sit down. I obeyed. She passed me my phone.

"Pick a song," she requested.

"Like a sex song?" I clarified.

"Like a strip dance song," Stephanie giggled. My heart skipped a beat. I quickly chose a song.

The innocent image that the yellow dress portrayed was unraveled as she crawled on the floor to me. She opened my legs gently, running her fingers over every inch. She stopped before she reached my erection and stood up. She turned around, lifting her dress slightly then dropped it. This was pure torture. I was completely mesmerized. She eventually fully removed her dress showing a white thong and white bustier.

"Fuck me," I begged.

Stephanie walked over to me. She straddled me slowly undoing my belt and pants. She stood up so I could take them off. I did so at a record speed. She straddled me again, sitting below my boner. She kissed me deeply, pulling my hair slightly with her hands. She grabbed my shirt and removed it. My hands clamored to the back of her bustier trying to undo the clasps. Stephanie removed my hands and stood back up.

"No."

"Just fuck me."

She slowly undid it, clasp by clasp. I drooled in anticipation. Finally, her perfect breasts were visible. She took off her thong and tossed it. She walked over to me and straddled me sitting below my erection again, putting the condom on me.

"Please, fuck me," I pleaded. My body was hurting with need. Stephanie kissed me again; she rose her body over my throbbing erection, her hands in my hair. She moved one of her hands to position my penis correctly. Stephanie slowly lowered herself down. I could feel every inch enter her.

"Holy fuck," I groaned loudly.

Stephanie kissed me passionately as she began to raise and lower herself. She bit my lip. I moaned in pure ecstasy. Stephanie lowered her lips to my neck, occasionally kissing gently. Each movement, each touch, sending shivers down my spine. I was getting close to finishing, my breath quickening.

"Fuck me," she whispered in my ear, pulling me on top of her. I scrambled to position myself, desperate for her. Needing her. I pressed in.

"Fuck," I murmured. The bed squeaked as I began to pound her with vigor. Stephanie moaned, digging her nails into my back. The sharp pain from her nails sent electricity through me, it egged me on. I deepened my thrusts, the distinct slapping noise echoed through my ears. Stephanie tilted her head back, her moans turning to whimpers as she pleaded for me to continue. Everything else fell away. All that mattered was her. I gripped her ass tightly, pulling her into me as I thrusted her. Stephanie lifted her head up, kissing then biting my shoulder hard. "Fuck!" I yelled.

"Holy fuck, fuck, fuck," Stephanie groaned as she climaxed, her body pressing against me. That pushed me over the edge. I finished immediately, slumping over her in complete bliss. I removed myself, taking off the condom and tossing it into my trash can. I laid down beside Stephanie. "Did I deliver on the greatest sex?" she asked, smiling.

"You most certainly did." I kissed her, running my hands down her body. "God, I love you," I whispered in her ear.

"I love you more." Stephanie kissed me on the tip of my nose.

"Do you think everything will go all right tomorrow?" I questioned. Stephanie hit me with a pillow.

"I know it will go all right tomorrow. Let's play a game," Stephanie suggested.

"What do you want to play?" I asked.

"What about 'would you rather'?" Stephanie sat up. I nodded. She swung her legs over me. "Okay, would you rather burn alive or drown?"

"Jesus Christ, Stephanie," I laughed. "Are you okay?" I joked. "Uh, like the fire or can the smoke kill me."

"Fire."

"Damn, that's tough, uh, neither," I stated. Stephanie giggled and shook her head. "I guess, drowning. Okay, would you rather eat a live beetle or a live worm?"

"Neither are poisonous?"

"Neither are poisonous," I confirmed.

"Worm, it would just be fun spaghetti." Stephanie shrugged.

"You're such a weirdo."

"Uh, would you rather die by a gunshot or explosion?" Stephanie queried.

"Are you planning my murder, Stephanie?" I joked.

"No, I'll change it. Would you rather fuck Aidan or Lucas?"

"I think I would rather plan my murder."

"Answer," Stephanie insisted.

"Uh, I guess Aidan, I feel like he would be more enthusiastic," I commented. "Who would you rather fuck, Aidan or Lucas?"

"Aidan, hands down, Aidan. I agree, I think Lucas would just not be into it," Stephanie muttered. "Would you rather be able to fuck as many men as you want, or only be able to fuck me once a year?"

"Asking the important questions." I thought about it for a few seconds. "You once a year."

"You're lying," Stephanie accused.

"No, I wouldn't feel satisfied after all those men. I would much rather feel satisfied once a year than never," I justified. Stephanie nodded. "Would you rather fuck Jace one more time or Raphael?"

"Oh ew, you don't want to hear the answer to that," Stephanie pushed my shoulder gently.

"I do, I'm curious."

"Don't ever repeat this, it's Jace," Stephanie replied. "Same question to you."

"Who would I rather fuck? Or who would I rather you fuck?"

"Who would you rather fuck?"

"I think Raphael," I laughed.

"Wouldn't you be scared of him killing you?" Stephanie giggled.

"I feel like that would add something to it." I winked at Stephanie.

"Oh, very kinky." Stephanie pinched my nipple hard. I tickled her and she screamed with laughter. "Where do you want to go Friday? I'll pick you up at the sign at seven." Stephanie curled up to me.

"Let's just drive for as long as possible," I whispered. Stephanie nodded.

"Wherever we go, promise me one thing?" Stephanie looked up at me.

"Anything."

"You'll give writing a shot."

"Okay," I agreed. We laid down in bed and I held her tight as we fell asleep.

"Sweety," I woke up to my mom gently shaking me. I sat up abruptly. Stephanie was naked and still curled up at my side.

"What the fuck, mom?" I hissed.

"Raphael's on the phone." My mom handed the house telephone to me.

"What?" I demanded through the phone.

"Good morning to you too," Raphael laughed. "I wanted to make sure Stephanie was there with you."

"She is," I stated. Stephanie murmured slightly, her arm searching to cuddle me.

"Good, can I speak with her?"

"She's sleeping," I rubbed my face.

"Put her on the fucking phone!" Raphael yelled abruptly. I gently shook Stephanie. She woke up and smiled at me. She then saw my mom and quickly grabbed the blanket covering herself, looking at me, completely mortified.

"Raphael's on the phone." I passed her the phone.

"Yes, I'm here," Stephanie said. Mom's eyes glided over her, a look of pure sadness crossing her face. I looked over to see the now dark bruises. The car accident must have been bad. "Yes, we understand... I'm sorry... yes... yes... I know... we're almost there... same... I know... we don't have a problem with

that... it's brilliant... I'm sorry, I should have called..."
Stephanie giggled. "Yes, we'll see you this afternoon. Okay, ya, ya, I'll see you tonight... nothing's changed, no... ya ... bye." Stephanie hung up and passed the phone back to my mom. Mom smiled and left the room.

"Stephanie," I took her face gently in my hands, gently tracing the bruises.

"Ya, just stupid, wasn't paying enough attention," Stephanie frowned. She straddled me and kissed me deeply. The door of my room reopened.

"Mom, get out!" I shouted.

"Just wanted to let you know that breakfast is ready," mom called. She closed the door behind her. Stephanie smiled mischievously and without warning stuck my penis in her mouth and began sucking.

"Sweet Jesus," I murmured in shock. She cupped my balls with one hand using the other hand to support my penis as she began to take my entire shaft. Her tongue flicked my tip whenever she got to the top. The door of my room opened.

"Just wanted to deliver this. That man, uh, started with an E. Oh shoot, what was his name. Anyway, he dropped this off," dad said, stepping into the room, holding a bag.

"Dad, get out," I gripped my covers tightly in terror. Dad looked at me confused before seeing a lump under the covers. He nodded and left the room. Stephanie continued on. Within seconds, I climaxed in pure satisfaction. Stephanie popped out from under the covers.

"Your parents need boundaries," Stephanie whispered.

"The only one in your house with boundaries is Eli, so you have no leg to stand on here," I replied. Stephanie laughed and got out of bed.

341

"Can I shower?" Stephanie queried, picking up the bag dad just dropped off.

"Ya, down the hall to the left," I instructed. Stephanie nodded and threw her yellow dress on, leaving. She came back fully dressed in a long-sleeved, black, thin turtleneck and jean shorts, her hair still wet and makeup done, bruises covered. I pulled on my clothing, and we walked downstairs together.

"Good morning," Stephanie waved at my parents.

"Good morning," my parents responded. My mom passed Stephanie and me a plate of bacon and eggs.

"I apologize for the intrusion this morning, I did not realize you guys were... busy," dad shifted.

"I think it best not to talk about this morning," I requested.

"Then about last night, for future reference the room is not soundproof," dad voiced, taking a sip of coffee. Stephanie giggled.

"I'm sorry, this isn't funny, I've just never had parents," Stephanie laughed. "Sorry, continue," she motioned to my dad.

"We are glad you two are being safe—" mom began.

"We just would like to be able to sleep," dad muttered.

"Okay, I think that has been sufficiently embarrassing and I vote that we just stop talking about it," I suggested.

"We are going to put a box of condoms in your dresser for the future and we want you two to continue to have fun, safe sex," mom continued. I buried my face in my hands.

"Yes, Levi is uncomfortable with this conversation, but I think it's very sweet," Stephanie put her hand gently on my arm. "I apologize if our activities last night were too loud, uh, we're just used to my house. And I live with a lot of guys, so there's a lot of claps and back pats for Levi there."

"Please don't engage in this conversation, Stephanie," I

groaned.

"But it won't happen again," Stephanie nodded.

"You are welcome over any time," mom smiled. "Are things okay at home?"

"Ya, just one of the guys wasn't being very nice. He got really drunk and high last night and just wouldn't let the argument stop."

"Was Raphael home?" mom asked.

"Ya, but he's one of the 'family' so no one really says anything." Stephanie began picking at her jaw.

"Is he violent?" Dad leaned forward.

"My dad's an ex-cop turned psychologist," I explained to Stephanie who let out a wavering breath. "We have to get to class," I announced. Stephanie nodded and got up quickly. She left to grab her bag from upstairs.

"We'll be talking about this later," dad stated.

"Oh, I certainly expect so," I laughed. Stephanie came down the stairs.

"It was such a lovely breakfast, thank you," Stephanie called as we left. I shut the door behind us. We got into her Aston Martin. "Your father used to be a cop and you didn't think that was important to tell me?"

"I was going to mention it today," I defended. "It never feels like a good time to tell your criminal girlfriend that your dad used to be a cop."

"I guess that's fair enough." Stephanie shrugged, obviously still irritated. "I'll tell Raphael and give him a heads up."

"Okay, is everything ready?"

"Everything is ready," Stephanie confirmed. "You have your burner phone?"

"Certainly do." I pulled it out of my pocket.

"So where do you want to go when this is all going down?"

"Well, not my parents, I want us to be able to help if something goes wrong," I replied. Stephanie nodded. "Can we see them before it goes down? Not to talk or anything."

"We can go to the cottage." Stephanie smiled. "It may be nice for you to say goodbye to it too, it's where this all happened."

"Ya, it doesn't seem real that we're all leaving," I breathed.

"I remember my first time. It didn't feel real until a week after we moved."

"Do you ever regret going into this?" I stared at my hands.

"It gets frustrating at times, but no, I've never regretted it." Stephanie murmured. I nodded, taking a deep breath. "The fake identities will be delivered today, so you'll learn your new name in the car." Stephanie pulled up to the university.

Chapter 17

"Stephanie and you were planning to just drive? No further plans?" the green-eyed lady asked.

"No further plans, just a tank full of gas and some fake IDs." I smiled thinking about how amazing that seemed. To be on the road with her, just the two of us. "I've lost everything, why is it even a question that I did this?"

"The gun was found in your possession," the brown-haired lady advised.

"I've explained it to everyone, Raphael gave me the fucking gun!" I yelled.

"We understand this is frustrating, we're almost done," the green-eyed lady reassured me.

***

Classes were excruciating. I was watching the clock the whole time. Aidan and Lucas tried to figure out what was up, but I went under the guise that Stephanie and I had a big fight. They seemed to be satisfied with that answer. Finally, it was time.

Stephanie and I walked out to the Aston. We didn't say anything the entire trip to the cottage. We pulled into the driveway. The men were loading up different vehicles with their selected instruments.

"The vehicles are all stolen and will be returned to the place they were stolen from. It confuses the police," Stephanie explained.

"Everything is thought through," I muttered.

"Comes with experience." Stephanie shrugged. We got out of the vehicle.

"Come to wish us good luck?" Eli smiled. Stephanie continued on to Raphael.

"Ya," I replied. Raphael held a different gun to his normal one. The long silencer made this gun impossible to conceal. He wore his driving gloves. Raphael laughed then shrugged.

"Are you nervous?" James questioned.

"Yes, I can't imagine how you guys must feel," I scratched my head.

"Never felt better, that pre-robbery adrenaline, better than any drug," Jace gleamed. Stephanie was giving Raphael a long hug. She pulled away gently, putting her hand on his neck. She pulled his head in until their foreheads were touching. She whispered something to him. Raphael nodded.

"I wouldn't worry about it, they're just saying goodbye," James put his hand gently on my shoulder. Raphael pulled her into another hug, his eyes closed to take in the moment. He whispered something to her. Stephanie nodded.

"I know," I nodded.

"Just please don't die," Stephanie stated, walking over to us, Raphael on her heels.

"Now why would I do that?" Raphael smiled.

"That goes to all of you," Stephanie announced. Everyone nodded. Eli hugged her tightly.

"If I was going to die, I would've chosen a better moment to do so," Eli commented. He pulled away cupping her face gently and looking into her eyes. Stephanie nodded.

"I am just immortal," Jace pulled Stephanie into him. He

kissed the top of her head. In all of this, I hadn't even considered the possibility of someone dying. "And if we get caught, you and Levi will have the challenge of breaking us out of prison," Jace joked, pulling out of the hug.

"I just have a very strong guardian angel," James smiled, gesturing to the scars on his left arm. He picked her up and spun her around. Stephanie giggled.

"Levi, get in here." Jace pulled me in for a hug. "We're gonna miss you." Jace patted my back, pain radiated from his aggressive gesture. James was quick to follow and embraced me tightly. I turned to Eli.

"You'll return home to us soon." Eli patted me on the back. I looked at Raphael. Raphael nodded to me respectfully. I nodded back.

"Hey, we'll see you soon." Raphael turned to Stephanie. "Everything will go fine. I promise." Raphael placed his hand on the back of her neck. "We'll see you soon, everyone free as can be and safe, right?"

"Right," Stephanie grinned.

"Right?" Raphael turned to the men.

"Right!" James, Jace, Eli and I agreed. Stephanie nodded. Raphael kissed her on the forehead.

"I love you and I don't plan on leaving you alone anytime soon," Raphael said, kissing Stephanie's cheek.

"Raphael, we should get going," Eli announced. Stephanie pulled away.

"Okay, everyone be safe," Stephanie called, retreating into the cottage. I turned to Raphael.

"We'll talk tonight," Raphael stated.

"Be safe, we need you," I remarked before I followed Stephanie into the cottage.

"That part doesn't get easier," Stephanie rubbed her face. "It's worse when you're not there."

"It's a safe robbery," I rubbed her back gently.

"No such thing." Stephanie bit at her nail.

"We need something to distract you," I grinned at her. "We can play 'would you rather'?" I suggested. Stephanie shook her head. "We can go for a drive?"

"Okay," she nodded. We left and got into the Aston Martin. Stephanie revved the engine before we began driving and blasted the music, rolling down the windows. Just over an hour into driving around aimlessly the burner phone rang. I looked down at it. Stephanie pulled over to the side of the road. Rolling the windows back up. I picked up the phone.

"Dealer's a no show. I'm calling your uncle now, get him to come down," Raphael's voice rang through the phone.

"Okay."

"Hello?" My uncle greeted.

"Hey, I just wanted to drop something off as a thank you, I'm at the doors," I lied.

"Oh, aren't you generous. I'll be right down," my uncle hung up the phone.

"It's a go," Raphael said, hanging up. The line went dead. That was it. Stephanie took a wavering breath.

"Take out the SIM card and break it," Stephanie ordered. I obeyed. "Wipe your fingerprints and throw the phone out," Stephanie instructed.

"Okay," I murmured, throwing it out the window.

"They won't take long; we should head back." Stephanie did a U-turn and began driving to my house. Neither of us spoke.

We eventually pulled up in my driveway. Raphael was already there, his Bentley in the driveway. We walked into the house.

"Ah, there you guys are!" mom cooed.

"I was thinking you guys got lost, I switched vehicles after work and still beat you," Raphael joked.

What a stupid thing to say.

I sat down beside Raphael at the kitchen table. My eyes were on him, he hadn't bothered to change clothing. His all-black outfit and tattooed arms making it impossible to think of him as anything else but a criminal. He leaned back, his cocky smile slithering on his lips as his eyes set on my dad.

"How was work today?" Stephanie sat down beside me.

"Went without a hiccup." Raphael shrugged, taking a sip of beer. Stephanie smiled and nodded. My heart jumped in relief. My mom placed bowls full of food on the table. Raphael put some potatoes on his plate. "I'm sorry Stephanie intruded last night; I hope she didn't disturb your Wednesday night."

"Oh, nonsense." My mom dismissed, putting some roast on her plate. "Stephanie is welcome anytime."

"Oh, I don't think it'll happen again," Raphael stated, his voice coming out more as an order than a presuming reply. "Just young love, it's hard to keep them away from each other," Raphael laughed.

Dad sat forward, his eyes narrowing. "From what Stephanie and Levi have told us, she had every right to leave."

"As I thought I made clear, we handle these matters within the family," Raphael's jaw hardened, not breaking eye contact.

"So, my test went well today," I interjected.

"That's wonderful to hear," Dad beamed. Raphael's burner phone went off.

"My apologies, I have to take this," Raphael stood up and answered the phone while walking out of the room.

"Yes, I'm very proud of him," Stephanie cooed, leaning into me slightly. Raphael came back to the kitchen and sat down.

"Well, that was certainly quick," mom chuckled.

"One of our friends is proposing tonight, he was just saying that he bought the engagement ring, no problem," Raphael explained.

"Oh, how exciting!" my mom smiled. Raphael nodded toward Stephanie, I kissed her on the cheek. "Who's the lucky girl? Do you know her quite well?"

"Him. They're both men," Raphael corrected. "We're familiar with him, it has moved very quickly though. But he's obviously in love, I've never actually seen him so in love. So, I'm very excited for them."

"Wow, so exciting," mom gleamed. "Maybe we'll have a proposal not too long from now." My mom gestured to Stephanie and me.

"Maybe," I kissed Stephanie on the cheek. A diamond ring would be the first thing I'll buy with my cut. The biggest one she's ever seen to make sure no one made the error in assuming she was available. I would do it spontaneously, nothing too scripted. Just the first night we're away together with our retirement fund. Maybe in bed after I tired her out from sex, maybe in the bath while drinking champagne, maybe in the morning. But it would happen soon, that much I had decided.

"What would you say to that, Raphael? A big family wedding?" Dad watched Raphael closely.

"Whatever Stephanie wants." Raphael smiled faintly, trying to act the part. Dad nodded slowly. He knew something was up. "So, uh, Levi tells me that you're an ex-cop? Why did you leave the force?"

"I forced him," mom giggled. "He was a fantastic detective,

but after Levi was born, I wanted him safe. So, I persuaded him to go into a career in psychology instead."

"Surprisingly close to being a detective," dad laughed.

"A detective? Levi didn't say you made it to that rank, very impressive," Raphael chirped and took a sip of beer.

"Yes, I always found it amusing to catch people in a lie," dad smirked.

"Yes, always fun. So, you had a fun time with the kids last weekend?" mom queried.

"Oh yes, they're always a joy to be around. I had hoped to teach Levi a thing or two about poker, but we unfortunately didn't make it to the casino," Raphael finished off the food on his plate.

"I think my son could beat you in poker," dad kissed his teeth, his glare unrelenting. He wasn't going to let this go.

"Perhaps we should have a game after this?" Raphael suggested.

"That sounds like an excellent idea!" mom said, cleaning up the plates. Raphael's phone went off.

"Levi, come answer this with me," Raphael ordered. I nodded and we left the room. Raphael picked up the phone. "Good," he replied, before hanging up. "It's done." A wide grin crossed his face.

"Fuck yes," I sighed, complete relief coming over me.

"I wanted to thank you, this wouldn't have happened without you," Raphael said sincerely. He pulled out his gun, wiping down his fingerprints.

"You brought this into my house?" I hissed.

"Shut up for two seconds, this is hard for me to say," Raphael retorted. "I'm sorry for being difficult with you. You are family, proved it today." Raphael took a deep breath. "You can come

back to us anytime. In the meantime, I want you to have this."
Raphael passed me his gun with his shirt. "I need you to protect
her." Raphael looked at me desperately.

"I will," I put the gun in my back pocket.

"If you don't, I'll kill you." His expression made his words
unmistakably true. Whether she chose him or not, she was the
love of his life. He would murder for her without a second of
hesitation.

"Oh, I believe that. I'm going to put this upstairs," I
muttered. Raphael nodded. I walked up the stairs and into my
room. I felt honored and proud. I was fully accepted. I was
charged with protecting his mouse. He trusted me to do that. He
required me to do that. I placed the gun in my bedside table.
Looking at it for a second as I puffed out my chest.

I won.

He needed me to take care of her because she chose *me*. My
hands moved to shut the drawer, giddily walking down the stairs
and into the kitchen. Everyone was cheering.

"Oh, I'm so excited, will they have a big wedding?" mom
demanded.

"Oh, of course. James loves parties," I said sitting down.
Stephanie kissed me on the cheek, beaming with excitement. We
had just received more money than people dream of.

"You'll look so cute in a suit standing up there as a
groomsman," mom leaned forward, pinching my cheek.

"My goal is always to look cute," I commented.

"And you always do," Stephanie giggled.

"Now, I have tiramisu for dessert, we can eat that while
playing some poker?" mom suggested.

"Sounds great, dear," dad replied. Mom began dishing out
the dessert as dad set up the poker game. "Do you know how to

play, Stephanie?" dad queried.

"She's a brilliant poker player," Raphael interjected. "I taught her when she was in foster care, I find it to hold so many life skills."

"I agree, but I was asking Stephanie," dad snipped.

"We often have poker games, the guys are very serious about them," Stephanie laughed.

"People can be serious about it without really knowing how to play. Poker isn't about the cards or the money, it's reading people." My dad sat next to Stephanie. Raphael had a chip in his hand and was twirling it, his vicious gaze on my dad. "See how your brother is sitting—"

"Foster," Raphael interrupted. Dad grinned. He was looking for that.

"That means he's frustrated," dad finished. "He's more likely to play the game taking a lot of risks."

"Roll up your sleeves, Raphael," Stephanie instructed. Raphael laughed; his frustration instantly melted away.

"I win honestly," Raphael rolled up his sleeves.

Raphael cracked his knuckles as my dad dealt the cards. My mom sat down. "Take it easy on me," Raphael winked at Stephanie. She smirked and shook her head. Dad burned and put down three cards face up. The game was highly strung. My mom, Stephanie and I were the ones taking this as a fun game. Dad and Raphael were locked at beating each other. To them this was a battle with extreme stakes.

My mom was the first one out, I was the second. Stephanie sat there staring at Raphael. Dad folded quickly. Raphael had raised it a grand.

"Can you read me?" Raphael chuckled.

"Like a book," Stephanie winked. "I call." She pushed the

extra chips in front of her. Raphael revealed his cards, nothing. Stephanie laughed and collected her chips. Raphael grinned.

I dealt out the hand, burned and flipped the first three cards. Raphael watched Stephanie. The table went through a few rounds of checks until I turned over the final card. Stephanie winced slightly. Raphael beamed, catching her mistake. Dad also caught it and nodded to himself, noting the reaction. Dad turned his attention to Raphael who was already watching him. They stared at each other.

"You have a terrible poker face," dad commented. "All in." My dad pushed his chips forward. Raphael laughed.

"All in." Raphael pushed his chips forward.

"All in." Stephanie shrugged, pushing her chips forward.

"Queen pair," Raphael placed his cards down.

"Ace pair," dad announced. Dad laughed joyously, smacking the table in victory.

"Don't celebrate just yet," Stephanie smiled. My dad and Raphael turned to her confused. "Royal flush." She placed her hand down.

"No fucking way," Raphael laughed.

"Well done." Dad praised. Stephanie did a little dance. Raphael shook his head smiling.

"Well, I think we have sufficiently humiliated Levi's dad. We should head out." Raphael stood up. Stephanie followed suit.

"Thank you for having us Mr. and Mrs. Davis, everything was amazing," Stephanie cooed. I stood up and kissed her.

"Let's head out," Raphael repeated. Stephanie nodded.

"I'll see you tomorrow," Stephanie quickly shot that look of love that made my heart stop.

"I'll see you tomorrow," I beamed, kissing her hand. We would be free. Together and free. Nothing seemed to be more ideal. Stephanie and Raphael left, the door shutting quietly behind them.

"Well, that was fun," mom commented and cleaned up. I helped my dad put away the poker set. "Well, I'm going to go to sleep," mom announced.

"I'll join you soon," dad kissed her cheek before she left. Mom's footsteps echoed up the stairs. Dad went to the fridge and grabbed two beers.

"Sit down," he ordered, passing me one. I obeyed, opening the beer and taking a sip. "You won't get in trouble for anything you say in this conversation, I need you to tell me the truth." Dad leaned back. I nodded slowly, sudden panic rushing through my veins. I took a deep breath.

"Will you tell the police?"

"Are you involved?" dad calmly took a sip of beer. I nodded. "Then no, it will stay between us."

"Okay."

"Raphael drives a Bentley, Stephanie an Aston Martin, he's obviously not in construction."

"Correct."

"So, he's a contract criminal."

"Yes."

"Raphael winced whenever you came close to Stephanie, he can't stand the term brother. He's obviously in love with her."

"Correct."

"He's the man Stephanie talked about this morning," dad stated. I nodded. "Is he dangerous?"

"Yes, very."

"Will he hurt Stephanie?"

"No, never."

"She had bruises on her jaw and her arms," dad narrowed his

eyes at me. That strong evaluating mannerism that reverberated through my childhood.

"She flipped her car," I replied. My dad nodded slowly.

"Will he hurt you?"

"No, he considers me family.".

"Raphael was on a job today; I'm assuming you and Stephanie were too."

"How did you—"

"He drives a Bentley but answered a flip phone. Did the job have something to do with your uncle's building blowing up?" dad asked. His eyes cutting into me like knives. I nodded. "Your uncle hasn't returned home."

"He's not hurt. Raphael promised no harm would come to him."

"Are you going to go on the run?" dad looked down, beginning to pick at the label on his beer.

"I'm leaving tomorrow morning," I croaked. Dad nodded. We sat in silence. Neither of us knowing what to say. The chilled distance burning me alive.

"I never thought this is how you'd grow up," dad murmured. The words tore at me. I wanted him to yell, I wanted him to shriek at the top of his lungs. But he just sat there. His heartbroken gaze not lifting from me. Keeping in his miserable silence.

"I'm sorry," I whimpered.

Dad shook his head. "It's nasty out there, you need to stand by your decision, or you'll be trampled."

"Any other advice?" I exhaled a laugh, uncomfortable and miserable as I faced him.

"Something's not right." Dad breathed. "The bruises." He kissed his teeth.

"I'll protect her," I vowed.

"I'll pray you can," he muttered. His eyes pierced into me for a few more moments. The unspoken words falling loudly into the tension filled air. Dad got up to leave. He rested his hand gently on my left shoulder. "You will always have a safe house here," dad's voice cracked. He continued up the stairs. I sat there in silence. I looked around the kitchen saying my goodbyes to it before going upstairs and into my room.

I set my alarm and lay in bed. My heart sounding loudly in my throat. A sweet and appalling mix of agony and euphoria waving through my body. I stared at the roof until I fell asleep.

My alarm broke through the silence. I got out of bed instantly, throwing my clothes on, grabbing the gun and stuffing it into my back pocket. I ran down the stairs and headed out the door then began the walk to my university. The sign seemed like a dignified flag. A beautiful welcome into my new life. I was escaping with the love of my life. Nothing could be better.

I waited until seven a.m. rolled around. No Stephanie. My heart started pounding, what if something had happened to her? I started to pace. My head started to race; my hands got sweaty. Seven thirty.

Nothing.

Do I run on foot?

No, that would be ridiculous. How far could I possibly get like that?

Cop cars from every direction appeared. Their sirens blaring. They parked in front of me. The sudden pierce into my daydream caught me by surprise. My mind racing to catch up to the reality that was happening. My eyes darted around at each of the cars.

Maybe they weren't here for me. That's it. Stephanie would appear any second and swoop me away. This was just a coincidence. A very bad coincidence.

The cops got out of the car; all their eyes were on me as they drew their guns. I put my hands up. My heart now puncturing through my chest as pure terror consumed me.

"Get down on the ground, hands behind your head," a cop shouted, her hands firmly on a gun. I obeyed, getting down instantly. Another cop came behind me, pulling the gun out of my pocket. He clipped the handcuffs on my right hand, forcing it back and connecting them to my left hand.

"You are under arrest for the murder of Larry Gray, armed robbery, and—" the cops voice yelled in my ear. I couldn't hear past murder. My uncle was dead. The handcuffs were tight. My breathing was quick. My heart pounding at lightning speed. The cop pulled me up to my feet and led me to the car. An audience was gathering as he pushed my head down and shut the door behind me. I watched as students stared as I was driven away. I looked out the window desperate to see Stephanie's car. I needed to know she was okay.

There was nothing.

Chapter 18

"You know the rest, I was miraculously released on bail, my dad hired your firm, and here I am," I summarized.

"We want you to realize what we're up against here. The gun that shot your uncle was in your possession," the green-eyed lady said.

"It's not that we don't believe you, this is just a hard defense to pull off. There's no record of a Stephanie Anna Gibson who studied history at your university. The cottage that you told the police about is owned by an elderly couple on the other side of the country," the brown-haired lady stated.

"I understand what's going against me. Holy fuck do I understand. But I didn't kill anyone. I just made a call," I hissed.

"Levi, we do understand, we're going to represent you, but realistically you're not going to walk away from this without jail time. Unless Stephanie, Raphael or one of the other ones come forward," the green-eyed lady sighed.

I put my face in my hands. "This isn't fair," I groaned.

"Okay, so we've heard your story, now let us talk to the prosecutor and see if we can get you a deal. Your mom is in the lobby," the brown-haired lady smiled. They both stood up and left the room. I followed and went to the lobby. Mom stood up giving me a hug. She walked me out to the car, we got in and we began driving back home.

"How did it go?" she asked.

"I'm fucked, royally fucked," I muttered.

"Please don't use that language."

"Mom, I'm literally on trial for murder, I don't think my language matters," I laughed.

Mom shrugged. "You didn't do it though, how can you get convicted when you didn't do it?" Mom demanded.

"Because Raphael wanted Stephanie, that's how," I placed my head on the seat looking out the window as the streets passed by. It had been two weeks since I had seen her. Every thought I had led back to me wondering if she was okay.

"They haven't reached out?" mom asked. I shook my head. "Well, these lawyers are supposed to be really good," mom reassured me. "Dad reached out to his old friends; they're trying to find them."

"They're ghosts," I murmured as I watched as the outside became familiar. "Mom, can we stop?" I asked, looking at my university.

"I don't know, sweety," mom hesitated.

"Please? I really want a muffin." I looked at her and smiled faintly. She nodded and pulled into the parking lot. I got out of the car and went to the café. I breathed in, smelling the familiar aroma. I walked over to the chocolate muffins. "I'm glad you have them in stock," I joked to the cashier.

"We're never out of stock, they're not very popular," the cashier replied confused. I laughed.

"I seem to remember coming here and not being able to buy any. It was a pretty important day to me," I replied somewhat aggressively.

"There was that one time where a gentleman came early in the morning and asked to buy them all. Very odd, they're terrible," the cashier pondered, ringing the muffin through. I put cash on the counter.

"Can you tell me what this man looked like?" I requested.

"What, do I look like a camera?" the cashier snipped. I nodded slowly, grabbing my muffin and walking away.

"Don't go there," I whispered to myself. I walked out of the university getting back into the car with my mom.

"Did you get it?" my mom questioned. I nodded. We drove home.

The days were full of nothingness. I sat on the floor drinking a beer and staring at my wall. Someone knocked gently on the door. Dad came in without waiting for an answer. At least I wasn't getting a blow job, I laughed to myself.

"How are you feeling?" dad queried.

"Fine." I looked at him.

"You don't look fine," he observed, coming over and sitting beside me. "What if Lucas and Aidan came over?"

"I'm on trial for murder, robbery and a hell of a lot of other things, I doubt they would want to," I chuckled.

"They're your friends."

"So were Raphael, Jace, James and Eli. Oh, and Stephanie. But look how that turned out." I took a swig of my beer.

"We don't know how many of them actually wanted to set you up, you said Raphael was their leader, they may have not had a choice." Dad put his hand on my shoulder.

"They had a choice."

"So did you, I refuse to allow you to sit up here and feel sorry for yourself. I'm sorry this happened, I really am, but you decided to run with the wolves and sometimes when you run with the wolves you get bit," dad stated. The room fell silent.

"You're right."

"I'll call Lucas's and Aidan's parents." Dad grabbed the beer out of my hand and left. I continued to sit there staring at the wall blankly. The day passed slowly.

"So, I promised Lucas's parents that everyone would remain at the kitchen table. I also had to promise we didn't have any handguns laying around, so that was fun," dad announced, rubbing his face. Aidan and Lucas sat down across from me. "Your mom and I will be in the living room," dad said to me, I nodded. He left.

"The cops took my only handgun," I joked. They didn't laugh. Come on, that one was good.

"Man, this is serious," Aidan stated.

"Really? I hadn't noticed. I should call up a lawyer," I rolled my eyes.

"What did it feel like to do it?" Lucas leaned in and whispered.

"Do what?" I questioned.

"To kill someone," Lucas murmured.

"I wouldn't know, that was Raphael. I wasn't even close to the building. He promised me my uncle wouldn't get hurt so I don't know," I sighed.

"How are you feeling?" Aidan queried.

"Not great, these last few months are just questions. What was real? Who was in on it? The other day, the cashier said that on the day Stephanie, and I met, someone came in and bought up all the muffins. I thought about that and only that for days. I'm driving myself insane." I shook my head.

"Stephanie loved you," Lucas insisted.

"I know," I looked at the table. "Every part of me just wants to know she's okay."

"Raphael is protective of her," Lucas stated.

"Raphael called me 'family' then shot my uncle and gave me the gun. I'm having a hard time believing hurting Stephanie is out of the question," I retorted. I rubbed my face with my hands. "This is what I mean, I'm unraveling. How are you guys?"

"Good, university is the same old, not as fun now that you're not there," Aidan replied.

"Ya, we miss you. It feels like we haven't seen you in forever," Lucas whined.

"I miss you guys too," I murmured. I hadn't spoken to them since the day of the robbery. The conversation felt strained. So much had changed since.

"We promised our parents we would only stay here for thirty minutes," Aidan announced. "We have to go, but we'll come back soon," Aidan promised. Lucas and Aidan left. I sat at the kitchen table alone. Everything seemed dark now. My life completely changed in a blink of an eye, and I was struggling to find the fragments to put it back together. I grabbed a beer from the fridge and went upstairs.

A few days of boredom passed. I sat at the kitchen table late in the evening drinking a beer. My mind racing but thinking of nothing. There wasn't anything more to grapple with. I would never know the answers I craved. There was a knock at the door.

"Levi, someone's here for you," dad popped his head into the kitchen. Mom and dad went upstairs, giving me a smile. I walked to the doorway.

"You're late," I sighed, taking a sip of my beer. Stephanie stood there in a light blue sundress. I looked past her to a mattified black Cadillac in the driveway. Eli stood beside it and waved. I nodded to him.

"Why didn't you tell me Raphael was watching me?"

Stephanie bit at her nail.

"Why didn't you tell me you planned to kill my uncle?" I retorted. Stephanie nodded slowly. She pushed past me and sat at the kitchen table. I shut the door and turned around sitting next to her. "Gun on the table, please," I ordered. Stephanie took her gun out of her purse, wiped off her fingerprints and set it in the middle of the table. She reached in her purse and pulled out a bundle of documents, setting them in front of me.

"Come with us," Stephanie urged. I looked at the documents. A fake passport, driver's license and credit card lay there.

"Are you forgetting we had this conversation before? You were meant to pick me up but instead the cops did," I mused. A mix of pure anger and tipsiness working in my favor to not just wrap my arms around her and forgive her instantly. Stephanie stood up grabbing two beers from the fridge. She handed me a new one. "I have been kicked out of university for this, I'm on trial for this, what punishment did you get?"

"We didn't know Raphael was going to set you up. Come with us, you don't have to go down for this," Stephanie pleaded. She reached out her hand. I picked up the passport, Carson Hall, a piece of paper with her number written on it fell out. I nodded slowly, my heart pounding and my mind spinning.

"Can you answer a question for me?" I queried. "What was real?"

"Us, your relationship with the guys, they love you. Raphael hates you." Stephanie smiled to herself then looked down. Her focus turned to the table, intent to win a staring contest with this inanimate object. "Why we came into your life was less than honest but then we got to know you and we all fell in love with you. Raphael convinced us to stick to the original plan, which was just to leave you. But after we left, we all realized how stupid that was. I love you, Levi, please come with us."

"Okay," I leaned in close to her. Willingly ignorant. Realizing that I would much rather live in her lie, than exist in a truth without her. "Where are we going?" I whispered to her.

Stephanie beamed. "As far as we can drive," Stephanie giggled.

God, I had missed that giggle.

Stephanie pounced forward, collapsing her lips on mine. I grabbed her hair, pulling her into me. She quickly went for my pants and belt, undoing them. My hands glided over her perfect body. She straddled me on the chair as we kissed frantically. Desperate to feel every inch of each other. I picked her up and pressed her against the wall pulling her thong to the side. I shoved myself into her.

"Yes," Stephanie whimpered. My breath quickened as I began to pound her. Forcing every inch into her quickly as I clung onto her, kissing her neck, my body needing her after all this time. Stephanie moaned in my ear, threading her fingers through my hair.

"Fuck," I groaned as I finished inside her, pure bliss washing over me. I placed her down softly. Her dress was uneven, showing her left shoulder slightly.

My heart sank. "Is that a hickey?" I demanded. Stephanie repositioned her dress to cover it again.

"It didn't mean anything," Stephanie insisted.

"Get out of my house," I commanded, everything was suddenly clicking.

It was you.

All of this time, all of these lies.

It was always *you*.

"Levi, I chose you," Stephanie stepped forward.

I stepped back. "No, you chose Raphael." I snarled. "Get out of my house," I muttered, rubbing my face. Stephanie didn't move. She stood there staring at me pleadingly. Her eyes on me as they welled with tears. I couldn't tell if they were real. I couldn't tell if anything was real anymore.

"Get out of my house!" I shouted. Stephanie shook her head. I grabbed her gun, pointing it at her. Stephanie shook her head again, tears falling down her cheeks as she began to sob. "I spent all this time thinking you were a fucking victim in this. But Jace told me Raphael didn't have the brain for complicated cons. This one seems pretty *fucking* complicated to me."

"I fell in love with you after—" Stephanie whimpered. Her voice croaking through the blubbering.

"No, you didn't. It's been Raphael, it's always been Raphael. All those whispers, all the laughs. You're in love with him, not me. You're just scared he'll do the same thing to you as he did to me." My eyes watered. "I was just a fucking pawn—"

"You have it wrong—"

"No, Stephanie, I think for the first time I have it right. If you loved me, you wouldn't have left me. You wouldn't have fucked the guy who sent me to prison!" I screamed through tears, looking down the barrel of the gun at her. "GET THE FUCK OUT OF MY HOUSE!" I cried.

I felt a gentle press on my arm. "Son, put the gun down," dad urged softly.

Stephanie ran out of the house.

"Shh," dad gently took the gun from my hand. I fell to my knees, sobbing. My parents surrounded me, holding me tightly as I wailed uncontrollably. Everything suddenly hit me.

I was nothing to her.

My life was shattered into unrecognizable fragments as she

walked away fine. My life was destroyed by someone I loved more than anything. Someone I had trusted more than anything.

My life was gone.

The police swarmed our house. Dad explained what happened while my mom held me close on the floor. They took the gun as evidence and took dad's statement. I gave an empty statement through tears. They left and my dad rejoined us on the floor.

We all sat staring at the wall. My dad took something out of his pocket and put it on my lap. It was the fake identity.

"You shouldn't go down for something you didn't do," dad said, tears streaming down his face. "Just call us from burner phones."

"And write, whatever works," mom moved the hair from my face.

"Take a few days to think about it," dad muttered, holding me close. We all cried together. The magnitude of the situation finally hitting us.

A day passed before I could look at the documents Stephanie had left for me. I stared at the bank card standing at an ATM. I looked down at the number Stephanie had given me, debating if I should call her for it or go in. I took a deep breath in.

"Levi? I'm so happy you called," Stephanie's voice rang through the phone. I could hear the guys talking in the background. I clenched my jaw.

"What's the PIN?" I demanded.

"What?"

"The PIN for the bank card," I growled.

"Three-Four-Seven-Eight. Levi, can we please talk?" Stephanie pleaded.

I hung up instantly. My body trembled with anger and sadness. Everything in me wanted to forget what she did to me, to forgive her and continue on. I put the bank card in and typed in the PIN.

I took a sharp breath as I came face to face with my share. My eyes watered in relief. I laughed to myself. My phone rang. I picked it up.

"Do you have access to it?"

"No, it's all yours," Stephanie replied. I hung up. My phone rang again. I ignored it. I walked away from the ATM and got into the driver's side of the vehicle.

"So?" dad looked at me expectantly.

"All of it is there," I beamed. Dad laughed boisterously.

"Okay, brake, drive and pull out," dad instructed. I nodded and followed his instructions, pulling onto the road and beginning the drive home. "You've picked this up quickly," dad gestured to the car.

"Nothing motivates you more to drive than the fear of being completely stranded," I mused.

"Have you decided where you're going to go?" dad queried quietly.

"I'm going to drive until I can't drive anymore," I replied. Dad nodded. We drove the rest of the way in silence.

"Okay, brake gently, put it in park and shut the car off," dad instructed. I did so effortlessly. "Well done," dad commended putting his hand on my shoulder. I nodded.

We left the vehicle and walked to the front door. Sitting there was a bottle of Dom Perignon. I grabbed it as we entered the house. "What is it?" dad inquired. I placed it on the kitchen table as my parents gathered around me.

"It's Stephanie's favorite," I muttered.

"Thank you – Raphael," dad read the note attached to the top. I sat down, my heart pounding. "What would he be thanking you for?"

"I rejected Stephanie," I murmured, staring at the bottle. "She's gone back to him." I sat there bewildered at this predictable fact.

Of course, she would go back to him.

"Why don't we call Aidan and Lucas and have them over. They can help take your mind off this," mom cooed, I nodded slowly, barely comprehending what she was saying. My brain still fully focused on Raphael and Stephanie.

I knew Stephanie loved him, but a bit of me had clung to the hope that I was wrong. That she left him for me. I stood up and walked to my room, falling into bed and going to sleep.

I will cope with this tomorrow.

The morning passed by slowly. Aidan and Lucas were coming over in the afternoon and I was eagerly awaiting the visit. They came through the door and sat down with me at the kitchen table.

"How are you?" Aidan questioned.

"I keep having this recurring nightmare that Stephanie's fucking Raphael and Raphael is just watching me and smiling," I muttered.

"So not great then," Aidan said.

"Why would you think she was having sex with Raphael?" Lucas asked.

"She came over a few days ago," I murmured, picking at the table.

"Oh shit, is that why the police were swarming over here? My mom was wondering if you killed someone else," Lucas leaned in.

"No, I have never killed anyone." I rolled my eyes.

"How did it go?" Aidan demanded.

"She told me she didn't know Raphael was going to set me up, tried to get me to come with her, we had sex, I saw a hickey on her shoulder and pointed a gun at her head until she left. Typical meeting with your ex," I joked. Lucas and Aidan looked at me wide-eyed.

"You guys had sex?" Aidan asked.

"But it was just sex with Raphael? She wanted to bring you," Lucas stated slowly.

"I think she's more concerned about the details I'll give the police."

"Also, you've never told us they ever had sex, maybe it was just another guy?" Aidan suggested.

"Oh, they fucked. James and Jace told me they used to be together. I thought she would choose me if it came down to it. I knew Raphael loved her, but I thought I knew she loved me." I shrugged. "Oh, and after I rejected her, I found a bottle of Dom Perignon on my front step. The note said, 'Thank you – Raphael.'"

"Jesus," Aidan grumbled.

"You deserve better, what a bitch," Lucas advised.

"A little bit of an understatement."

"At least it's a bottle of Dom Perignon," Aidan smiled.

"Eli said 'rejection is easier to swallow with an expensive gift.'" I smiled to myself at the memory.

"They all deserve each other." Aidan shook his head. My phone rang. Stephanie. I ignored it.

"Just Stephanie, she's been calling me." I shrugged.

"They can't track the call?" Lucas questioned.

"They couldn't pull fingerprints off her own gun, I doubt she'd be stupid enough to let me track her," I mumbled. Aidan's phone rang. He picked it up and looked at me. Aidan hung up.

"I'm sorry man, we have to go." Aidan stood up. I nodded. Lucas and Aidan left; the front door shut behind them. My parents came and sat down with me at the table.

"I have to go," I announced. Mom nodded. Dad placed his keys in the center of the table.

"Drive until you can't drive anymore," dad urged softly. I nodded. I went upstairs and quickly packed a small bag. I walked out and threw it in the back of the car. Mom hugged me tightly.

"Come back whenever you can and let us know you're safe," mom sniffled.

"I will always love you, son," dad embraced me. I nodded, tears welling in my eyes. I got in the car and reversed out of the driveway, my parents waving to me as I left. I had no idea if or when I would see them again. I got on the freeway and drove.

The cars became a blur as I left everything, I had ever known for nothing. My heart felt empty, my head cluttered with attempts at an explanation of how my life had become this. I continued to drive well past the sunset. The lights merged as I tried to stay awake. I finally decided to pull over.

I pulled into a motel. I walked to the office and got a room for the night. I checked in under my new name, Carson Hall. My room was at the top of two stories. Room number two. The white paint on the railing was decaying. I walked into the room and checked for bed bugs. It was fine. I sat on the bed and turned on the television.

There was a loud knock on the door. I panicked. My heart beating quickly. I looked through the peephole and saw blackness. The police had found me.

I opened the door slowly. Stephanie stood there in a pair of shorts and a black, long-sleeved corset. Eli stood beside her in a black shirt and jeans.

"How did you find me?" I demanded.

"Well, to start you didn't change your car or phone,"

Stephanie sighed. She tossed keys at me. "These are to the Audi," Stephanie gestured to a black vehicle on the other side of the parking lot.

"Where's my car?" I looked around the parking lot.

"Oliver – sorry, Jace is getting rid of it," Stephanie explained. I frowned.

"Here, for your safety," Eli cleaned a gun and passed it to me.

"Last time I accepted one of those, I got arrested," I mumbled. Stephanie grabbed the gun from Eli and licked it.

"Ew, what the fuck?" Eli whined.

"My DNA," Stephanie huffed, passing the gun to me. "We're in the motel across the street," Stephanie grumbled and turned to leave.

"Why?" I demanded.

"Why what?" she turned back toward me, her glare was harsh and cold.

"Why are you doing this?" I questioned.

"What don't you get about this? Uriel fucked up; you weren't meant to go down for this." Stephanie raised her voice.

"Who the fuck is Uriel?"

"Raphael." Stephanie rubbed her face, she looked exhausted. "No one was meant to go down for this. If anything happens to you, it's on us." Stephanie spun on her heels and walked down the stairs.

"What about my uncle? Why is that not on you?" I yelled after her.

"He wasn't meant to get hurt." Stephanie turned and looked sincerely into my eyes. "No one was meant to get hurt."

"Stephanie—" I called, running after her, I grabbed her arm gently, I saw her wince.

"My name's Courtney." Stephanie yanked her arm away from me and continued to walk away.

372

"Whether you like us or not, we're family." Eli squeezed my shoulder and nodded to me.

Eli walked behind her as they crossed the street. Uriel stood there at the corner of the motel. He watched me intently as he smoked a joint. As Courtney walked by him, Uriel turned his head toward her, watching her closely; she didn't even glance his way. He looked back at me and dropped the joint, putting it out with his foot. Uriel nodded at me and left the corner following in Eli's footsteps.

I returned to my motel room. I took a deep unsteady breath in and grabbed the bottle of Dom Perignon from my bag. I went to the bathroom and opened it over the tub.

"To losing everything and continuing on," I muttered to myself.

Uriel controlled the group. He controlled her. I was an idiot for thinking she was anything else but his.

The beauty of power.

I took a swig from the champagne bottle. The smooth and familiar flavor reminding me of my perfect moments with her. I set it down on the desk, grabbing my laptop from my bag, my mind buzzing around the events of the last few months. A few months had changed the entire course of my life. I was determined to make sense of it all. I took a deep breath and began to write my story.

"Start from the beginning" The woman leaned back, her green eyes piercing into me.

Manufactured by Amazon.ca
Bolton, ON

44479067R00217